Also by WILLIAM BERNHARDT

CAPITOL BETRAYAL

CAPITOL BETRAYAL

A NOVEL

WILLIAM
BERNHARDT

BALLANTINE BOOKS • NEW YORK

Copyright © 2010 by William Bernhardt

All rights reserved.

Published in the United States by Ballantine Books, an imprint of The Random House Publishing Group, a division of Random House, Inc., New York.

BALLANTINE and colophon are registered trademarks of Random House, Inc.

ISBN 978-0-345-50301-5

Printed in the United States of America on acid-free paper

www.ballantinebooks.com

2 4 6 8 9 7 5 3 1

First Edition

For Marcia
my eternal flame

How wonderful it is that nobody need wait
a single moment before starting to improve the world.
—ANNE FRANK

CAPITOL
BETRAYAL

Prologue

APRIL 14
9:17 A.M.

When the second shot blasted, the crowd panicked.

Seamus McKay swore under his breath. This sort of thing never happened in the deserts of Afghanistan, where there were rarely any crowds to panic. He never should've accepted a domestic assignment. But it was too late to worry about that now. There were four terrorists in there, at least three of them armed. He had kept his weapon holstered to avoid exactly the frenzied chaos that now surrounded him. But there was no point in remaining unarmed now. He drew his Glock 23 and pointed it into the air. The sooner all these tourists dispersed, the better.

He had no idea why the four men he was tracking had come to the Washington Monument, one of the most popular tourist attractions in D.C., but none of the possible answers was good. A fully capable nuclear suitcase had been stolen from a top-secret Arlington armory, and Seamus was convinced these men had it, or knew someone who did. He mentally combined all the possible reasons terrorists with nuclear capability might come to the Washington Monument . . . and every potential explanation sent chills racing down his spine.

Seamus fought his way through the crowd, both hands on the gun, making his way toward the front door against the flow. Why were they inside the monument, where several hundred tourists would be traveling up and down the elevators or perched at the top at any given moment? He needed to get there before they made it to the elevators. He stepped sideways, hands over his head, doing his salmon-swimming-upstream act, all the while being battered by screaming teenagers and overweight men wearing T-shirts and ball caps.

Another gunshot rang out, causing the stream of maddened tourists to move even faster and with less care for their surroundings. He had to keep his mind on what he was doing, without distractions. There were four of them and one of him, and although he had faced worse odds over the course of his CIA career, it wasn't something he looked forward to reexperiencing. The clichéd thought would be: I'm getting too old for this. But in the present case it had nothing to do with age. It was more the desire to live a real life, to experience what other men were doing in middle age, to settle down with—

Someone cuffed him on the back of the head. Damn it all, that would teach him to let his mind wander. He swung the gun around in a perfect one-heel pivot—

And brought it smack in the face of an elderly woman wearing a "Virginia Is for Lovers" lightweight jacket. She was carrying an umbrella, which was apparently the weapon of mass destruction she had used on him.

The gun didn't intimidate her. "You stepped on my foot!"

"Beg pardon, ma'am," Seamus said, bowing his head, then moving along again, back on his line drive toward the front entrance.

He jumped the turnstile.

The lobby was more spacious than you could ever believe possible just from looking at the tall, lean, sleek marble obelisk from the outside. At the far end, he saw the two elevators, and between them the famous bronze statue of George Washington designed by Jean-Antoine Houdon, the French neoclassical sculptor who had immortalized most of the great men of the late eighteenth and early nineteenth centuries. Though the lobby was large, it was still jam-packed with tourists. Why? There had been three gunshots, for God's sake. What were they waiting for, the city bus?

He scanned the crowd but didn't see any of the men he had been chasing. That was frustrating. Were they already riding to the top? Seamus didn't think there had been enough time. So where were they?

At least he didn't see any corpses lying on the floor. That was a relief. Those men must have fired for a reason, but as far as he could tell, it was not to kill. Probably just herding crowds out of their path or, perhaps, trying to instill terror. That was what terrorists did, right? It gave him cold comfort to see how ineffective they had been. There were still far too many people in here. But he could deal with that.

He raised his gun into the air, aimed toward a window (because damaging a national treasure could really dock his pay), and fired.

"Listen up!" Seamus bellowed at the top of his lungs. "I'm a federal officer. This is an emergency situation. As long as you remain here, you will be in danger. I want everyone to leave the building and the immediate vicinity of the monument. Now! Understood?"

In response, he heard a mixture of squealing and gasping and grumbling, even a muttered "Will they refund our tickets?"

Seamus fired his gun again. "So get out now, or I'll shoot you myself!"

That got the crowd moving. He had to suppress a smile. Yes, if nothing else, a decade in the Middle East trained you to be good at scaring people. In a few seconds, most of the spectators had cleared out. Now if he could just find—

Something hard bashed against the back of his head, and this time he was certain it was not an old lady's umbrella.

He fell forward but caught himself with his free hand and rolled around. One of his quarry was standing over him, grinning, his automatic weapon in his hands. He'd slammed Seamus with the butt and he was eager and ready to do it again. He had a deep scar—or perhaps a burn—on the left side of his face that made him both instantly identifiable and instantly threatening.

Seamus brought his gun hand around but the terrorist was too quick for him. He knocked the gun away. It skittered across the floor and disappeared in the distance.

Great.

While he was ducking, Seamus brought his fist around and pounded his assailant in the solar plexus. While he was doubled over, Seamus hit him again and again. When he saw the man's fingers weaken, he knocked the gun out of his hand, then followed through with another blow to the neck. Hard.

The man dropped to the floor like a withered flower. Seamus had literally knocked the wind out of him. He wasn't dead, but he would be out of the game for a good spell. That meant—

Another gunshot whizzed by just inches from Seamus's head. Damn. Another one. Where was he?

Early retirement was sounding better all the time. As long as he wasn't retired to a coffin.

More gunshots rang out. Seamus dove behind the priceless statue of George Washington between the elevators. He tried to spot the shooters. Staying low enough to be safe, he managed a quick survey of the lobby.

Two men were down on the floor, at opposite ends of the lobby. And the third was above him, on a raised platform in the north corner. Probably a security roost. But perfectly adapted to becoming a sniper's nest.

Seamus crouched beneath the statue, pinned down like a bug. Eventually someone would tell the police what was happening, but he would be dead long before that came about. He needed a weapon, or some plan of action.

But instead he got a major complication. He heard a sharp, abrupt ringing sound.

His blood went cold. The elevator to his right had arrived.

He turned just enough to see the doors opening. It was almost full of tourists who were in all likelihood going to become the next victims unless he did something fast.

Seamus executed another perfect sidewise somersault right into the elevator. Luckily, the tourists inside made way. Before the shooter had a chance to react, Seamus reached up and pushed the button to make the door close.

"Wait a minute!" a middle-aged man in striped Bermuda shorts said. "What the hell—"

And then the gunshots rang out. The man stopped talking.

Seamus saw the dents the bullets made in the door, but fortunately they closed before anyone was hurt. He pushed another button and the elevator began to rise. He could play it safe, ride all the way to the top, get out, and hope that help came quickly.

But there was that troubling matter of a nuclear device that they must have brought to this hallowed monument, this symbol of democracy, for a reason.

He pushed the button to stop the elevator midway up the shaft, then turned to face the eight people in the elevator. "What have you got?"

They looked at him as if he were out of his mind.

He grabbed an older woman by the shoulders. She had big beauty shop hair and a purse the size of a suitcase. That might be useful. "I'm asking what you've got! Answer me!"

She appeared to have difficulty speaking. "I—I don't have . . . anything."

He didn't have time for this. He grabbed her purse and spilled the contents onto the floor. She didn't say a word.

He sifted through the contents. A compact—useless. Wallet—useless. Kleenex—useless. Bobby pins, car keys, chewing gum—useless.

Hair spray. He tested it. Not a pump spray, but the old-school kind that used old-school fluorocarbons. An aerosol spray.

Useful.

And then he spotted what his mother used to call a rattail comb—a metal comb with a long, thin handle.

Also useful.

He crammed them into his pocket and barked at the others, "What have you got? Now!"

All at once, the two women and the teenage girl in the elevator dumped their purses on the floor. The men emptied their pockets. Seamus didn't know if they thought he was insane or if they thought he was dangerous, and at the moment he didn't much care, so long as they complied.

He sorted through all the junk on the floor. A Bic lighter. Absolutely useful. A rubber band. Well, you just never knew, did you? He didn't see anything else of value. Was this really all there was?

"Anyone else have anything?"

The man in the Bermuda shorts shrugged—but Seamus noticed a bulge in his Windbreaker pocket. He helped himself.

A glass flask.

"Scotch?"

The man avoided his gaze. "How'd you know?"

"Smelled it on your breath." Seamus shoved everything into his pockets. "Just stay here. It isn't safe down there. When the coast is clear, the police will come and rescue you. Now, who can give me a boost?"

The man in the Bermuda shorts bent over, and Seamus stepped up onto his back. He pushed open the escape panel and, with arms conditioned by years of gymnastics and regular exercise, pulled himself through the opening.

He was inside the monument. He knew that, once upon a time, people had been able to walk down the steps, but the stairs had been closed due to concerns about safety and vandalism on the many commemorative plaques. These elevators had originally been constructed to haul materials to the top, then, after it was completed, converted to use for transporting visitors.

He was about to use them for something completely different.

He could see the other elevator shaft about ten feet away. The cage was below him at ground level, but the cables were right there waiting for him.

He should be able to jump the distance. He had jumped farther, though not in a long time, and in this instance, if he didn't make it, he wouldn't just lose a medal. He'd lose his life, after falling about two hundred feet and splatting down on the cage below.

Well, nothing ventured . . .

He felt confident, even if he wasn't quite as light as he had been in younger years. He stepped toward the far edge of the elevator, then took a run at it. He flew through the open space between the elevators . . .

And overshot the mark and collided with the cables. His face burned against the main cable, which stung like hell. But he managed to get a grip on the cable and hold on to it.

He'd made it.

After that point, it was a simple matter of lowering himself to the elevator box below him. Simple until he arrived, anyway.

As quietly as possible, he opened the escape panel at the top. The doors were open.

He knew he would have no chance to survey the scene once he appeared in the opening. He had memorized the positions of the two men on the ground level just before the elevator doors closed. He hoped they hadn't moved too much.

He gripped the edge of the escape hatch and took a deep breath.

Showtime. Five, four, three, two . . .

On one, Seamus flew through the opening, swinging outside the doors and several yards beyond. The terrorist on the far right had drifted, but not so far that Seamus couldn't accommodate the difference with a quick course correction. The man brought his gun around, but Seamus was too fast for him. Seamus wrapped himself around the man's legs and brought him down to the ground. He squatted on top of the man, pounding him in the face before he had a chance to resist. He pressed his gun down with one hand and grabbed the rattail comb in the other. In one swift, sure movement, he drove the long thin tail of the comb into the man's temple.

The terrorist didn't even have a chance to scream. He was dead in less than a second.

And a second after that, his friends reacted. Seamus grabbed the dead man's gun and responded, which sent the others flying. It appeared the remaining man on the ground was not armed. That would make Seamus's job simpler. He ran under the ledge so the man above couldn't see him, then pulled the trigger.

Nothing happened.

Out of ammunition. Could he never catch a break?

The other man had a knife, a big ugly one, almost a machete. He was running toward Seamus, a desperate expression on his face, the knife raised above his head. And Seamus had . . .

Hair spray.

He would have to make it work for him.

He waited until his attacker was most of the way to him, because he knew that if he stepped out from under the ledge he was a dead man. When the man was ten feet away, Seamus brought up the hair spray, pushed down the button, and ignited the spray with the Bic lighter.

A stream of fire blazed through the air, smacking the other man in the face. He screamed and dropped the knife as his hands reflexively went to his face. All at once, his features became liquid. The flesh of his face began to blacken and burn.

Seamus gave him two swift kicks to the kneecaps, just to make sure he didn't go anywhere, not that there was much chance. This poor loser's only concern would be his pain.

That left the man upstairs.

While the hotshot with the automatic rifle was still trying to figure out what had happened below, Seamus leaped up and grabbed the edge of the balcony ledge, pulled himself up into a crouch, then pushed off the bottom edge into the air. He found himself above the balcony and just in front of the man with the gun.

While still in midair, Seamus kicked out, knocking the gun from the man's hands. On his way down, he brought his elbow into the man's nose.

The cartilage shattered instantly. Blood spewed out in all directions. That had to hurt.

But it didn't stop him. On his hands and feet, he crawled toward his gun. In less than a second, Seamus calculated what was going to happen and the likely result. No matter how fast he was, the other man would reach the gun first. He'd mow Seamus down before he got halfway there.

Unless Seamus did something to stop him.

Seamus removed the glass flask from his pocket and pitched it with his best Nolan Ryan speed at the man on the floor. The alcohol drenched his lower body.

Seamus had maybe two seconds before the man reached the gun. In that time, he pulled out the Bic, ignited it, used the rubber band to pin down the click switch, keeping it ignited, and threw it at the man crawling across the floor.

An instant later, he was engulfed in flames.

He beat desperately at the fire, but there was nothing he could do. The inferno spread with alarming speed. Five seconds later, his entire body was immolated. The cries sizzled down to whimpers and soon after that were gone altogether, lost in a hideous sea of flame and flesh. His body fell to the floor, motionless.

At that point, Seamus stopped looking. He knew where this was going. He didn't need to witness it.

He lowered himself off the balcony and dropped back down to the floor. The man he had used the hair spray on was still writhing on the ground.

But the first man he had attacked, the man with the hideous scar, was gone.

And he still had not found the silver suitcase.

He crouched down beside Hair Spray Man. The flames had burned out, but he was in shock, shaking and immobilized by pain.

Seamus didn't care. He grabbed him by his hair—very hot—and jerked his head backward.

The terrorist's eyes flew open. He made a gurgling noise. Seamus knew that in his condition, he could suffocate easily.

He whispered into the man's ear, "I'll give you one chance to answer. If you don't, you're dead. If you lie to me, you'll die and I'll make you hurt even worse than you do now." He leaned in closer. "Where's the suitcase?"

The man was trembling so badly he could barely speak. "G-g-gone."

He pointed in the general direction where the man with the scar had been. Damn! "What were you planning to do here?"

"S-s-s—" For a moment Seamus doubted he would ever get it out, but he finally managed. "Send your president . . . a message."

By blowing up the Washington Monument and irradiating everyone in the nation's capital? Yeah, that would probably screw up the president's plans in the Middle East. "Where is your friend going with the suitcase?"

"I don't know. R-r-really." Given the circumstances, Seamus didn't doubt him. He couldn't lie, not now, and his eyes showed just how desperate he was to comply, to be believed.

"What are you planning now? What are you going to do next?"

Seamus couldn't be sure, but despite the man's pain, despite his almost certain knowledge that death would soon be forthcoming—or perhaps because of it—the corners of his lips turned upward. He was smiling.

"You're too late," he said as his eyelids fluttered closed. "No matter what you do to me. Or anyone else. You're too late."

Part One

The
Bunker

1

Ben Kincaid stood rigid and still as his wife, Christina McCall, adjusted his tie, smoothed the lie of his shirt, and ran a lint brush over the shoulders of his navy blue suit coat.

"There," she said, taking a step back to survey the view. "Now you look like someone who's ready to advise the leader of the free world."

"That's a relief."

"Remember to smile and say something nice about his wife. And don't remind him about—" She stopped in midsentence. "Wait just a minute." She hiked up the leg of his blue slacks. "Are you seriously wearing red socks?"

Ben's eyes moved downward. "They're my lucky socks."

"No."

"But I need all the luck—"

"No." She pointed toward the clothes closet. "Change."

Ben obeyed without further protest. Of course, he always made a great show of being put out when Christina made these sartorial demands, but in truth, he didn't mind a bit. Given that he had no sense of fashion and was partially color-blind, he needed all the help he could get and was capable of accepting it without feeling his manhood was threatened. For years his mother had picked out and paired up all his clothes. Now she had passed the torch to his wife. All this meant, he reminded himself as he changed into a pair of blue socks, was that he was a very fortunate man.

The irony was that, once upon a time, Christina had been known for her dubious fashion sense, for dressing more like a member of the Sex Pistols than a practicing attorney. All that had changed last year when Ben made his run for a Senate seat. In addition to the five thousand other consultants they'd consulted, they'd hired a fashion consultant to tell them how to dress for formal functions, casual events, and television appearances. For Christina, it was a road-to-Damascus experience. Now she had the reputation of being one of the sharpest dressers in Washington. Ben had been asked more than once if she had acquired a fashion degree at some point in her past. With her gorgeous red hair styled in a fetching shoulder-length coif, Ben found her absolutely stunning. Not that he was prejudiced or anything.

"That's more like it," she said when he reemerged. "And just for the record, you're not wearing those Superman boxer shorts, are you?"

"I'm not planning to strip at the White House."

"Yes, and nothing unplanned ever happens to you, does it?"

"Good point. No, I'm clean."

"Thank you." She smiled, and the smile made his spirits soar. Such a beautiful woman. Her face seemed to absolutely glow. Was it all his imagination? She even seemed taller these days. Although he supposed that could have something to do with the heels. "Anything else you need, *mon cher amour?*"

"No. I'd better go. Traffic is terrible this time of day. And it still takes half an hour to get cleared to enter the White House."

"Still?"

"Yup." Ben had been working for almost two months now as a member of the president's legal team. Robert Griswold was the official special counsel to the president, but he had a staff of four lawyers. After his Senate defeat Ben had been appointed to fill a temporary vacancy on that staff. Despite the loss—not exactly unusual for a Democrat in Oklahoma—Ben's rankings in popularity polls remained high nationwide as a result of his work during his brief time in the Senate, particularly his work on the controversial Emergency Council bill, which garnered nationwide daily coverage. His oration on the floor of the Senate was widely credited with being the cause of the bill's ulti-mate defeat, which endeared him to many, especially in the Democratic party. Still, he'd been flabbergasted when the newly elected president, Roland Kyler, invited him into the White House. "I want the president to have a chance to read my brief. So I'm out of here."

"Did you have Jones proofread it?"

"I'm an adult, Christina."

"And you're the worst speller on earth. Spell-check is not enough for you. Email it to Jones now. He'll have it proofed by the time you get to the White House."

He raised his chin a bit. "If you insist. Parting is such sweet sorrow, but—"

"Wait." She took both of Ben's hands and snuggled close to him. "Can you believe that sometime today you're going to see the POTUS?" Christina had always loved hip slang and catchphrases. She'd picked up on the Beltway acronyms in no time at all. "You work hard and try to help him. He's a good man."

"You just say that because he did you a favor."

"No, I say it because it's true."

"You're talking about his inspirational politics?"

"I'm talking about him, the human being. He's good to his wife. That's the surest sign of a good man."

Ben arched an eyebrow. "Is it indeed?"

"Yes. I read that he's given up smoking after twenty years because his wife didn't want smoke to ruin the White House—or him. That can't be easy, but he's doing it for her. So you help him out, Ben. He doesn't need any extra trouble."

"I'll probably get ten minutes with him. If I'm lucky."

"Look at you!" She grinned and pulled him closer. "You're talking about meeting with President Kyler all calm, cool, and collected. I re-member when you couldn't think about talking to a judge without your knees shaking so badly you could barely walk."

Ben shrugged. "Times change. People grow up."

"They do indeed." She wrapped her arms around him. "And may I just say, Mr. Kincaid, that I like the way you've grown up, very much." She pressed herself against him and squeezed.

"Oh, I almost forgot." Ben grinned. "I have a surprise for you."

"What a coincidence. I have a surprise for you also."

"Well, you'll never top mine."

"Never say never."

"No, that's what you always do. You always top my story. But not this time."

"Okay," she said, "you go first."

Ben beamed. "Robert says there's a good chance that after this temporary appointment expires, I might be appointed to the president's energy commission."

"That's terrific! Who better than a good Oklahoma boy to advise the president on energy concerns?"

"Well, he knows we have to shift over to natural gas, the sooner the better. Our dependency on foreign oil is killing this country on numerous fronts. And we simultaneously need to develop alternative energy sources—"

Christina held up her hands. "Hold on, tiger. I've already heard the speech. Save it for the president."

"Right. Sorry. But isn't that great news?"

"Terrific."

"So what's your news, huh? Go ahead and try to top a presidential commission appointment."

She batted her long eyelashes. "I've signed LexiCo as a firm client."

Ben's lips parted. "No."

"Yup. We're their counsel for all litigation matters, civil and criminal."

"No!" Ben knew LexiCo was a huge East Coast technology firm that Christina had been courting for months. Having them on the firm roster would not only generate much revenue but start a precedent. Where LexiCo went others would surely follow. Ben had been concerned about the firm and its nascent D.C. satellite office, especially after he went "Of Counsel" so he could take the White House appointment. Now it appeared that Christina had landed a client who could keep the firm busy well into the future. "That's fantastic!"

"Yup. I'm hiring a new associate. Just in case I want to take some time off."

"Good thinking."

"And?"

He sighed. "And your news is bigger than mine."

"Like I said, never say never." She pulled him close once more.

"Can we make a date to watch *Jeopardy* together tonight?"

She made a small moue. "Because you've read, like, every history book ever written? I don't think I can stand to hear you ace all the history questions again."

"Hey, at least you don't have to listen to someone talking about how sexy Alex Trebek is."

"I only did that once!" She squeezed him all the tighter. "It's just 'cause he reminds me of you, you smarty. So tell me the truth—do you like me a lot, or do you really truly love me, Mr. Kincaid?"

He hugged her with all his heart and soul. "Yes."

2

As it turned out, Ben's estimates were all wrong. Traffic was so jammed as he left their K Street apartment that it took him forty-five minutes to get to the White House, but only twenty-five minutes to pass through all the security protocols and get to his office. It worked out the same. Only a few minutes after he reached his office, the president's chief of staff knocked on his door.

"The president is ready to see you."

Ben rose to his feet. He knew Sarie Morrell didn't like it, but his mother had taught him to always rise when a woman entered the room, and old habits died hard. Sarie was the president's chief of staff, one of the few females to ever hold that position. Her crisp efficiency, not to mention her good looks and snappy dress, often reminded Ben of his wife. Sarie was a blonde, with long, straight hair that stretched past her shoulder blades, but she shared with Christina that most valuable of all assets: the ability to get things done. Other White House staffers dithered, changed their minds, vacillated, but not Sarie. Once she made a plan, she stuck to it and pushed to make it a reality. In the short time he'd been in the White

House, Ben had seen what an asset she could be to President Kyler, whom he believed to be a good man with his heart in the right place.

"Do I need to bring anything?"

Sarie was an Alabama girl and spoke with a pronounced southern accent. "Just a notepad and your razor-sharp brains."

"I think I left them at home."

"Then fake it. That's what the rest of us do."

Ben grabbed his legal pad and followed her into the corridor. She moved fast, and he had to make an effort to walk with her, rather than in her wake. The legal office was at the far edge of the West Wing, near the elevator the First Family used to get to their personal rooms. The corridors were crowded today, but then, they almost always were. He was amazed by how much business, in so many different arenas, was conducted in the White House on a daily basis.

Ben still considered this sprawling mansion, which insiders called "the Residence," a large Greek labyrinth. He had learned to negotiate his way by noting landmarks. In a few moments they passed the Red Room, a favorite of his because he knew it was a favorite of Eleanor Roosevelt's and had been refurbished under the direction of Jacqueline Kennedy. Barely a half minute later, given Sarie's brisk pace, they were whizzing by the Green Room and the Blue Room, both of which he knew had been substantially improved by Pat Nixon. Her husband had covered up FDR's swimming pool and added a bowling alley. Pat had brought in more than six hundred fabulous artifacts and artworks. How did those two ever live together?

They turned right into the main corridor and almost collided with Dr. Henry Albertson, the president's chief physician, who entered at the same time from the opposite side. Ben was surprised to see him. He knew the White House medical office was located at the far opposite end of the corridor.

Ben nodded at the doctor. "You're walking briskly this morning."

Albertson was an avuncular man in his mid-sixties, his hair still brown and his cheeks the color of radishes. "You do anything else in this joint, you'll get trampled."

"Not on your way to an emergency, I hope."

"No. Just headed for the Oval Office."

Ben's eyes narrowed slightly. "Now? Are you involved in the off-shore drilling case somehow?"

"No, no. I just like to drop in from time to time. To observe what's going on."

"You mean with the president?"

"Just every now and again. Whenever Sarie thinks it's a good idea."

Out the corner of his eye, Ben saw a look pass from Sarie to the doctor. The expression on Albertson's face gave him the distinct impression that she thought he should close his mouth. He did.

As Ben continued walking down the corridor he attempted to break what had become an uncomfortable silence. "Any progress with the Speaker of the House, Sarie?" President Kyler was a Democrat, but the Republicans controlled the House, and as a result, Kyler had been unable to pass any of his major objectives so far. The Speaker, Congressman Wilkins, was extremely charismatic and high-profile, probably nursing presidential aspirations of his own. "Surely there must be someplace they can compromise."

"If so, I haven't found it. And believe me, I've tried." She flashed him a quick smile. "I've turned on all my southern-girl charm and then some. Even offered to come by the House cafeteria and whip up a batch of my grandmama's hominy grits. He didn't go for it."

Ben shook his head. "The man must be made of steel."

"Well, he's from New Jersey. They don't know what good food is."

"Wait a minute," Dr. Albertson said. "I'm from New Jersey."

"And have you ever eaten my grandmama's hominy grits?"

"Well, if the opportunity arose . . ."

"I brought some to the potluck at Vice President Swinburne's house last month. And I made careful note of who partook and who did not. You were not among the partakers."

Albertson cleared his throat. "Well, I would've been." He patted his stomach. "But that darned spastic colon of mine was acting up."

Sarie gave him a long look. "Do tell."

"I don't think I've ever had grits," Ben said.

"Well, you're a man of culture and refinement," Sarie replied. "I feel certain you would adore them."

"Doesn't that pretty little wife of yours fix you breakfast?" Albertson asked.

"She does," Ben replied. "She makes a fantastic spinach omelet. When she has time." And when she didn't, he did not add, or when she wasn't looking, he dug into his secret stash of Cap'n Crunch. Living with a health food nut could be so challenging at times.

A deep, gravelly voice cut into the conversation. "This must be the Three Stooges. On their way to tell the emperor he's got no clothes."

Ben veered left and saw his least favorite person in the entire White House, Admiral Wilson Cartwright, the head of the White House Military Office. He was a stocky older man, about a foot shorter than Ben, but if you judged by his bearing and manner, you would think he must be at least three feet taller.

Ben had never been very good with the military. But Cartwright seemed to have an absolute antipathy for lawyers. Whenever possible, Ben just tried to stay out of the man's way.

"We're off to see the wizard," Ben answered.

Cartwright made a guttural growling sound. "Then you can follow me."

Of course. It would have to be that way. Cartwright led the way down the corridor.

"Are you interested in offshore drilling?" Ben asked.

"Oil reserves are first and foremost a military concern," Cartwright replied in a tone that suggested Ben was a total idiot for asking.

"Yes, but this is a legal matter. The injunction—"

Cartwright's eyes moved closer together. "Maybe you've been too busy chasing ambulances to notice what's been going on in the Middle East for the past fifty years or so, but it's the greatest threat to this nation, so I don't have the luxury of looking the other way."

Ben knew it was foolish to even reply. Anything he said would be twisted around to fit into the man's monomaniacal worldview. But the perverse imp within Ben wouldn't let it lie. "I still don't understand why the military needs to attend a legal strategy session."

"Well, I don't know why Robert Griswold appointed you to his staff. A man that age normally has more sense. But I do know this: as soon as we enter the Oval Office, you'll do your bleeding-heart routine about the environment and you'll oppose every sensible approach to reducing our dependence on foreign oil. Someone with some perspective has to be there."

So that was what this was all about. "I'm all for reducing our dependence on foreign oil," Ben said. "But I won't sacrifice our natural resources for another basin of oil or two. The only long-term answer is alternative—"

"I don't have the luxury of dwelling on so-called long-term solutions. I have to deal with the threats that confront us in the here and now."

"I still don't understand—"

Cartwright stopped abruptly. "You don't have to understand, Mr. Kincaid. All you have to do is file your little lawsuits and stay out of the way of the men who are doing the real work to protect this nation. You understand what I'm telling you? Stay out of my way."

Ben tucked in his chin. "You may have been confused by my snappy attire, but I am not in the military. I am not under your authority and I do not take orders from you."

"Everyone in this building takes orders from me, mister." To some extent, Ben knew that was true. As head of the White House Military Office, Cartwright was in charge of the entire building and everything that transpired within, including communications, food, medicine, emergency procedures, and all forms of executive transportation. If the president wanted something done here, it went through Admiral Cartwright. And if Cartwright wanted to attend this meeting, there was no way that Ben could stop him. "So my advice to you is to stay out of my way. I do not like enemies and I do not treat them kindly."

"Oh, look," Dr. Albertson said, clapping his hands together. "We've arrived. What a shame this engaging conversation will have to come to an end."

Ben noted that Sarie had to bite down on her lip to keep from smiling.

They approached the northeast door to the Oval Office. Ben knew there were four entrances to the executive office. The northeast door opened onto the president's secretary's office; the northwest door led to the main corridor of the West Wing; the west door connected to a small study and a dining room; and the east door led directly to the Rose Garden. This was the primary way in for visitors, perhaps because it made it easier for his secretary, or the chief of staff if she was available, to prevent unwanted intrusions.

They were greeted by the press secretary, Alden Meyers, a tall man from Connecticut whose background was in advertising.

"The president may be delayed," he told them in a hushed voice. "There's a crisis. We're preparing a statement."

Ben immediately thought of the Speaker of the House and the legislation now being debated. "A legislative crisis?"

Meyers lowered his head gravely. His voice dropped at least an octave. "No. A nuclear crisis."

3

8:44 A.M.

Admiral Cartwright moved rapidly to the forefront. "Nuclear? Has there been an detonation?"

"No," Meyers replied. "Not yet, anyway. But a nuclear suitcase bomb has disappeared from a secret Arlington armory. The CIA has some leads and they've been tracking suspects."

"Terrorists."

"That would be the worst-case scenario. It's always possible it was misplaced—"

"Someone misplaced a nuclear bomb?"

"—or relocated. One of those left-hand-doesn't-know-what-the-right-hand-is-doing situations. But the circumstances suggest theft by foreign agents, so the CIA has been investigating."

"Have they apprehended anyone?"

"Not yet. There's an agent in the field who thought he had something important, but we haven't heard anything back from him yet."

"Are we going public with this?"

"The president says yes, even though he knows there will be negative fallout. It will undoubtedly cause panic and criticism. But the people have a right to know. And he's afraid that if he doesn't and a bomb goes off, he'll look like he didn't know what was going on."

"I think that's a mistake," Cartwright grunted, looking at the Oval Office door. "But I guess I can tell the man myself."

"Look," Ben interjected, "my little meeting can wait. Sounds like the president has more important things—"

"No," Meyers said. "Your meeting may be brief, but he wants it to happen. The president wants to continue doing business as usual. It's important not to let a possible terrorist threat interfere with the work of governing. And we don't know at this time that there's any immediate threat."

Ben shrugged. "Whatever the man wants."

Sarie knocked on the door. "Roland?"

The door opened, and on the other side, Ben glimpsed the POTUS himself—the president of the United States.

"Come on in, gang."

Cartwright, predictably, entered first, though Sarie was racing so hard they almost bumped shoulders passing through the doorway. Albertson followed close behind. Ben was content to be fourth. Meyers moved in the opposite direction, presumably off to prepare a press release.

Sarie and Cartwright sat on the two facing sofas with such speed that Ben wondered if they had assigned seats. Albertson stood at the north end of the room beside the portrait of George Washington. Ben wasn't sure where to go, but the president gestured toward two high-back Martha Washington–style lolling chairs in front of the fireplace. Ben took the seat on the right. He had noticed during previous meetings that the president always sat on the left. He wasn't sure why, but given how every move any president made these days was carefully calculated and orchestrated in advance, he was sure there was a reason.

President Kyler was a tall Californian who had managed to maintain his tan even in the often inclement climate of Washington, D.C. He had the sort of distinguished senior-statesman good looks that photographed well on television, an essential these days for anyone hoping to be elected to the highest office in the land.

Ben couldn't resist smiling when he saw Kyler, even though these days he normally saw him at least once a week. The thrill never died. He had been a huge supporter of Kyler during his campaign, though at certain times and places he'd had to keep it to himself—he didn't want his own failing senatorial run to impact negatively on Kyler's. Christina was the one who had singled Kyler out early in the campaign as the best hope for the nation. After his predecessor's tumultuous, saber-rattling administration, Kyler looked like a much-needed breath of fresh air. He favored all the progressive people-first programs that the previous president had ignored. He pushed education and alternative energy and, best of all, dreamed of augmenting diplomatic missions to ease world tensions and render future invasions and wars unnecessary. His speeches had so inspired Christina that anytime she could spare time from Ben's campaign, she devoted it to his.

This had become important barely a month after Ben started work-ing for Kyler, when Christina needed a favor. Ben was barely comfort-able speaking to the president, much less asking for a favor. He knew how busy the president was and doubted he could find time to do any-thing for them. He was wrong. Kyler remembered that Christina had been one of his earliest and most ardent supporters. He put her prob-lem at the front of his executive to-do list and had the whole mess cleared up in less than a day. It was hard not to admire someone like that, someone who could take the highest office in the land and still not forget who his friends were. Ben never forgot anyone who had been kind to his beloved wife, especially not someone who had taken time to do her this favor. He owed the president a debt of kindness he would always remember, and which he would be happy to pay back any way he could.

"Please, everyone, take a seat," the president said. He seemed pre-occupied, which was not surprising, given what Ben had just heard.

Kyler had installed a wide-screen video monitor over the fireplace, which Ben knew was capable of receiving every television channel known to mankind, satellite transmissions, closed-circuit transmissions, and just about anything else the president might ever wish to view.

The president launched into the discussion exactly the way Ben had expected—a discussion between two men, the president and his legal counsel. "You'll forgive me if I'm brief, Ben. There's a lot going on right now. Not only—"

Admiral Cartwright interrupted. "What's the latest intel on the stolen suitcase?"

Kyler blinked a moment but remained unflappable and turned to answer the question. Ben marveled at the temerity of a man willing to interrupt the president of the United States.

"Nothing concrete. We had a promising report from a field agent, but he's been out of contact for over twenty minutes now and we don't know his location. Seamus McKay."

"I know McKay," Ben said, then immediately wished he hadn't, after every head in the room turned to face him. "It was just a little . . . I mean, nothing—" He cleared his throat. "I met him once, when I was a senator. Gave him some advice. Seemed like a good, capable man."

"He's the best we have," the president rejoined. "Spent almost two decades in the Middle East. He's like Superman. James Bond on steroids."

"But you haven't heard back from him," Cartwright said.

"No."

"I hope someone hasn't pulled off Superman's cape."

"Exactly." The president paused. "Still, the investigation is ongoing. We have no reason to believe there is any present danger."

Cartwright made a dismissive noise with his lips.

"The situation in Kuraq concerns me a good deal more. As you know, we've had aircraft carriers and troops poised in the Gulf for some time, ready to invade Kuraq if they don't back off their occupation of the Benzai Strip. They've been threatening to instigate a genocidal war against the natives. The UN is still debating, but I'm not going to stand still and do nothing while they slaughter thousands of people."

"What's the new development?" Ben asked.

"A Red Cross helicopter on its way to Benzai went down just over the Kuraqi border. We think at least some of the passengers are still alive. But the military leader, Colonel Zuko, won't give us permission to recover them."

"Why should he?" Cartwright said. "He's not blind. He can see you're preparing to invade. You'll be lucky if he doesn't grab them all and turn them into hostages."

"Yes, thank you, that possibility had occurred to us."

"Then what are you doing about it?"

"Everything we possibly can, Will." Ben couldn't help admiring how well Kyler kept his cool, even when being openly challenged by that tinhorn brass hat. He supposed some people might see it as weakness, but Ben admired a man who didn't need to get into a cockfight to show who was boss. The president of the United States had no need to prove himself. He was the commander in chief, whether Cartwright liked it or not.

"But this isn't what I wanted to talk with you about, Ben. As you know, the SageTech firm has filed for injunctive relief from federal regulations preventing them from offshore drilling near the coast of Virginia. If they are successful, it could upset my entire energy plan. Are they going to be successful?"

"Predicting the outcome of lawsuits is a fool's game," Ben replied.

A corner of the president's mouth tugged upward. "I must be paying you for something."

"Here's the reality of the situation. There are many places SageTech could've filed this lawsuit. They undoubtedly chose Virginia because the state's supreme court leans heavily to the right. Regardless of what happens in the lower courts, it will eventually end up before the state supremes, and some of them might be tempted to vote their politics instead of their legal precedents."

"But then we could appeal to the U.S. Supreme Court."

"Yes, but it's also heavy on the Republican side."

"They can't just ignore the law."

"No. They'll say the law is unconstitutional and argue that is should be set aside."

"I assume you'll have a response."

Ben raised his eyebrows. "Now that *is* what you pay me for." Ben removed a stapled bundle of papers from his legal pad. "I've prepared three drafts exemplifying different approaches we could take. All of them are geared toward one thing."

"Winning in the Supreme Court."

"No. Winning everywhere. Because we don't want a lower-court loss. Even if we can later get it reversed, the press will be all over it, the Speaker of the House will declare it a victory, and your energy plan will suffer."

"You're exactly right."

"So we need to win, not just in the last court, but in every court."

"That would be a miracle."

Ben shrugged slightly. "Miracles are kind of my specialty."

President Kyler extended his hand. "Kincaid, I don't know if I've mentioned this before, but I like you. And I'm glad to have you on my staff."

"The feeling is mutual, sir."

"I hate to break up this lovefest," Cartwright barked, "but when the Middle East is on the brink of disaster, don't we have more important things to discuss than some damn lawsuit?"

Kyler sighed. "Stay calm, Admiral. It's not as if the United States has never intervened in Middle Eastern affairs before."

"Don't I know it! There's been too much of it. Never comes to anything good."

"That's not—"

"We have no jurisdiction there," Cartwright said adamantly. It seemed he was willing to address the newly elected president in the same officious manner he used to address Ben.

To Kyler's credit, he took it all in stride—though this close up, Ben did notice a tiny twitch in his eye. "Will, there's no point in being the leader of the free world if you're not willing to lead."

"All you're doing is asking for more trouble in the Middle East, as if we hadn't had enough already. And for what? A bunch of overfed, overpaid sheiks who blow their money on fancy hotel rooms instead of building a nation?"

"That's only a small percentage of—"

"It doesn't matter. America's first concern should be America."

"And it is. But when we wield so much power, it would be immoral to stand idly by and—"

"If you send in those troops, you'll leave a gaping hole in our national defense."

"A hole? A hole?" Kyler smiled and, to Ben's amazement, began to sing. "There's a hole in the bucket, dear Liza, dear Liza. There's a hole in the bucket, dear Liza, a hole."

The room fell silent. Ben saw Dr. Albertson and Sarie exchange a meaningful glance.

Kyler continued grinning. While the others watched silently, he rose from his chair and walked to his desk.

Ben knew he had been under a good deal of stress during his first few months in office. Was the strain already starting to get to him? His eyes seemed unfocused and distant.

"I love this desk," Kyler said, rubbing his hand lightly over the inset leather blotter. "It's called the Resolute desk. Do you know why? It was made from the timbers of the British frigate HMS *Resolute,* which was discovered by American whalers after it was stranded in the ice and abandoned by all hands. The ship was repaired by the U.S. Navy and returned to England. This desk was a reciprocal gift from Queen Victoria to President Rutherford B. Hayes. Can you imagine the great minds that have sat at this desk? Great minds. Great minds."

"Mr. President," Cartwright said, his bushy eyebrows tightly knitted together. "Can we talk about Kuraq? I assume—"

Kyler flung himself across the desk. "Ha! But you should never assume. Because when you assume, you make an ass out of you and me. *A-s-s, u,* and *m-e.* Get it?"

Dr. Albertson quietly rose to his feet. Somehow a sphygmomanometer had materialized in his hands. He approached the president. "Sir, I'd like to take your blood pressure and conduct a small examination, just to make sure—"

"Oh, leave me alone." Kyler turned and faced the large window behind the desk. "So much history has occurred in this room. So much history. Did you know that the White House—which they used to call the Executive Mansion—originally didn't even have a West Wing? True. You can thank Teddy Roosevelt for this. Before him, this whole wing was covered by gardens and greenhouses. Teddy was the one who decided he needed a retreat from his wife and children and pets and nieces and nephews. He had the West Wing constructed to give himself a private retreat where he could actually get some work done. Taft enlarged it, and every president since has worked right here, in this office, gazing out at this magnificent view."

Albertson tapped him on the shoulder. "Sir, I really must insist—"

"On what? A round of croquet?"

"On invoking my authority as White House physician to do a spot examination to make sure you're of sound mind and body."

"Of course I am. Go away, Henry."

Ben noticed Cartwright was watching this exchange carefully.

"Give me two minutes and I can confirm that you have not suffered a cardiac arrest or a brain hemorrhage. That will do for now. Later we can—"

Without warning, the northwest door flew open and four men streamed through the opening. From their dress, Ben assumed that they were Secret Service agents. In fact, Ben recognized one of them—Max Zimmer. He had met Zimmer during the second tragedy in Oklahoma City.

"Mr. President, please come with us."

President Kyler seemed even more befuddled. "Come with you? You come with me!"

"No, sir." Without further comment, Agent Zimmer placed his hands under the president's arms and hoisted him into the air.

"Up, up, and away, in my beautiful, my beautiful ballooooooon!" the president sang. "Where are we going?"

"To the PEOC, sir. Immediately."

The PEOC? Ben wondered. Had he heard right? What—or where—was that?

The Secret Service men took no notice of the president's behavior. Ben wondered if that was because they were so professional and focused—or because they were used to it.

Another agent grabbed Ben's arm. "You'll have to come, too, sir."

"Me? I'm just a lawyer."

"Our instructions are to relocate everyone in the Oval Office immediately."

"Can I call my wife first?" Ben asked, taking out his cell phone.

"No, sir," the agent said, snatching it away from him. "You may not." He gave Ben a push and herded him toward the doorway. Ben saw the other agents doing the same for everyone else in the room.

Just as they almost had him through the door, President Kyler put his foot down—literally. He pivoted in the doorway and faced them.

"Just one damn minute," he said forcefully. He seemed like his previous self once again. "I'm the president of the United States. I demand to be informed why I am being relocated."

Agent Zimmer shook his head. "There isn't time, sir."

"Then make it quick."

Zimmer paused. "We have reason to believe that short-range theater ballistic missiles may be headed toward the White House."

The president's eyes widened—just like everyone else's. "Ballistic missiles! How could they get this close to Washington without being detected earlier?"

Zimmer pressed his lips tightly together. "They're ours."

4

Christina made her way through the front door of the offices of Kincaid & McCall on C Street. They were not as plush as the old digs at Warren Place in Tulsa, but arguably the location was better. Particularly when your husband was jumping from one political appointment to the next. And that was the key to real estate, wasn't it? Location, location, location.

Jones was sitting in the front office, taking phone messages, answering email, and watching CNN out the corner of his eye.

"What's happening?" Christina asked, flinging her briefcase up on the counter. "What's new in our world?"

"Nothing unexpected. Just me managing the office all by myself. As usual."

Jones was a fabulous office manager, so the martyr streak was something she and Ben had learned to ignore. "Gosh, sorry. What am I, two minutes late? *Excusez-moi!*"

"I thought you were coming in at eight now."

"Did I say that? Well, I thought better of it."

"You've got about a zillion calls from someone at LexiCo. Are they a client?"

"They are now," she said proudly.

"Great. More work. When is Ben coming back?"

"Not anytime soon, I'm afraid. Fear not, Jones. We'll survive."

"Yeah. But I miss seeing the Boss."

She didn't bother to ask why she wasn't the boss now. She knew that for Jones, there was only one Boss, and it wasn't her—and it wasn't Bruce Springsteen, either. "I'm sure he'll drop by from time to time. But he's very busy. Such a big shot. Working for the president."

"Yeah, yeah. Very impressive."

For a moment Christina was afraid he was going to cry. She would have to make sure Ben came by for a visit. "Anything else going on?"

"You've got three youngsters wanting to interview for the associate position."

"Swell."

"You didn't tell me we were hiring another associate."

Christina sighed. "Jones, we're—"

"As the financial comptroller of this outfit, shouldn't I have been consulted? So you could determine *if* we can afford a new associate."

"This LexiCo work should pay for an associate's salary and then some."

He sniffed. "Let's hope so."

"Any phone messages?"

"Yes," he said, lightening somewhat. "My wife got a job at the Library of Congress."

"That's wonderful. Paula will be able to stay with you here full-time. I'm glad. I don't think a married couple should ever be separated for long."

"Well, you know, we've been married awhile. We're not as googly-eyed as you and Ben."

"I'm sorry to hear that."

"I'm not. I have trouble keeping down my dinner when I'm around you two."

She grinned. "Anything else? You know what I want to hear."

"Sorry. No word from Loving."

She frowned. Their longtime investigator Loving had taken a tough beating some time ago when he was tracking cesium smugglers during an investigation relating to one of Ben's cases. He'd survived, but the trauma of the experience had hit him hard. He'd asked for some time off—an investigative sabbatical, so to speak—to relax, recover, and try to get his head together. No one had seen or heard from him since.

"If that changes, let me know immediately."

"I will."

"Anything I can do for you?" she asked.

He pressed his hand against his chest. "No, no, you just go on about your business. I'll take care of all the logistics and payroll and everything else that's difficult or—" His eyes darted to the television screen. "Wait a minute. What's going on?"

Christina edged around the counter so she could see. The screen was displaying a stock picture of the White House.

" . . . don't have the details, but we are told that the terrorist alert warning is at its highest and that there is a concern that we may be facing an imminent threat. Inside sources say that the president and everyone else in the White House have been evacuated to an undisclosed safe location. Repeated rumors are circulating that the White House itself may be in danger and . . ."

Christina stared at the screen, her face turning ashen. "Ben!"

5

The president and Agent Zimmer continued to exchange words while moving, but the whole evacuation procedure became so frenzied Ben could no longer hear what was being said. He felt as if he were a cow in a slaughterhouse. The Secret Service agents didn't quite use a prod on him, but almost. If he delayed or hesitated, his personal shepherd pushed up against him, nudging him along.

They quickly passed through Cross Hall, which connected the State Dining Hall and the East Room. A few seconds later they were in the East Wing, where the First Lady and the White House social secretary kept their offices. Where were they going?

As they entered the corridor, they encountered another squadron of agents with two political heavy hitters of their own: Michael Ruiz, the nation's first Hispanic to fill the office of secretary of state, and secretary of defense, Albert Rybicki. Just before they turned the corner, Ben thought he caught a glimpse of another platoon of agents whisking someone in the opposite direction—someone who looked like the vice president of the United States. Could that be? Why wasn't he coming with them?

But once he thought for a moment, he realized that made perfect sense. Even if there wasn't time to transport everyone else, they would take the VP to another location. They didn't want the president and his immediate replacement in the same place. Just in case those missiles made contact.

After they had traveled about halfway into the East Wing, the Secret Service agents herded them into a large elevator. It had the spacious, no-frills appearance of a freight or cargo elevator, but given how many of them there were, Ben was grateful for the extra space. Agent Zimmer pressed a button and the elevator descended. In the small and relatively quiet space, Ben was able to pick up more of their conversation.

"I'm confused," the president said. "I thought that in the event of an imminent air strike, the plan was to put me on Air Force One and get me the hell out of Dodge."

"Based on our current intel," Zimmer explained, "we're not sure there's time." Zimmer was dark-skinned and the black suit and tie made him seem even darker. His clipped manner of speaking and emotionless delivery might make him seem cold to some, but Ben had learned to appreciate his rare ability to remain totally cool in a crisis. "At any rate, we're not taking the risk. We're taking you to the PEOC. We're sending the vice president off in the plane."

"But if there's not enough time for me . . ." The president didn't finish his question. He figured it out for himself. "Oh."

If someone had to be at risk, it wasn't going to be the president. It would be the man chosen as his running mate.

"Thank heaven the First Lady is in California. How can we be under attack from one of our own missiles?" the president asked.

"We're not sure yet, sir. But a missile has been fired."

"How close?"

"The missile has already entered P-fifty-six airspace." Ben had been around long enough to know that was a reference to the zone of restricted air traffic surrounding the White House.

"Can't we bring it back?"

"We cannot, sir."

"Divert it?"

"No."

"I specifically recall being advised that our computer guidance systems had the capability to—"

"Sir, we've lost control of the guidance systems." Zimmer probably didn't intend to raise his voice, but he did, and it had the effect of silencing everyone in the elevator.

The agent took a deep breath, then slowly continued. "We'll give you a full briefing as soon as we have you safely in the bunker."

The elevator doors opened and they all streamed outward. Zimmer and two other agents steered the president toward a door on the far left. Dr. Albertson went with him, presumably still eager to complete his examination. Everyone else was herded toward a set of double doors directly before them. Cartwright, predictably, tried to break loose from the pack and follow the president, but one of the agents gently but firmly kept him moving toward the double doors.

Ben was escorted into what at first glance appeared to be a fairly standard White House briefing or conference room. There was a long table in the center surrounded with chairs, a three-seat communications terminal, a video monitor like the one in the Oval Office, a programmable illuminated map of the world, a writing easel, telephones, the ubiquitous coffee station, and on the north wall the seal of the president of the United States. When he looked more closely, though, and more important, looked up, he realized that the room was far from conventional. It had a rounded, almost tubular shape. The ceilings curved at the corners and, above the faux-wood paneling, the walls were gray. There was also something odd about the air, although it took him a moment to identify what he was subconsciously sensing. There was nothing natural or fresh about the air. It was all being pumped in from somewhere else.

Agent Zimmer entered from a side door not far from the presidential seal. "Please take your seats."

Everyone complied. Sarie took the seat nearest the coffee and poured herself a tall one. Ben knew she was a coffee junkie. He drank the stuff on occasion to make a good show, but in the privacy of his office, he always preferred a cup of chocolate milk. Cartwright was still grumpy, so Ben stayed out of his way.

"Welcome to the PEOC," Zimmer continued.

"The what?" Ben said, apparently too loudly.

Zimmer smiled slightly. "You're not the only one who doesn't know, Ben. I guarantee it. Dick Cheney said he didn't even know this place existed until we brought him here on September eleventh. PEOC stands for the Presidential Emergency Operations Center. It's an underground bunker buried deep in the basement beneath the East Wing of the White House. It's designed to withstand a nuclear attack."

Ben swallowed. "Then you believe—"

"We do not at this time believe there is a nuclear threat, no. But with an extremely powerful conventional missile in the air and a nuclear suitcase gone missing, this seemed the most prudent response."

"How long are we going to be here?" Ben asked.

"I have no way of knowing the answer to that question."

"Can I call my wife?"

"Not at this time, no. This bunker is shielded so intensely that ordinary cell signals cannot get out. The only way to make contact with the outside world is through this communications station. I'll let you know as soon as that situation changes."

"Enough of this blather," Admiral Cartwright said. "Tell us what's going on. What's this about one of our own missiles heading toward the White House?"

"I'm sorry. I'm not at liberty to disclose that information."

"Do you know who I am, mister? I'm the head of the—"

"Yes, sir, I know very well who you are," Zimmer said without blinking. "And that information still can only be disclosed on the president's direct order."

"What about me?" Ruiz asked. "I'm the secretary of state. Can you tell me?"

"Not at this time."

"If you can't tell me, whom can you tell?"

"The president is being briefed. After that's completed, he can make a determination about what information he wants released and to whom."

"Are you listening to me? I'm the secretary of state!"

"Yes," Agent Zimmer said, absolutely stone-faced. "I knew that already. I also know that your wife's name is Marjorie, that you have two daughters named Olivia and Danette, you keep a bull pup named Tiger, you graduated eighty-sixth in your class at West Point, and your favorite book is *Pride and Prejudice*." He paused. "I really don't need a briefing on who you are. But thank you anyway."

Ruiz sat back in his chair, apparently chastised.

"Does anyone else require identification, or may I proceed?" Zimmer was looking directly at Cartwright as he said it.

Cartwright mumbled, "Proceed," then he turned toward Ruiz, eyebrows knitted. "*Pride and Prejudice*?" he whispered. "That's not a man's book."

"Have you read it?" Ruiz shot back.

"Well . . ."

"So shut up."

Secretary Rybicki leaned forward. "Can you at least tell us if this is about Kuraq?"

"No," Zimmer said, "I can't even tell you—"

All at once, the lights in the room shimmered on and off. Someone shrieked, startled. Ben noticed that the power to the monitor and communications panel flickered off as well.

"What was that?" Cartwright demanded.

Zimmer's face barely changed, but it was enough for Ben to be concerned. "I don't know. I'll investigate."

"Damn it all, man, are we safe or not?" Cartwright said, rising to his feet. What he lacked in height he made up for in bluster. "Can they get to us?"

"Nothing can get to you in this bunker."

"Apparently something is shorting out the electrics!"

"I wouldn't jump to that conclusion. Power blips happen, even in the White House."

"Don't give me your flippant speculation. I want facts."

"Then give me a chance to investigate," Zimmer said, with just enough edge to get his point across. Cartwright sat down.

Ben found himself admiring Zimmer even more than he had before.

Zimmer moved to the communications station and talked to someone on the other end. Ben tried to eavesdrop but the chatter was too soft and too fast.

Sarie's brassy southern drawl interrupted his reverie. "Somehow this wasn't what I had in mind when I decided to go into politics."

Ben nodded. "Wasn't exactly what I was thinking when I went to law school."

"I'll bet you went to law school with grandiose notions of saving the world and helping those less fortunate than yourself."

Ben shrugged. "Mostly I just wanted to irritate my father."

Sarie laughed a little, which did a good deal to elevate his spirits. "Come to think of it, I think that was why I married my first husband."

Zimmer returned to the table. "I have news," he said. His eyes seemed to focus on the center of the table. "The missile just went down into the Potomac."

Several jaws dropped. The silence spoke volumes. Ben knew what he was thinking, what they were all thinking. It really happened. It really happened.

"It exploded underwater. We don't know of any casualties. At least not at this time. But as I'm sure you're all aware . . . the Potomac is not far away."

"How could this happen?" Sarie said quietly. "It's impossible. Impossible."

"Apparently not," Ben replied quietly.

"We believe it was a theater ballistic missile—a short-range missile, basically. Range between three hundred and about thirty-five hundred kilometers. So called because it's designed to be used against nearby targets—within the theater, so to speak. Although the warhead is capable of carrying a nuclear or even biological payload, this one, happily, did not."

"But the next one might," Cartwright spat out.

Zimmer ignored him. "That power blip was likely an EMP—electromagnetic pulse—from the explosion. It's an electrical disruption that often follows a major detonation, even one non-nuclear in origin."

"I still want to know what this is all about!" Cartwright said. "Is it Kuraq? Is that who's doing this?"

"Sir," Zimmer said, "I already told you I'm not authorized to—"

"Well, I am." Behind him, Ben saw the president entering the room. Dr. Albertson followed just behind him.

Everyone began to rise, but he waved them back into their chairs. "Please remain seated. Is everyone comfortable? I mean, within reason, given the circumstances. Is there anything I can do for you?"

"You can tell us what the hell is going on," Cartwright barked. "You're the president, not a damned flight attendant."

President Kyler gave him a patient, long-suffering look. "Can someone get me some coffee?"

"I'll do it," Zimmer said quickly. Ben was surprised to see a senior Secret Service agent fetching coffee, but he supposed it was a security measure.

The president took a sip of the hot coffee and then answered the admiral's question. "Unfortunately, Admiral, I don't know much more about the situation than you do. No one has claimed credit for the attack. We've been attempting to contact Colonel Zuko, but as you may be able to discern, he doesn't always take my calls."

"How are they doing this?" Secretary Ruiz asked.

"Somehow the enemy has managed to infiltrate our national defense computer systems. We're not sure how. We believe they may have a high-tech satellite—maybe even something as low-riding as a dirigible—capable of penetrating our networks. But that's speculation. Truth is, the only reason we suspect this . . ." He paused before continuing. "Is because we've been working on something like it ourselves."

"Don't we have antisatellite weaponry? Isn't that what Sky King does?"

"It has been unable to locate the satellite. Or whatever it is."

"How is that possible?"

The president's shoulders rose and fell. "This is speculation, but our techies believe it must be equipped with some sort of cloaking device."

"Cloaking device? I've never heard of that."

"Sounds vaguely familiar, though," Cartwright mused. "Have I heard about that at a briefing? Maybe related to the hypersonic attack missile project? Or from the papers on the planned orbiting antiballistic missile laser?"

"*Star Trek,*" Ben said softly.

"What?" Every head in the room turned his way, and Ben wished, not for the first time that day, that he had kept his mouth shut.

"That's where you've heard the term. The Romulans had them on *Star Trek.* Cloaking devices. Made a ship invisible to another ship's sensors."

"But that's poppycock!" Cartwright sputtered.

"Unfortunately," President Kyler said, "whatever it is these people have, it's all too real. And all too effective."

"Isn't there something we can do?" Rybicki asked.

"Believe me, we're working on it. But so far we've been unable to get the invader out of the system. Or to detect the cause of the invasion."

"How extensive is it?"

"We know they control the Vernon missile silo—the one closest to the White House. They've blocked us out of the whole control system."

"Can we depower the system? Take them offline? Or drain the missiles of their fuel?"

"Unfortunately, the invaders are also capable of igniting that fuel and have sent an email indicating that they will if we attempt to drain or depower the missiles. Those missiles use RP-seven fuel. It burns at about five thousand degrees Fahrenheit. In other words, if it's exploded, it will do almost as much damage as if they had fired the missiles."

"How is this possible?"

"Whatever these people have, it appears to be at least two, three years down the technological line from anything we've developed."

"So in effect, someone else is controlling our military weaponry," Cartwright said.

"To the extent that our weaponry is controlled by computer, yes. But not the entire arsenal. Only a small portion of the missiles located on the East Coast. And none of them is believed to be a nuclear weapon."

"So what is this small portion of non-nuclear missiles capable of doing?"

"As I understand it," the president said grimly, "they could take out about half of the population of the East Coast." He paused. "Some of the most densely inhabited parts of the United States."

Secretary Rybicki jumped in. "This is unacceptable."

"I agree," President Kyler said firmly. Ben admired his steady resolve in the face of a major crisis. He was the absolute antithesis of the man Ben had witnessed only a few minutes before, the one who'd been singing about a hole in a bucket. "We're exploring all possible options. And our intelligence forces are attempting to find out who's behind it. In the meantime—"

"Mr. President!"

Kyler jerked his head around, his eyes fierce. It was just possible he had been interrupted one time too often.

"My apologies," Agent Zimmer said. "But I thought you'd want to know this."

"Well, what is it, then?"

Zimmer cleared his throat. "We have Colonel Zuko on the phone."

Kyler's eyes widened. "Thank God. How did you track him down?"

"To tell you the truth, sir, he called you."

"What? But how—why—"

"He says he wants to talk to you." Zimmer paused. His voice deepened. "He also says he wants to know how you enjoyed the gift he sent you. The one he had delivered to the Potomac."

6

*B*en felt a thudding in the pit of his stomach. So it was true. Kuraq—and its military dictator—were behind the attack. How else could Colonel Zuko have known?

"How did he get this number?" President Kyler whispered. He looked as if he had had the wind knocked out of his sails.

"I don't know, sir," Zimmer replied. "But I imagine that would be substantially simpler than infiltrating our military defense computers."

"Good point. Can I take it in the briefing room?"

"Sorry, sir. The only phones are here. At the communications station."

Kyler grimaced. "Put it on speaker."

Zimmer nodded and pushed a button.

Ben knew Zuko had been educated at Western universities, and the combination of the elevated British accent and the clipped Middle Eastern tones was unsettling, particularly coming from a voice that seemed permeated by false congeniality.

"Good morning!" the voice over the intercom boomed, with such ebullience you might have thought it was coming from one of the president's long-lost friends. "How are you, my American counterpart? Are you enjoying your life underground? And did you like your present?"

In this instance, the president's unflappability was perhaps the only thing that kept most of the people in the room from descending into total panic. "I take it that you are claiming credit for the firing of a short-range missile into the Potomac."

"My dear Mr. President," the dictator said, "I take credit because it was I who did it, with the assistance of my scholars and advisors. Isn't it amazing, the technological advances that are coming from . . . what is it you like to call us? The third world? Maybe it is time we were promoted." The colonel chuckled, a bone-chilling laugh that had no mirth in it. "Perhaps it is you who represents the third world. Or the fourth. Possibly the fifth."

"Colonel Zuko," the president responded, "we have reason to believe that you have knowingly and purposely interfered with our defense computer networks. I am formally demanding that you cease and desist all interference immediately."

"But my dear Mr. President, you are not in any position to make demands. So long as we control your missile systems, we can send a weapon to destroy any target in the eastern United States within five minutes." He paused, and when his voice returned, it was slower, heavier, and absent the false amiability. "From here on out, it is I who will be making the demands."

"We'll find your satellite eventually," the president said.

"Perhaps yes, perhaps no. But I believe time is on my side. You can rattle your sabers and desperately run about trying to catch up to me. In the meantime, I can destroy your people simply by making a phone call."

"My people tell me that your control is spotty and inconsistent. You may be able to launch a few missiles, but certainly not all."

"Mr. President, how many missiles do you think I need to bring your puny nation to its knees?"

The president's voice dropped to a whisper. "You are the new Hitler."

"Hitler? You self-righteous fool. Perhaps you should ask your secretary of defense to give you a history lesson when we are done talking. I understand he is a student of history. I am no Hitler, my friend. I'm the new George Washington. I am a freedom fighter. Everything I do is to free my people, to cast off the yoke of the bully tyrant nation that attempts to control us and treat us like slaves."

"That's absurd. We never—"

"Do not attempt to persuade me with your ethnocentric view of the world. The American oppressor interfered in the Middle East for fifty years, and now you are planning to bring your oppression to my country. I will not sit idly by and let my nation become the next Iraq. We will fight. I have a duty to my people."

"You weren't even elected by the people. You took over by military force."

"And if I recall correctly, there was much military force involved in the formation of your own country, true? Of course there was. But I did not call to debate history. You have declared war on my nation. And this is a war I intend to win."

"We never declared war on Kuraq."

"Your troops are just outside our gates! I can see them now on our radar. Do you expect me to wait until it's too late to respond? I will not."

"If you fire another one of those missiles, people will die."

"In every war there is collateral damage. But still the war must be fought. The price of freedom is eternal vigilance. Did George Washington take lives at Yorktown? I believe he did, but he did it to defeat Cornwallis and to secure a new nation. I will do nothing less for my own. You may label me a madman if that makes it easier to carry out your aggressions. But I am a patriot, sir. A patriot. And like any good patriot, I will defend my nation till my dying breath."

"What's this all about, Zuko? Why now?" While he spoke, the president was gesturing to Zimmer, who was quietly whispering into another line. Ben couldn't know for certain, but he assumed they were making an effort to trace the call. Did that mean they thought he might be somewhere nearby? It seemed impossible. Or perhaps they knew he was in Kuraq and were trying to target him for some kind of military strike. "All we've asked is that you let our people cross your border and perform a simple rescue operation."

"Do not treat me like a fool, Mr. President. I may be many things, but foolish is not among them. I hold all the cards in this poker game. Do not pretend that we do not both know that your military forces have been swarming around our borders for weeks. We have intelligence, too, sir. I have seen your aircraft carriers in the Gulf."

"They are in those waters on peaceful missions and with the permission of the Saudi Arabian government."

"Do not treat me like a child!" Zuko barked. "I know what the planes aboard that ship are capable of doing. You have a least a thousand troops ready to invade at your command. I know that you have aircraft in Saudi Arabia that can be in our airspace in fewer than twenty minutes! I know you have planned an invasion of my sovereign state. Your own people have confessed it to me. Under torture, yes, but they confessed just the same."

The mention of torture cast dread into the hearts of everyone in the room. Zimmer was at a computer keyboard now. He appeared to be pulling up some kind of logistical or tactical information. Aerial maps came and went with such speed that Ben could not identify them.

"Does that mean you're responsible for the Mymidon attack and kidnapping?" the president asked.

"I assumed you would know it was me, given how flawlessly the operation was executed. Today's exercise will be no different. You are but the sand of the desert in my hands, Mr. President. You will bend to the shape and will of my hand, or you will slip through my fingers and fall apart. Permanently."

The president sat down in the chair at the head of the table. He leaned in very close to the speakerphone. "And was it also your highly efficient men who raided the Arlington armory a few hours ago?"

Ben held his breath and waited for the answer. If this sadistic madman had a portable nuclear device, they would be permanently helpless, even if they did recover control of the computer networks.

"Do you not understand, Mr. President? We are everywhere. We control everything. And now you will do everything I request—everything! Or the consequences will be horrible."

"Colonel Zuko, I will not permit you to commit genocide in the Benzai Strip."

"What action I take I do to secure our borders. And that is no business of yours! But it does not matter. There is nothing you can do about it."

Although he wasn't taking notes, Ben had been clenching his pencil with a white-knuckled grip throughout the entire conversation. He dropped his pencil, and without really thinking about it, bent down to pick it up.

While bent over, he looked under the table.

The president's feet were moving. Not swaying. Not tapping. But tap-dancing. Moving back and forth in a sprightly manner that did

not affect what the others saw above the table. One of the darker secrets in Ben's past was that in the second grade his mother had forced
him to take tap-dancing lessons. He knew a shuffle-ball-change when
he saw it.

A foreign dictator was threatening to take out a large portion of the
nation. And the president was tap-dancing.

The president and Zuko continued talking. Ben knew his expression must have changed, because Sarie gave him a concerned look. "Is
something wrong?" she whispered.

He pointed under the table and mouthed, "Look."

"Trying to get a look at my cleavage?"

Ben's face flushed. He continued pointing.

She looked.

When her face came up again, it was ashen.

"What's going on?" Ben whispered.

She spread her hands wide in a gesture of bafflement and helpless-
ness.

Ben didn't know what to make of her reaction. But the situation
didn't seem to be shocking her as much as it was him. He asked: "Have
you seen this before?"

She hesitated before making any response, then, with considerable
reluctance, nodded.

"What's going on?"

She shrugged.

"What does his doctor say?"

She shrugged again, then added quietly, "He's concerned."

Ben was glad to hear Dr. Albertson understood the president was
exhibiting strange behavior, but somehow *concerned* didn't seem
nearly adequate.

"How long?" Ben asked, careful not to attract attention.

Sarie thought for a while before answering. "Month or so."

"Who else knows?"

She shrugged again.

Ben thought about that for a moment. More than once he had been
amazed by the number of people the president met in the course of a
single day. If he had been exhibiting these strange symptoms for a
month, anyone could know.

Even the dictator of a foreign nation.

Ben began to whisper again, then caught a glance of Admiral

Cartwright on the opposite end of the table, glaring at him. He felt as if he were being scolded for telling secrets in class.

The conversation with Zuko must have been reaching a fevered peak, because for the first time ever, Ben heard the president raise his voice.

"Colonel Zuko, the United States will not tolerate this!"

"When will you get it through your sun-baked brain that you have no choice in the matter?"

"We do not stand alone in the world, Colonel. The United Nations will not—"

"The United Nations is only as strong as the United States, and at the moment the United States is helpless."

"We are not the only superpower."

"Who do you think will come to your rescue? Russia has far greater ties to the Middle East than to you. China owns you. You may have allies on paper, but what can any of them do for you? You stand alone in the world. You stand at my mercy."

In the corner, Zimmer, still wearing communications headphones and staring at a computer screen, gave the president a signal. Ben didn't know what it meant, but his face seemed to have at least a trace of optimism.

"My people are already working on this problem, Colonel. It won't be long before we pry you out of our computers."

"It will be too late, Mr. President, because you have only thirty minutes before I let the next missile fly."

"You're making a mistake."

"No, it is you who is making the mistake, a tragic one. You will withdraw your troops, and not just away from my borders, but from the entire Gulf. You will withdraw your forces from the Middle East, from our borders, from Saudi Arabia, from Iraq. Everywhere."

"That's insane!"

"My spy satellites are watching you. I know the truth, even if you do not care to reveal it to me. And I will not tolerate this." He paused. When his voice returned, it was somewhat calmer. "I am not a barbarian. I am a civilized man. I will give you thirty minutes to order your men to retreat. If you have not begun to retreat in that time, I will launch the next missile. And this one will find civilian targets. That I can guarantee you."

"Colonel, be reasonable—"

"Do not presume to give orders to me! I am not the one poised to invade your soil!" He sounded agitated, his voice jumping wildly in pitch and volume. "We do not meddle in the affairs of others. We do not attempt to play gendarme for the entire world. The American reign of terror has come to an end. You have meddled in the Middle East long enough, as your thirst for oil brought you to increasingly stupid decisions, extending your resources, living beyond your means, living the decadent lifestyle of high consumption and low productivity. Those days are done, Mr. President. You will withdraw your forces immediately. Or your people will face the consequences."

"I can't do that, Colonel. Not while you still occupy the Benzai Strip. Do you hear me?" There was no response. *"Do you hear me?"*

Still no response.

"I won't abandon our personnel. The people who went down in that helicopter are U.S. citizens. We have the right to retrieve them!"

Still no response.

"Are you listening to me, Colonel?"

When the colonel's voice finally returned, it possessed an eerie calm that Ben found positively chilling. "Your time begins . . . now."

7

Seamus McKay climbed into the driver's seat of the beat-up Dodge the Company had loaned him for in-city work, grousing once more about how screwed up the whole system really was. The terrorists had better weapons than they did, better intel than they had, and perhaps most gratingly, better cars than they got. And yet they were supposed to track these people down and apprehend them—while of course being scrupulous about not violating their civil rights.

Good luck.

Come to think of it, he might have violated eight or ten civil rights during that brawl at the Washington Monument, but he had prevented the ugly obelisk from being blown to pieces, so he hoped that would be the primary focus of the debrief. Well, he could hope, anyway.

His whole midsection ached. He must've sprained something when he pulled his entire body weight up to the second level where the sniper was perched. He needed to get to the gym more often than he did, keep those abs in shape. But as his chronological age crept ever closer to fifty, the urgency of befriending the Nautilus machines seemed to subside. Wasn't he getting too old for this life? Coming stateside had been a step in the right direction. Did he really want to spend the rest of his life chasing after the kind of scum who would rob a nuclear armory?

Speaking of which, he'd better phone in an early report. The security cops at the monument must've contacted his office by now. He'd better make sure his superiors got his side of the story, as quickly as possible. As he pulled onto the parkway, he dialed his cell with his left hand.

"Zira?"

"I'm here, Seamus. What the hell is going on?"

As succinctly as possible, Seamus tried to bring her up-to-date, explaining how he had followed the trail from the Arlington armory, using a tip from a trusted informant, caught up to the thieves just as they left their hideout, and followed them all the way to the Washington Monument. He left out most of the details of the fight, just mentioning in passing that he had taken out several men single-handedly.

"But one got away? With the suitcase?"

Count on Zira to accentuate the negative. "Unfortunately. I couldn't be in four places at once."

"So you took down three men of no importance and let the one with the nuke escape?"

"I took the fourth down, too. Unfortunately, he got back up again."

He could hear a tsking sound on the other end of the connection. "I think this is another example of incredibly poor judgment, Seamus. Just the latest of many such instances."

How had he ever ended up with a female operations chief, anyway? With her high heels and her perfectly tailored suits, she wouldn't have lasted ten minutes in Afghanistan. Did someone in Washington think this was politically correct?

"I saved the monument," Seamus said curtly. "And there were no casualties."

"Yet," she rejoined without waiting a breath. "But since there's a maniac out there with a nuclear device, how long will that remain true?"

Seamus stifled the instinct to swear. "Look, I've still got some leads. I saw a couple of things out there that might indicate where this guy will go next. I'll follow up."

"No, Seamus. You won't."

He swerved his car onto M Street and pulled into the far lane. "Are you kidding? I'm the one who found these clowns. No one knows more about them than me."

"Nonetheless, you—"

"I'll come in and do a full debrief and report later. Promise. But I've got to cover the field while the trail is still hot."

"No, you don't."

"Are you listening to me?" Seamus practically shouted into the receiver. "These guys stole a nuke and they're planning to use it."

"Yes," Zira replied, "and sadly enough, that is not the most urgent threat facing our nation today."

"What are you talking about?"

"How much do you know about Kuraq and its current leader, Colonel Zuko?"

Seamus resisted the temptation to say, "A hell of a lot more than you." "Plenty. Kuraq isn't that far from Afghanistan or Iran. I've seen Zuko in action, back before he took control."

"Good. How would you describe him?"

"Smart. Western-educated. Insecure about his military position, which is likely to make him dangerous."

"You're certainly right about the last part. Zuko has somehow infiltrated our military defense computers and seized control of some of our ballistic missiles."

Seamus's eyes bulged. "More nukes?"

"No, conventional explosives, at least at this time. But very powerful. Capable of making a very big hole in the ground."

Seamus ground his teeth together. "How did he do it?"

"Our computer guys are still investigating. The most popular theory is that he's launched a spy satellite that has a powerful computer-hacking ability."

"His computer geeks came up with something before our geeks did?"

"It's looking that way."

Seamus took a deep breath. "You know what this means, don't you?"

"You'll be putting in overtime."

"More than that. Think about it. Someone robs a highly secret and heavily guarded nuclear armory. Someone hacks into our computers and seizes control of our missiles. Both on the same day? You got to think it's the same people, executing some well-planned and highly coordinated attack against the United States. And there's only one way that would be possible."

"Do enlighten me, Seamus."

He hesitated several beats before he could make himself say it. "We've got a mole."

"You can't be serious."

"I am. It's the only possible explanation. Zuko shouldn't even know about the Arlington facility. Most people don't. And I don't care how good his hacking program is—I don't believe he could get into the military defense system without inside help. Someone passed him some back doors to ease his entry."

He was gratified to hear that, for once, Zira didn't immediately snap back with a response. "That is a singularly disturbing possibility."

"And a very real one. You need to start running the A-Alpha Shadow protocols. Find the mole. Look for someone on the inside who has been making unexplained phone calls to unlisted numbers. Especially foreign numbers. Find out if anyone has recently had a significant unexplained cash infusion to their bank account."

"I know how to find a mole, Mr. McKay, thank you very much."

Seamus smiled. It gave him pleasure to think he had gotten that officious bureaucrat's goat.

"And what will you be doing, if I may ask?"

"I'm not sure," Seamus replied. "I guess I'll consult my computer expert. Find out how this might have been done. Who could have engineered it. If you really think this takes priority over the nuclear suitcase."

"It does. We have no direct evidence—other than your unsubstantiated suggestion that they were going to detonate it in the monument—that the suitcase will be used anytime soon. But we have a direct threat from Zuko that a missile will be launched shortly. If you can figure out how to get him out of our computers, we need that intel immediately."

"Then that's what I'll do."

"Good. Get to it." She paused. "Don't bother calling in to the president. He's in the bunker. You can't get through. I can contact him via his Secret Service detail. I'll pass along what you've learned."

"Okay." Seamus swerved his car around into the opposite lane and headed back the way he came. This new assignment called for a course correction.

"Call me the moment you learn anything."

"I will."

"And Seamus." The edge fell out of her voice, but it was replaced by something darker and more urgent. "Understand that this is not just another assignment. You may have done decent reconnaissance work in the Middle East, but this isn't contingent or theoretical. Those missiles are pointed right down our throats. This threat could bring down the presidency. This threat could take hundreds of thousands of lives and revert the East Coast to the Stone Age." Her voice dropped another notch. "This could be the end of the United States as you and I know it."

8

9:33 A.M.

Agent Zimmer rose to his feet, one hand pressed against his left
earpiece. "We've lost the connection, sir."

"Get Zuko back!" the president snapped.

"We didn't lose him." After a moment Zimmer added quietly, "He
hung up."

A brief silence ensued as Ben and everyone else in the bunker con-
templated the confidence of a man who felt sufficiently secure to hang
up on the president of the United States.

"I want him back on the line as soon as possible," the president
said firmly.

"Yes, sir. But Mr. President . . ." Zimmer pointed toward a screen
at the top of the communications station.

They were marking the colonel's countdown. Time was slipping
away, all too fast.

"I know I can make the man see reason," the president said. "Just
get him back on the line."

"I'll do my best, sir." Zimmer sat and returned his attention to the
screen.

All at once, the lights and power began to flicker again. The lights shuddered on and off for several seconds, then actually went out alto-gether.

"What the hell?"

"What's going on?"

"Who's in charge here? Is anyone in charge?"

Ben recognized the last voice as Admiral Cartwright's, but the panic and tumult were becoming so frenzied that after that it was hard to hear anything.

Then the lights came back on. A few moments later, power re-turned to the communications station and the screens. Ben heard the familiar whirring sound that told him computers were rebooting.

"What just happened?" the president said evenly.

"I don't know," Agent Zimmer said, motioning to another agent. "I'm sending people topside to find out." Two of the agents streamed out the door.

"Aren't all these power lines secure?"

"They should be, sir. The bunker has its own power conduits, and like the bunker itself, they're designed to withstand a nuclear blast. Even the EMP from a nearby missile detonation shouldn't cause more than temporary interference."

"Find out what's happening!"

"Already on it."

"Good." The president leaned forward, one hand squeezing the bridge of his nose.

Cartwright saw his opening. "Mr. President—"

President Kyler held up his hand, silencing him. "Just give me one damn moment." He breathed in deeply, then released it, then did it again, then again, each time digging more desperately for air. He began to wheeze. "Doctor?"

Dr. Albertson walked to his side and presented what appeared to be an asthma inhaler. Ben had had no idea the president suffered from asthma. That had never been mentioned during the campaign or, to his knowledge, afterward. How had they kept it a secret? Or was this a symptom that had developed more recently, perhaps another sign of the great strain of the presidency?

President Kyler took two gigantic whiffs from the inhaler. A few moments later his breathing began to normalize.

"Mr. President," Cartwright launched again, but Kyler waved him away.

"Zimmer," he said, his voice subdued and remarkably calm, given the circumstances, "I want all the monuments on the National Mall closed. No, on second thought, make that all the monuments in Washington. Close them down and tell the folks to go home."

"But Mr. President," Secretary Ruiz objected, "if you do that, it could cause a panic."

"I'd rather have panic than casualties. Colonel Zuko will be looking for symbolic targets. Dramatic demonstrations of his protest against our way of life. I think there are many in D.C. that would serve his purpose all too well. Close them down."

Zimmer nodded. "Will do, sir."

"Send a memo through military channels to other high-profile potential targets on the East Coast. Wall Street. The Statue of Liberty. Disney World. They need to know that today might be a good day to close up shop."

"If Wall Street shuts down early—"

"They can come up with some explanation that doesn't involve a terrorist threat. They've done it before." The president turned toward the communications station, where Zimmer was already hard at work. "Can you get me an update on the people who went down in that helicopter behind the Kuraqi border? I'd like to know if they've already been captured. If they're POWs."

"And if they are?" Secretary Rybicki asked.

"Then we have an even better excuse to bring our troops across his border."

"Did you not listen to the man? He's launching a missile in only a few minutes. If you invade, he's likely to fire them all."

"I assure you, Mr. Secretary, that I heard every word Zuko said. And I don't have time for a review. Ben?"

Ben looked up abruptly. He had become so absorbed in the ongoing drama that he had almost forgotten that he was technically a member of the president's staff, too.

"Yes, sir?"

"Give me a very quick brief on our international rights with regard to Kuraq. What's the law? Does he have the right to defend himself in this way? What difference does the presence of our troops make? After all, we're there with the express permission of a Middle Eastern nation."

Ben took a deep breath. "As you probably know, sir, what we call international law isn't really law at all. It is simply a hodgepodge of various conventions and agreements that have arisen over time, starting in the Middle Ages in, ironically, the Middle East. These have established values and procedures over time—but they are hard to enforce with a nonparticipating nation. You can get a judgment in the World Court, but how do you enforce it? You can get a proclamation from the United Nations, but what impact will that have on a nation such as Kuraq, which has refused entry to UN weapons inspectors for the past five years?"

President Kyler nodded grimly. "And I think now we can see why. They've been working on something big. Something they didn't want anyone else to know about."

"Last I heard, our ships were still waiting outside the twelve-mile limit, in international waters. If they come within twelve miles of the Kuraqi coast, however, we will be violating their territory as defined by the relevant UN charter agreement."

"But we have the invitation of the Saudi Arabian government."

"I know. But since when did one nation have the ability to waive the rights of another? Never, I hope. Does Canada have the ability to authorize Kuraq to invade U.S. airspace? I hope not."

"I see your point. But this is different. Our intelligence data suggest that they plan—may have already begun—the systematic slaughter of the people on the Benzai Strip."

"Then the appropriate course of action would be to obtain UN authorization. That's what George Bush did—the first one. The UN Security Council authorized an invasion after Iraq invaded Kuwait. Over three dozen member nations participated, although of course the United States played the primary role."

"His son didn't have UN authorization to invade Iraq."

"No, he didn't, and partly as a result, his coalition was much feebler and the action never gained worldwide support. Most foreign nations viewed it as a war of aggression, not of liberation."

"I've had my men working on the UN for weeks. So far we haven't been able to get anything."

"You're suffering the negative fallout of previous U.S. actions in the Middle East. Just when it looked as if we might finally be getting out of the Middle East, here we come again, wanting to invade someone else."

"I know, I know." The president's fingers began to bounce on the tabletop. Maybe it was just Ben, but the pattern looked all too much like the same little dance he had seen the man's feet performing under the table. "But we can't stand by and watch this barbarian slaughter an entire region!"

"But we do not have authority to invade."

"Clinton sent our troops into Bosnia."

"Yes, but Clinton was acting under the direct authority of NATO, and there was clear evidence of the planned genocide against Bosnian Muslims and had been for years. After those broken and emaciated faces played on television, he had the support he needed—at least for a while. Our evidence about what's going on in Benzai is—forgive me, Mr. President—considerably more sketchy. And we don't have the authority of NATO or the UN or anyone else."

"At this rate, Ben, if I wait for that, those people will be dead. Tens of thousands of them."

"I understand your position, Mr. President. But my job is to advise you on the law. And that's what it is."

"Pardon me for butting in," Cartwright said.

Ben's eyebrows knitted together. Had Cartwright ever shown the remotest reluctance to butt in before?

"I thought you were working on some energy lawsuit, Mr. Kincaid. Since when did you become an expert on international law?"

"I'm like a well-tuned PC," Ben replied. "I can multitask. I've been around awhile, and I've held many different positions. And with respect, Admiral, all I did was answer the president's questions. I never suggested I was any kind of expert."

The president waved the strife away. "I know this much, Admiral. He's the leading expert on international law currently in this bunker."

Cartwright grudgingly acknowledged the point.

Kyler turned back to Ben. "What about his claim that he has the right to fire our missiles?"

"I can't imagine that there's anything anywhere in international law that would support that claim, regardless of what we've got next door to him in Saudi Arabia. So long as we remain in international waters—"

"But that's the problem."

The president's interruption caught Ben—and everyone else in the bunker—by surprise. The short hairs on the back of Ben's neck stood on end. He had the distinct feeling this case was about to get a good deal more complicated.

"I gave the commanders the order to start moving in this morning. Slowly! But still, they've crossed into Kuraqi waters."

Secretary Ruiz leaned forward. "Why wasn't I told about this?"

"You would've been told in due time."

"In due time? I'm the secretary of state!"

"I think we all know that, Mike."

"You have an obligation to consult with me on major foreign policy matters."

"I did consult with you, Mike," the president said wearily. "I just didn't do what you wanted. I'm pretty sure I have that power. I think it comes with the presidential seal."

Ruiz folded his arms across his chest and glared.

"I'm afraid this does change everything," Ben said, filling in the dead air.

The president did not respond immediately. Ben assumed that was because he already knew what the answer would be.

"How do you mean, Ben?" Sarie asked.

He decided to answer, if not for the president, for the sake of everyone else in the room. "If we have crossed Kuraq's borders, the colonel could easily call that an act of war. Come to think of it, he was talking about war during that phone conversation, wasn't he?"

"I can't stand by and let him butcher those people!" the president said. His lips trembled as he spoke. His eyes watered. Ben hoped to God he didn't cry.

"I understand the consequences. But we have invaded his territory."

"And his claim to the Benzai Strip is feeble at best."

"But we haven't invaded Benzai, right? We've invaded Kuraq. And if Colonel Zuko deems that an invasion, he can make a retaliatory declaration of war. And at that point—well, let's face it. He can do anything he wants. Anything he can get away with."

"Even explode bombs on our land?"

"Is there some rule that wars must always be fought on other people's soil? I don't think so. In World War II, we firebombed Dresden. We nuked Japan. I think in Colonel Zuko's mind, he's in exactly the same position we were then, and has the same right to take action. To destroy his enemy. To win the war."

President Kyler brushed his eyes clear, then rose. "Agent Zimmer, have you done as I asked?"

"Yes, sir. All federal institutions in D.C. are closed or closing."

"Good."

"Haven't gotten an update on the men who went down in the helicopter. But we're working on it."

"Please do. I'd feel better about this if I knew that those people were safe."

Ruiz made a harrumphing sound. "How can anyone be safe while that madman is controlling our missiles?"

"Zimmer," the president continued, "I want you to find the vice president and patch him into this conversation. He needs to know what's going on. Just in case . . . you know."

Zimmer cleared his throat. "That's going to be a lot easier than you might imagine, sir."

The president tilted his head, obviously puzzled. "And why?"

At that moment the main doors opened and the question was answered without a word.

The new addition to the ranks of those locked down in the bunker, flanked by four Secret Service agents, was Vice President Conrad Swinburne.

9

Seamus pulled his Dodge up the driveway beside an apartment at the south end of the Georgetown Flats, residential housing for graduate students at Georgetown University. He wondered if he should have called ahead. On one hand, there was always value in surprise, particularly if you were planning to ask for a big favor and didn't want the target to have much time to consider all the sound reasons to say no. On the other hand, a little warning might give his informant time to conduct research or, at the very least, be home when Seamus arrived.

It was a difficult decision, but as usual, Seamus came down on the side of surprise. Perhaps it was the result of too much time in the Middle East, where his targets had a tendency not only to not be at home but to be in another country if they knew he was dropping by. Maybe it just better suited his personal style.

He got out of the car and glanced up at the second-story apartment. No lights visible in the window, but that didn't mean much. It was morning, and besides people like this target didn't have much need for overhead lighting. They could survive by the dim blue glow of the computer screen.

Seamus had first encountered RossumRulz not quite a year earlier, while doing research on a new algorithm that was being used to break into scientific facilities, including some covertly operated by the U.S. government. They had suspected terrorists at first—that was everyone's first-blush instinct in the post-9/11 world. Turned out to be industrial espionage, corporate spooks hoping to discover the next big thing before their competitors did. But in the course of doing research on the Internet—where else?—he came across someone who worked under the name of RossumRulz, a tribute presumably to the inventor of the Python operating language. Not only was he more knowledgeable about these decryption algorithms than anyone else Seamus had encountered, he was able to deduce that there were only three people capable of devising such a program.

Turned out he was right. Seamus nabbed the culprit on his second try and brought the whole security breach to a satisfying conclusion. He had offered to treat RossumRulz to a steak dinner at the Four Seasons, but the informant had declined. Apparently he wanted to maintain his anonymity. Which made Seamus all the more determined to know who and where he was. Just in case.

That part was a cinch. People talked about how there were no skid marks on the information superhighway, but there were, especially when you had the ability to serve a subpoena on the ISP. RossumRulz had cleverly disguised his server by doubling back through several blind alleys and having his own home miniserver, but Seamus still found him. He didn't introduce himself. He had no need to at that time. But he definitely filed the name and address away for future reference. For when he needed it.

The time had come.

Seamus walked briskly up the outside stairs to the top level, then knocked on the door.

Maybe a minute later, a kid opened the door. Seamus knew he was twenty-three, but he didn't look it. He was maybe five foot four and had dark, shaggy, curly hair that fell down on all sides as if he were using gravity for his styling gel. Perhaps a latter-day tribute to the early Beatles. He wasn't obese but soft in the middle, which was about what Seamus might expect from someone who spent his whole life in front of a computer, seeing the light of day only when a new *Star Wars* picture was released.

"Here's twenty bucks," the kid said. "Where's the pizza?"

Seamus smiled. "I'm not the pizza boy."

"Oh, sorry." He started to shut the door.

Seamus wedged his foot inside, stopping it. "I want to talk to you."

"I don't need any magazine subscriptions."

Jeez, was his suit that bad? "I'm not selling magazines."

"Whatever it is you're selling, I don't want any. I buy online exclusively from Cheap Deals."

"I'm from the government," Seamus said.

The kid's expression froze. "Are—are you a cop?"

"Sort of. I'm looking for Arlo Patterson."

"Oh. Oh!" He slapped his forehead in a particularly unconvincing display. "Arlo doesn't live here anymore. He moved two apartments over." He leaned in a little bit. "I think he was trying to get a line on the girls' dormitory. He can do amazing things with that telescope of his. His parents actually believed that he was interested in astronomy. Isn't that incredible?"

Seamus smiled thinly. He hoped this kid didn't use a webcam to tell chicks he was buff, because he was the worst liar Seamus had met in his entire career. This guy had probably never lied in his entire life, except when his friends asked if he was still a virgin. "Look, Arlooo," he said, making the name sound as stupid as possible, which didn't take much, "I'm investigating a major terrorist threat and I don't have much time, so are you going to let me in or am I going to knock you down, tie you to the radiator, and torture you till you tell me what I want to know?"

Arlo's voice jumped an octave. "Come on in."

Seamus stepped inside. The apartment was even more revolting than he had imagined. He had expected the inches of dust and decaying pizza boxes. But the Captain Picard action figures? That was just embarrassing.

"Look," Seamus began, "we know each other. Sort of. You helped me find the people who broke into the Merski Institute. I was working under the user name BoldDragon."

"BoldDragon. Sure, I remember. Very modest."

"Well, it was my code name overseas."

"And I'll bet you chose it. You should really work on those self-esteem issues."

"I need your help again, kid. There's a Middle Eastern kook who has hacked into the military computers that control some of our East Coast ballistic missile systems."

Arlo made a long whistling sound. "Sweet."

"Not so much, kid. Especially since the next missile might be coming right to your backyard."

"Is that what happened out in the Potomac? I knew that wasn't any gas explosion. That was a cover story, right?"

"I can neither confirm nor deny. But give me the benefit of your expertise. They think this guy may have a satellite that's programmed to do the hacking. How would that work?"

"They'd need an operations base. Probably not too far from the computers they're hacking into. They'd also need a seriously invasive program. I'm assuming the Pentagon has pretty decent firewalls in place."

"I think that's a safe bet. So how hard would this be?"

Arlo walked to his desk and plopped down in the swivel chair facing his computer screen. The computer itself and its ancillary parts covered not only the entire desk but half the available floor space. "Know anything about GhostNet?"

Seamus searched his memory. That rang a bell . . . perhaps a memo he had half read. The tech stuff wasn't his strong suit. It had never had much relevance out in the desert. "Refresh my memory."

"Back in '09 it came out that this vast electronic spying operation had infiltrated one thousand two hundred ninety-five computers in government and private offices in one hundred three countries."

"One hundred three? That's, like, every country with computers."

"Just about. They got caught by a brain trust up in Toronto. They stole documents, most of them classified. They hacked into embassies, foreign ministries. The program was being operated out of China. Which might explain why—get this—they even hacked the Dalai Lama. Can you imagine? What kind of people sic malware on the Dalai Lama?"

"Seriously bad people."

"I guess so. They also concentrated on the South Asian and Southeast Asian countries."

"Definitely the Chinese."

"And they were able to do it because they had a really good program. This malware—that's short for malicious software—didn't just phish for random information. It whaled for particular targets. Important stuff. Totally Big Brother. It could even turn on deactivated webcams and mikes to eavesdrop."

"Get out of here."

"It's true."

"Did they get the United States?"

"Not as far as we know—but if the Chinese could do it to others back then, how long before someone else can do it to us? Not long, I think. All they need is the right program. And if they've got a satellite to direct it, there's even less chance of the infiltration being detected."

"And what if they've got a mole inside the military?"

"Someone who could feed them passwords and tell them about back doors? Cakewalk. Hell, I could probably do it with that information."

"Could you stop someone else from doing it? Boot them out of the computer system?"

Arlo thought a few moments before answering. "Maybe. It's hard to reverse-engineer malware. And I'll bet those Pentagon boys are already working on getting that virus out of their system."

"That's a safe bet. What would be the safest—or quickest—way to terminate their control over the computers?"

Arlo pondered. "If you could find the operations base, you could shut down the command signal. If no one's guiding the satellite, then the satellite stops hacking."

Seamus stepped forward eagerly. "Great. How do we find this base?"

Arlo shrugged. "I have no idea."

"Who would be capable of doing this?"

"The Chinese."

"I mean domestically. If you were looking for a hacking expert, whom would you call?"

He didn't have to think long. "Me."

Seamus arched an eyebrow. "Who's got self-esteem issues now?"

"Hey, I'm good enough to be your expert."

"Yeah, but I assume you'd remember if you'd designed any malware for Middle Eastern dictators."

"I should hope so. The only gig I've ever done anything like that for was— Oh. Wait a minute. Oh, no. Ohhhh, nooooo."

Seamus pulled him up to his feet. "What is it? What did you do?"

"It was so long ago, I barely remembered. Almost a month."

"What did you do?"

"These guys wanted to prank the university, so they wanted some targeted malware, something that could hack into a well-protected system. But they weren't Middle Eastern. They were preppies. They were—"

"Employees, most likely, you stooge."

"They didn't say they were going after the military."

"Imagine that."

"And they said nothing about a satellite."

"Because they're not stupid."

"And even as good as I am, I don't think it was good enough to hack into the military defense system. It might be able to seize control once it's in, but there's no way it could get past all the firewalls and defenses."

"But what if the people you sold the program to also had top-secret passwords and back-door information?"

Arlo's mouth formed a silent o. "That would be bad. That would be real bad."

"Yeah, it is. Come on, kid." Semus tugged forcefully at his elbow. "You're coming with me."

"But I've got class today."

"I'll give you a note from the doctor. Bring a copy of your program."

"I don't have one!"

"What?"

"That's part of the deal. They bought exclusive rights. No copies allowed."

"Did you keep any notes?"

He shrugged. "Not so much."

"Could you at least explain what you did to our computer experts?"

"I guess I could try."

"Good. I want you to try very hard." Seamus led him toward the door. "I want you to think about it in advance so when we get there you—"

Seamus was cut off by a sudden spray of broken glass flying across the room.

"Duck!" he shouted, shoving the kid to the ground.

He watched as a parallel line of bullets crashed into the opposite wall. He heard a harsh rat-a-tat sound, followed by more flying glass and another spray of bullets.

"Great," Seamus muttered. "Stay down!"

He reached under his coat and pulled his pistol out of its holster. He brought his arms up over the desk and fired wildly out the window, pointing downward. He covered a wide range. He couldn't possibly see who was firing from this angle—but the shooter didn't have to know that.

It didn't suppress fire for long. Another long rain of bullets came flying through the windows. Seamus huddled over Arlo. He didn't think the bullets could get them here, but even glass could be deadly at this velocity.

He returned fire.

Arlo stared at his gun. "What the hell is that?"

Seamus grunted, speaking as he fired. "That is my official Company-issued weapon."

"But the guy outside's got a submachine gun! How do they expect you to take on guys like that with a peashooter?"

Tell me something I don't already know, Seamus thought. He squeezed off another round, then ducked behind the desk.

"Who is that?"

"Don't know. Probably one of those preppies you work for."

"You think he wants his money back?"

"No. I think he wants you dead."

"Why?"

"So you won't tell anyone what you just told me."

"But it's too late!"

He shook his head. "Not if he kills me, too."

He fired another round, then ducked back behind the desk.

The bullets stopped.

"Does that mean he went away?" Arlo whispered.

"In the first place," Seamus said, "I wouldn't assume there was only one. In the second place, I doubt it. We're totally pinned down. Why leave? Why not finish off the job?"

"Oh."

"Look, kid, focus on the door. When I count to three, I want you to make a run—"

His sentence trailed off as more glass blasted into the room. A small canister plopped down on the floor only a few feet away from them.

It was round and indented like a pineapple.

Arlo made a sucking sound with his throat. "Is that—a grenade?"

"I'm not sure," Seamus said, inching forward, careful not to get in the way of another round of bullets. "It might just—"

The lid popped off. Seamus heard a hissing noise, then, a moment later, a colorless gas sprayed out of the canister.

"Oh, no," Seamus said. "Oh, Jesus God."

"What is it?"

"Bad news."

Arlo grabbed his arm. "Bad? How bad?"

Seamus shook his head. "We're dead."

10

President Kyler stared at the vice president with something like a combination of horror and disbelief. "Good God, Connie—what the hell are you doing here?"

Swinburne smiled faintly. "Good to see you, too, Roland."

"Don't take it personally, man—you were supposed to be a long way from here by now."

One of the agents guarding Swinburne handed Zimmer a sheet of paper. Zimmer glanced at it, nodded. "They didn't make it out, sir. We didn't move fast enough. I take full responsibility for this failure."

"I don't care about who is to blame, Zimmer. I want to know what happened."

"We got the vice president to Air Force One, but before they could take off, the missile in the Potomac exploded. We deemed it too risky to take to P-fifty-three airspace with the possibility of guided missiles that near. And now we know Colonel Zuko controls some of our missiles—"

"I get the picture, Zimmer. You did the right thing." President

Kyler stared at the next person in the line of succession to his office. "I'm glad you're safe, Connie. But I'm not glad you're here."

"Understood, sir. If you'd like, I can retire to the other room."

"Don't be ridiculous. If you're stuck here, you should know what's going on. But Zimmer—notify the Speaker of the House. Just in case."

Just in case they should have to tap the third in the constitutional line of succession? Ben felt a chill run right down his spine.

He watched the interplay between Kyler and Swinburne carefully. Even though they had been running mates, Ben knew they were not close. Kyler was far more liberal and they differed on many key policy issues, differences Swinburne had been forced to bury to get the vice presidential ticket. They were almost fifteen years apart in age—Swinburne was older—and they had radically different backgrounds. Kyler had grown up poor; Swinburne was privileged. And they came from opposite ends of the country. Swinburne had originally run for president and accepted the vice presidential slot only after it became clear Kyler had clinched the nomination. Even then, the selection was not made based upon any mutual respect. It was a simple matter of self-preservation. Swinburne was from Florida, which had progressively become the most important swing state in every presidential election. Kyler had chosen Swinburne because he needed him, not because he wanted him.

"Sarie," the president said, "would you bring the vice president up-to-date?"

Ben didn't question why he had chosen his chief of staff to perform a task that anyone in the room could've done, including the cabinet members. She had a fine ability to synthesize materials and to deliver the key points in an economical fashion. Even without notes, she was able to summarize their desperate situation succinctly.

"And now, Ben, please fill him in on the legalities as you see them."

Ben complied, trying to mimic her efficiency. What was there to say, really? The president had taken an action for humanitarian purposes that a sovereign leader was interpreting as an act of war. So he was coming at the United States with everything he had. Which, unfortunately, turned out to be quite a bit.

"You think he's acting within his rights?" Swinburne asked.

"I wouldn't go that far," Ben answered. "But I think we've given him the ammunition he needs to justify his extreme actions to the world, at least for a while."

"That will change as soon as people start dying. We may be in his waters but we haven't killed anyone."

"True," Ben felt compelled to say. "But if war does break out, there will be casualties on all sides. And all anyone will remember will be who started it. Zuko is determined to make the world think that was us. To paint us as the aggressor."

"Why do you all keep talking about war?" Secretary Ruiz said. "We don't want to go to war with these people. Do we?"

"Not at the moment," the president said. "As long as they control our missiles, we would be at a distinct disadvantage." He pivoted and turned back to the communications station. "Any progress on getting that maniac out of our computers?"

Zimmer shook his head. "They're trying every antivirus program we've got, but it isn't working. They tell me that if they could find the satellite or whatever it is, track the virus to its source, they could learn how it works. That could lead to a cure. But so far they haven't found it."

"Cloaking device," the president said grimly.

"What?" the vice president replied.

"Cloaking device."

Swinburne shrugged. "Beam me up."

President Kyler smiled faintly. "I wish I could."

The vice president's eyes went to the clock on the station ticking down Zuko's countdown. "Seventeen minutes left?"

Zimmer nodded.

"Is there any chance we'll break this man's lock on our missiles in that time?"

Zimmer hesitated before answering. "Not really. But I believe they'll do it eventually."

"Any reason to believe he's bluffing?"

Zimmer hesitated. "This is just my opinion. . . ."

"Well, let's hear it, man."

"I actually lived in Kuraq for a time, before I joined the service. I lived with a family near the Benzai Strip. There was a woman . . . well, you don't need my life story. The point is, I saw Colonel Zuko on a regular basis during his rise to power. I think I know the kind of man he is. He's not crazy. He may be desperate, given to desperate means. But that is how he took control and that is how he has maintained it ever

since. The truth is, he's the worst possible adversary we could have."
He paused. "And no, I don't believe he's bluffing. Military men don't
bluff. They get the biggest gun and then meet the enemy head-on.
That's what he's doing now."

The president covered his face with his hands. "Damn."

Zimmer cleared his throat, then set another Styrofoam cup before
him. "Here's your coffee, sir."

"Yeah. Thanks."

"Sounds to me as if we're in dire straits," the vice president said.
"We need quick and decisive action to protect ourselves. And I don't
know whom we can trust other than the people in this room."

"If that," Ben said.

Ben looked up and once again saw the whole room staring at him.
He was really going to have to learn to keep his thoughts to himself.

"What the hell are you talking about, shyster?" Cartwright asked.

Ben turned his hands palm side up. "Am I the only one who noticed?"

"Noticed what?"

"The colonel knew the president was in the bunker. He called
here."

The president waved the thought away. "We've covered that already. Anyone who can launch a U.S. missile by seizing control of our
computers can uncover my phone number."

"Yes, I get that," Ben said. "But how did he know you were down
here? I heard the Secret Service say that the usual protocol would be to
whisk you away on Air Force One to a safer location. There just wasn't
time. But how does Zuko know that?"

The people at the table began to look at one another.

"And he specifically mentioned Secretary Rybicki, remember? The
history buff."

The president shrugged. "It's only logical that I would consult my
secretary of defense."

"Yes, of course. But Zuko knew more than that. He knew Rybicki
was here in the bunker. Even though that is not standard emergency
evacuation protocol. So how did he know? How could he possibly
know?"

Ben looked down one side of the table, then the other. He heard no
response.

"There's only one possible explanation," Ben said, speaking the words no one wanted to hear. "Zuko is getting information from someone."

Secretary Ruiz spoke with dry lips. "You mean . . . from someone inside the administration?"

Ben looked him directly in the eyes. "I mean from someone inside this room."

11

Seamus knew what it was as soon as he smelled it. Some sort of lachrymatory agent—what the rest of the world called tear gas. It was highly concentrated and potent. He could already feel his eyes watering. Probably phenacyl bromide, given how fast it was taking effect. By his estimate, they had about five seconds to do something. But the only thing they could do was run outside—where the sniper would be waiting for them. Either way, they were dead in the water.

"What are we gonna do?" Arlo screamed. Tears were streaming down his face.

Seamus didn't really know, didn't have a plan. But he couldn't just sit there and choke. He grabbed the kid by the arm. "Come on."

"Out the door?" Arlo said, coughing.

"That would be much too obvious." He could feel the mucous membranes in his ears, nose, lungs, and throat swelling up. If he didn't get away from that canister soon, he'd be gone. It was tempting to grab it and throw it, but he knew that if he came that close, he'd never have time to make the pitch.

On the opposite side of the apartment, he spotted another small window. He dragged Arlo along with him. The kid was coughing so badly he could barely see straight.

Fire escape. And just a few feet beyond that, his parked Dodge.

Of course, if the sniper had any sense—or had a partner—they'd surely be watching that. His only chance was to move fast.

"Ever been parachuting, kid?"

"Are you crazy? No!"

"That's okay. Just follow my lead." He fired a few rounds out the front, just to throw them off guard. Then he wrapped himself around Arlo and hurled the both of them out the window.

They crashed down onto the fire escape amid a clatter of iron and shattered glass. The gunfire paused for a moment as the sniper tried to figure out what was happening. Seamus didn't wait. Still holding on to the kid, he rolled sideways, right off the fire escape. By the time the bullets reached the fire escape, they were gone.

They free-fell for five feet, then slammed down onto the hood of his Dodge. He rolled so that the impact hit him on the back, the place he was best able to absorb it, protecting the boy. All the air was sucked out of Seamus's lungs and he wasn't entirely sure the weight of the kid hadn't broken one of his ribs. Didn't matter. He didn't have time to think about it.

He rolled off the hood of the car and tumbled to the side—the side facing away from the shooter. Gunfire soon followed, but just as before, it was a nanosecond too late.

"What the hell was that?" Arlo screeched.

"I was saving your punk-ass life," Seamus grunted. He pulled out his gun and fired a few shots over the car, then ducked back down for cover.

"You saved my life? How? All we've done is move from dead behind my desk to dead behind your car!"

"Yeah. But my car moves. Come on."

Seamus opened the driver's-side door and, careful to keep down, pushed Arlo across the seats. Seamus scrambled in behind him. Bullets pounded against the side of the car, but nothing came through. These Company cars might not be flashy, but they were well reinforced. Not exactly Cadillac One, but close.

Seamus kept his head well below seat level and shoved the key into the ignition. The car started immediately.

"Thank God," Arlo wheezed. "Get us out of here!"

"That's what he'll expect us to do," Seamus muttered. He shoved the car into reverse, then yanked the wheel and floored it.

The car practically exploded backward and rolled onto the yard. A second later, he spotted the shooter.

"Stay down, kid."

He threw the car into drive and plowed across the grass. The man with the gun—who actually did look kind of preppy, or perhaps like an aging preppy who hadn't gotten the memo that the eighties were over—panicked as he saw the Dodge's grille bearing down on him. A moment later he recovered and brought his submachine gun around. It was a moment too late.

The car hit him square on. He was flipped up and flung sideways. He hit the lowest branch of a dogwood tree, then fell to the ground with a thump.

"Ow." Arlo winced. "That's got to hurt."

Seamus didn't doubt it, but his attention was focused in front of him, as always, securing the playing field. There was a second shooter, as he had suspected. And he had an equally nasty-looking Uzi.

He floored it toward the second shooter. The creep managed to get off a few rounds, shattering the windshield. Seamus closed his eyes. Arlo ducked into the footwell beneath the glove compartment. Seamus couldn't see anymore, but he didn't let that slow him down. He targeted where he knew the man had to be and kept barreling across the lawn.

A few seconds later he felt the impact, perhaps the most satisfying thud he had experienced in a good long time. Two seconds after that, the flying body thumped onto the trunk of the car.

"I hope these thugs carry insurance," Seamus grunted as he stopped the car and crawled out.

He started with the first shooter he had downed. The one who hit the tree. His neck was snapped cleanly. Seamus didn't even bother checking for a pulse. He was dead and gone.

He moved quickly to the other felled assassin. His leg was twisted behind him at a bizarre angle. Seamus didn't need a surgeon to tell him that leg would never function again. The guy probably died when—

Wait a minute. He wasn't dead. He was spitting blood, coughing. His face was racked with pain.

Seamus got right down in his face. "No promises, you son of a bitch. But I think it's just possible you might live. If I call an ambulance immediately."

The man teared up. His eyes were pleading. "P-p-please—"

"I know you and your friends used this kid to hack into the defense computers. I know you came here to kill him to cover your tracks. What I don't know is: Where's your base of operations? The one you're using to control the satellite."

The wounded man's head was shaking. His whole body began to tremble.

"You'd better tell me, if you want any chance whatsoever to live. 'Cause if you're thinking you're headed to some afterlife with wine and honey and virgins, all I can say is, you've got a hell of a lot of misery between you and that." He paused. "I can make that misery last a good long time. Longer than you can endure without going stark raving mad. And just FYI, there's no heaven for filthy terrorists who try to shoot college kids when they're not looking."

Truth was, the man was fading and would probably be gone in thirty seconds or so. But he didn't know that. "So talk! Where's the base?"

"D-don't . . . I—I d-don't know. . . ."

Seamus leaned forward, pressing his knee down on the broken, twisted leg. The man screamed.

"Last chance, chump. Where's the base?"

" I don't . . . know. . . ." He was crying, spitting out blood between syllables. He wasn't lying. Seamus was sure of it. He didn't have the capacity to bear this kind of pain without trying to end it. Probably no one did. Damn.

"What about the missile?" Seamus pressed. "What's Zuko's target for the missile?"

The man looked up at him pleadingly, not answering.

"Answer me or my thumb goes into that gaping gash in your leg! I'll pull the bone out with my bare hands!"

"Nooo! Please, no!"

"Spit it out! Or I'll start putting bullets in your appendages one at a time!"

"It—it—it—"

"Tell me!"

His eyes and mouth opened. He was giving up the ghost, almost literally letting all the fight seep out of him.

"J-J-Jeffffff . . ."

"Jeff? Who the hell is Jeff?"

"The J-J-Jeffff . . ."

"The Jeff? What in the hell?"

Behind him, Seamus heard the rustling of grass and then Arlo's voice. "Don't you get it, man? He's not saying Jeff. He's trying to say Jefferson. As in the Jefferson Memorial."

Seamus grabbed the man's collar and hauled him upward. "Is that right? Is that what you're saying?"

The man's lids were heavy and he was beyond speaking, but his head trembled up and down in a manner that approximated a nod.

"Jesus God." Seamus threw him down, then stared up at the sky. "I should've known. First Washington, now Jefferson."

"Why would they want to do that?" Arlo asked. "It's just a big hunk of marble."

"It's a symbol, kid. A very important symbol. And more to the point, it's a symbol visited by thousands of people every day. Thousands of people who will be slaughtered as soon as that missile hits."

12

9:48 A.M.

The room was silenced by Ben's disturbing but inescapable conclusion.

"If there's a mole in here, who can I trust?" President Kyler asked.

"That's the key question," Cartwright said, arms folded across his portly chest.

"And the question none of us knows the answer to," Ruiz added. "Well, maybe one of us does."

"Or more," Secretary Rybicki said.

"If Kincaid is right and there is a mole down here," Cartwright said, "who the hell is it?"

All those seated at the table began to look closely, too closely, at the people sitting around them. Ben could feel the heat of scrutiny, the weight of too many eyes bearing down on him at once. He was well aware that in many respects he was the outsider in the room: not a member of the cabinet, not really a member of the president's staff, and a presence in the White House for only a brief period of time. The two secretaries probably didn't even recall meeting him before today.

As it turned out, paranoia did not reach out to him first. "Agent

Zimmer," Cartwright said, "exactly how long were you in the Middle East?"

Zimmer still had the headphones on and appeared to be conducting about three conversations and watching six screens at once. He made a waving gesture that clearly conveyed a message: I'm too busy to talk to you.

"Hmph," Cartwright said, frowning. "Convenient."

"Sorry to bring this up, Mike," Vice President Swinburne said to the secretary of state, "but weren't you formerly friends with Colonel Zuko?"

Ruiz looked stricken. "Friends? Hardly. I've met him a few times, long ago. We were both at Oxford at the same time. I was a Rhodes scholar and he bought half of Queen's College. But I certainly wouldn't say we were ever friends. I don't think I've spoken to him since he returned to Kuraq."

The president's head tilted slightly. "Didn't Zuko help out with your first campaign?"

"What, you mean back when I ran for mayor in Laramie?" Ben spotted distinct patches of red popping out on Ruiz's cheeks. "Yes, he made a little contribution. I'd forgotten all about it. But it was his idea. I never talked to him."

Even Cartwright didn't bother to respond to that. No one could make Ruiz look more incriminated than the job he was doing on himself.

"I don't understand why these accusations are coming my way," Ruiz said defensively. "I'm a statesman, not a military man—unlike you, Admiral Cartwright. I daresay you know more about our missile defense system than anyone in this room."

"What are you getting at, Ruiz?" Cartwright replied.

"I'm just pointing out that Colonel Zuko is not a computer genius. Someone had to give him some assistance."

"Are you accusing me of treason, man?" The admiral's eyes looked as if they might pop out of his skull. "If that's what it is, stand up and do it to my face!"

Ruiz looked away. "I'm just saying. . . ."

"You were in charge of the Middlemarch study, weren't you, Will?" The president spoke soberly, but his voice seemed weak, almost feeble.

"Yes," Cartwright replied. "And I guess this proves the importance of that effort!"

"Middlemarch?" Sarie looked just as puzzled as Ben was. "I haven't heard of that. What is it?"

"That's the code name for a top-secret study to assess the vulnerability of our national defense computer system. Basically, we were trying to determine if we could be infiltrated . . . well, in exactly the manner Zuko is doing right now."

"Really?" Rybicki said. "What was the conclusion of the study?"

Cartwright pursed his lips. "That we had a lot of work to do to make this country secure."

"And was that work done?"

"Some of it. We haven't had time—" He stopped short. "Well, we haven't!"

Ben was wishing now he had never spoken. He'd thought it was obvious to everyone already that Zuko had inside information. But it seemed all he had done was magnify the already massive sense of paranoia in the room. In any case, he thought the bunker needed an immediate change of subject before this turned into a bloodbath.

He noticed that Zimmer had stopped talking for a moment, and so he seized the opportunity. "Agent Zimmer, I know you're busy, but given the exigent circumstances . . . is it possible I could make a brief phone call to my wife?"

Zimmer shrugged. "The problem is, if I let you make a call, I need to do the same for everyone."

Ben frowned. Since there were eight people down here, plus the Secret Service agents, and only about ten minutes left on the clock, that was clearly a deal breaker.

"I don't need to call home," Cartwright said, to Ben's surprise. Was he being generous, or did he just consider anyone who wanted to call his wife during a crisis a pantywaist? "My Brenda has been a military wife for thirty-nine years now. She knows the drill."

They took a quick poll of the room, and as it turned out, Ben, Rybicki, and Sarie were the only ones who wanted to make a call, so Zimmer allowed it, though he limited each call to one minute.

Sarie went first. She looked terrible. Ben wondered whom she had called. She wasn't currently married, and he didn't think she was close to any family members. Her work was her life. But there was someone she wanted to talk to before it was too late. She trembled as she spoke, which was more than unfortunate. When you had to get a call completed in one minute, it's a poor time to develop a stutter.

Secretary Rybicki made a brief call, then it was Ben's turn. "Remember," Zimmer said, "you can make no reference to the missile crisis, Colonel Zuko, or anything else that is not currently public knowledge."

"Understood. One minute."

Zimmer smiled slightly. "Well, for you, Ben . . . perhaps I can make it two."

Zimmer turned his back and took a few steps away, presumably to give Ben a tiny quantum of privacy. Ben quickly dialed Christina's cell phone.

"How's my favorite wife?"

"Ben! Oh, my gosh. Is it really you? I've been so worried! The news said that the White House might be in danger, then they said there was a gas explosion, but people on the Internet are saying a missile exploded, and I didn't know where you were or— What happened? Where are you? I went to—"

"Christina, I'm sorry to interrupt, but I only have two minutes."

"What?"

"I just wanted you to know that I'm safe. I'm still at the White House—sort of—and I'm with the president and we're all safe. I may not be able to come home for some while, though, so I wanted to assure you that—"

"Oh, my gosh, Ben. They've closed all the monuments on the Mall. Something big is going on out there."

"Yes, I know—"

"What is it?"

"I can't talk about it."

"Spoilsport."

"But I'm safe, honey. And when I get home, I'll have big news. You'll never top this."

"I'll bet I can."

Ben felt an irritable gnawing in his stomach. "No, not this time, sweetie. There's just no—"

"Your mother is going to redecorate the spare room."

"And you're telling me this now? When the whole country—"

"Didn't you say I could decorate the room?"

"Well, yes, but—"

"Good. She has excellent taste. And isn't family more important than politics?"

"I suppose," he said. She didn't need to know how serious this crisis really was.

Out the corner of his eye, Ben saw Zimmer holding up all his fingers. Ten seconds.

"Honey, I have to go now. I just wanted to tell you not to worry. I'm safe. And I love you very much."

"I love you, too, you goofus. Get your sexy butt home soon."

Ben flushed and hung up the phone.

When he returned to the conference table, everyone else was engaged in a heated debate.

"We can't give in to terrorists!" the president insisted.

"We should've pulled out of the Middle East a long time ago," Ruiz said. "Found our energy somewhere else. Let the damn camel jockeys obliterate one another."

"Look," Vice President Swinburne said, "I don't know where you were in your deliberations before I made the scene, so I'll just jump in—if you don't mind, Mr. President. I know I'm not technically a member of the cabinet."

"I always value your opinion, Connie."

The expressions Ben read on both faces suggested that neither of them believed a word of that statement.

"Then let me be blunt. I think we have to tell our forces to retreat. Get us the hell out of there. Before this countdown runs out."

The president slowly lowered himself into his own chair. "Are you seriously suggesting that we give in to this terrorist?"

"But he isn't a terrorist, Roland. He's the internationally recognized leader of a sovereign nation."

"He seized power in a bloody coup."

"That's ancient history. He is the leader of Kuraq and he has a legitimate beef." Swinburne spread his hands wide. "Look, I don't want to see all those people in Benzai slaughtered, either. But if it's a choice between losing them or losing some of our own people—well, I hope I don't have to explain what side I come down on."

"We're the most respected nation in the world, Connie. We can't always act in our own interests. We're citizens of the world."

Ben could see that Swinburne was becoming agitated. "Then let me put it to you even more bluntly, Roland. Do you have any desire to be reelected?"

"I hardly think this is the time—"

"A poor decision here could tank this administration."

"That's my decision to make."

"And you won't just be dragging yourself down. I'd like a shot at your job when you're finished. And that isn't going to happen if the people learn that you traded American lives for those of some non-Christian foreigners most people haven't even heard of before!"

"This is a time for cool-headed foreign policy statesmanship, not political maneuvering!" the president shouted.

"This is a time for pragmatism, not boneheaded idealism!" Swinburne shouted back. "And if you won't do what needs to be done, I will."

"Over my dead body!"

The vice president looked at him levelly. "I can think of an easier means to get you out of the way than that."

13

Seamus called 911, then snapped his cell phone shut. "Come on, kid."

"Do I have to?"

"You're not safe here. And I'm not done with you."

Seamus moved toward the car, but Arlo hesitated.

"What are you waiting for? A papal bull?"

"I just—I—" Arlo shook his shaggy head. "You were seriously harsh with that guy."

"He's a terrorist who tried to kill you, kid. Remember?"

"You tortured him!"

"I wouldn't put it that way. I . . . persuaded him."

"You tortured him."

"Look, he was fading fast, and if I was going to get anything out of him, it was going to have to happen fast. He's working with people who have pointed our own weapons at us and are threatening to launch them at any minute. I don't have time to say pretty please."

"Yeah, I get that, man. I just—I don't know why you had to go all Gitmo on him."

"Have you forgotten that this guy came here to kill you?"

"No. But if we start using the same tactics as the bad guys, doesn't that make us just like the bad guys?"

Seamus swung the car door open. "I don't have time for a philosophical debate. Get in!"

Arlo did as he was told. Seamus turned the car around and started back toward downtown. The National Mall. And all the monuments on and near it.

He punched in a highly classified number on his cell phone. A few seconds later, someone picked up.

"Seamus?"

"Zira, listen. I got—"

"Seamus, where the hell are you? I didn't give you the go-ahead to—"

"Zira, for once would you shut the hell up?" That explosion would probably cost him some vacation time. Possibly his job. But she needed to hear what he had to say, as quickly as possible. "Just listen to me, Zira. I'm cutting to the chase. I tracked down the computer expert who may have inadvertently helped Zuko's people infiltrate our computers. Some terrorist thugs showed up to silence him. I managed to interrogate one of them."

"Why didn't you bring him in?"

"There wasn't time."

"Seamus, I certainly hope you didn't do anything inappropriate. Maybe you can get away with those strong-arm tactics out in the desert, but you're in the civilized world now and—"

"Zira, close your trap and listen!" Oh, man, was he going to pay for this. "Zira, they're targeting the Jefferson Memorial."

For once she was actually quiet. For a second. "Are you certain about this?"

"I don't think my informant had any incentive to lie. He was . . . in an awkward situation."

"Tell me what happened. I need to evaluate the intel."

"No, Zira. You need to evacuate the memorial."

"Actually, the president just gave an order to close all the Washington attractions, so it's already in progress."

"That's not good enough. You need to evacuate the whole Mall. Get the people out of there! There can't be anyone within a mile radius of the memorial."

"Do you think the suitcase is involved?"

"I don't know. I'm headed that way now."

He heard her barking orders to someone else. When she came back on she said, "I've started the evac. The contingency plans have been in place ever since the first Oklahoma City bombing. They'll move quickly."

"How quickly?"

"The E-one-oh-one blueprint says the entire Mall should be clear in seven minutes."

"Does that assume all the tourists cooperate? No one stops to take pictures?"

"I think it's five minutes if they all cooperate. What are you going to do?"

"I could head to the memorial."

"Why? So they can evacuate you, too? You're good, Seamus, but I don't think you can stop a ballistic missile."

"You've got a point. My informant thinks there must be some sort of operations base in the area. Some Computers R Us outfit that sends instructions to the satellite or whatever it is up there."

"Does he know where it is?"

"No."

"Find it, Seamus."

He couldn't resist. "Well, okay, if you're sure. If you'd rather, I could come into the office so you can debrief me."

"Just find the goddamn base, Seamus."

"All right. Since you asked nicely."

"Call back when you can."

"I will. Bye."

He snapped his phone shut.

"Do you always talk to your boss like that?" Arlo asked. "'Cause I worked at Taco Bell once, and my supervisor didn't even understand what sarcasm was. Which is probably why I only lasted three weeks."

Seamus blew air through his nose. "Listen, kid, I'm not used to having someone hovering over my shoulder. When I was in the Middle East, I went weeks without any contact with anyone. Including superiors. And none of my superiors was—" He used better judgment and buried the end of the sentence.

"You were in the Middle East?"

"For the better part of ten years."

"In the Iraq war?"

"Not exactly. In . . . um, contingency operations."

"You were a spy!"

"I can neither confirm nor deny."

"You were!" Arlo pounded the dash of the car. "You so were. That must be where you learned all those moves."

"I guess you could say that."

"Did you go after bin Laden?"

"Yeah. Damn near caught him, too."

"Sweet!" Arlo bounced up and down like a kid meeting his favorite superstar. "You're, like, one of America's heroes."

"If so, it's a well-kept secret."

"Have you ever been shot?"

"More times than I can count."

"Have you ever had to kill anyone?"

Seamus closed his eyes briefly and sighed. "More times that I care to remember."

"That is so razor. You know, I've done some counterintelligence work myself."

Seamus arched an eyebrow. "You have?"

"Oh, yeah. I mean, in a video game. But it was a highly realistic simulation."

"No doubt." Seamus kept his eyes on the road. "Kid, have you given any thought to how we're going to track down Colonel Zuko's base of operations?"

"We? Did you say we?"

"Don't have a stroke. Yes, I said we. How are we gonna do it?"

"Geez, I don't know. Do you have any leads?"

"You're my lead, Arlo. How are we going to find it?"

"How would I know?"

"An operations base like you described must need staff. There can't be many people in the area with the techno-gizmo whiz kid qualifications to help terrorists hack into our defense computers."

"True."

"Where would we find these people? In the Washington area."

"How would I know?" Arlo pondered for a moment. "A lot of brainiacs hang at the university."

"Georgetown? Maybe. But what about when they're not working?"

"I really don't know."

"Well, what do you do in your spare time?"

"I don't have spare time. I mean, besides computer work. Programming. Facebook. World of Warcraft."

Seamus rolled his eyes. "Don't you ever go out?"

"Um, out?"

"Like, to meet friends. Perchance even go on a date?"

"I generally eschew frivolous and meaningless social encounters."

"You have no friends."

"That's not true!"

"When was the last time you went out on a date?"

"What does it matter?"

"Are you gay?"

"No!"

"Then it matters." Seamus took a hard left and merged onto the parkway. He was driving too fast, but hell, he was in a hurry. Traffic was thick, but in the opposite direction. He wondered if that was because the evacuation had begun. "How can I say this, kid? You need to get a life."

"I have a life! I have a very rich and rewarding life—"

"Filled with megabytes and malware and perhaps, on a really good night, Internet porn."

"You don't know anything about it!"

"No, *you* don't. And you need to, because I need to know where to find the other people like you."

"D.C. Bytes."

Seamus processed a moment. "Is that a critical evaluation?"

"No. That's a deli and coffeehouse. Frequented by the upper echelon of the programming/hacking/phishing community."

"Fine. Where is it?" Arlo gave him the address. "Then that's where we're headed." He glanced over his shoulder. "I'll turn the car around and—"

At the edge of his peripheral vision, Seamus saw something in the air. It would be impossible to describe—if he had never seen anything like it before. It looked like a horizontal crayon mark streaking across the sky and moving very fast.

"Oh, my God," Seamus said breathlessly.

"What? What?" Arlo jumped up in his seat and turned toward the back. "What is it? What's happening?"

"We're too late," he said. His eyes traced the crayon mark as it passed over them. "The missile is on its way. And heading straight toward the Mall."

14

"All right, all right." Secretary Rybicki jumped out of his chair and came between the president and his VP. "Let's all cool down. We only have a few minutes left to make a very important decision. And we aren't going to accomplish that with an alpha-male smackdown. Remember what Lincoln said: cool heads prevail in torrid times."

"We need a show of strength," Vice President Swinburne said. "The strength to make a tough call."

"I don't think most of the people I know would consider retreat a sign of strength," Rybicki countered. "We can't let this maniac go unchecked. I wonder if the president is doing enough. I think it's time for scorched-earth tactics."

"That's crazy talk."

"Forgive me, Mr. Vice President, but I don't recall seeing you at the military academy. You went to Yale and studied geology, right? I'm sure that's useful in some arenas. But I have studied military tactics, and I say we should go in with everything we've got, leave nothing intact. Scorched earth worked for the ancient Scythians. They put Persia in its place, back in their day. Maybe we should try the same thing. What do you think, Mr. President?"

"You're right. You're right." The president fell back into his chair and pinched his nose. "I just wish . . . I wish . . ." His eyes seemed to detach, to lose their focus. His gaze drifted off to the side, somewhere vaguely in the direction of the presidential seal on the wall. "Here's the story . . ."

Ben couldn't quite hear what he was saying. Without making a show of it, he leaned in closer.

". . . of a lovely lady . . ."

Ben glanced at Sarie. Sarie looked back at him, dumbfounded.

He wasn't mistaken. The POTUS was singing the theme song from *The Brady Bunch*. In a time of crisis, with only a few minutes left till disaster, with the entire eastern seaboard facing possible destruction, he was singing the theme from a cheesy seventies sitcom.

Ben quickly scanned the room. Everyone else seemed just as incredulous as they were. He particularly scrutinized the vice president's expression but found it very difficult to read.

To Ben's amazement, the president played air guitar and made the sound of an electric fuzz during the song. "That's the way we became the Brady Bunch." He extended one arm across the table. "Yeah!"

Not a person in the room spoke. All eyes were focused on the leader of the free world—and then on the countdown on the wall.

"What's the matter?" the president said, grinning. "No one has a sense of humor?"

Swinburne cleared his throat. "Um, Mr. President . . ."

"I don't like that tone in your voice, mister. I don't like it at all." Abruptly the president looked at Ben. "You know what I wish, Ben?"

"Um, no . . ."

"I wish I could be a butterfly. Don't you wish you could be a butterfly?"

Ben swallowed. "Well, I think you have to be a caterpillar first. I don't think I'd care for all that slithering. And don't they have short life spans?"

"But you could fly, Ben. Fly!' He shot to his feet and stretched out his arms. "Wouldn't that be wonderful?"

Off to the side, Ben saw the vice president make a motion toward the doctor. A moment later, Dr. Albertson crossed the room to his patient.

"Sorry, Roland. Need to take a few readings."

"Why?" he said petulantly. "There's nothing wrong with me!"

"Just want to do a spot check." He removed his stethoscope. "Check your heartbeat, make sure there's no cardiac arrest. Check your blood pressure. Make sure there's no aneurysm. I'd like to take some blood, too, but I couldn't analyze it without going topside. . . ."

He looked across to Zimmer. Zimmer gave him a firm no.

"Well, just let me see what I can do with what I have available." He took out the inhaler. "Why don't you take a hit from this? Might help. Maybe your airways are constricted. That can make a person . . . light-headed."

"I am not light-headed!" Kyler replied. "Leave me alone!"

"Sorry, but when it comes to your health, I'm the boss." He took the better part of a minute—one of the few they had left—to complete his examination. "My friends," he said when he was done, "I detect nothing overtly the matter with the president's health."

Ruiz sputtered, "Well, there's obviously something wrong!"

Swinburne's brow was creased. "Doctor, I don't want to seem opportunistic. But we don't have time for any nonsense. We are in a crisis situation. This nation needs to be led by someone who is in full control of his faculties."

"The law is the law," Dr. Albertson said firmly. "And Roland Kyler is the president, whether you like it or not."

"I know you've read the Twenty-fifth Amendment, Doctor. If the president becomes incapacitated—"

"I see no evidence of that."

"Open your eyes, man!"

"I won't declare any man incapable based on a little odd behavior."

"Be reasonable. This could cost thousands of American lives."

"I'm aware of the possible consequences."

"Then *do* something!"

Dr. Albertson shook his head. "Physiologically, so far as I can tell from the instruments available to me down here, the president is in perfect health. So he remains in charge."

"Not if—"

The vice president never got to finish his sentence. Agent Zimmer cut in. "Sir, Colonel Zuko is back on the line."

"Put him on."

Ben looked up and, to his astonishment, saw that the president had snapped back to his normal state. He looked as strong and sturdy as ever.

What the hell was going on here?

Ben didn't have much time to ponder. The colonel's eerie, disembodied voice was soon back on the speakerphone.

"I greet you again, Mr. President. And your loyal second, Mr. Swinburne. I hope you are all comfortable down there."

"Get to the damn point," Kyler barked.

"As you wish. I'm sure you have noticed that you have one minute left on the clock. One minute to save countless lives. May I ask your decision?"

"There's no decision to make, Colonel."

"Roland!" Swinburne said, but the president shushed him.

"There will be blood on your hands, Mr. President. I have given you every possible opportunity to stop it, but you have chosen to take another path. The path of death and violence."

"You're the one threatening to kill people."

"And you're the one threatening my people."

"You can stop it!"

The vice president whispered softly, "You can, too, Roland. Please do. Please!"

"The United States will not negotiate with terrorists, Zuko," the president said firmly. "Not now. Not ever."

Even over the phone line, Ben thought he heard Zuko sigh. "Then you have made your decision. I am sorry." He paused a moment. "I will call you again. After you have had time to count the dead."

The room was silent. Everyone stared straight ahead.

"He doesn't mean it," Rybicki said, breaking the silence. "It's a threat. That's all. We called his bluff."

"You think so?" Admiral Cartwright asked.

"Of course. Even a crazy bastard like that must know that—"

He was interrupted by a loud beeping sound coming from the communications station.

They were all too afraid to ask.

"My God, no!"

Zimmer turned, suddenly aware that everyone present had heard what he just said.

"Are you sure?" Zimmer said into his mouthpiece. "Are you ab-solutely sure?"

A pause. Zimmer's eyes closed.

"Continue all evacuation efforts. Shut down the subway system. Get people out of there as fast as you can. Everyone. Law enforcement, emergency rescue. Everyone! As fast as possible!"

"What's going on?" the president asked in a quiet voice.

Zimmer rose slowly to his feet. His face was ashen. "I'm—I'm—" He choked. He swallowed, then tried again. "I'm afraid I have confir-mation, sir."

"And?"

Zimmer paused only a few seconds before answering, but it seemed an eternity. "A missile has been launched."

"Do you know where it's going?"

Zimmer was still listening to his intel source in one ear. "I'm afraid I do, sir. It has almost arrived."

"And?"

"And . . . it couldn't possibly be any worse."

The president pressed his fingers against his temples. "Just spit it out, man."

And then Zimmer told them.

"Oh, my God. Oh, my dear God. Not that. Anything but that!"

15

Seamus pulled his car over to the side of the street and stared at the vast destruction before him. Even at this distance it was impossible to miss the devastation that lay before him.

He had seen the missile strike. He had spotted it when it was on its way, quickly found a good vantage point, and parked the car. Arlo stayed inside. Just as well. He might want to tuck his head under his hands, for that matter. Seamus wouldn't blame him. No one needed to see this. He had seen missiles strike before, but this was different. This was not out in the barren, mostly unpopulated desert.

This missile struck at home.

The targeting was perfect. He had to give the terrorists—or perhaps their computer guru—credit for that. It struck dead on the roof of the Jefferson Memorial and instantaneously exploded it into billions of pieces. In less than the blink of an eye it was transformed from a marble masterpiece of neoclassical architecture to a field of rubble.

Chunks of marble and metal flew through the air in a grotesque pyrotechnic display. Seamus saw large chunks splash into the Tidal

Basin Memorial. He saw another large piece crash down on the rooftop of the George Mason Memorial. No telling what damage that might have done, not to mention what treasures might have been destroyed.

Fortunately, as far as he could tell, all the tourists had been evacuated in time. Maybe Zira was right and they really could clear the area in seven minutes. He hoped so. He didn't see how anyone in the immediate vicinity could have survived. If the explosion hadn't killed them, the flying rubble surely would.

Seamus pulled a pair of binoculars out of the trunk of his car, but it was almost impossible to see anything. The billowing smoke and ash and fire rendered Seamus unable to get a clear view. All he really got was a portrait of devastation. A bleak landscape. A barren wasteland.

He had seen this before, possibly even seen it worse. But that had always been somewhere else. This was the first, the only time he had seen it on U.S. soil.

He heard the shuffling of Arlo's feet behind him. "You should stay in the car," Seamus told him.

Arlo didn't listen. "Jesus. Is that—the Mall?"

Seamus compressed his lips. "What's left of it."

"They did it. They really did it."

"They really did."

"Is it over?"

Seamus shook his head. His upper lip began to curl. "No. If they were willing to do this, they won't stop now. Zuko knows he's going to be the pariah of the world community. He doesn't care."

"What does he want?"

"I don't know. What does it matter? Every terrorist wants something. The important question is, how do we stop him?"

"What are you—" Arlo lurched into a coughing jag. The smoke had made it into his lungs. It was becoming difficult to breathe.

"Let's get out of here," Seamus said. They crawled back into the car. He started it up and headed in the opposite direction.

Behind them, the sky looked as if an enormous hand had reached down and ripped a swath out of the heavens. It was devoid of birds, of clouds, of any signs of life or beauty. Now it was only fire and ash. One of the key symbols of democracy, of the great truism that all people are created equal, was no more.

When Arlo spoke again, his voice was hoarse. "What are you going to do next?"

"Isn't it obvious, kid?" Seamus gripped the wheel so tightly his knuckles turned white. "I'm going to stop the bastards who just blew up my favorite memorial."

Part Two

The Twenty-fifth Amendment

16

The president slowly lowered himself into his seat. The formerly bickering room became silent, motionless. The giddy, infantile exuberance of only a few minutes earlier seemed completely replaced by the grave despondency of a leader who realizes a tragedy has just befallen his nation.

And, Ben imagined, who realizes that he might have prevented it.

Ben kept his eyes focused on Zimmer. At this moment, the Secret Service agent knew more about what was going on out in the world than anyone else in the room.

"I want updates in real time," President Kyler said to Zimmer. "I want to know what you know, when you know it."

"Yes, sir." Zimmer covered the mouthpiece. "The reports are coming in slowly. Our people got out of there in time, but I'm getting intel from two agents in helicopters."

"And?"

"It isn't good, sir."

"Just tell me, damn it, and stow the commentary."

"Yes, sir." As always, even in the face of presidential wrath, Zimmer remained totally implacable. "The Jefferson Memorial has been obliterated. It's gone. Chunks of white marble are scattered across the Mall. We don't know of anyone who was still in the building—but we can't rule out the possibility."

"Understood. The target was destroyed. Collateral damage?"

"I would imagine quite a bit, sir, given that the Jefferson Memorial was just struck by a ballistic missile. We can assume damage all across the area, all the buildings, monuments, statues, everything. There's still a lot of smoke and dust, hampering visibility, but I think we can assume that our men will find considerably more damage with time."

"Tell me about people," the president said softly.

"I've also got a report that the Metro is down," Zimmer continued, and Ben wasn't sure if this was supposed to be an answer to the question, the one on everyone's mind. "Apparently the station closest to the detonation has collapsed. There was no train in the station, but no trains can get through there, either, so the line is effectively disabled. It probably shouldn't be run until we've had a chance to get structural engineers out to check over the entire system. There's no telling where the foundations might have been weakened."

"People," the president said, with a little more force than before. "Tell me about people."

Zimmer took a deep breath, then continued. "We had begun the evacuation of the National Mall before the missile struck. Theoretically, there should have been enough time to complete it. We don't know of any casualties there or anywhere else in the vicinity." He paused.

"But?" the president said. "I sense we are coming to a *but*."

Zimmer sighed heavily. "But there is no way I can guarantee no one was in that building or any other structure in the area. I can't guarantee no one was in the Metro station. There's no way of knowing what the shock waves from the explosion might have done in the surrounding area."

"Numbers, Zimmer. I need numbers."

"I don't have them, Mr. President. But I would be astonished if there were not a casualty somewhere. Probably . . . several."

"Damn," the president said. His fist tightened. "Damn. On my watch."

"This might not be a welcome comment, sir . . ."

"No, go ahead. You've earned the right."

"I know you think Colonel Zuko is a madman. But the truth is, he chose a target that was largely symbolic—not all that lethal. He probably knew we were evacuating the Mall. If he'd wanted to take lives, he could have sent the missile elsewhere."

President Kyler stared at him with astonished eyes. "Are you saying . . . Zuko did us a favor?"

"Of course not. I'm saying it could have been much worse. If he had moved the target a mile in any direction, it would have been."

"Thank you, Zimmer. For whatever that's worth." Kyler rose. "If you'll excuse me, my friends, I'm going to step into the other room for a moment. Please let me know if—"

"Mr. President!" Zimmer said suddenly.

"Yes?"

"I have Colonel Zuko back on the line."

Kyler's eyes closed wearily. "What does that malicious bastard want now? To gloat? To rub my face in it?"

"I don't know, sir. He's just asking to talk to you."

Kyler pressed his head against the wall. "Put him on."

"President Kyler." There was no levity in the colonel's voice this time, no urgency, and, to Ben's surprise, no malice. "I'm sure you are not anxious to talk to me. I am calling to express my regret for what I was forced to do."

"Regret?" Kyler exploded. "If you regret it, why'd you do it in the first place?"

"You left me no choice."

"We always have a choice, Colonel Zuko. From the day we're born. The choice to do good. Or the choice to do evil."

"If my experiences in the world have taught me anything, it is that in real life, conflicts can rarely be reduced to anything so simple as good and evil."

"Is that why you called, Colonel? So we can debate philosophy?"

"No." There was a pause. Ben thought he might be projecting, but he sensed a certain degree of reluctance in the colonel's voice. "I have called to again request that you remove the invaders from Kuraq's borders."

"You're asking me to bargain with a terrorist."

"According to my sources, your men will touch ground in a little over two hours. We will have to meet them with force to defend our land. Bloodshed will inevitably result. I would prefer to avoid that."

"Then do."

"And allow your soldiers to invade unimpeded? To take over my nation?"

"They're just coming in to rescue the men who went down in that helicopter."

"With all due respect, Mr. President, I don't believe you. They were out there before the helicopter went down. And their number is far greater than would be necessary for a simple rescue operation."

"I don't have to convince you of anything, Colonel. And I'm not taking orders from you."

"All I ask is that you respect our sovereign soil."

"And I'm telling you that the United States does not negotiate with terrorists and the United States does not retreat!"

All at once, Vice President Swinburne rose to his feet, an incredulous expression on his face. His message to the president seemed self-evident: What the hell are you doing?

"I am sorry that you do not see the need to respect international law," the colonel said, and Ben sensed genuine sorrow in his voice. "I am hoping that your advisors will be able to talk you into a more sensible position, so I will give you more time to reflect before we strike again. If you do not retreat, however, the next missiles will launch in two hours. At twelve noon, your time. Precisely."

Ben felt his spine stiffen. Not again. Please, not again.

"And this time, Mr. President, this time—" To Ben's astonishment, the colonel's voice cracked as he spoke. He started again. "This time I will not be able to do you the courtesy of choosing a symbolic target. This time there will be civilian casualties. Many of them."

"You can't do that!" the president spat out.

"I have no choice. If you have not withdrawn your troops in two hours, we will send three missiles into neighboring residential areas. I will not bother telling you where so as to save you the trouble of attempting an evacuation. There is no time, no possibility. This time thousands of your people will die. People you could have saved. The collateral damage will be the blood of innocent Americans. And you will have to answer to the world for your own aggression."

The line went dead. Silence blanketed the bunker.

The vice president broke the silence. To everyone's surprise—and horror—he walked right up to the president and grabbed him by the lapels. "Are you insane?"

Everyone watched dumbfounded as the vice president shook Kyler back and forth in rhythm to his words. "I'm asking you a question! Are you completely insane?"

The president said nothing, but looked back at Swinburne with a mixed expression Ben didn't know how to read—horror, shock, confusion, defeat. In any case, it was not what the VP wanted.

Swinburne threw the president down into a nearby chair. His eyes were wide and bulging. "My God," he said, "you are, aren't you? You're completely insane!"

Dr. Anderson rose slowly to his feet. "Now wait just a minute—"

Swinburne waved him away. "Don't bother. It's obvious now. It's been staring us in the face the whole time. How else can you explain this bizarre behavior we've witnessed?"

"The president has been under a tremendous amount of stress. . . ."

"Every president has stress. Everyone in this room has stress. But most of us aren't singing TV show themes."

"Now just you look here. I'm the medical man in the room—"

"And I'm the vice president of the United States!" Swinburne barked back. "And I am not going to sit here and let that monster take thousands of American lives for no good reason."

"We both know there's a reason."

"Not a good one. Not for a sacrifice at that level."

"The president has a free hand to make decisions in the foreign policy arena."

"Not if he's insane!" Swinburne clapped his hands down on the president's shoulders. "Roland, listen to me! Pull back those troops. At least until we get that murderer out of our computer system. You can always go back later."

"The United States cannot be seen backing down," Rybicki said. "If we do, every tin-plated madman in the world will come after us."

"They will understand this exception. We're acting to save lives."

"It will set a precedent. If we back down this time, who will be next? Who will be the next petty dictator with a grudge?"

"I don't care!" Swinburne bellowed. Ben had to wonder if he was bordering on the brink of crazy himself. "I just don't want thousands of Americans to die for nothing."

Kyler folded his arms across his chest. "I will not alter my decision."

Swinburne spoke through gritted teeth. "Then you, sir, must be insane. And due to your mental incapacity, you must be replaced."

Dr. Albertson stood again. "Mr. Vice President—"

Swinburne reached into his back pocket and threw something down on the table between them. It hit the tabletop with an impressive thwack.

Ben leaned forward to peer at the cover.

It was a pocket-sized copy of the United States Constitution. Just like the one Hugo Black used to carry in his back pocket. It seemed Conrad Swinburne had the same habit.

"You know what it says as well as I do, Doctor. The Twenty-fifth Amendment. When the president is incapacitated and unable to perform his duties—as this man clearly is—he will be replaced by the vice president. That's me. So I'm taking over right now. Before this horrific day gets any bloodier."

17

Ben picked up the small booklet and began turning to the amendment in question, the one that governed presidential succession. He
had read it before, of course, but not recently. And never before had it
been so relevant.

"You can't do that!" President Kyler roared. "As long as I'm still
standing, I'm the president."

"Not if you're incapable of performing your duties!" Swinburne
shouted back.

"I don't become incapable just because we have a difference of
opinion."

"No, you're incapable because you're insane!"

Ben scanned the amendment as quickly as he could. He didn't
enjoy watching the president when he seemed so beaten and ineffec-
tual, and it was hard to forget the bizarre behavior he had witnessed
twice that morning. He forced himself to remember the Roland Kyler
he had followed throughout the campaign, the inspirational leader
who had given the country new hope, the possibility of alleviating the
problems, both domestic and foreign, that confronted the nation. That

was the man he wanted to remember, and that was the man he wanted to see rise again.

He also reminded himself, not for the first time that day, of the gigantic favor Kyler had done for Christina. This man, despite being probably the busiest person on earth, had taken time to do a kindness for his wife.

Ben would not let him down when he needed a return favor.

He quickly read the amendment. *Section 1. In case of the removal of the President from office or of his death or resignation, the Vice President shall become President. . . .*

"You don't have the authority to take me out of office on your own," President Kyler said.

"The Constitution gives me the right to take over in the event the president in stark raving mad!"

"As determined by the vice president? If that were the law, no president would be in office very long. Especially not if you were their vice president!"

"Gentlemen," Secretary Ruiz said, "please calm down. This isn't a playground. The nation is in peril. Let's proceed with this in a calm and orderly fashion and—"

"Proceed with what?" the president asked. "The delusions of this man who would be king? President Swinburne's thinly veiled political coup?"

Ben read all the faster.

Section 4. Whenever the Vice President and a majority of either the principal officers of the executive departments or of such other body as Congress may by law provide . . . their written declaration that the President is unable to discharge the powers and duties of his office, the Vice President shall immediately assume the powers and duties of the office as Acting President . . .

Swinburne continued. "In the event that the president is found to be mentally unbalanced—"

"You don't have the authority or expertise to make that decision."

"I shouldn't have to!" Swinburne glared at Dr. Albertson. "Look, Doctor, no more mollycoddling. It's time for you to step up to the plate. I know Roland is your longtime friend, but there are lives on the line now, so you're going to have to cowboy up."

Albertson coughed into his hand. "I don't—I don't know what you're saying, or implying, but—"

"I'm saying I know how it pains you to have to make a decision, particularly if someone might get a little mad at you, but the time has come. You've seen the president's aberrant behavior. You know he's off his rocker. So say so. Make a formal medical declaration that he is unfit for office. So I can take over and save thousands of lives."

Albertson looked down at the carpet. "I'm just—I'm—I'm not prepared to—"

"If you need to make a little examination or something, then do it already. Get on with it!"

"No, I'm saying, I don't—I mean—I don't believe—I don't want—"

Swinburne slapped his forehead. "Would you stop stuttering already? Give me what I need. All you have to do is say the word and it's a done deal and we can get the country out of this mess!"

"Actually, you're wrong," Ben said.

Everyone in the room looked up. Ben had spoken so much more quietly than anyone else who had spoken recently that it had the impact of a cry of "Fire!" in a library.

"What are you saying?" Swinburne said, his neck twisted to one side.

Ben cleared his throat. Here we go . . . "You don't have the authority to declare the president incapable. Not even if you have the support of the president's doctor. I'm sure his thoughts are worth hearing—nothing personal, Doctor—but the Constitution doesn't mention the president's doctor at all."

"It mentions the vice president."

"True. But you have the authority to displace the president only with the agreement of the majority of the leaders of the various executive departments. In other words, the cabinet."

"Do you see the cabinet down here, Mr. Lawyer?"

"Only two members. The secretary of state, Mr. Ruiz, and the secretary of defense, Mr. Rybicki. But even if you have their votes, they don't constitute a majority or even a plurality, so you still don't have the constitutional requirement for forcing the president out of office."

"Look, if the rest of the cabinet is unavailable—"

"That's not what the Constitution says. It doesn't cover that contingency. I'm sure the framers of this amendment never foresaw a situation like this one. But the fact remains. You don't have the authority."

Swinburne came right up to Ben, hovering over him. "Do you want to see innocent people killed, you fool? What are you doing?"

"My job. Advising the president on the law—and, if necessary, enforcing it."

"This isn't just a game, kid!"

Ben stood up and looked the vice president squarely in the eye. "No, sir. It is not. This is very serious. And that is why it is so important that the law be strictly followed. To the letter."

"We don't have time—"

"These constitutional protections were inserted into the amendment for a reason—to protect the president against any undesirable power plays or conspiracies."

Swinburne seemed inflamed. "Are you suggesting—"

"All I'm suggesting is that the president, like any other U.S. citizen, is entitled to constitutionally provided procedural protections. Like due process. Like the right to a fair trial. Part of the reason these constitutional guarantees were created was to prevent hasty, reactionary decisions in difficult times that would undermine the fundamental philosophy of the nation."

Swinburne turned and slapped his hand on the table. "Then what do you suggest, know-it-all? I for one will not just stand here yapping while this man takes us to the brink of disaster. I won't be paralyzed just because we can't contact the other members of the cabinet."

Seemingly out of nowhere, Agent Zimmer popped into view. "Actually," he said, "we can."

Ben walked toward him. "Do you know where they are?"

"Yes. The other cabinet members have all been moved to—" He stopped short. "A safe location." Ben was glad to see that someone in the room hadn't forgotten that they very likely had a mole in the bunker. "But I am in contact with them. I can put them on speakerphone. I can arrange for them to hear all of you in here. In fact, I can use my webcam to set up a video line so they can see what's going on."

"Perfect," Ben said.

"Wait just a minute," Swinburne said, stepping between them. "What are you talking about?"

"What I'm talking about," Ben said, "is a trial."

"Are you joking? We don't have time for a trial."

"You're going to have to make time. The Constitution sets out a procedure. We will follow it."

"But the missiles will be launched in—"

"I understand your opinion. However, the Constitution doesn't make allowances for the suspension of constitutional rights in the event that the vice president is in a big hurry. Or even for a national emergency. The Constitution guarantees due process. To all citizens."

"What is this, Kincaid, some kind of power trip? Indulging your ego? The trial lawyer wanting to pull everything into his arena? I won't stand for this!"

"With respect, sir." Ben took a deep breath. "You don't have any choice."

Swinburne slapped the table again and walked away.

Cartwright spoke up. "If we're going to have a trial . . . even a quick one . . . don't we need some kind of procedure?"

"To the extent possible, we can follow the normal federal rules of civil procedure," Ben explained. "We might have to make some adjustments, since as far as I know I'm the only lawyer in the room. But I think the vice president has made it clear he can argue his case forcefully. He can be the acting prosecutor, presenting the case for removal. With his permission, I'll represent the president—in effect, the defendant." He shrugged. "It's kinda what I do. Normally, anyway."

The president gave him a little salute. "I'm honored to have you in my corner."

Ben was touched by his response, although also mindful that the president at this point didn't have a wealth of choices.

"Why does he need a lawyer?" Swinburne barked. "Can't he represent himself?"

"The right to a fair trial includes the right to counsel. Surely you're familiar with *Gideon v. Wainwright*?"

Swinburne made a grunting sound. "I think I saw the made-for-TV movie."

"Well, as you may recall, the happy ending came when Henry Fonda got a new trial, with a lawyer. Which totally changed the outcome."

"That's all well and good," Admiral Cartwright said. "But if this is going to be a trial—a real trial—don't we need a judge?"

"We do," Ben said hastily. He could see already that with stakes this high—and tempers high as well—this would rapidly descend into chaos without some sort of restraint. "Perhaps Agent Zimmer can patch in the chief justice."

"I think that's a poor idea," Zimmer said. "I can understand contacting the cabinet. It's necessary, and they all have top-level security clearances. But that doesn't extend to the judiciary. Let me just remind you all that these are extremely sensitive matters and we don't want any leaks. Especially to the wrong people."

Admiral Cartwright tossed down his pen. "Well, then, I guess this is where I have to make my ugly confession."

Swinburne squinted. "What?"

Cartwright rose to his feet. "I guess none of you are aware of the fact but . . . well, Kincaid, you're not the only lawyer in the room."

Ben arched an eyebrow.

"I was a lawyer back in the day," Cartwright said. "Spent years in the JAG Corps, till I moved onto bigger things. Never cared to look back, either. But I still remember the drill."

"What are you saying?" Swinburne asked.

"I'm offering to be your judge," Cartwright said succinctly.

Ben pondered a moment. Cartwright had the qualifications, and he was here. On the other hand, did Ben really want the judge to be the person in the room who hated him most?

"Well, Kincaid?" Swinburne said. "Don't just stand there like a damn wax statue. Say something!"

Ben realized that Cartwright was now no longer the person in the room who hated him most.

"The defense will accept you as the judge for this constitutional proceeding," Ben said.

"And so will I, if it moves this thing along any faster," Swinburne said. "Have you people forgotten that we are facing a dire countdown?"

"I haven't," Ben said. "But before we can proceed . . . Mr. President?"

He seemed almost dazed, slow to respond. "Yes, Ben?"

"Does this proposed procedure meet with your approval?"

Swinburne slapped the table once again, right in front of Ben, making a thunderous noise. "I don't approve of the procedure, but that didn't matter to you. Why does he get to decide whether he approves of the procedure?"

Ben slammed the table equally hard, bringing his hand down nearly on top of Swinburne's. He leaned forward and gave Swinburne a cold glare right in the eye. "Because, at least for the moment, he's the president of the United States. Got it?"

Swinburne slowly drew his head back. "Fine. Let's just get started."

"Mr. President?"

Kyler nodded. "Yes, Ben, it does meet with my approval. And . . . thank you." He crossed the room and took the seat beside Ben. Apparently this side of the room was going to be the "defendant's table."

"Don't thank him yet," Swinburne muttered.

"I'm thanking him for restoring some sense of law and order to this potential modern-day lynching."

"Oh, give me a break." Swinburne waved a hand in the air.

"It's true," Sarie said, looking up at him with the first friendly eyes Ben had seen in a good while. "Thank you for intervening, Ben."

Ben tilted his head to one side. "It's nothing."

"I disagree. Right now, Ben, you're the most important person in the room. Maybe the most important person in the country."

Well, geez, he hadn't thought about it like that. Nor did he want to.

Ben turned to Agent Zimmer. "Do you have the rest of the cabinet?"

"Yes," Agent Zimmer said, pushing several buttons at once. "I'm patching them in right now."

One of the overhead screens came to life. The blackness flickered away and was replaced by a ceiling-eye view of thirteen men and women seated around an oval table. Ben had no idea where they were located, but he could see that they were all present and waiting.

"I'm Ben Kincaid," he informed them. "I'll be representing the president. I assume you all already know the vice president, who will be acting as prosecutor. Have you all been briefed on the situation?"

The man in the center pulled a microphone toward him. Ben recognized him as Arnold Cross, the secretary of the treasury. "Yes, Ben, we have. I've been chosen to act as spokesperson on this end."

"Good. Can everyone hear me?"

He saw many heads nodding.

"If you lose the signal or lose track of the argument at any time, please let me know."

Cross nodded. "We will, Ben. We're ready."

"Very well." Ben saw that, while he was talking, Admiral Cartwright had taken a seat at the head of the table. "Your honor, I believe we're ready to proceed."

Cartwright nodded. All at once, his expression was blank and unemotional. Judicial. He apparently had the ability to rein in his hyperactive emotions when the situation called for it. "Very well, gentlemen.

We don't have a lot of time here, so let's get started. I will ask you to both keep everything brief and to the point. No unnecessary legal games or tricks or stunts. We just don't have time for it. Call the witnesses you need and then get the hell out of the way. Understood?"

Ben and Swinburne answered together. "Yes, your honor."

"All right then." Cartwright leaned back in his chair. "Mr. Prosecutor—call your first witness."

18

10:09 A.M.

Seamus gripped the steering wheel tightly and kept his eyes fixed on the road ahead.

D.C. Bytes was in Anacostia, and it was taking them forever to get there. Traffic was never good this time of day, but now they were caught in a steady stream of people fleeing the Mall, not to mention the chaos that can be expected anytime a ballistic missile has been exploded in the vicinity. He wasn't normally given to fits of road rage, but on this occasion, when every second was precious—could be the last— he had a different attitude about people who drove slowly in the passing lane and grandpas who left their turn signal blinking.

He and Arlo had both been silent since they turned away from the scene of devastation. Seamus could see something was on the kid's mind, but at least for now, he was content to let the silence extend as long as possible.

But nothing good lasts forever.

"Is the Jefferson Memorial really your favorite?" Arlo cleared his throat. "I think, statistically, the Lincoln Memorial is the most popular."

"Lincoln was a great man," Seamus answered succinctly. "Jefferson was a genius."

"Oh, yeah? He was the guy who slept with his slave, right?"

Seamus ground his teeth together. "Jefferson was the third president of the United States. The second vice president. The founder of the University of Virginia. The architect of Monticello. And, oh yeah, the guy who wrote the Declaration of Independence. Maybe you've heard of it."

"Is that the one that starts, 'Fourscore and seven years ago'?"

"No," Seamus said, tucking in his chin. "That would be the one that begins, 'We hold these truths to be self-evident, that all men are created equal.' "

"Oh, yeah, yeah, yeah, yeah, yeah. I remember now. That's a good one."

"You could say so."

"I think I memorized part of it in the sixth grade or something. No wonder you like Jefferson."

"It's more than that. Jefferson was brilliant. The most learned man of his time. A serious scholar. A man with a heart." He paused. "Couldn't balance his checkbook and was constantly in debt. But that's the way it usually is with geniuses."

"That's cool. I should read more. I mean, you know. Offline. The old-fashioned way."

"Yeah, you should. There's more to life than killing computer zombies."

"You read much? I would think it would be hard to keep up with the latest bestsellers when you're out in the caves with bin Laden."

"You might be surprised, kid. If you want something bad enough, you find a way to make it happen."

"So you really do like to read?"

"I was an English major in college before—"

"*What? You?*"

Seamus looked suddenly embarrassed. "Never mind."

"Seriously. You? Gliding down the *New York Times* bestseller list?"

"I don't worry about the latest bestsellers. They come and go. I much prefer the classics. The books that have stood the test of time."

"Who are your favorite writers?"

"Like you're gonna recognize the names?"

"Try me. Who's your all-time favorite?"

Seamus took a deep breath. "Dickens."

"Charles Dickens? As in 'Please, sir, I want some more'?" His voice took on a sepulchral tone. "As in 'I am the Ghost of Christmas Yet to Commmmmme'?"

"There's a lot more to Dickens than that. He was a reformer. He cared about other people, the events of the day. He wrote about the evils in his society and exposed wrongdoing. His writing changed the world in which he lived."

"Oh. That's cool."

"Yes, it is." Seamus screwed his hands tighter around the wheel. "I wish someone would write a book that changes the world we live in. For the better."

"Maybe you should do it."

"I've tried to write. But I can't find the time. I start something, and then—" He stopped short, suddenly embarrassed. "And why are we talking about this?"

"I don't know. I'm just trying to get to know you. As a person."

"Why?"

"Well, we've been hanging out together. This is our chance to bond."

"I'd rather not."

"Ah, don't be so tough-guy macho. You must have a human side in there. Somewhere. Let's really get to know each other. You saved my life."

"If you say, 'I love you, man,' I'm throwing you out of the car."

"All right, stay calm."

"We're trying to stop a madman from firing missiles at American citizens. Not starting a bromance."

While he drove, Seamus called Zira, who gave him the latest updates. Specifically, on the positive side, that so far no fatalities from the missile launch on the Jefferson had been detected. On the negative side, Colonel Zuko was promising a flurry of additional missiles in less than two hours if the president didn't give in to his demands. Which the president seemed keenly disinclined to do.

The conclusion was inevitable, Seamus thought as he snapped his phone shut. They needed to find the terrorists' base of operations. As soon as possible.

Seamus pulled into the downtown commercial part of Anacostia.

The streets were mostly deserted. Probably everyone wanted to be safe at home after a missile explosion so nearby. He remembered that after 9/11, the streets of New York City had seemed almost barren for days, at least by comparison with the usual crowds. It would be even easier for most Washingtonians to avoid the main arteries of commerce—the most likely targets.

He was making a sharp right turn when he heard Arlo shout so loudly he almost jumped.

"That's him!"

Seamus put his foot on the brake and slowed, staying several feet behind the figure on the side street. "That's who?"

Arlo jumped up and down in his seat. "You remember me saying there were only so many people in the area with the level of computer expertise to be useful to these terrorists?"

"Yeah."

"Well, the only one who isn't in prison just came out of D.C. Bytes. That guy in the Lisa Loeb glasses."

Seamus glanced at the tall, skinny man in the turtleneck—which seemed a little heavy for April in D.C. Still, he had a grown-up hair-cut—unlike Seamus's current companion—and very nice shoes. Guccis, if he wasn't mistaken.

"This guy isn't poor."

"No. Well, he might be now. Not a few months ago."

"Explain."

"Harold Bemis is the inventor of the Cobra operating system, probably the most widely used system in business and industry world-wide. Anyone too intelligent to use Microsoft uses Cobra. He got filthy rich—until it was discovered that Cobra contained a tiny little worm that surreptitiously fed information about the computer in which it resided to the Cobra central office, where Bemis then sold it off to the highest bidder."

"Ouch. I'm guessing some people weren't happy."

"You would be guessing correctly. Lawsuits flew, all around the world. He settled them eventually, trying to stay out of the papers and out of prison. But it cost him a fortune. To be specific, his personal fortune."

"A rich boy suddenly poor. Exactly the sort of person who might welcome the opportunity to make some quick cash."

"You mean like from terrorists?"

"That's exactly what I mean."

"But that would be against the law."

"He probably thinks he's too smart for all that. Leopold and Loeb with a pocket protector." Seamus followed Bemis till he reached his car. There was no way to stop and wait without being obvious, so he passed him and circled around the block. He wanted to remain unobtrusive, which wasn't easy when you were driving a car with a shattered windshield.

By the time he returned to the same street, Bemis was pulling away in his BMW.

"Any idea where he might be headed, kid?"

"Beats me. Home? Girlfriend?"

"Do you computer types have girlfriends?"

"I think the ones who can afford to drive BMWs do."

"Well, let's hope not." Seamus squinted, his eyes trained on the back of Bemis's car. "Let's hope he's seen that the first mission was accomplished, so now he's going to return to the tiger's lair to help them target the next wave of missiles. Because if that's his game, he's headed back to the operations base."

"And you're going to follow him?"

Seamus kept his eyes on the back of Bemis's car. "Exactly."

"And once you get to the base? It's bound to be swarming with terrorists and guns and . . . you know. Crazy people. What are you going to do then?"

"Don't know," Seamus said. "Tell you when I get there."

"You mean you're just making this up as you go?"

"That's how all us geniuses operate, kid."

"Give me a break. You're no Thomas Jefferson."

"No," Seamus said quietly, leaning into the wheel. "Jefferson never hurt anyone. But I will." He drew in his breath. "I'll do whatever it takes to make sure these killers don't fire another missile. Ever again."

19

Vice President Swinburne seemed more subdued as he stood and smoothed the line of his suit coat. It was amazing, Ben thought, how the merest suggestion of a courtroom, even when the participants hadn't altered their location, altered people's behavior. Civilized them, in a way. At least until the accusations and objections started flying.

"The prosecution calls the president's doctor, Dr. Henry Albertson."

Dr. Albertson stood, his hands extended. "What do I do?"

Ben pointed to a vacant chair next to Sarie. "Let's make that the witness stand."

Albertson took the chair as directed.

"Since we don't have a bailiff," Admiral Cartwright said, "I hope no one will object if I administer the oath." No one objected. "Let me just point out that even though I don't have a Bible, this oath is still binding, and anyone who lies under oath will be subject to the penalty for perjury, which is a federal crime."

"I don't tell lies," Albertson said. "And I don't reckon I'll start now."

"Do you swear to tell the truth, the whole truth, and nothing but the truth, so help you God?"

"I do."

"Please take your chair. Mr. Prosecutor, you may proceed."

To save time, Cartwright announced that all witnesses could describe their backgrounds in brief narrative form, rather then through the usual question-and-answer process. Ben learned much that he had not known about Dr. Albertson: Dr. Albertson and President Kyler had known each other since they were college roommates at Yale, he had been named the national doctor of the year twelve years before, he was a widower, and he kept a cocker spaniel named Pierre.

"Have you had a chance to observe the president recently?" Swinburne asked.

"Of course. I see him almost every day."

"Does he have any health problems or conditions of which you are aware?"

The doctor hesitated before answering. Ben saw him glance at the president.

"The witness will answer the question," Cartwright said.

"It's all right, Henry," the president said softly. "You're under oath."

"Yes," Swinburne echoed, "you are under oath, so tell the truth. The complete truth."

"I understand my oath," Albertson said, "and I don't need lessons on telling the truth from you. But I'm this man's doctor, understand? He's my patient. My only patient at present. That means we have a privileged relationship, and I'm honor-bound to keep his confidences and medical condition private."

"He's right," Cartwright explained. "He can claim privilege. In fact, I think he has to." Cartwright paused. "But the patient always has the option to waive privilege."

"I waive it," the president said without hesitation.

"That doesn't mean I have to say anything," Albertson said.

"No," Cartwright agreed, "it doesn't. But may I remind you of the magnitude of the stakes here? Literally the leadership of a nation. And may I also remind you that we are very pressed for time?"

Dr. Albertson tightened his lips, glanced at the president again, and finally nodded. "Just as you say, then. I'll answer the question." He looked at the vice president. "Yes, I am aware of a few health issues. Nothing that should impact the performance of his duties."

"Could you please tell us what those conditions are?"

"For the past few weeks, the president has experienced what I would call a mild form of asthma. Just a little trouble breathing."

"Has he ever experienced this before?"

"Not to this degree. He's always been a bit of a wheezer. Lots of allergies. But nothing like this."

"What, in your medical opinion, could bring on asthma attacks at this stage in his life?" Swinburne asked.

"Well, the obvious answer would be stress. There are lots of stressful jobs out there, but nothing like being president of the United States. He's the leader of the free world, for Pete's sake. Everyone is watching him. Everyone is either counting on him or waiting for him to make a mistake. You try making policy in a pressure cooker and see if you don't wheeze a bit."

"We're all familiar with the strain of public office."

"With respect, sir, no one is familiar with the strain of being the president unless they've experienced it firsthand. Not even the vice president."

Swinburne made a grumbling noise but added nothing.

"He's only been in office a few months," Dr. Albertson continued, "but he's had to move, to meet hundreds of people, to totally alter his way of life. He's had to change his traditional habits—had to break some bad habits. He's been separated from his family for extended periods of time. Eventually the strain will show. His hair is already dramatically grayer than it was before he took office. There are new lines on his face, especially around the eyes. So it's easy to see where his respiratory ailments might be exacerbated."

"Have you prescribed any treatment?"

"All I've done is given him an inhaler. ProAir HFA. It's a minorleague bronchial stimulant, but it seems to be sufficient to take care of the problem for now."

Vice President Swinburne pondered a moment. "Haven't I seen you passing him that inhaler?"

Albertson nodded. "I am the president's doctor. Always at the ready with whatever he needs."

"Couldn't he carry his own inhaler?"

"We tried that, but it always seemed to end up in the same place as the man's car keys. Lost."

"Doctor, tell us the truth. Could this respiratory condition affect the president's ability to reason?"

"No," Albertson said flatly.

"Could the medication you've prescribed affect his ability to reason?"

"Absolutely not."

"But if he's unable to breathe, surely that could render him unable to function. Disabled."

Ben winced as Swinburne used the magic word from the amendment. If the doctor agreed that the president was disabled, the trial would be over.

"No, not at any time," Albertson insisted. "His condition would have to be significantly worse than it is at this time before I would agree that he was disabled, even for a brief period of time."

"I see." The vice president batted a finger against his lips. He was thinking. Ben could almost see the wheels whirring in his head. "I noticed you used the plural earlier, Doctor. You said the president had medical conditions. What are the other ones?"

Albertson's lips thinned again. It was evident he did not want to proceed.

The president gave him a nod.

"The president," Albertson said with a sigh, "is diabetic."

Ben could feel the shock waves filtering through the room. Everyone stared at the doctor, surprised and incredulous. Even Agent Zimmer looked stunned, and he rarely even changed his expression.

"How can that be?" Swinburne said finally. "There was no mention of this during the campaign."

"No. There wasn't."

"His medical records were revealed."

Albertson nodded. "As with the asthma, this condition did not become evident until after he took office. He has chosen not to disclose it to the general public."

"How did you discover this condition?"

"The president was complaining of headaches, excessive urination, constant thirst. When I heard that, I didn't really even need an examination. That's a textbook case of the symptoms that accompany the onset of diabetes."

"Is this also induced by stress?"

"Well, I don't have any science to back me up, but I sure wouldn't be surprised. When you put a body under that kind of strain, it starts to weaken, pure and simple. Things fall apart, to quote Yeats. The body is no exception."

"Thank you for your opinion," Swinburne said, with a tone that did not suggest much gratitude, "but what would be the cause according to medical science?"

"It occurs when either the body does not produce enough insulin or the cells in the body ignore the insulin. It's the product of a disordered metabolism. The result is abnormally high blood glucose levels."

Swinburne seemed to be having trouble believing the president was a closet diabetic, but then, so did everyone else in the bunker. "Is he receiving any treatment?"

"Yes. He's controlling the condition with a combination of diet, exercise, medications, and insulin injections."

"So the president is dependent upon these insulin injections to sustain his life?"

"At the present, yes."

"Doesn't that leave him . . . vulnerable?"

"No more so than any of the other twenty-four million diabetics in the United States. As long as he receives his treatment, he's fine."

"Is there a cure?"

"The only real cure at this time is a pancreas transplant."

"Has the president considered that?"

"Yes."

"Will he have it done?"

"Not while he's in office."

"Why not?"

Ben knew he could object here—Swinburne was asking one witness to explain another person's reasoning. But the doctor apparently knew the answer, and given the time restrictions they were functioning under, Ben suspected Admiral Cartwright would not appreciate any unnecessary objections.

"If the president were to have surgery of this nature, he would have to be rendered unconscious by anesthesia. That would mean that, for a few hours, anyway, he couldn't govern. Therefore, under the Twenty-fifth Amendment, he would have to transfer power temporarily to the next in line."

"Yes? And?"

Albertson averted his eyes. "And he said he'd turn into a pillar of salt and die before he'd turn the presidency over to you."

20

Ben saw Admiral Cartwright cover his mouth and turn away. The judge couldn't be seen laughing at the prosecutor, right? But it was good to know that, behind his stern exterior, Cartwright had a sense of humor.

Swinburne threw back his shoulders. He looked mad, not that he had exactly appeared delighted before. "So the president has been hiding not one but two serious medical conditions?"

"I wouldn't use the word *hiding*. He's chosen not to make these matters public. That's his right."

"The public has a right to know the condition of the president's health."

"Do they really? Why do they need to know?"

"Well—"

"And of course if they know, then so does everyone else. Does Colonel Zuko need to know the intimate details of the president's health? What about the leaders of North Korea? Pakistan? Do they need to know when the president is not feeling at his best?"

"If he's not fit for the job," Swinburne countered, "he should step down."

"Let me tell you something, mister. No one has perfect health. And even if they did, one month in this job would wreck it. Nonetheless, the president's health is not something that should be detailed to anyone who does not have an immediate need to know. If nothing else, it's a national security issue."

"That's your opinion."

Albertson smiled. "Well, son, that's what you asked for."

"Dr. Albertson, I assume that if the president's diabetes were not treated, or were not treated properly, he might exhibit some . . . odd behavior."

"Mental symptoms are possible," the doctor replied. "But what you'd more likely see is a man in pain, perhaps a man in shock or even a coma."

"You're sure about that?"

"Yes. And anyway, what's the point? His diabetes has been treated. There has been no time since his diagnosis when he suffered for want of treatment."

"But he has been exhibiting aberrant behavior."

Ben felt his eyes twitch. This was where things were bound to get sticky.

The doctor pushed himself up in his seat. "Was that a question?"

"You witnessed the sorry spectacle of the president of the United States, just a short while ago, reacting to a crisis with the behavior of a three-year-old. Singing, laughing . . ."

Albertson shrugged. "He's the president. He can sing if he wants to sing."

"The theme from *The Brady Bunch*?"

"If he wants."

"So a foreign dictator has flung one of our own missiles at a domestic target—and you think the appropriate response is to sing sitcom songs?"

"I think different people release stress in different ways. Who cares? Whatever works."

"Objectively speaking, if you didn't know the president personally and you heard that a man in his mid-fifties was behaving in this manner, what would you think?"

Albertson tried to appear casual—not entirely convincingly. "I try not to be judgmental. I'm not a psychiatrist. Different strokes for different folks."

"Well, then, since the members of the cabinet who are watching on the webcam did not see this themselves, let me describe it. And then you can tell them whether I described it accurately." Swinburne took a deep breath. "Abruptly, in the middle of a discussion regarding our response to the colonel's threat to launch one of our missiles, the president began singing the *Brady Bunch* theme song. If I recall correctly, he also played the air guitar."

Ben observed the faces of the ten men and two women in the cabinet on the closed-circuit screen. When Swinburne mentioned singing, their expressions became somewhat quizzical. When he mentioned playing air guitar, their expressions became concerned.

"He did that for maybe a minute," Dr. Albertson said. "Then he stopped and—"

Admiral Cartwright pounded on the table. "This is not a time for making speeches. The witness will restrict himself to answering questions."

Ben arched an eyebrow. Usually it took a judge more than ten minutes before he contracted "judgitis."

"The point is," Swinburne said, turning his attention back to the witness, "for a period of at least five minutes, the president was not behaving as a capable leader. He was behaving like someone suffering from mental illness."

"Objection," Ben said, rising to his feet. "Sorry, your honor, I know time is of the essence. But that was not a question and the prosecutor is not qualified to render a medical opinion."

"Sustained," Cartwright said. "Try again, Mr. Swinburne."

Swinburne pursed his lips. "Dr. Cartwright, did you not find the president's behavior during this episode . . . disturbing?"

Ben glanced over at his client. The president was keeping a good poker face, but he clearly did not like being talked about as if he were not there. Particularly when the subject of the conversation was his sanity.

"As I said, he's under a lot of stress."

"And it would appear he snapped under that stress!"

"It would appear to be that he was letting off some steam, perhaps as a coping device." He looked up at the camera. "But I did not at any time see anything that I took to be a sign of mental illness or incapacity. Never!"

Ben hoped that this ringing declaration made an impact on the de facto jurors on the closed-circuit television, but he had a disturbing intuition they were still hung up on the reference to air guitar.

Swinburne paused for a moment and took his chair. Ben had started to wonder if the examination was over when Swinburne said, "Dr. Albertson, isn't it true that the president saved your life?"

An audible murmur ran through the room, reassuring Ben that he was not the only one who did not know this story.

More eye contact passed between the two men. They were sitting only about five feet apart, but for the moment, Ben felt as if a gulf had come between them that was immeasurably wider.

"Yes," Dr. Albertson said quietly. "Yes, that is true."

"When did this occur?"

"When we were in college. We were at a party. A private organization. Something for those who were too cool—or too poorly connected—to be members of Skull and Bones. I'd had a few—well, more than a few. Way too many more than a few. I was up on the roof, messing around like an idiot. Like most damn fools that age, I thought I was invulnerable."

"What happened?"

"Long story short, I lost my footing. Went tumbling down the roof. I would've been a big drunk blood splatter on the pavement—except Roland Kyler grabbed my foot and held on for dear life. I was dangling off the edge, watching my life play before my eyes. I must've weighed a ton. But he held on to me. Held on for almost twenty minutes, sweating and straining, his bones aching, but he never gave up, he never let go, until finally some help arrived." Albertson paused reflectively. "These people have heard me say that President Kyler is the only reason I'm here today, and they think I mean because he appointed me White House physician. But they're wrong. I mean that if it hadn't been for him, I wouldn't be alive. I wouldn't have gone to medical school, wouldn't have been doctor of the year, wouldn't have been anything. But for him."

"That's a great story," Ben said, rising, "but I don't see the relevance."

"The relevance is this," Swinburne said. "Dr. Albertson, you are totally loyal and devoted to the president, aren't you?"

"One hundred percent."

"That is why, even when he exhibits clearly disturbed behavior, you refuse to draw the obvious conclusion."

"That's not true. I—"

"What's true is that this man could be standing on his head wearing a bunny suit and you still wouldn't acknowledge that there was anything wrong with him!"

"Objection!" Ben said.

"Sustained," Cartwright replied, but Ben knew it didn't matter. Swinburne had made his point.

"That's all right, Judge," Swinburne said. "I think I've established this witness's obvious bias. It's unfortunate that a personal friend—particularly one with a debt of gratitude—was given an important executive post, especially since it has significant ramifications. But I can't change that now. What I can suggest is that the members of the cabinet take the witness's bias into account and consequently disregard his medical assessment. If there's going to be an unbiased determination as to the president's sanity, it's going to have to come from the cabinet."

Ben looked at the closed-circuit screen and saw several of the cabinet members nodding in agreement. That was not a good sign.

Swinburne had established that the president was acting insane and that the president's physician would never declare him insane, no matter what he did. Which meant it was a job for the vice president and the cabinet. And Ben had no doubt they would do it, and quickly—unless he gave them a reason not to.

21

*B*en thought a moment about how to proceed. Normally, on cross-examination his job would be to undo whatever damage had been done to his client's case by the witness. In this instance, however, the doctor himself hadn't done any damage to President Kyler, at least not directly. Technically, the only person Dr. Albertson had damaged was himself—his own reputation and credibility. But Ben knew that was going to have a negative impact on President Kyler's case. He needed to find some way to salvage Albertson's credibility as a medical witness who believed Kyler was absolutely sane.

"Dr. Albertson," Ben began. This tiny room in the bunker made for an awkward ersatz courtroom. Under normal circumstances Ben had some distance from the people he was grilling, not to mention the judge. That was done for a reason. Given the raised tempers that attended most trials, it was important for the participants to have some space. Here they were practically on top of one another, breathing down one another's necks, with no room to maneuver or escape. "Let's start with that last bit of business first. You've testified that President Kyler saved your life once and you are grateful to him. The unanswered question is whether your gratitude renders you incapable of issuing a reliable medical opinion."

"Absolutely not."

"Well," Ben said, playing the devil's advocate, "that's easy to say, but—"

"Mr. Kincaid, I have been a doctor for almost thirty years now. I know what I'm doing." Good. Ben had managed to raise his dander a little, which was exactly the reaction he wanted. The doctor needed to get a little feisty if he was going to salvage this mess. "I took the Hippocratic Oath. I have an obligation to the AMA. So when it comes to rendering a medical opinion, it's just as if I were under oath—every time I do it. I give the truth, the whole truth, and nothing but the truth, no matter what. No matter who it is."

"So you're saying your friendship with the president has not influenced your medical opinion."

"That's exactly right. My testimony is based upon observation and constant, almost daily mini medical evaluations, plus a complete workup done not two weeks ago. There is simply no evidence of negative brain function, nor of any physical ailment, such as a stroke or brain tumor, that might affect his mental condition. The president may have unique coping mechanisms, but so what? The question here is whether he's sane. And that question I can answer with certainty. He is."

Beside him, Ben could see his client sitting up a little straighter. He was glad he'd had this opportunity to rehabilitate the witness.

"Let me ask you a few questions about the coping mechanisms you mentioned. Can you explain what you mean?"

"Of course. We all deal with stress in different ways, some healthier than others. Some cope by drinking too much, or turning to drugs, or other alleviators. Nixon became an alcoholic in the White House. Some think Clinton became a sex addict. Those are obviously unhealthful coping mechanisms. Roland, on the other hand, likes to sing and act a little childish. So what? He isn't hurting anyone. It's not as if he's on national television. And it's a good sight better than drinking himself to death."

"So you see no problem with it?"

"Why would I? He has to do something—he's got the weight of the world on his shoulders. He's given up some of his favorite stress relievers. Why not let the man have this one harmless indulgence?"

"Would it be fair to say everyone has coping mechanisms?"

"Of course. Everyone." Albertson pointed. "Even the esteemed vice president."

Ben saw Swinburne sit up a little straighter in his chair. They definitely had his attention now.

Dare he press further?

"Okay, I'll bite. What does the vice president do?"

"Have you not noticed how often his hand goes into his suit coat pocket? And then his arm gets all stiff and tense. I think he's got one of those squeeze balls, those stress relievers you buy in Hallmark stores. Either that or a big wad of Silly Putty."

Ben turned slightly toward the vice president, as did almost everyone in the room.

A moment later Swinburne somewhat sheepishly reached into his pocket, then rolled a yellow squeeze ball onto the table. It looked like a tennis ball but obviously had a different, squishier consistency. The impressions of Swinburne's fingers were still visible on it.

"Nice work, Sherlock," Swinburne said.

Albertson grinned, probably for the first time since he took the witness chair. "Elementary, my dear Swinburne."

"Thank you, Doctor," Ben said. "No more questions." Ben felt he had done about all he could do. Most of Albertson's testimony had been favorable. He had shored up the holes as best he could. The cabinet might still suspect that Albertson was not an impartial witness, but Ben had given them a plausible alternative explanation for the president's behavior. He hoped that would be enough—at least for the present.

Vice President Swinburne rose to his feet. "Judge, may I redirect?"

Cartwright tapped a pencil against the tabletop. "May I remind you that we have a countdown ticking here?"

"No one is more aware of that than I, Judge. The whole point of this trial is to make sure no more people die when that countdown is completed. But I do think I have something valuable to bring out."

"I have to object," Ben said. "And I don't want to protract this unnecessarily, either. But he had his direct examination and he rested. He cannot bring out new matters on redirect."

"This is not new," Swinburne insisted. "This is simply a continuation of what was said before." He looked directly at Cartwright. "I would beg the court's indulgence. It's not as if we had time to prepare for this trial. We're all working off the cuff here. What is paramount is that all the most relevant information is revealed."

Ben started to protest, but the judge cut him off.

"Very well," Cartwright said. "I'll allow it. But be brief!"

"Yes, sir. I will." He turned toward Dr. Albertson once more. "Doctor, during your previous testimony, you mentioned hyperglycemia. Would you please explain the difference between that and hypoglycemia?"

"Well, hypoglycemia is just the opposite—it's abnormally low blood glucose."

"Does this condition ever occur to people suffering from diabetes, such as the president?"

"It's rare, but it does happen. Usually as a reaction to treatment. Too much insulin, or insulin delivered at the wrong intervals, something like that. Sometimes excessive exercise can bring it on."

"The president exercises regularly, does he not?"

"Yes. That's one reason he's in such good shape."

Swinburne nodded. "Can you describe the symptoms of hypoglycemia?"

Albertson slowed considerably. Ben suspected he was beginning to understand where this line of questioning was headed.

"Most commonly, it produces agitation, sweaty palms, that sort of thing. Patients suffer from sympathetic activation of the autonomic nervous system, which can produce altered emotional states such as dread and panic."

"You're saying they can experience panic attacks."

"I guess that's one way of putting it. Panic attacks to such an extreme that they can become immobilized. Consciousness can be altered or even lost, which can lead to the induction of a comatose state, seizures, or even brain damage and death."

Swinburne pounced, as Ben knew he would. "You said consciousness can be altered?"

"Yes."

"Meaning the victim's behavior might be altered."

"But this is very rare—"

"Could this altered behavior involve things such as . . . well, singing at inappropriate moments?"

Dr. Albertson's lips pursed. He did not answer.

"I'm waiting for your answer, Doctor. The truth, the whole truth, and nothing but the truth, remember?"

Albertson frowned, then replied. "Yes, I suppose that it is theoretically possible. But that doesn't mean it is the cause of the president's behavior."

"But it could be."

"I disagree. I have personally monitored his insulin intake to make sure he doesn't get too little or too much."

"Doctor, is it possible for even a very experienced, capable physician to make an error in judgment?"

"Of course, but if he had hypoglycemia, I'd know it."

"How? Are you able to do lab work on his blood down here in the bunker?"

"No. But I have a blood glucose meter and—"

"At this moment in time, you don't know if he has hypoglycemia or not. Correct?"

"I suppose I can't rule it out as a medical certainty. But there are other symptoms I ought to be able to observe, and they aren't present."

"So far as you know."

"Right."

"And let's be honest—even if he didn't have those symptoms now, he could develop them in the future, right?"

"Well . . . anything is possible."

"So the president is quite literally a ticking mental time bomb."

"That's an overstatement."

"This disease he has hidden from the public eye could have a profound impact on his ability to govern. Perhaps that's why he's chosen to hide it."

"Objection!" Ben said forcefully.

"Sustained," Cartwright replied, but it didn't matter. The damage was already done. The seeds of doubt were planted in the cabinet members' minds.

Dr. Albertson leaned forward. "I keep a careful eye on our president. Nothing is going to happen to him without my—"

"Have you had a chance to do blood work today?"

"No, but I could if—"

"Have you performed a psychiatric examination?"

"I don't have—"

"And you won't till we get out of this bunker."

"Well, true, but—"

"So at the very least, for the period of time we are restricted to this bunker, you cannot make any guarantees about the president's health or sanity."

Albertson flushed, obviously angry. "How can I—"

"Exactly!" Swinburne shouted, cutting him off. "How could you?" He paused a moment and let everyone ponder the question. "I'll answer that one for you. You *can't*."

Swinburne turned his attention to Admiral Cartwright. "I'm finished with this witness, Judge. No more questions."

Ben glanced at the president. He was still keeping his poker face on, but Ben knew he was concerned. Who wouldn't be? The doctor was likely the most favorable witness they could possibly get, but Swinburne had still managed to use him to make his case—and Ben had done little or nothing to stop it.

He didn't have time for recriminations. He had to focus on the future, not the past. He had to make sure he did the best he could with the next witness and stop Swinburne's momentum.

Before it was too late.

22

Seamus remained focused on the back of Harold Bemis's BMW. The sky was overcast, but he didn't know if that was a Washington spring rain coming in or the smoke from the explosion at the Jefferson Memorial drifting across the city. The streets were still mostly deserted. He and Arlo were passing one of the most popular shopping malls in Georgetown—in fact, in the whole D.C. area—but it appeared largely empty. Presumably the hideous news of a missile strike so close to home was keeping most everyone indoors. That was understandable. What kind of person could watch the CNN footage of a disaster of this magnitude and think it was time for a new pair of shoes?

The happy advantage of this depopulation was that it made it easier to track a suspect. The downside was that it greatly increased the chances of being spotted. And Seamus did not want to be spotted. He couldn't afford to lose him. He wanted to catch the people behind the attack on the Jefferson Memorial so much that he could feel it in the marrow of his bones.

Harold Bemis pulled his car to the side of the road to parallel park. Seamus managed to find a place for his own car before he passed him—

something that would have been impossible on a normal day in this neighborhood.

"What do you think your boy genius might be visiting in the mall?"

Arlo shrugged. "There's an Apple Store in there. I think there's a GameStop."

Seamus shook his head. "I just don't see the guy in the Gucci shoes dropping by to pick up an iPod. He probably has people to do that. A personal shopper. Possibly a fleet of them."

"He probably got his hand-delivered by Steve Jobs."

"Yeah. Something like that."

"But now that he's fallen upon hard times—"

"I can't see it. People don't change that much. Even when they've fallen on temporary hard times."

Bemis got out of the car and headed toward the double glass door entrance to the mall.

"Stay here. I'm going to follow him."

"Wouldn't it be smarter to just stay here until he returns to his car?"

"How do you know he's going to return to his car?"

Arlo's head bobbed. "I suppose you have a point."

"You stay in the car. That's an order." He scribbled a number on a scrap of paper. "If you see anything suspect, call me. Otherwise— don't."

"Got it, chief."

Seamus trailed Bemis into the mall, careful to keep a discreet distance, which was all the harder because there were so few people milling about. Seamus was a little surprised it was even open, but he supposed that time and retail wait for no man.

He was barely a hundred feet inside the mall when Bemis slowed his steps. Seamus could tell by his shoulders he was about to turn around, so he ducked behind the nearest escalator.

Now he couldn't see Bemis. How could he know how long he needed to stay out of sight? This was impossible. He counted slowly to ten, then inched back into the open.

Bemis was gone. Damn. Had Seamus waited too long? Or worse, had the man suspected he was being followed and intentionally turned in an effort to ditch him?

He walked toward the fountain in the middle of the common area.

It was on a raised platform and gave him a better view of the surroundings. Attempting to remain as casual as possible, he cast his eyes
around the interior.

Where was Bemis? How could he have disappeared so quickly?
Was there some secret hideaway in here somewhere? Maybe he'd
ducked into a tailor's shop and entered the secret terrorist lair . . .

Shades of *Man from U.N.C.L.E.* He was really going to have to
stop letting his imagination carry him away.

Seamus spotted him. Somehow Bemis had gotten to the upper
level. He was entering the food court.

Seamus raced to the bottom of the escalator and bolted up the
steps. He didn't want to attract attention, but he knew that if he moved
fast enough, he could get to the court before Bemis had a chance to—

A gunshot whizzed by his ear, so close it felt as if it had sizzled itself into his tympanic membrane. A second shattered the glass panel
just a few inches from his leg.

Seamus flattened himself against the moving metal steps. The sharp
edges cut into his chin—but that was the least of his worries. Another
bullet hummed its way just above his head.

He heard several cries of alarm, both from above and below him.
Whatever few people might be shopping that day, they'd heard the
shots, too. The next sound Seamus detected was of rapidly moving feet.
That was good. Given what had just happened at the Jefferson Memorial, they didn't need any urging to take this seriously, and that was all
for the better. He couldn't help them right now, but he didn't want any
collateral damage.

He reached for his gun—but what would he do with it? He didn't
know where the shooter was. He would nail Seamus long before Seamus spotted him. He was pinned down—trapped on this escalator. And
even if the sniper was the worst shot in the entire terrorist cell, he'd hit
his target before Seamus reached the top.

Only one chance if he wanted to live. It was a long way down—but
it wasn't getting any nearer.

Seamus pressed both hands on the moving black handrail and side-
jumped off the escalator.

He plummeted at least twenty feet down to the tile floor, just a few
yards from the fountain. The impact hurt. How many times had he
fallen too far in the last few hours? Too many. His right ankle stung. He
had probably sprained it, but given the distance, he was lucky it wasn't

broken. Didn't matter. He had no time to think about it now. He shook it off and kept moving.

Gunfire rang out again, but it came from farther away this time. As long as Seamus kept moving, he could stay ahead of his assassin. A moving target was much more challenging to catch.

It wasn't Bemis firing. He was certain about that. The shots came from the wrong direction, plus Bemis just didn't seem the assassin type. Quisling and technical advisor, sure. Sharpshooter, no. In a situation such as this, Beamis would be useless.

Seamus raced down a branch of the mall. Even if the shooter was following him from above, he would have a hard time getting a bead on him over here. Seamus ducked into the nearby Macy's.

He hated the smell of the perfume counter that greeted him at the door. It was nothing against their selection; he just had yet to encounter a perfume that didn't make him wish women would simply let themselves smell the way they smelled. But he would have to tough it out. If that killer wanted a piece of him, he would have to leave his safe perch and come out into the open.

Seamus found a safe place behind the jewelry counter and waited. He didn't have to wait long.

Two minutes later the sniper entered the store.

No doubt Seamus's many years of experience were helpful when it came to spotting gunmen. It also helped that there were so few people in the mall. But he felt confident that he would know this clown was trouble anytime, anyplace, even if he had met him during a game of blindman's buff. Some people just smelled like trouble, and that was a smell Seamus received loud and clear, even when he was inundated with artificial musk and clove and a thousand other laboratory-concocted aromas.

The killer wore a black Adidas warm-up suit with black-and-white sneakers. It was the pimps, then the gang members, who had first adopted this form of casual wear for their everyday enterprises. Now it had apparently infiltrated the terrorist world. He looked scruffy and nervous. Seamus didn't need a close-up of that bulge under his zip-up jacket to know that it wasn't a potbelly.

His first instinct was to jump out into the middle of the walkway and start shooting, but his experience told him that wasn't the right play. The guy might still get the drop on him, if he was quick enough, and there were still employees manning the counters who might be hurt in any cross fire. If possible, Seamus needed to take this man down without an exchange of bullets. Slowly he stepped back and waited patiently for the shooter to come to him.

As soon as the man had passed him, Seamus swiveled back into the walkway behind him. He brought the butt of his gun down hard on the back of the man's head. The gunman hurtled forward and crashed into a glass jewelry display counter.

Glass shattered, flying in all directions. Seamus heard several cries behind him.

"Get out of here!" he shouted. "And stay down!"

He hoped the sales personnel would listen and obey. He didn't have time to check. The assailant was already scrambling to his feet, trying to crawl out of the debris. Reaching inside his warm-up jacket, he pulled out a gun with a long nose. Seamus recognized the compressed-air silencer. The high-speed ammo it fired would do a hell of a job on his stomach.

He wasn't about to give the punk the chance. Running forward, he kicked the gun out of the man's hand before he could fire. Then Seamus brought his shoe down hard on the man's gut, like he was stomping a particularly virulent spider. The man cried out, his face reddened, and his head crashed back on the floor amid the shattered glass and blood.

Seamus bent over him, but the man suddenly lurched forward, a shard of glass clutched in his hand. Seamus scooted backward. The jagged blade missed him by less than an inch.

That dirty son of a bitch. Well, fine. If that's the way he wants to play it . . .

Seamus picked up a nearby glass bottle of perfume and hurled it at lightning speed. It shattered against the assassin's forehead.

Blood erupted. Head wounds were the worst. On top of that, the pungent alcohol-based mix dripped into the wound and the man's eyes. He screamed and clutched at his face, desperate to remove what could not be removed.

Seamus crouched down and grabbed him by the collar. He slapped his hands away. "Maybe now you're ready for a little chat?"

The man whimpered, babbling incoherently. Temporarily blinded, he was undoubtedly wondering if he would ever see again.

"If you tell me what I want to know, the pain might not get any worse. Though I'm not promising anything."

The man spoke through sobs and clenched teeth. "I want . . . immunity . . ."

"You've been watching too many cop shows on TV. Immunity is not a option. I don't have that power and I don't have time to get it. Your choices are pain or no pain. And you have five seconds to decide."

There was no immediate response, which really pissed Seamus off. He realized he had a short fuse, but given what he had been through today, who could blame him?

He pressed his finger into the wound on the man's forehead.

The man screamed. "I'll talk! I will! I'll talk!"

"Thank you," Seamus said, smiling. "I appreciate a positive attitude. Now tell me where the operations base is. Don't hold anything back or—"

Seamus was cut off by a sharp blow to the back of his skull. He lost his balance and fell forward, tumbling into the broken glass.

His head ached, and he had trouble seeing clearly, but he rolled over onto his back, trying to react, trying to salvage himself before it was too late . . .

He looked up.

Harold Bemis was hovering over him, clutching a metal jewelry case.

Guess the geek wasn't quite as harmless as I thought, Seamus realized dazedly.

"Why the heck couldn't you just stay in the car with Arlo?" Bemis said in a nasal, high-pitched voice. "Now we're going to have to kill you."

23

Christina sat in her office and stewed. She was embarrassed at her-self and her lack of productivity, but she just couldn't help it.

She was worried about her husband.

She had canceled the interviews with the three candidates for the associate's position. With missiles flying through the skies, the couldn't focus on business. Besides, she didn't like deciding on these business matters without Ben. Even if he was currently "of counsel," he was still her partner, in every possible way, and she preferred working with him to working without him.

And the fact that he wasn't here just reminded her that she didn't know specifically where he was or what kind of danger he might be facing. Ben was a good man, smart as they came, in an intellectual sort of way. Not necessarily in a self-preservational sort of way. When things got sticky, he needed her there. She had a different kind of smarts: seat-of-the-pants, save-your-neck street smarts. She filled his gaps. That's why the relationship worked so well, in her opinion. That, plus the fact that he was the most terrific man she had ever known.

Thank goodness he had managed to make that call to her. At least she knew he was alive. But the call had raised almost as many concerns as it assuaged. She would never really feel safe until this crisis—whatever it was—was over and she and Ben had their arms wrapped around each other again, preferably in bed. Only then would the story come to an end.

She heard a knock on the office door.

Jones poked his head through the opening. "Anything I can do for you?"

"No, thanks. I'm inconsolable."

"Make a decision on the associate?"

"No, I can't. Toss a coin."

"Tempting, but I think I'll wait for you to pick." He paused. "That guy at LexiCo is still calling."

"Take a message."

He frowned. "In my role as office manager, client relations come within my purview, and I think—"

"Stow it, Jones."

"Ooookay." He thought a moment. "Look, I've been monitoring the news. So far, no one knows anything."

"Like who blew up the Jefferson Memorial?"

"If CNN knows, they're not talking."

"Then they don't know. Is there a pending threat? Are there going to be more explosions?"

"Beats me. But the general consensus seems to be that the danger is not over."

She pressed her lips together.

"I'm sure Ben's fine," Jones hastened to add.

"I'm sure he is, too. But I still want to see him."

"I know." Jones shuffled his feet on the carpet a minute. "I'm going out. Anything you want?"

"I want my husband!"

He nodded. "I'll let you know if I hear anything." He closed the door behind him.

Great. Now she felt guilty, too. She hadn't meant to be sharp with Jones. She wasn't fit for human companionship right now.

It just wasn't right. It wasn't fair. She and Ben hadn't even been married that long. She had waited so long for this! To think that she might lose him just when—

Just when she had a message she wanted to give him.

She glanced at her watch. She would give it another hour. Tops. Try to get some work done. And if nothing happened by then . . .

Then she would make something happen.

24

The president requested a short recess before the next witness was called, and Admiral Cartwright granted it—with a strong emphasis on the word *short*. Kyler and Ben stepped into the small adjoining room where the president had received his initial briefing from the Secret Service agents.

"Ben," the president said, "I appreciate all you're trying to do for me. But this trial isn't off to a good start."

"I know," Ben said, "and I'm sorry. Swinburne turned out to be a much sharper prosecutor than I expected. Has he been to law school?"

"No, he came straight out of the oil industry. But I think he has all the DVDs of the old *Perry Mason* series."

"Well, that explains it."

"There's something you need to know about that jury you've got." President Kyler leaned forward and spoke confidentially. "I know you're probably thinking we have the edge, since I appointed them. You're probably thinking they'll be loyal, indebted, or at least self-interested enough to keep me in office. But the truth is I just barely won this thing, as you know. If Florida had gone the other way, I'd be toast.

I had such a thin mandate, I had to make compromises when I selected my cabinet. Try to appeal to all interested parties."

"And how does this relate to the current trial?"

"What I'm saying, Ben, is that at least half the people in the cabinet, I don't really know or like all that much. And the feeling is mutual."

Well, that was just peachy. "Any other secrets you'd like to let me in on?"

"Yeah." Anytime his client broke eye contact, Ben knew it was going to be bad. This time proved no exception. "The truth is—I haven't been feeling . . . quite myself."

"What do you mean?"

"I don't know exactly. I just don't feel quite . . . right."

"Are you telling me you have a problem?"

"I don't know what it is."

"Let's cut to the chase, Mr. President. Should you step down?"

"No! No!" He waved his hands in the air. Ben had never seen the man look weaker. Was he doing the right thing here, trying to keep him in office? Or should he step aside and let the Swinburne locomotive take the presidency? "You can't do that. I mean—you shouldn't. You can't. You know what Swinburne would do."

"Pull our troops out of Kuraq."

"Exactly."

"And that would be bad."

"We cannot do that!" the president insisted. Ben wasn't sure if this was a show of strength or desperation. "We can't abandon our troops. And especially not the men and women who went down in that helicopter."

Ben stared into the man's eyes, wondering what was going on in there. He felt more confused than ever.

"Mr. President, please just answer this one question for me. I've seen you experience these . . . episodes. Twice now. How do you explain them?"

The president shook his head helplessly. "I can't."

Ben winced. "Do you remember them?"

"Yes. No. I mean—sort of. It's . . . hazy."

"Do you feel as if you lose control?"

"No. I mean—I feel like I'm in control, but afterward . . . it's like being drunk. Have you ever been drunk, Ben?"

"Can I plead the Fifth?"

"It doesn't matter. I'm not incompetent. And I'm not crazy."

Ben swallowed. "Mr. President, forgive me for saying so, but it sounds to me as if there is . . . something going on inside your brain. Something not right."

"I've been under enormous stress. Did you not hear what the doctor said? The question is whether I'm competent to govern. I don't have to be perfect. Just competent."

Ben supposed that was true enough.

"And I am competent. More than that. I'm ready and able to work. And I won't sell this country out when the going gets tough, like Swinburne wants to do. Not on my watch."

Ben nodded. He wasn't sure what was going on with the president. But, at least for the moment, he seemed capable, if not a tower of strength. And he shouldn't be displaced just because his ambitious vice president differed with him on a matter of foreign policy.

And he had done that favor for Christina. Ben would never forget that.

"All right, then," Ben said. "I'm sure they're getting agitated out there. Let's go back. And I'll try to do a better job with the next witness than I did with the last."

25

*B*en reentered the main room, followed by his client, the president of the United States. Now that, he thought, was a line he'd never expected to see on his résumé.

As he made his way back to his station at the table, he passed close to the secretary of defense, Albert Rybicki. He felt something brush up against his hand.

He looked down quickly.

Rybicki had just passed him a note.

What was this, grade school? Was note passing really necessary? But when he thought about it for a moment, he realized that, trapped down here in this pressure cooker with everyone else, it would be very difficult to have a private conversation—and impossible to do it without the others knowing.

So he palmed the note and remained quiet.

As soon as he was back in his chair, Ben casually unfolded the note, careful not to attract attention.

Beware Ruiz, it said. *He'll do anything to get our troops out.*

Down at the bottom, in smaller writing, Ben saw a postscript: *Ask about Apollo.*

The sun god? The corporation Ben used to work for, way back when?

What did it mean?

Ben glanced up at Rybicki and made a curt nod. Rybicki returned nothing. Ben really wanted to ask a follow-up question or six, but he got the distinct impression Rybicki would not welcome it. If he had wanted to chat, he wouldn't have passed a note.

Rybicki wanted to be helpful without anyone else knowing about it. Interesting.

What was going on in this cabinet? Was Ruiz another dissident who was not really friendly toward the president? How many others like him and Swinburne were there, people working with this president but more than willing to bring him down given the opportunity?

In a way, Ben was almost sympathetic; he had opposed the latest Iraq war and he had always believed he would do anything to get the troops out. But did that include undermining the commander in chief? In effect, a political coup? Plus Kuraq was not Iraq. What Zuko proposed in Benzai was genocide, pure and simple, and there was little doubt about what would happen to the people who'd gone down in that helicopter if Zuko found them first. Should Kyler be deposed because he didn't want to see those people slaughtered?

Somehow, that just didn't seem right, even if the ultimate goal— saving the troops—was understandable.

Ben's reverie was broken as Swinburne called his next witness. "Your honor, I'll call Michael Ruiz to the stand."

Ben couldn't help wondering about the coincidence—or was it?— as he watched the man take his seat on the makeshift witness stand. First Rybicki had warned him about Ruiz—and now he was being called to the stand. Had Rybicki known he would be next? If so, how much more did he know? Had there been a conversation of import in here while Ben was in the other room?

Swinburne began with an abbreviated run-through of Ruiz's qualifications. It was even briefer than Albertson's. Although some of the cabinet members might not have known the president's doctor, they all knew the secretary of state. Most of them had worked with him at one time or another. He had been in Democratic politics for most of his adult life, had served four years as an ambassador to the Court of St. James, and had briefly served as national security advisor for the last Democratic president. There was no question—when it came to foreign policy, Ruiz knew what he was talking about.

"I'm sure everyone reads the newspapers," Swinburne said, "and is aware that Kuraq is currently a hot spot of unrest, but they may not know all the salient points about that nation and its dictator, or their relationship to the United States. Could you please give them all a quick and dirty primer on the situation? Sort of a *Kuraq for Dummies*?"

Ruiz smiled slightly, then complied. "Kuraq is located in the Middle East, with one border on the Gulf of Hormuz. Although a relatively small nation, it is a major oil producer and a member of OPEC. It ships millions of barrels of oil each year into the world market via tankers traveling out of the Gulf. This export has made it important to the global economy, not only to the United States but also to Russia, China, and many other nations.

"Unfortunately," Ruiz continued, "like all too many of the nation-states in this region, its importance to the world economy is accompanied by a perpetually unstable government. Kuraq has been buffeted through a series of different leaders going back to the fifties, many of them theocrats. Diplomatic relations with the United States have varied depending upon the reliability of the government in question."

"If you would, sir, please give us the essentials about Colonel Zuko."

"Zuko is a military leader who managed to take over the country from the previous Sunni religious leader. Like Osama bin Laden and so many other honchos in this region, he fought in Afghanistan in the 1980s against the Russian invasion, with the United States. Yes, that's right. He was on our side back then. His later enmity toward us has nothing to do with Israel and nothing to do with oil. It's all about Afghanistan, specifically the way the United States abandoned Afghanistan after we won there against Russia. And let's face it—the man has a point. What we did in Afghanistan was shameful. We left the nation in total disarray. No infrastructure whatsoever. No educational system, no working economy. Our attitude was, as long as the Commies aren't invading, we'll take our money and go home. Millions were left destitute, hungry. This tumultuous situation gave rise to groups such as the Taliban and al-Qaeda, many of the strongest terrorist enemies of the United States.

"Colonel Zuko didn't resort to terrorism, at least not initially. He had lived in the West. Been educated at Oxford. It's possible this gave him a different perspective on geopolitics. At any rate, he preferred to work with the military and to strengthen his home nation from within. His plan was to build Kuraq up first, then go after revenge against the United States. It was a smart plan. He was one of the first to use the army he controlled domestically to shore up struggling businesses and maximize oil production. As Kuraq's economy became more robust, so did his control. By the onset of this decade, Kuraq had one of the strongest economies in the region. That was when Zuko decided it was time to control more than just the military. He staged a coup, planned so effectively and efficiently that it was almost bloodless. He removed the religious leaders and took over, though careful the whole time to do so in the name of 'the one true religion.' In a sense, he didn't replace the theocracy. He simply replaced the previous ayatollah with himself. The only difference is, this ayatollah has an iron grip on the army."

Ruiz looked up. "So you can see the difficulty. When one guy controls a booming economy, the military, *and* the religious establishment, good luck getting rid of him."

"Do we want to get rid of him?" Swinburne asked.

"Certainly the president would like to do so." Ben noticed that Ruiz was looking up and to the right—careful not to let his eyes wander anywhere near the president of whom he spoke. Was he one of the cabinet members not all that attached to their commander in chief? "He's been obsessed with the desire to topple Zuko almost from the first moment he took office."

"Objection," Ben said. "The witness is, at best, expressing an opinion. Not stating facts."

Cartwright nodded. "The court would appreciate it if the witness would limit his testimony to what he has actually seen and heard."

Ruiz nodded obediently. "Yes, your honor."

Swinburne resumed. "Can you tell us the first time you recall the president addressing the subject of Kuraq or Colonel Zuko?"

"Of course. I'm sure you recall that just a few days after the president took office, an unidentified terrorist bombed our marine headquarters in Lebanon. No one took credit in the immediate aftermath, and we were scrambling to determine what had happened. We were getting intelligence reports from all over the world, most of them contradictory and inconclusive. But when it came time for the first briefing and planning session, the first day after the incident, the president sat down and immediately said, 'Tell me what Zuko has to do with this.' "

"What did that question suggest to you?"

"What it suggested was that the president had already determined that Zuko was responsible or, worse, that he wanted to pin it on Zuko regardless of what really happened. I found that appalling. We were trying to find out what happened, but the president didn't seem to care. He just wanted Zuko's head. As you know, in the weeks that followed, his rhetoric against Kuraq only increased. First he applied the most extreme economic sanctions. Insisted upon a total embargo of the country, which resulted in short- and long-term shortages of food and medicine within the country. Soon thereafter we were sending troops and positioning them just outside Kuraq's borders."

"Excuse me," Swinburne said, "but weren't those troops sent in response to the Kuraqi occupation of the Benzai Strip?"

"That was the official explanation. Whether you want to believe it or not is another matter."

"Is there any reason to doubt it?"

"As I already mentioned, the president seemed strangely preoccupied with Zuko and his country. And there was nothing new about their claim to the Benzai Strip."

"Moving in troops was new, wasn't it?"

"Yes. But Zuko's explanation was that he needed to seize their food and medicine stockpiles to help his own people, which is understandable under the circumstances. Outside aid was still reaching Benzai, but not Kuraq."

"What about the alleged genocide?"

"I would put a heavy emphasis on the word *alleged*. A few people were killed during the struggles relating to the initial occupation, but we haven't confirmed any deaths since. We hear rumors of Zuko's genocidal plans—but so far there has been no known attempt to actually start a massacre. That's why the president has been unable to get support for a UN resolution against Kuraq."

"They haven't found any evidence of genocide, either?"

"No. In the eyes of too many around the world, this looks like another excuse for American imperialism. We come up with excuses for every invasion we've made into the Middle East, but in the eyes of many, those excuses are just that—rationalizations for doing what we want to do, even if it amounts to little more in reality than a war of aggression or a flat-out theft of natural and economic resources."

Swinburne stroked his chin thoughtfully. "Is there any reason the president would be so obsessed with Kuraq?"

"Objection," Ben said. He suspected this one was not going to do much good, but at the very least it would interrupt the flow of this damaging assault on the president's credibility. "Calls for speculation about a third party's motives."

"Not really," Swinburne responded. "The question goes toward the president's mental state. Shows that he may not be exercising the intellectual prowess we would want from our president. That is very relevant to this proceeding."

"No," Ben insisted. "The fact that the president may have a different opinion than the secretary of state does not in any way suggest mental instability. Surely we're mature enough to be able to differ without labeling opposing viewpoints as crazy."

"I understand what you're saying," Admiral Cartwright said. "But I think this is relevant. I'm going to allow it. I will caution the witness to avoid speculation, however."

Ben frowned. This was not going to be helpful. He felt certain Ruiz could accomplish his goals without violating the judge's rule against speculation—at least not too obviously.

"I think President Kyler blames Zuko for taking away his honeymoon. You know, the first one hundred days or so of a new presidency when the press and the public are still excited and his approval ratings are high and a president can typically start instituting a good deal of his campaign agenda. The bombing so preoccupied political thought that Kyler didn't get that grace period. But why he assumes that Zuko was responsible and has obsessed on him so, I just couldn't tell you. It doesn't seem rational to me."

"Objection," Ben said, rising.

"I'm sorry," Ruiz said quickly. "I don't mean to testify about the president's mental state."

Ben found this apology profoundly unconvincing.

"I'm just trying to understand why I and many others at State were mystified," Ruiz continued. "It didn't make any sense. There are worse dictators in the world, and bigger threats to the security of our nation. North Korea. Pakistan. Just to name two."

"Maybe he's just being careful," Swinburne suggested. "Is there any downside to being careful?"

"In this case, yes. Kyler has committed so many of our resources to this region that, in the event that a real threat developed, we would be hard-pressed to mount an effective response quickly. Furthermore, it's extremely damaging to world opinion about the United States. I just don't think the rest of the world is going to tolerate another Middle Eastern invasion by American forces. At least not unless we have positive proof that they were behind the bombing. Or that people are being slaughtered in Benzai. And at present we don't."

"Have you seen any further evidence that the president is obsessed with some kind of personal revenge against Zuko?"

"Objection, leading." Ben hated to make so many objections. He knew that excessive objections irritated the jury, who usually would like to hear the answer to any question interesting enough to draw an objection. He could only imagine the effect on a group of cabinet members, people used to getting their information in succinct briefings, and in this case, people who could see the deadline till the next missile launch approaching all too quickly.

Cartwright tilted his head to one side. "Well . . . it was a leading question, Mr. Swinburne. Do you understand what we mean by that term?"

"I think I've got the general idea, judge. I'll try again." Swinburne cleared his throat. "Have you observed any indications of what might be the basis for the president's preoccupation with Kuraq?"

"I think he wants revenge," Ruiz said.

Ben rolled his eyes. Swinburne had used the inappropriate leading question to tell Ruiz how he wanted him to answer. If he needed cash after his vice presidency, he could have a fine career as a prosecutor.

"Why would he want revenge?"

"The attack could have come during the previous administration. Whoever was behind the attack seems to have purposely waited until Kyler was in office before they made the strike. But there seems to be more to it than even that."

"How do you mean?"

"It's hard to explain. It's almost as if there were . . . some sort of grudge match between Kyler and Zuko. As if the president has personal reasons for wanting to put him down. I'm sorry I can't explain it any better. But it really does seem to have a personal aspect to it."

"And how is that not speculation?" Ben said, rising.

"The man's doing the best he can on short notice," Cartwright said curtly. "It's not as if they've had time to rehearse their testimony."

Point taken. Ben sat down.

"One last question, Mr. Secretary. Excluding what you have witnessed today in the bunker—I assume everyone has already heard enough about that—have you observed any behavior by the president that you considered irrational?"

"I think sending troops to the Kuraqi border was irrational. More than just a mistake. It was wrong on so many levels that I believe it was not the action of a man in full control of his faculties. I think his ongoing aggression toward a petty Middle Eastern dictator shows a lack of clear reasoning. And I think his refusal to withdraw troops when Zuko has control of our ballistic missiles and possibly a nuclear suitcase is positively insane!"

"Objection," Ben said again. "He's not qualified to render that opinion."

"I don't think he's using the term in the sense of a medical diagnosis," Cartwright said. "He's just saying that what has happened doesn't make any sense to him."

"That's exactly right," Ruiz said.

"So your objection is overruled. Honestly, Mr. Kincaid, we need to move faster so we can get this job done within our deadline."

Ben sat down, frowning. And by "this job," did the judge mean simply finishing this trial—or booting Kyler out of office?

"I have no more questions," Swinburne said. "But before we proceed any further, judge, I have to ask if we can't bring this matter to an immediate close."

Ben stood beside him. "What are you talking about?"

"I'm just trying to be reasonable. This isn't a real trial. "

"It isn't?"

"We can be flexible. And we've already had evidence of the president's irrational decision making, of erratic behavior, of a life-threatening medical condition that could potentially affect his reasoning and that for all we know may be the cause of his unstable behavior."

"Is this a motion," Ben asked, "or a closing argument?"

"I just think we've heard enough, judge. And we have too little time before Zuko strikes again. I say we ask the cabinet members for an immediate vote. Right now."

26

10:47 A.M.

"What?" Ben said incredulously. "I haven't called a witness. I haven't even cross-examined this one."

Swinburne shrugged. "I just don't see that it will make any difference."

"I'm sure you don't," Ben replied. "And I'm sure every prosecutor would like to end the trial before the defense has a chance to put on their case."

"I'm not—"

"Gentlemen, please." Admiral Cartwright held up his hands. "I understand what you're saying, Swinburne, but I think due process—"

"Due process may be fine for other trials," Swinburne said, "but not when deadly missiles could be fired at any minute!"

Cartwright's expression darkened. If Ben had had any doubts before about how quickly and thoroughly he had taken to the role of a judge, it disappeared instantly when he saw that—like every other judge on earth—Cartwright did not like to be interrupted.

"Mr. Vice President, I know you're not trained as a lawyer, so let me give you the basics right now. You never interrupt the judge. Never!"

"But—" Swinburne started, though he had the good sense to stop before it went far.

"Believe me, no one is more aware of that ticking clock than I am. But we can't honestly say that the Constitution has been honored if we haven't given Kincaid a chance to put on a defense."

"Exactly," Ben said.

"Now, if you'd like to speed things up, Mr. Swinburne, you can rest your case with this witness."

Swinburne looked down at the floor and made a grumbling noise. "Well, I have one more person I want to call."

"Then why don't we dispense with this preemptive strike and get on with it? Motion overruled."

Well, at least it wasn't going to be over that quickly, Ben thought as he returned to his position at the table. Although he had to wonder whether it would ultimately make any difference.

Before he launched into his cross, he took a card from Secretary Rybicki's deck and passed the president a note: *Why does Ruiz think your actions in Kuraq are personal?*

The president responded with lightning speed: *Because they are.*

Ben crumpled the note in his hand and put it safely into his pocket. This was just great. They would have to talk later. For now, he needed to cross-examine this witness.

"Mr. Secretary, your testimony seems to express your opinion that the president is not acting objectively."

"To say the least," Ruiz replied.

"Are you?"

Ruiz seemed taken aback at the question. He stumbled a few moments before answering. "I—I believe so."

"To me, sir, you seem just as rigid in your belief that we should not be in Kuraq as the president is in his belief that we should."

"I hardly think—"

"Would it be fair to say you have made up your mind on this subject?"

"Well, yes."

"And you firmly believe that we should pull out of Kuraqi waters?"

"Yes."

"So how do you differentiate your firmness—some might say your obsession—from the president's? They sound like much the same thing to me."

"But my decision is based on a rational analysis of the available facts."

"And we know that how?"

"Well—because—because—"

"I'm sure if we ask him—and we will—the president will say exactly the same thing. I'm sorry, Mr. Secretary, but it sounds to me as if you're labeling the president's decision making as irrational and insane because he has the temerity to hold an opinion different from your own."

"No, not at all."

"This isn't really about the president's purported insanity. It's about your intolerance!"

"Hear, hear," the president said, clapping.

Cartwright thumped the table. "The defendant will refrain from comment and interruption!" he barked. Then he added, as an afterthought, "Even if he is, you know, the president of the United States."

Ben couldn't help smiling.

"Let me explain something," Ruiz said, sounding a little strained. "I've been working in the foreign policy arena for almost twenty years. I know my stuff. So I probably don't have as much patience as I might when I know someone is making a wrongheaded decision. I'm sure you feel the same way, Mr. Kincaid, when someone makes an incorrect statement about the law. But this goes far beyond just making a bad decision. This is a position that simply makes no rational sense—especially now, when we're under attack from our own missiles!"

"Have you never before heard anyone say that they will not negotiate with terrorists?"

"Well, of course."

"Is that irrational?"

"No, not—"

"Isn't that basically what the president is saying now?"

"Perhaps that's what he's saying, but I think there's a lot more to it. Even Ronald Reagan, the cold warrior, ended up working with terrorists in the Iran-contra mess. He didn't like it, but he thought it was necessary given the circumstances. Similarly, President Kyler needs to realize that this is a time when he needs to step back, if only temporarily, and give Zuko what he wants. For the security of the nation."

"But other leaders have stuck to the no-negotiation policy, have they not? Even when there were serious consequences? And they weren't removed from office. Right?"

"I suppose. But—"

"Thank you, Mr. Secretary. You've answered the question." Ben tried to comfort himself with the knowledge that he had gained something. It might not be much, but it was something. "And speaking of bias, sir, didn't we hear earlier that you know—or at least knew—Colonel Zuko personally?"

"Yes. I knew him slightly in college. So?"

"Well, perhaps that's why you don't think he's as much of a threat as the president does. You still remember the larky good ol' days going to keggers and frat parties."

Ruiz's upper lip actually curled. "They don't have fraternities at Oxford. But I suppose you wouldn't know that."

"No, I wouldn't. I went to school in Oklahoma, where everyone has the sense to know that anyone crazy enough to seize control of our missile systems is a serious threat."

"I know he's a threat," Ruiz said, cutting off Swinburne's objection. "I just don't believe the president is handling the threat in the right way. And to continue sending in troops when we can't get him out of our computers is nuts!"

"Isn't it possible that Zuko might back off when he sees our troops marching up his front lawn?"

"I think the U.S. East Coast will be gone before that happens."

"That's your prediction. I asked if it was possible."

"Anything's possible."

"So it's possible the president is right."

"I don't think so."

"I didn't ask what you think. I asked if it's possible."

"I suppose. Remotely possible. Very remotely. More remote than the Andromeda galaxy."

"But possible."

"Remotely."

Well, at least he'd gotten that concession. If you could call it that. But there was still something nagging at the corners of Ben's brain.

"Secretary Ruiz, didn't we learn earlier that your relationship with Colonel Zuko is deeper than a mere college friendship? That he actually contributed to your first political campaign?"

Ruiz shrugged his shoulders. "It was a tiny contribution. Maybe five hundred dollars. I don't really remember."

"And he never contributed again to any subsequent campaign?"

"No." He paused. "Colonel Zuko never contributed to any of my subsequent campaigns."

Ben thought a moment. Something about the way Ruiz said it bothered him. Yes, he looked up and to the right as he said it. His good friend police detective Mike Morelli had told him once that that was the sure sign of someone who either had extreme attention deficit issues—or was lying. But Ben also noted the way he'd said it. He hadn't used the pronoun *he,* as one normally would in response, since Ben had just used his name. Instead he'd said "Colonel Zuko never contributed"—as if he were making some sort of distinction in his own mind.

"Secretary Ruiz, did someone else make a contribution to your subsequent campaigns?"

Ruiz's brow knitted. "I would guess something like several thousand people made contributions to my subsequent campaigns. What are you getting at?"

"I'm asking about contributions that may be relevant to this proceeding."

"I'm afraid you've lost me."

Ben thought for a moment. He felt certain he was close to something. He just wasn't sure how to get there.

Beside him, he saw President Kyler tilting his head and making bug eyes. Was he having another episode? No, he was trying to tell Ben something.

And then he remembered Rybicki's note.

"Secretary Ruiz, did you ever receive any contributions from . . . Apollo?"

As soon as he spoke the word, Ben saw Swinburne twitch a little. That was a good sign.

Ruiz leaned forward slightly, looking confused. Ben was pretty sure he wasn't. "Apollo?"

"Yes. You know what it is, don't you?"

Ruiz looked at Swinburne. Swinburne looked away. On your own, buddy.

"Are you . . . talking about the energy company?"

Ben took a shot. "Obviously."

"Sure. I've heard of it. Hasn't everyone?"

"And did they contribute to your campaigns?"

Ruiz acted nonchalant. "I . . . think they may have done so on occasion."

"And what's their connection to Colonel Zuko?"

"Is there one?"

Ben was getting tired of this cat-and-mouse game. "Yes, there is one, and I want you to stop wasting our time and tell the cabinet about it right now."

Ben saw Swinburne twitch again. He was probably thinking about objecting but didn't want to do so in a futile effort that might give the appearance he was trying to cover something up.

"I don't know any of this firsthand."

"Tell us what you do know, Secretary."

"It's my understanding that Apollo may have some drilling leases . . . in Kuraq."

At long last. "And that would require the express consent and involvement of Colonel Zuko, right?"

"I suppose so. He pretty much runs the whole economy."

"And if the colonel is removed from office, Apollo would lose those leases."

"It's possible."

"So Apollo has a direct financial interest in the perpetuation of the colonel's dirty little dictatorship."

"I wouldn't put it that way."

"I'm sure you wouldn't. Because Apollo has you deep in its pockets."

"Objection," Swinburne said. "I don't know what the technical ground would be, but that can't be permissible."

"I think the ground might be that it's argumentative," Cartwright suggested. "Or perhaps failure to ask a question."

"Fine. I object because of those."

"Objection granted. Mr. Kincaid, you've made your point. Save the rest for your closing."

Sound advice, but Ben wasn't ready to take it. "Secretary Ruiz, are you suggesting that your relationship with Apollo doesn't have any impact on your reasoning?"

"Exactly."

"Then why were you trying to cover it up?"

"I wasn't!"

"Well, you certainly weren't forthcoming."

"I didn't see what it had to do with the matter at hand. I still don't!"

"Let me ask you a hypothetical question, Mr. Secretary. If you found out a member of your staff had been receiving money from a company with financial holdings in North Korea, would you send him out there to negotiate a nuclear arms treaty?"

"Of course not. But that's totally—"

"So you admit that financial interests could potentially influence decision making?"

"No. I mean—sure, but I don't—" He paused and took a deep breath to clear the befuddlement. "Look, just because Apollo contributed a little campaign money does not mean they own me."

"So I guess you've never done a favor for someone who contributed to your campaign?"

"Well . . ."

"Of course you have. Probably everyone has. The question is, how do we know you're not paying back a campaign contribution right now?"

Swinburne shouted his objection, but Ben plowed on ahead. "How do we know you're not paying Apollo back by protecting their leases—by ensuring that Colonel Zuko remains in office?"

Cartwright banged on the table, Ruiz protested—and Ben kept right on going.

"How do we know you're not trying to help out your buddies at Apollo—and the colonel—by eliminating his greatest threat, the president, and advocating the removal of our troops from Kuraq?"

Ruiz rose to his feet. "That's preposterous!" he shouted. His words echoed through the tiny room. His face was red. "I would never do that. It's just a contribution. It's—"

"No more questions," Ben said, turning away.

"But I'm not done," Ruiz sputtered.

"Apparently you are," Admiral Cartwright said. "Please step down."

"But he's accusing me—"

"We all heard it, Secretary. We don't need a recap. Step down!"

Ruiz reluctantly tucked his head and left the witness chair. Ben wanted to lean over and give Secretary Rybicki a big kiss, but he restrained himself. If the man wanted to remain in the background, so be it. His intel had salvaged that cross-examination and, Ben hoped, given the cabinet members a reason to disregard Ruiz's testimony.

But would that be enough to make them disregard the disturbing image of the president of the United States singing the theme from *The Brady Bunch* while the world was on the brink of disaster? That was another question altogether. And as long as they held that image in their heads, it would be hard not to vote him out of his office.

27

Seamus lay helplessly on the department store floor, gazing up at the high-level geek who had just knocked the hell out of him and sent him crashing down into the shattered glass.

Life was just full of ironies sometimes.

"So . . . what do you want me to do next?" Harold Bemis said, in a voice so shockingly high that Seamus wondered if it was possible the man had not yet been through puberty. Who would know? He doubted there were any women who could testify on the topic.

The fallen sniper lying only a few feet away slowly pushed himself up. He was cut in about a hundred places and his forehead was caked with blood. He was obviously having trouble seeing. The perfume and blood mixture still stung, but he was managing.

"Son of a bitch," the assassin growled. As soon as he was fully on his feet, he reared back and kicked Seamus right in the ribs.

Seamus winced. That hurt, and the man had kicked him exactly where he had been injured before. He had suspected he might have damaged a rib earlier. Now he was certain of it.

And just to add a little more pain to the situation, the bastard kicked him again.

"Goddamn Americans," the man swore. He spat into Seamus's face. "All you know is the torture!"

Seamus suspected it wouldn't help him to remind the guy that this had all started because he was trying to kill Seamus in cold blood. Logic probably wasn't his strong suit.

"Can we get out of here?" Bemis said nervously. "It's only a matter of time before mall security shows up."

"Then I will shoot them down like the dogs that they are," replied the sniper.

"Yeah, unless they get you first. Let's just get out of here."

"And let this scum live?"

Bemis shrugged in a goofy way that suggested that he couldn't decide whether he wanted vanilla or rocky road, not that he was deciding whether someone lived or died. "I don't care. Whatever you're going to do, just do it already."

"Perhaps I should call Ishmael."

Ishmael, Seamus thought. Almost certainly a code name for some high muckety-muck in the terrorist cell. Of course to him, Ishmael brought to mind *Moby Dick*. But to these people, it was much more likely a reference to the second son of Abraham. The progenitor of the Islamic faith. The ancestor of Muhammad.

"Don't you think he has enough on his mind right now? He asked you to bring me to the location. As quickly as possible. I gather there's a problem."

"Yes. The military are fighting against your virus. They are making some progress."

Bemis nodded. "I'm not surprised. I warned him they would react quickly if you announced what you had. Better to just do it."

"That is not what the colonel wanted."

"Whatever. We don't have time for this. Do it and let's get out of here."

Seamus glanced one way, then the other. No one was visible. Had no one called in a disturbance?

He looked all around himself for a potential weapon—and found nothing. They had him pinned down like a dead butterfly. There was simply no way he could do anything in time.

The assassin recovered his gun from where it had fallen, then crouched down on one knee and pressed the pistol against Seamus's left temple.

"If you have a God you pray to, this is your last chance."

"You know we'll stop you, don't you?" Seamus said defiantly. "You and all your buddies. You'll end up in prison. Or dead."

"It is you who is about to die."

"There won't be any virgins at the penitentiary. And the only sex you'll be involved with will be exceedingly unpleasant."

"Goodbye, American pig." He smiled a little as his finger tightened on the trigger.

At first Seamus couldn't tell what had happened. The killer looked at him quizzically, then his neck stiffened, and a moment later he dropped to the floor like an anvil.

Keys were sticking out of the back of his neck. Two were embedded deep in his flesh. He wouldn't be getting up for a good while. If ever.

Seamus didn't wait for an explanation. He pushed himself up as quickly as possible and grabbed the gun. He whirled around—

Arlo was pointing a weapon at Bemis.

"What are you doing here?"

Arlo kept his eye trained on his fellow geek. "Saving your butt, that's what."

"I told you to stay in the car!"

"Well, I disobeyed. Which is why you're still alive."

Seamus squinted. "What is that you've got, anyway?"

Arlo twitched. "Have you got the gun?"

"Yeah."

"Good." Arlo flipped the black object around. "It's a thumb drive. Take it with me everywhere I go."

Bemis's brow creased. "I thought it was a taser, man."

Arlo smiled. "You need to get out more."

Seamus took the little piece of plastic and metal. "Does it shoot bullets?"

"Nah. It doesn't do anything, unless you've got a USB port. Except it turns out to be useful against particularly stupid archcriminals."

"I saw you in the car following me, Arlo," Bemis said. "Why are you helping these clowns?"

"Why are you helping terrorists who are trying to blow up the country? I mean, I knew you were hurting for money, but this is treason!"

Bemis rolled his eyes. "Don't be stupid. It's all just a big game."

"Well, your game almost got me killed this morning, Harold. And almost killed my friend just now." He grinned. "Until I showed up to save the day."

"Don't get too proud of yourself, kid," Seamus grunted.

"Why? You had a gun, and you ended up flat on your butt. I saved the day with a flash drive and your car keys."

Seamus decided to let that go. The kid had handled the situation well, even if Seamus was never going to admit it aloud.

He grabbed Bemis by the collar. "Tell me. Now."

"I—I don't know what you want."

"I think you do," Seamus said, tightening his grip. "Spill it. Where's the operations base? Where are they controlling the satellite?"

"I don't know," he said helplessly.

Seamus didn't want to believe him, but at this point, he seemed well past any ability to dissemble. Or to do anything else other than possibly wet himself. "Didn't I hear you say you and your friend were going there next?"

"Yeah, but I don't know where it is. That's why he was supposed to pick me up here. He was going to take me."

"You weren't there when they fired the first two missiles?"

Bemis shook his head furiously. "They didn't need me."

"But they do now."

"Apparently so. I got a text. Want to see it?"

"Yeah. As a matter of fact, I do." He took Bemis's cell phone and began punching buttons.

"I think he's lying," Arlo said.

"I am not. I never lie."

"Last week at D.C. Bytes you said you hadn't done any programming in months."

"Well . . . that wasn't a lie. That was a cover story."

"Same diff!"

"Children, please," Seamus said. "I need information, not quarreling."

Bemis stared up at the ceiling. "I'm not telling you anything. I don't care what you do to me. I won't talk."

"I'll bet you would. In about ten seconds. But unfortunately, I don't think you know anything."

"So I can't tell you where this base is."

"Ah," Seamus said, pressing a hand against his aching rib cage. "That's where you're wrong. You're going to tell me everything I need to know."

28

Ben dearly desired to take the president into the other room for another confab, but he knew Cartwright was already impatient with the progress of the trial. Moreover, he'd seen several of the cabinet members on the big screen glancing at their watches. Understandably so—the clock had barely more than a hour left till the colonel had promised to deploy the next missile. He didn't want to risk their ire by requesting another delay.

Oh, well. If the president had something to tell him, he could always slip him a note.

Swinburne cleared his throat. "Your honor, I'd like to call the president's chief of staff to the stand. Sarie Morrell."

Everyone was surprised, but Sarie herself was absolutely stunned. She pressed her hand against her chest. "Me? Why me? I don't have anything to say to that polecat."

Swinburne smiled, possibly the creepiest smile Ben had ever seen in his life. "Why don't we determine that on the witness stand?"

Sarie looked pleadingly at the president. He smiled reassuringly and nodded toward the witness stand.

Sarie headed toward the chair. As she passed Swinburne, Ben heard her mutter under her breath, "You're making a big mistake."

Swinburne did not appear particularly threatened.

At first blush, Ben would've thought Swinburne was making a mistake, too. Secretary Ruiz's loyalty to the president might have been in question, but Sarie's was not. She had been with the president for many campaigns, not just the last one. She had served as his chief of staff when he was governor, too. She was renowned for her efficiency, her hard work, and her dogged devotion to her boss. She was known to go to great lengths, to stay up all night, to plunge into the lion's den—or a nest of Republicans—to help her boss obtain his goals. Her loyalty was simply not in question.

But Swinburne was not a stupid man.

So why would he call such a potentially dangerous witness?

Well, he wouldn't, Ben realized. Unless he had a very good reason. Unless he had a specific goal he wanted. Some information he thought he could get out of her.

What did Sarie know?

This time Swinburne didn't waste time on her credentials or background, even though Ben knew both were impressive. Perhaps he wasn't interested in making her look good. Perhaps his goal was exactly the opposite.

"Please state your name."

"Sarah Lynn Morrell." Ben loved the way her accent gave the last vowel in *Morrell* about three syllables.

"And your current position?"

"I'm the president's chief of staff."

"How long have you worked for him?"

"Counting previous positions, almost fifteen years."

"So it would be safe to say that you like working for him?"

"Well, I'm not one to abandon ship while it's still in the water."

"Would it be safe to say you like the man personally?"

"I've never known a better man than Roland Kyler in my entire life. And I've known a lot of good men. If I didn't know better, I'd swear he was a southerner."

"And I suppose that makes you somewhat devoted to him?"

"Absolutely."

Swinburne turned toward Admiral Cartwright. "Judge, given the witness's obvious inclinations—one might say biases—I ask permission to treat her as a hostile witness."

Ben arched a eyebrow. For a nonlawyer, he was making a savvy move. If she was a hostile witness, he could ask leading questions. Which might be necessary to lead her into whatever snake pit he wanted to visit.

Cartwright turned toward the witness. "Ms. Morrell, do you understand that Mr. Swinburne wants to declare you to be a hostile witness?"

She frowned. "*Hostile* isn't a strong enough word for it."

"So . . . that motion will be granted. Proceed."

Swinburne adjusted the tie of his suit jacket. "Ms. Morrell, please tell the members of the cabinet what happened on the morning of March twenty-eighth."

She stared back at him blank-faced. "Are you kidding? That was two weeks ago. Do you have any idea how busy I am? How would I know?"

"Are you saying you don't remember?"

"Can I look at my Filofax?"

"Is it down here?"

"No." Just as well. If she had used it to refresh her recollection, Swinburne would have had the right to examine the entire calendar. Heaven only knew what he might have found.

"Let me try to help you, Ms. Morrell. That was the day of the Easter egg roll."

"Oh." Sarie's face seemed to flatten, as if someone had sucked all the life out of it.

"Ringing any bells yet?"

"Well . . . it was a very busy day."

"No doubt. What happened?"

"Well, of course, they bused in all those schoolchildren. Lots of adorable little runts, most of whom had no idea where they were or why it was important. Dragged here by teachers, followed by parents chasing after bragging points. One kid slugged another over a pink plastic basket. Another tried to urinate in the rosebushes. A fight broke out over who got to stand at the front of the line. So they could chase after those inedible wooden eggs." She sighed. "Lovely event."

"And did the president play any role in this festivity?"

"Well, yes. He opened up the ceremony."

"Was he on time?"

A stricken expression came across Sarie's face. She looked as if she had been caught in a trap. Perhaps she had. Swinburne was frighteningly well informed.

"No. He did not appear on schedule."

"What did you do?"

"Well, I'm his chief of staff. A big part of my job is making sure he is where he's supposed to be. On time. So when he didn't show up in the Rose Garden, I went to look for him."

"And did you manage to find him?"

"Eventually. It took a good fifteen minutes."

"So I will assume, knowing how quickly you move, that he wasn't in any of the first fifteen or so places you looked for him. Where did you finally find him?"

Sarie pursed her lips. "In the Portrait Hall. Just beyond his secretary's station outside the Oval Office."

"And what was he doing there?"

"He was . . . looking at the pictures."

"What pictures?"

Sarie took a deep breath, her shoulders heaving. Ben didn't need a sixth sense to realize this was something she really didn't want to talk about.

"Each incoming president gets to choose which of the full collection of presidential portraits in the White House gallery they wish to have hanging in the hallway, where they are bound to see them almost every day. Most everyone keeps Washington and Lincoln, but there's room for more. Clinton chose Jefferson, because he was named for him. Dubya chose his father, an obvious gesture of respect. Reagan chose Coolidge, because . . . well, no one really knows why he chose Coolidge. Silent Cal had been in the basement so long they weren't sure they could get all the dust off him."

Even Swinburne smiled a little. "And whom did President Kyler choose?"

"Kennedy. And FDR."

"And what was he doing in the gallery with these pictures?"

Sarie looked away. "Well, I don't know that he was doing anything, exactly . . ."

"Ms. Morrell," Swinburne said sternly, "you are under oath. Tell the cabinet members what he was doing."

She sighed. "He was talking to them."

Beside him, Ben saw the president avert his eyes, toward the floor.

A discernible susurrus flowed through the room. Swinburne appeared incredulous, although Ben suspected he wasn't even surprised. He must've known what he was fishing for. "He was talking to the portraits?"

"Oh, you know how you do when you're alone and you don't think anyone is listening. You just start saying your thoughts out loud. It's no big deal. I remember a deb who talked to the centerpiece at her coming-out party."

"What exactly was he saying?"

Sarie squirmed uncomfortably in her chair. "I believe they—I mean he—was talking about . . . God."

Swinburne blinked. "God?"

"Sure. I guess you're probably unfamiliar, but he's the head deity who created the universe and—"

"I know who God is, Ms. Morrell," Swinburne said, confirming what Ben had long suspected: he had no sense of humor whatsoever. "What was the president saying about God to the inanimate portraits on the wall?"

"He was asking JFK if he believed in God."

Swinburne nodded several times. "And did he?"

"Objection," Ben said, without great hope. Mostly he just wanted to break up Swinburne's maniacal flow. "How are JFK's religious beliefs relevant to the matter at hand?"

"The point of the testimony," Swinburne said with a sneer, "is to demonstrate the depth of the president's delusional mental state."

Cartwright nodded. "I'm afraid I'll have to allow it."

"So," Swinburne said to Sarie, "did JFK believe in God?"

"JFK didn't answer," she said, smiling. "At least not so as I could hear him."

"What did the president have to say on the subject?"

"He said he wondered about JFK's immortal soul. He said that JFK mentioned God from time to time but that he doesn't seem to have been very religious. He mentioned that JFK didn't seem to observe at least one of the Ten Commandments."

"I see."

"He wondered if JFK had placed his faith in God when his PT boat was sunk. Then he asked FDR if he lost his faith when he contracted polio. And he asked about FDR's lack of attention to the same commandment."

"Anything else?"

"Well, I didn't just stand there eavesdropping. I went to finishing school, you know. I have manners."

"Of course. What did you do next?"

"I cleared my throat and made a lot of noise. I didn't want to startle or embarrass him. Then I approached and laid my hand on his shoulder and told him the kiddies were waiting."

"What did he say?"

"He . . . didn't answer at first."

"And then?"

Sarie looked like a caged cougar. Ben wondered how many other people knew this story—and who might have been able to call her on it if she hadn't come forward with the details. "Then I noticed that he was crying. Big-time tears. All over his face."

"Crying. I see. Did he say anything?"

"Yeah. He grabbed my hand and asked me if I would pray with him."

"Excuse me?"

"Oh, you heard what I said, you big bowl of grits. He wanted me to pray with him."

"And what was your response?"

"Well, I'm aware there is some precedent for this sort of thing in the White House. I didn't see as it would hurt anything. And we were celebrating a religious holiday. In a pagan sort of way."

"So you prayed with him."

"Sure. Why not? Nothing I didn't do every week back at the Southern Baptist church in Birmingham. He did all the talking."

"What did he say?"

"He prayed for guidance. He prayed for insight. And he prayed for, um, his immortal soul."

"His immortal soul? Did he actually use those words?"

"He did."

"Was there something he was concerned about? Felt guilty about?"

"If there was, he didn't share."

"Did he pray for anything else?"

"Yes. He also, um—" She cleared her throat. "He prayed for God to forgive JFK and FDR for their marital indiscretions and to take their souls up to heaven."

"I see," Swinburne said, steepling his hands. "How thoughtful of him."

"Yeah. I thought so."

"How did he look when all this took place?"

"I don't know what you mean. He looked like himself."

"Eyes, complexion, posture . . . ?"

"His eyes were red, but he had been crying. His face seemed red, too. Kinda puffy. He's so tan, though, sometimes it's hard to tell about that. He was slouching. He didn't have his presidential aura. He seemed tired."

"And what happened after that?"

"Nothing. After we finished with the praying, he cleaned up a bit, then followed me outside and opened the egg roll. Just like nothing had ever happened."

"No more odd behavior."

"No. He was completely himself again."

"But for a time, when he was talking to the pictures and all—he did not seem himself?"

Sarie thought for a moment. She had pretty much opened herself up to this one with her last remark, and she knew it. "I suppose not. Or perhaps it was just a side to him I hadn't seen before."

"In fifteen years of working with him."

"Right." Her eyes lowered. "Right."

"Ms. Morrell, since President Kyler took office, how many other such erratic episodes have there been? Instances of the president behaving oddly."

Ben wanted to object—it was clearly a leading question and assumed facts not in evidence. But since she was a hostile witness—albeit a pretty cooperative one—he knew Swinburne could get away with it.

"I don't know. Most of the time he has been perfectly normal. Sharp as the best needle in my mama's sewing kit."

"But how many times has he been . . . odd?"

Sarie shrugged. "I dunno. Once or twice, maybe."

"I'll assume that means at least twice. Would you tell us about those incidents, please?"

She tossed her head back, swinging her long hair out of her face. "Well, there was that deal in the White House swimming pool. That was kinda . . ." She looked at the president apologetically.

President Kyler smiled. "Weird?"

She smiled back. "Your word, not mine."

Swinburne made his trademark grunting noise again. "I will ask the witness to address her comments to me."

"My pleasure, cutie pie," Sarie responded.

"What happened at the swimming pool?" Swinburne demanded.

She leaned back. Ben got the impression this story was going to take a while. "It was another one of those disappearing-president deals. He was supposed to be taking a meeting—come to think of it, he was supposed to be meeting you, wasn't he?"

"Was this the Tuesday before last?"

"I think so, yeah."

"He was supposed to be meeting with me. He kept me waiting for more than an hour."

Ben sighed. Now the prosecutor was actually testifying—but it would be pointless to object. They had to get the evidence before the cabinet as expeditiously as possible.

"Right. Well, speaking as the keeper of the president's schedule— you got off easy. Next time bring a book to read."

"I'll try to remember that. So what was he doing in the swimming pool?"

"Strange as it may seem, he was swimming."

"I'm guessing there was more to it. Otherwise, you wouldn't have brought this up as an example of odd behavior."

"Well, I didn't notice anything out of the ordinary at first. Till I stepped up to the edge of the pool to talk to him. That's when I noticed . . ."

"Yes?"

"He wasn't wearing any clothes. Forgot the ol' swimsuit, you know what I mean?"

Ben saw several low-key looks exchanged across the room—and on the closed-circuit screen. The president was staring intently at the floor, making eye contact with no one.

"I mean, it's not that unusual, is it? I know when I was growing up, the boys used to go to the Y early in the morning and they'd all swim naked. I don't know what that was all about, but it was why Daddy never took me to the Y on Saturday mornings."

"But the president apparently didn't have your daddy's scruples."

"I don't think the president expected me to drop by."

"Wouldn't he always expect his chief of staff to come get him when he's overdue?"

"I think perhaps he had lost track of the time."

"What was he doing?"

"Laps."

"Did he say anything?"

"Eventually. Once he noticed me. He, um, asked if I wanted to get in."

Swinburne arched an eyebrow. "How agreeable of him."

"Yeah, I thought so."

"And did you?"

"No."

"But why not?"

"I didn't have my suit."

"Apparently that's not a requirement in the presidential pool."

"It is for me."

"Did the president seem embarrassed by his nakedness?"

"Not really, no."

"Did he provide any kind of explanation?"

"Well, I guess at one point he did say that he longed to be free, free like a butterfly, free like the wind. Maybe that had something to do with it."

"And was he surprised when you declined to get in with him?"

"Actually, yeah. He was. A bit cranky about it, too. Almost as if he had forgotten about, you know, gender differences and such."

"What happened next?"

"Oh, I eventually managed to get the little butterfly out of the water. I held out a towel—well, I held it between us to block the view, if you know what I mean. He was jabbering exuberantly about how good it was to be alive! Jumping up and down like an eight-year-old. At one point he asked if I thought it would be a good idea to hold the next cabinet meeting at a nudist camp."

Ben saw several necks stiffen on the television screen.

"And your reply?"

"I told him I thought it would be an interesting experiment, but he would have to get a different chief of staff because I wouldn't be there."

"Thank God for that," Swinburne said. "You may be the only thing that's kept the executive branch from descending into total chaos."

"Well, I try to help out where I can."

"Was there anything else unusual about this encounter?"

"Wasn't that unusual enough?"

"Any crying or praying? Talking to imaginary friends?"

"Not this time, sugar."

"Fine. I believe there was at least one other instance of unusual presidential behavior that you observed."

Darn. Ben had been hoping he might forget. He scanned the room, wondering if anyone else was as tired of this as he was. Unfortunately, all he saw was rapt attention. He decided that objecting on the grounds of repetition might be ill-advised.

"Yes. There was. Just one other. Three days ago." Her face lost all traces of attitude and humor. Ben got the disturbing feeling that this episode was going to be the worst of them all.

"And what did he talk about on this occasion? Butterflies?"

"No," Sarie said, lowering her eyes. "Suicide."

29

With one word, Ben knew Sarie's testimony had transformed from an account of eccentric behavior to something far more dire.

"Had the president gone missing again?" Swinburne sounded almost hopeful.

"In a sense. It was late at night. After hours. He wasn't missing any meetings. His wife just wondered where he was. I think he was late for their weekly gin game or something."

"Is tracking the president in your job description?"

"I was doing it as a favor for Sophie."

"I see. How long did it take you to find him this time?"

"Over an hour."

"Really? I would've thought a hyperkinetic sort such as yourself could've covered the entire White House in an hour."

"Twice. But I still couldn't find him. Because he wasn't there. Not exactly."

Ben wondered if she would wait for the obvious question. She did. There could not be any surer sign of her reluctance to proceed.

"Where did you find him?"

Sarie took a deep cleansing breath, then released it slowly. "On the roof."

Swinburne went bug-eyed. "What?"

"His keepers were going nuts, naturally. He hadn't logged out—not that he would've been allowed to leave by himself—but they couldn't find him. He might still be up there if we hadn't heard from a cook. Turns out there's a service panel in the corner of the kitchen. Climb through and you're out on the roof."

"Sounds like a potential security hazard."

"Of course it was bolted, but on the inside. Who even knew it was there?"

"The president, apparently."

"Well, yeah. The cook just saw the tips of his shoes before they vanished out of sight. When I inquired, she pointed out the passageway to me and I dutifully scrambled up it. I really should be paid more than I am, you know?"

"As should we all."

"So I grabbed this little iron ladder that looked as if it'd been there since John Adams first moved in, and pretty soon I was on the roof. Can you believe it? The roof of the White House. Who even knew that was possible?"

"Not me. But I didn't know there was an underground bunker before they dragged me here today."

"Good point. So the wind was horrible—practically blew me off the roof—and I knew this couldn't be safe because we were probably vulnerable to snipers and such, but I toughed it out and looked around. Over by the railing—and by that I mean the edge of the roof—that's where I found the president."

Ben wondered if he should object on grounds that the witness was employing a horrendously run-on sentence. He decided Cartwright probably wouldn't be amused.

"What was he doing?"

"He was . . . laughing."

"Laughing? Not crying?"

"Well, that too. It was strange. He was doing both at the same time. And talking."

"What was he talking about?"

"Oh, many things. Rapidly. One topic after another."

"Let's take them in order. From the top."

Sarie frowned. "Well, at the start, he was talking about flying."

Swinburne did a double take. "Flying? Like a butterfly?"

"I suppose. He said, 'Wouldn't it be wonderful if I could get away from it all? Just fly away.' "

"Then what did he do?"

"He stood up." Sarie licked her lips. It was obvious that this had been a difficult experience for her, one she did not relish recounting. "That was a bad idea in and of itself. I told you how strong the wind was up there. An accident would be easy. But he didn't seem to notice. He extended his arms in front of him, like Superman, you know? He shouted, 'Up, up, and away!' Bent his knees and sort of . . . sprang. 'I can flyyyyyyyy!' he shouted at the top of his lungs. 'Flyyyyyyy!' " She paused, caught her breath. "I thought he was really going to do it. I panicked. I grabbed desperately for his feet. The irony is, he wasn't actually trying to fly, but my stupid groping almost knocked him off the roof."

"Did his feet leave the roof?"

"No, thank God. But that seemed to puzzle him. He acted as if . . . as if he really thought it was going to happen."

"As if he really believed he could fly?" Swinburne suggested.

"Yes," she said quietly. "That was my impression. He expected it to happen and it didn't. So he was perplexed."

Beside him, Ben saw the president shaking his head. Did that mean it wasn't true? That it hadn't happened like that? Or just that the president was miserably embarrassed by this testimony?

"What happened next?"

"He sat down, eventually. But his mood had changed. He wasn't talking ninety miles a minute anymore. There was a lot more crying and a lot less laughing. Somehow the fact that he had failed to fly seemed to have really depressed him. He became despondent. Difficult to talk to. So mostly I just listened."

"What did he say?"

"I don't remember it all. He just seemed so . . . hopeless. Helpless. Deep in despair." She turned toward President Kyler. "I'm sorry, Roland."

"You just go on telling them what you saw," he said softly but firmly. "There's never any harm in telling the truth."

A noble sentiment, Ben thought. But he knew from personal experience that it was the truth that could often be the most damaging.

"Please continue," Swinburne said, urging her on.

"He was sobbing. Tears were streaming down his face. He said things like, 'What's the point of it? What's the point of going on? No one cares if I live or I die.'"

Even Admiral Cartwright, he of the stoic judicial face, reacted to this. This testimony was getting darker by the moment.

"He said he was barely getting started but he was already a terrible president. He said he had let the American people down. He said he knew things were going to get worse before they got better and he just couldn't handle it. I tried to talk to him, tried to tell him that wasn't true, that he was a good man, that people all around the world had tapped into his optimism, his desire for change, for world peace. But it was no use. He was inconsolable. That was the greatest irony, I thought. He had brought hope to people all around the world. But he couldn't bring hope to himself."

Swinburne nodded sadly. "What else did he say?"

Sarie thought for a moment. "He was particularly overcome with tears when he started talking about parenting. He said he had been a horrible parent, a failure. He said if there were anything at all he could do over in life, it wouldn't be with his wife, or his education, or politics. He wanted a second chance to be a better father."

Like everyone else in the room, Ben knew the president had only one child, a daughter, Jenny Kyler, who had been something of a rebel ever since she left home. She'd gone to school at Smith and was apparently bright, but she'd frequently made headlines by getting caught out after curfew, underage drinking. Once when Kyler was governor she was arrested while protesting outside the auditorium where her father was about to speak. Sophie Kyler had referred to Jenny among friends as "proof that no good turn goes unpunished."

When Kyler had announced his candidacy for the presidency, it looked as though he might be the first candidate in some time with no children being used as campaign props. And then, to everyone's surprise, Jenny came on board. She was even useful. Ben had heard Sarie say that she was very good at keeping her father on schedule, which apparently was an ongoing problem. And then, just after the first debate, a journalist's microphone caught her referring to the opposing candidate as "a first-class asshole." The next day, that was splashed all over the papers. Kyler's campaign had no choice but to publicly apologize—since Jenny refused—and to remove her from the campaign staff. Jenny threw a fit, publicly vowing to never have anything to do with her father again. And she had been true to her word. Despite the best efforts of a number of people, she had not visited once in all the time her father had been in the White House. Ben had heard rumors that no one was even sure where she was.

Ben could understand how the loss of his only child could hit the president hard. Anyone could. But the thought of him blubbering about it on the roof of the White House was not going to encourage anyone to keep him in office.

"He said he couldn't stand to go it alone," Sarie continued. "He needed the support of his wife, his offspring. Without them, he was nothing." She paused, though she was clearly not finished. Her eyes darted from one side of the room to the other. Even though Ben was sure she didn't mean it this way, he knew the break was having the effect of giving particular emphasis to whatever blockbuster was yet to come.

"Yes?" Swinburne said. "Please go on."

Sarie licked her lips. "He said he didn't think he could stand to go on living."

There was an audible gasp in the bunker. Papers shuffled on the television screen. The secretary of education stood and got a drink of water. The president slid deeper into his chair.

A suicidal president? That was simply unacceptable. On any grounds. No one would care now whether he was crazy or not. A suicidal president had to go, by whatever pretext was possible.

"How did you respond?"

"Of course I tried to bolster his spirits. I told him that he was wrong, that he was a great president, that he had done everything he could for Jenny. That it wasn't his fault she was unmanageable. And I told him that in time she would come around. It's true. I was a bit of a rebel myself back in the day. Didn't talk to my parents for almost ten years over some grievance so petty I don't even remember what it was now. I told him everything I could think of to say. But nothing seemed to help."

"What else did he say?"

"He just went on and on in that vein, for probably almost half an hour. I didn't know what to do. I didn't want to get the Secret Service— I didn't want anyone to see him like this. So I waited it out."

"And he was still talking?"

"Yes. Eventually he wrapped his hands around his knees and began to rock back and forth—" She cut herself short. "He said he was going to kill himself, just get it over with. Just jump off the roof and be done. Over. I tried to get him to think about what impact that would have on his wife, his child. 'They'll never miss me,' he insisted. 'Oh,' he said, 'maybe they will at first, for a week or two. But they'll get over it. They'll move on. And they'll be much better for being rid of me.' "

The other people in the room were shifting in their seats, wishing there were someplace they could go. This would be uncomfortable to hear in the best of circumstances, but when the president was sitting right there, only a few feet from all of them, it was awkward in the extreme.

"Did he talk about how he might do it?"

"Yes." Another deep breath. "He realized in time that jumping off the roof might not be fatal, though it was sure to bring great pain. He talked about getting a knife from the kitchen and doing himself in hara-kiri style. He talked about grabbing a Secret Service agent's gun and shooting himself through the head. Then—then—"

She choked. Ben realized it must be incredibly difficult for her to do this. She wasn't presently married. As far as anyone knew, the primary man in her life was Roland Kyler. And now she was effectively betraying him, in what was perhaps his moment of greatest need.

"Then," she continued, with great difficulty, "he talked about doing it at a press conference."

The secretary of education gasped.

"He said he'd smuggle a gun in when no one was looking, and once the cameras were rolling he'd blow his head off in living color. That would show the bastards, he said. That would show Colonel Zuko and all the other people who were conniving to bring him down. He wouldn't give them the chance. He'd just do it himself."

Ruiz threw down his pencil and turned away. Rybicki covered his face. No one looked the president in the eye. The murmuring and whispering in the tiny bunker was so intense Admiral Cartwright had to pound the table several times. "There will be quiet in here! The witness is still testifying."

"I'm really not," Sarie said. "That's all there is. That's everything I've seen. Before today."

"Let me ask you one more question before you go," Swinburne said. "And let me thank you for your honest testimony. I know it wasn't easy for you and I appreciate it. But my question is this: when you witnessed this spectacle on the roof of the White House, did the president seem . . . sane?"

"Objection," Ben said. "She's not qualified."

Cartwright waved him down. "She sees the man virtually every day. She may be the best observer we've got of his daily condition. I'm going to allow her to answer the question."

"But she's not a—"

"I've ruled, Mr. Kincaid. Sit down."

Ben unhappily returned to his chair.

Sarie shook her head. "I don't know if I would call him insane. He didn't seem himself. I will say that. He didn't seem like the Roland Kyler I know. It's was as if somehow he had been changed. Altered."

"Incapable?"

"I'm not a psychiatrist."

"I'm not asking for a medical diagnosis. But you can give us your own opinion, based upon what you saw and heard. I'm sure the judge will allow it."

Sarie continued shaking her head, searching for the words. "I just don't know what was wrong with him that night, or in the pool, or before the Easter egg roll. I don't know what brings on these . . . episodes. But I know they're real. And I know they're scary."

"But Ms. Morrell, did he seem stable? When he was threatening to kill himself? In graphic and bloody ways?"

Her head hung low. "No," she said quietly. "I suppose not."

"Thank you," Swinburne said. "Your witness, Mr. Kincaid."

30

Very generous of Swinburne, but what the hell was Ben supposed to do with this witness? She looked as if she couldn't go on, at least not without a recess, something the judge couldn't and wouldn't grant. He didn't doubt that she had been telling the truth. There was no chance that he was going to impeach her on cross. Her credibility and honesty were ironclad.

Still, he had to do something. He just didn't know what that might be.

He stood and addressed the witness. Some of the people in the room were absolutely glaring at him. They didn't want him to go on. They'd heard enough.

"Sarie," Ben said, "I know this has been a terrible ordeal for you, and in most circumstances I would ask for a recess before proceeding. In this case, though, there just isn't time. Do you think you could answer a few questions for me? I promise I won't go on too long."

She looked up. Her face was pale. "I'll do my best."

"Sarie, the whole purpose of this proceeding is to determine whether the president is incapable of serving as president due to some mental infirmity. The president can be as odd as he wants. That doesn't matter. It's only important if it prevents him from performing him official duties."

"I understand."

"And I know you saw some strange things. But I haven't heard anything that suggests that the president couldn't do his job."

Ruiz slapped himself on the forehead, looking at Ben as if he had lost every marble he ever had.

"You've testified that these episodes come without warning or any discernible trigger."

"That's true."

"And you've said that they eventually pass."

"Yes."

"After a brief time, he seems normal again. Able to perform as president?"

"Absolutely."

"Has he failed to accomplish any work as a result of these odd interludes?"

"Never once."

"Has he ever been unable to respond in a crisis or to take an appropriate action?"

"Absolutely not."

"Does his ability to make decisions seem impaired?"

"Not after the episodes are over. He's the most decisive man I've ever known."

"Then would it be fair to say that you do not perceive him to be rendered incapable?"

"Yes, absolutely."

"But what about during the episodes?" Swinburne barked. "What if a crisis breaks out while he's having one? Like now!"

Admiral Cartwright glared. "It is not your turn to speak, Mr. Swinburne. Please desist."

Swinburne folded his arms across his chest. "My apologies," he grumbled.

"So, Sarie," Ben continued, "I gather you would not want to label the president incapable. Or insane."

She hesitated. "No. I would not want to."

Not quite good enough. Ben wanted her to distinguish these odd episodes from genuine and severe insanity. He tried again. "Sarie, do you have any experience with people suffering from mental illness?"

"Yes, actually I do." She folded her hands in her lap. "You may not know this, but one summer when I was in college I worked at a state hospital. In the mental ward."

Ben's stomach was churning. Why did he suddenly have the distinct feeling he was going to regret having asked this question?

"I spent the whole summer changing sheets and dishing out pills. Caring for the inmates. It was educational—but also very chilling. I had never been around such disturbed people in my entire life. I never got used to it. There was just something . . . different about them. I'm not talking about their behavior. I mean, when I looked into their eyes. Shakespeare says the eyes are the window to the soul, and I guess that's right, because whenever I looked into these people's eyes, it seemed like something was missing. Something was . . . wrong."

Ben tried to cut her off, but she ignored him. Tears began to trickle out of her eyes. "And when I sat beside President Kyler on the roof that night and I looked into his eyes, I saw the same look. The same vacancy. The same wrongness."

The whispering in the room spiked. Cartwright pounded on the table, but it made little difference. On the television, the cabinet members watched with gaping mouths.

Sarie tried to control her broken voice. "I'm sorry, Roland. I'm so, so sorry. You are a good man. But you are not well. You need help. And I hope you will get that help, because I know there is so much you can contribute to the world. But not now." Tears flowed. Her voice rose an octave, then cracked altogether. "I *am* sorry, but it's true. We're in a crisis situation, and we need a leader, someone dependable, not someone who might start having an irrational episode at any moment—might be having one now for all we know!"

She reached out to him with both hands. "Roland, you need to step down. You need to do it now. For everyone's sake. Please!"

After that, the room descended into chaos. Cartwright tried to regain control, but it was useless. Everyone was talking at once, expressing their opinion, their contempt, their outrage. Ben couldn't pick up the televised conversation, but he could see the discussion among the cabinet members was equally agitated. Everyone was talking.

Everyone except the primary subject of the chatter. President Kyler rose, quietly slipped into the other room, and closed the door behind him.

Swinburne moved toward Admiral Cartwright. "Judge, we rest our case."

"I thought you might."

"Furthermore, given what we've heard, and given the exigencies of time, I will ask again that we move to an immediate roll call vote. Honestly, Kincaid, what could you possibly put in evidence at this point that would change anyone's mind?"

Which was exactly the question Ben had just been asking himself.

Ben was not a quitter. Not ever. Went totally against all his instincts, all his training.

But what was there to do? Kyler had been shown to have a serious medical condition, diabetes, and to be dangerously unstable, threatening to kill himself in front of millions of people. It was obvious he couldn't function during these episodes. Wasn't it?

What was left to do?

Of course, Kyler could've said the same thing when Ben had come to ask him a special favor. . . .

Ben closed his eyes. He would not give up on the man. But he needed to talk to him. And he needed a minute to think. To plan. To come up with . . . something.

Because if he didn't come up with something fast, something new, something unexpected, there was no question about how the vote would go. Not only was Ben certain that the president would be removed if the vote were taken at that moment, but he suspected it would be unanimous.

Part Three

The President's Defense

31

"I'm telling you, I won't talk!"

Seamus had to stifle his laughter. Harold Bemis was clenching shut his eyes and mouth and standing rigid as a stick. He looked like nothing so much as a little boy who was determined to hold his breath till he passed out.

Seamus saw security arriving through a back entrance. Better late than never. He pulled out his ID and waited.

"Are—are you going to waterboard me? Then take those awful pictures?"

"It might come to that," Seamus said. "But for the moment, I think I'm content to extract information from your cell phone."

"What? How?"

Seamus pulled up the last text message Bemis had received and saw that the number was blocked. No surprise there. He checked the recent cell activity on the phone. Bemis had received a lot of blocked-number texts in the past few weeks. But the four that had come today were local, and a few knowledgeable taps into the inner workings of the phone showed Seamus that they had a different point of origination than the others.

Because today, Seamus surmised, Ishmael was at the base firing the missiles according to Colonel Zuko's orders.

The security officers started barking questions. That lasted about five seconds, until Seamus flashed his badge and demonstrated that they were not the top-ranking officers on the premises. He didn't like to be rude, but he was working under a deadline and he simply had no time for rent-a-cops, especially not ones who took about twice as long to react to a dangerous scene as they should have done.

"I've got to get out of here. Call my office when you're ready to write your reports."

"Yes, sir. We'll secure the crime scene."

"Right. Oh, except—" Seamus crouched down by the inert body of the man who had tried to kill him—and yanked his car keys out of the back of his neck. "I'll need these."

The security cops stared at him, their mouth gaping.

Seamus left the two suspects in their care and started back toward the street, hauling Arlo behind him.

"How do you know where the base is?" Arlo asked, walking fast, trying to keep up.

"I don't. Yet. But I will." He punched a few buttons on Bemis's phone. Someone picked up on the first ring. "Zira?"

"I'm here, Seamus. Have you found the base?"

"Almost. Two things first. Do you have a fix on my location?"

"Of course." Like everyone else in the Agency, Seamus had a cell phone equipped with a homing device that allowed the central office to track him at all times.

"Good. I just left two suspects about two hundred feet behind me in a Macy's department store. One is the computer genius who's been conspiring with the enemy. The other is muscle. Gun muscle, anyway. You might want to send some boys over to interrogate them. Although the muscle may be dead. I'm not really sure."

"Seamus, what in—"

"And I don't think the geek knows anything," he continued, ignoring her. "But it never hurts to try."

"Seamus, so help me, if you've done anything—"

"I haven't. Honest." He had to smile. Tweaking Zira was his only pleasure in this otherwise grim day. "But here's what I need you to do.

I'm calling you now on the geek's phone. Get a lock on the signal and look up his calling records. Someone has texted him four times today. The calling number was blocked. But I know you can get around that."

"In a New York minute." She began barking orders to some underling nearby.

"Can they do that?" Arlo asked while they walked.

"Which? Hack into a private citizen's phone records, or pierce the veil to learn who made a given call? Doesn't matter. Either way, they can." And the NSA does it a lot more than we do, he wanted to add. But some family secrets were best kept private.

By the time they reached the car, Zira had an answer for him. "The phone was purchased at a convenience store. We're triangulating on its signal to find its current location." She paused. "It's in northern Maryland."

"Got it."

"Call me as soon as you know something?"

"Always." He snapped the phone shut and slid behind the wheel. Arlo hopped into the passenger side.

"Um, look, kid . . . I think this is where you get off."

"What? No way."

"You've been helpful, finding Bemis and all. But this next stop is likely to be dangerous. I can't bring a civilian into it."

"I saved your life."

"And I appreciate what you've done—but not enough to let you get killed at the next stop."

"But what if you need me to identify some computer gizmo or something?"

"Like what?"

"I don't know. What kind of stuff do international terrorists usually have?"

Seamus smiled. "Get out, kid. I'll send you a postcard when it's all over."

"I refuse."

"Don't make me get rough."

"What if this isn't the base? What if you need to track down another computer geek?"

Seamus craned his neck. "Well . . ."

"It's possible."

"It's . . . remotely possible." He frowned, then put the car into drive and pulled out into the light traffic. "All right. You can stay. But you do everything I tell you to do."

"Got it."

"Most important, this time, when I tell you to stay in the car, you actually stay in the goddamn car!"

"Got it!" Arlo said, holding up his hands. "I understand. Completely!"

"Good." Seamus turned down a side street. He knew a shortcut that might get them to their destination ten minutes earlier. Especially since traffic wasn't bad.

"So," Arlo asked, "what are you going to do when you get there?"

Seamus shrugged.

"Right. You make it up as you go along. But if these people are launching missiles and hiding from the government, don't you think the place will be guarded?"

"I can handle guards."

"What about alarms? Motion detectors? Laser webs?"

"Been there, done that."

"Ugly men with big guns? More than you can take down at once?"

Seamus gave him a fierce look. "I'm bringing in the people who blew up my man's memorial. Before they can do something even worse. No matter what it takes." He paused, then turned his eyes back to the road. "Even if I have to die in the process."

32

Admiral Cartwright had granted Ben what was possibly the most generous gift he had ever received in his entire professional career: five minutes. From the fewer than forty they had left.

He joined Kyler in the briefing room. He had never expected to be in a position to woodshed the president of the United States, but that's what it had come to.

"You need to level with me," Ben said. "What's going on?"

President Kyler held up his hands helplessly. "I just don't know!"

"Do you know what brings these episodes on?"

"If I did, don't you think I would've done something to prevent it?"

"Do you remember what happened when they're over?"

"Sort of. In a hazy way. Almost as if I were recalling a dream. Something that seems almost real but isn't."

"Was Sarie lying?"

"I don't think so." He lowered his eyes. "I don't have any reason to believe so."

"Her account is pretty much the way it happened?"

"Yes," he said quietly.

"So you remember sitting on the roof talking about offing yourself on live television, but it never occurred to you that maybe you ought to get some help?"

"The president does not have the option of just getting help!" he exclaimed. "The president can't do anything without a hundred different people knowing. A thousand! I can't even get a prescription without it going through a dozen desks, and then they have to buy it under at least three assumed names so no one is sure what exactly, if anything, went to me. And there's a reason for that. Do you know what would happen to my standing in the world community if these medical issues came to light? Or what would happen to my chances for reelection?"

Ben was frustrated, but he supposed it was true. The president lived on display, and there was nothing he could do without someone somewhere seeing.

"All right, look. We'll try another approach. This business about you and Zuko—I don't believe for a minute that you're motivated by some idiotic executive alpha-male arm-wrestling match."

"Well, thank you for that, anyway."

"So what is it? Why are you being so hardheaded about Kuraq?"

Kyler drew in his breath. "The United States cannot give in to terrorists, even if they are the leaders of a powerful nation. If we start that, in no time—"

"Will you stop already?" Ben said. "I've already heard the standard line. I'm bored to tears with it. I don't believe you would put so many lives at risk over a matter of principle. That isn't the man I voted for, the one who talked about global peace and a new world order. There has to be something more."

No response.

"Well?"

Kyler's voice was quiet. "Those people who went down in the helicopter . . . deserve to be rescued."

"No one doubts that. But your best chances would be with a small razor-sharp task force. You don't need to send in every battalion you've got stationed out there."

"There's more to it than you know."

"I realize that!" Ben shouted. He took a breath and reined his voice back in. For all he knew, he was audible in the adjoining room. "So tell me already!"

The president looked at him reluctantly.

"I know you don't want to do this," Ben said. "Do you want to remain president? Because if you do, you need to tell me everything."

"You—you don't know what you're asking of me, Ben."

"No," Ben said, looking directly into his eyes, "I don't. But I know this: it's your only chance."

When Ben opened the door leading to the main room of the bunker, the buzz inside instantly disappeared.

Are we back in grade school? he wondered as he and the president entered. They gossip behind your back, then go all hush-hush when you return. Pretty soon someone's going to suggest that the president has cooties.

"Right on schedule," Cartwright said, glancing at the clock. "That's the way I like it. Are you ready to proceed with your defense, Mr. Kincaid?"

"I am."

"Please call your first witness."

Ben nodded. "Let me say in advance that I beg the court's indulgence—and that of everyone else in the room. We haven't had a chance to prepare properly, obviously, and the next witness has no idea he's about to be called."

Several heads bopped up at attention. Who was he talking about? Could it possibly be me?

Ben let the suspense build for about a nanosecond. That was all the time he had to spare. "For our first witness, the defense calls Secret Service agent Max Zimmer."

The people sitting at the table were surprised, even astonished—but there was no reaction from Zimmer, who was still sitting at the communications station, tapping on his terminal keyboard.

Ben realized he was still wearing his headphones, sucking in intel from the outside world. He hadn't heard that he had been chosen.

Ben walked over to him and pulled off the headset. Zimmer instantly whirled around, an angry expression on his face, his hand on the barrel of his weapon.

"Keep it in the holster, Shane." Ben smiled sheepishly. "You've been called to the witness stand."

Zimmer looked at him as if he were some strange species of bug. "Me?"

"I'm afraid so."

"I don't know anything."

"Then it shouldn't take long."

Zimmer shook his head emphatically. "I'm sorry, Ben, but I have to monitor the situation outside. We've got a crisis situation here."

"Can't one of the other agents handle it? At least for ten minutes or so?"

Zimmer clearly was not happy about this.

"We know this is an inconvenience," Cartwright said, "but this proceeding is of the utmost importance, so I would appreciate it if you would cooperate—immediately."

Zimmer frowned, then snapped his fingers. "Gioia?"

Another agent snapped to attention.

"Take over. You've got a direct feed from the CIA, the NSA, Homeland Security, our embassy in Saudi Arabia, the disaster relief team at the Mall, and about a dozen other operatives."

"Understood," Gioia replied.

"If anything of interest happens, or any significant intel is uncovered, I want to know about it immediately."

"You will, sir."

"Thank you." Still frowning, Zimmer smoothed out his suit, tucked in his tie, and looked around the small room. "So where do I sit?"

Ben directed him to the makeshift witness stand. After he was sworn in, Ben got his personal details out as well as the essential points of his résumé. After spending some time overseas, including in Kuraq, hopping from one job to the next, he'd finally returned to the United States. He had been with the Secret Service, now a division of Homeland Security, for thirteen years.

"How long have you worked at the White House?"

"A little over four years. I was first brought in during the Blake administration to guard the First Lady. At her request. She and I had, um, known each other many years before. After her untimely assassination, I was assigned to the president."

Ben could see from the tiniest cloud in his eyes that the memory of the First Lady's murder—when he was on duty and guarding her—still stung. "And do you still hold that post today?"

"I do. The incoming president, Roland Kyler, was kind enough to retain me on his personal detail."

"Before we go any further, Agent Zimmer, let me ask you about politics. Do you approve of the president's political positions?"

"To be truthful, I don't know that much about them."

"You must absorb something from being around him so much."

"Not really. I try to stay out of the political fray altogether. My job is to protect the president, and I think I can do that most effectively if I remain uninvolved with political issues. My dedication can't waver depending upon what position he's taken on the latest hot spot or political issue. So I might as well not know."

"Surely you have some thoughts about his position on Kuraq. Do you approve of U.S. troops being deployed there?"

"Haven't really thought that much about it."

"Come on."

"I assume the commander in chief knows far more about it than I do and is in a better position to make a decision about such matters."

"But you lived in Kuraq for a time, did you not?"

"Yes."

"So you must have a good deal of insight about the country."

"That was a long time ago. Before Colonel Zuko came to power. It was a different country. A different Middle East. A different world."

"And I believe you indicated that while you were there, you lived with someone with whom you became . . . close."

Zimmer's eyes seemed to burn air in a direct line toward Ben's. "Yes."

"Have you remained in contact?"

"No."

"And that experience didn't leave you with any personal feelings regarding this nation?"

"No. Especially not when I'm on duty. I protect the president, period. Doesn't matter who or what he says or does. If the people elected a baboon, I'd protect him, too. That's my job."

Ben took a deep breath. He could see he wasn't going to get anything more just by pounding at the man. It was time to move in a different direction.

"How do you like working for President Kyler?"

"We haven't had any serious problems."

"Any minor ones?"

"Well, as I gather Sarie mentioned, he does have a bad habit of wandering off. That's never going to go down well with your Secret Service detail."

"I would imagine not."

"As far as we're concerned, any moment he's not in our sight is a moment he could be in a sniper's sights."

Yes, Ben thought, especially if he's sitting on the White House roof. "What have you done about this problem?"

"I sat him down—" He looked up at the president abruptly. "I mean, with his permission. When time permitted. Because, of course, he's the boss. But we had a talk."

"What was said?"

"I told him why it was unsafe and unacceptable for him to continue using various and devious means to ditch his security detail. I told him that if he needed some privacy, that could be arranged in a secure fashion. But a rogue president running amok just wasn't going to work."

Ben would've loved to have been present for that conversation. "Was the meeting productive?"

"Very. He finally told me why he had been disappearing."

"Why?"

Zimmer squirmed slightly. "I don't think we need to go into that. It's not relevant. The point is, once I knew what it was about, it was easy to arrange some privacy for him in a safe manner."

Swinburne jumped up. "I object, judge. That question was posed by the defense lawyer to a friendly witness. It needs to be answered."

Cartwright harrumphed. "The witness will answer the question."

"No," Zimmer said. "Actually, I won't."

"Agent Zimmer, you swore an oath to this court."

"I realize that. But I also swore an oath when I joined the service. I won't reveal the confidences of those I'm protecting. Goes against the very nature of the job."

Ben knew Swinburne wouldn't be satisfied with that. "Can you at least give us a hint what this was about?"

Zimmer appeared supremely uncomfortable, but he eventually answered the question. "Suffice to say that there were times when the president wanted to . . . do things . . . without his wife knowing about it."

33

Ben's lips parted. Damn. That wasn't what he'd been expecting at all. The president was sneaking around on his wife? It sounded as if the president was doing something unlikely to endear him to anyone.

Ben decided the best thing he could do was to ignore it and move on.

"Agent Zimmer, I know the vice president is keenly interested in whether the president has engaged in any unusual behavior, so I'll just save him the trouble by asking you myself." Meaning that if this incriminating testimony had to come out—and it did—Ben would rather it happened while he was in control of the examination. If Swinburne tried to delve back into it later, he could object on the grounds that the question had been asked and answered. "Have you observed any unusual behavior by the president?"

"On occasion, though nothing like what we saw earlier today in the bunker. Very mild by comparison."

"Such as what?"

Zimmer reflected for a moment. "I recall one evening he got a call on his private cell. He didn't say but I assume the call was from his daughter, Jenny. He didn't give the details, but it sounded as if she were in some kind of trouble. After the call ended, he began talking about how he had failed as a father. He was very emotional about it."

It was a strange business, almost comic, Ben thought, listening to a man testify virtually without emotion about someone else being emotional. "Did he seem despondent?"

"I suppose. He thought he had failed in the parenting arena. I didn't know what to tell him. I've never had children. Don't know anything about it."

"Did he talk about killing himself?"

"No, no. Nothing like that."

Thank God. "Any talk about flying? I mean, without an airplane."

"No. Never. He talked about losing his freedom—but who wouldn't? The president lives on public display, with vultures circling around waiting for him to make the smallest slip. It's no life for anyone. I wouldn't want it."

Yes, but the vice president does. Which was why we're here. "Any other instances of unusual behavior?"

"Not really. Well, unusual is a matter of opinion, I suppose. There was that one conversation about streaking."

Ben blinked. "Streaking?"

"Yes. I was the only agent in earshot. We were making our way across the south lawn. And he mentioned that he would like to rip off his clothes, unchain himself from the suit and tie, and race stark naked across the lawn."

"I see. Did you think he was serious?"

"Not at first. But he wouldn't let it go. He continued talking about how freeing it would be, how he'd like to just take off and feel nature embracing him. He started rubbing his hands all over himself, getting this euphoric expression on his face. Tugging at his necktie."

"Did you find this disturbing?"

Zimmer shrugged. "All in a day's work."

"And did he in fact remove his clothing?"

"Nah. I talked him out of it. I reminded him that out on the lawn, it was impossible to know who might have a cell phone camera at the ready. The last thing any president needed was to be up on YouTube stark naked, showing the whole world his shortcomings."

Ben bit down on his lower lip. So the stoic Secret Service man did have a sense of humor after all. That was good to know.

"Any other remarkable incidents?"

"No. And honestly, I don't know how remarkable those are. I've seen some seriously weird stuff go on at the White House in my time. I think it's inevitable when you live in a goldfish bowl like the president does. And the First Lady. And really, the entire White House staff."

"So there was never a time when you thought the president might be insane?"

"Absolutely not. Though I'm not sure I would find that particularly remarkable. I think it's a miracle anyone can put in four years at this job without going insane."

"And you've never observed any behavior that made you think the president might be incapable of performing his duties?"

"No. To the contrary, even on the days when I observed the incidents I just recalled, I saw him functioning very well."

"Have you observed any pattern or frequency to these odd incidents?"

"Not really." He pondered a moment. "I guess, now that you mention it, both of the main incidents I described occurred just after he returned."

"Returned? From what?"

"From one of those . . . privacy moments I mentioned."

Ben was perplexed. Was the man meeting an intern in a private room while his wife wasn't looking? Ben could see where that might stress him out. In which case, why didn't he stop?

"Your honor," Ben said, "could I have a moment to confer with my client?"

"Didn't you just do that? I gave you five full precious minutes."

"I need more. Just one minute will do."

"I'm sorry, Mr. Kincaid. In another world I'd probably say yes. But we just can't afford all these time-outs. Please proceed."

Ben looked at the president and hoped he could read minds. The message he was sending was: Write me a note. Explain. Unfortunately, his telepathy must be waning, because the president did not begin writing.

He would have to proceed in the dark.

"Agent Zimmer, have there been any other occasions when the president took you into his confidence?"

Unlike the other witnesses, Zimmer was not bashful about looking where he wanted to look. On this occasion, he was looking at the president.

He was seeking permission.

This message the president seemed to understand. He gave a firm nod. Zimmer returned it, though the expression on his face was grim.

"And," Zimmer said, "you understand the consequences?"

It took Ben a moment to realize Zimmer was talking to the president, not him. Swinburne was slow on the uptake, too. He was just getting ready to object when the president answered.

"Do it."

Zimmer directed his next comments to Ben. "Yes, there was one such occasion."

"Can you tell us what happened, please?"

"The president contacted me because he wanted to arrange a visit with an individual living in Pennsylvania. A man named Abe Malik. It was a weekend trip, sandwiched between two speaking engagements."

Sarie sat up straight. It was obvious she hadn't known anything about this.

"Was there a reason he couldn't just arrange it in the normal fashion through his chief of staff?"

"Yes. He wanted it to be private. In fact, he didn't want anyone to know about it."

"Is that so hard?"

"For the president, yes. Remember, Air Force One carries reporters with it. They would notice an unexpected detour to Pittsburgh."

"So how did you manage it?"

"After his second speaking gig, which was only about a hour away from where he wanted to go, we put an agent who resembled him into Cadillac One—the president's usual car—and put President Kyler in another car almost equally well protected but not quite so high-profile. The press were told he'd gone out to do some shopping for his wife. When he finished with his meeting, he returned to Air Force One and no one was the wiser."

"Did you accompany the president on this journey?"

"Of course. Anytime he's out in public, I'm with him."

"So did you learn where he was going?"

"I already knew where we were headed. That was a condition of the arrangement. We had to check out the individual in advance. And we had to do a security sweep of his apartment, where the meeting took place."

"What was the reason for the meeting?"

Zimmer inhaled, then slowly released the air through his teeth. "The president wanted to talk him out of joining the Red Cross."

"But hasn't the president been an ardent supporter of the Red Cross?"

"So I gather."

"Why did he want to talk anyone out of joining?"

"The president felt the assignment was too dangerous. Mr. Malik was planning to travel to one of the world's most treacherous hot spots. The Middle East."

"The president wanted to keep him out?"

"Exactly. But his arguments were unavailing. Mr. Malik departed the next day. We tracked his progress as long as possible—till he was beyond our supervisory range."

"Once he was overseas?"

"Yes. At that point, he was beyond Secret Service supervision. But I wouldn't be surprised to hear that the CIA was asked to keep an eye out."

It was time to bring everyone else up to speed. Ben asked the critical question.

"Why was the president so concerned for the safety of this one individual?"

"Isn't it obvious? You've heard what was centermost in his mind. How often he lamented that he had been a poor father."

"What are you saying?"

Zimmer folded his hands in his lap. "I'm saying that, according to the president himself, Abe Malik is his son."

34

Judging from the astonished reactions in the room, Ben surmised that Agent Zimmer had done a very good job of keeping the president's secrets. "How can the president have a son that no one knows about?"

"A few people know. His wife. His daughter, Jenny. Me. Maybe a handful of others. He's several years older than Jenny. I gather it was a pregnancy in a prior relationship, before he was married."

So the president had an illegitimate son. A surprise—but did anyone really care these days? Sarah Palin's daughter had had a baby out of wedlock, but that didn't seem to stir up much controversy. Would this? Or would it just be passed off as a youthful indiscretion?

"Did Abe Malik join the Red Cross?"

"He did. He was a pilot, and they always need more experienced pilots. He was posted to the Middle East, as planned, where he ran several emergency supply runs of food and medicine. Most recently, he was piloting runs to the beleaguered people in the Benzai Strip."

"And where is he now?" Ben asked.

"Haven't you guessed?" Zimmer spread wide his hands. "He was flying the helicopter. The one that went down in Kuraq. The one the president has sent troops in to rescue."

At last it all began to make sense. Everyone was talking at once, barely bothering to whisper.

Cartwright pounded on the table. "I will ask again that everyone please remain quiet so that we can proceed. Our time is running out!"

The din slowly subsided.

Surely now, Ben thought, people would understand why the president was determined to send troops into Kuraq—and why he wouldn't back off and abandon the people who went down in the helicopter. Even when the missiles were pointed at his head, how could anyone expect him to abandon his own son?

Ben glanced down at the president. His head was hung, his eyes were downcast. Ben had brought out the testimony they needed if they were to have any chance of salvaging this presidency. But it had come at an enormous cost. His secret was out. And his powers of judgment were still in dispute.

Ben didn't know if Kyler was making the correct foreign policy decision or not, but he knew this: it was not insane to want to protect your own son. Zimmer had provided a perfectly sane motive for the president's decisions. And right or wrong, that was what they needed to keep him in office.

"I have no more questions," Ben said. "Pass the witness."

"Very well," Cartwright said. "Mr. Swinburne, it's your turn."

Swinburne skittered back to the table. He seemed eager to proceed. If this new development had caught him by surprise—and Ben was certain it had—he was adjusting admirably.

"Agent Zimmer," he began, "are you familiar with the Twenty-fifth Amendment?"

"Well, I've heard a lot about it since you showed up."

"Are you familiar with its provisions?"

"Not really."

"Basically, it provides for the removal of the president when he is rendered incapable. We primarily think about that in terms of situations involving death and disease, but those aren't the only possible events that could cause a president to be rendered incapable."

Ben knew where this was heading and he didn't like it, though to be honest, the same idea had already occurred to him.

"Isn't it possible," Swinburne continued, "that the president could be so personally involved in a political scenario that he is unable to be objective?"

"I suppose that's theoretically possible," Zimmer said.

"In this instance, we now know that the president's actions have at least in part been motivated by the fact that his only son is currently behind enemy lines. How is it possible that would not influence his decision making?"

"That's not for me to say, sir."

"But you must see how having a child at risk would skewer your thinking process."

"I've never had children, sir. I wouldn't know."

"Even if you haven't had children yourself, you must see my point. Couldn't his own personal ties to the crisis leave him incapable of dealing with it in a rational manner? Or make him susceptible to improper influence—especially if Zuko captures his son?"

"Objection," Ben said. "This whole line is inappropriate. Mr. Zimmer is a Secret Service agent, not a constitutional scholar."

"I think that point is well taken," Cartwright said. "Sustained."

"I'm not asking him to render a legal opinion," Swinburne said. "I want him to tell us, based upon his own personal observations of the president, whether he believes that the man can be objective when his son is in the line of fire."

"I have never seen anything that suggested to me that the president is incapable of fulfilling his duty, not in this situation or any other."

"Well, what about that streaking business? Was that just par for the presidential course?"

Zimmer shrugged. "It's not the strangest thing I've ever seen."

"Do you think the country would be well served by a naked president?"

"If I may remind you," Zimmer said with admirable calm, "he didn't do it."

"But he might've. You thought he was going to."

"That was my first impression. That changed later. But what does it matter? He didn't."

"Next time he might."

"Next time *you* might. Who knows? None of us can predict the future."

"I can assure you I won't be streaking. At least not until I lose thirty pounds." Nice attempt, but things had become too dark for anyone to appreciate humor. "The president has become utterly unpredictable. Talking about streaking and flying and . . . killing himself in disturbing ways. Sneaking off on secret assignations. And keeping secrets from the American public, secrets about his own family."

"I suspect President Kyler is not the first president who wanted to keep his family secret."

"Yes, but the others didn't. They faced up to the truth and took whatever hits came from honesty. President Kyler chose to hide."

"I don't know why he decided to keep his son in the closet. And I don't think you do, either."

"I think it's obvious. He had an illegitimate child whom he abandoned. Why else would he not acknowledge what had happened?"

"As I said, I don't know."

"Has he had any other contact with Mr. Malik?"

"Not to my knowledge."

"How did he learn that Malik was planning to join the Red Cross?"

"I don't know. But I suspect the message was transmitted by his daughter. As I said, she knows about Malik, and I believe they stay in contact."

"I would think most fathers would be proud to have their sons join the Red Cross."

"The president said he would support his participation in missions to any other part of the world. Just not the Middle East. President Kyler knew that the region was unstable, and about to get worse. Which proved correct."

"Wouldn't that be the time to acknowledge his son to the world? When he's about to make such a noble gesture?"

"I think it would be more complicated than that."

"How do you mean?"

"I believe this particular announcement would do critical damage to the president's support ratings—particularly in the South. And that consequently would erode his ability to lead."

"The South?" Swinburne took another moment. "Are you saying this son of his is of mixed race?"

"Exactly."

Swinburne took a step backward. The light was dawning. "So there would be immediate political consequences. Because the man is half African American."

Zimmer's head tilted to one side. "Uh . . . no."

"He's not part black?"

"No."

"But you said—"

"I'm sorry. I thought it was obvious. He's not of African descent." Zimmer paused just long enough to whet everyone's interest. "He's Middle Eastern."

Swinburne's jaw dropped so low it almost thudded against the floor. "Middle Eastern? His son is from the Middle East?"

"Well, his son's mother was." Zimmer frowned, glanced at the president, then added: "To be specific—she's Kuraqi."

35

Seamus sped down the highway toward a remote location in rural
Maryland. They were still near enough to D.C. that the traffic
from fleeing Washingtonians complicated travel, as did Zira's erratic
come-and-go information.

They had managed to triangulate on the cell phone's signal to determine its location. The signal was emitted, however, only when the
phone was turned on, and the user was apparently turning it on only
when he wanted to use it. He was probably savvy enough to know that
those times were when the phone was vulnerable, so he limited it as
much as possible. He probably did not count on the efficacy of the
CIA's latest Sidewinder triangulation program, which could track a cell
phone down in less than a tenth of the time it had taken the previous it-
eration.

Seamus pulled up beside what appeared to be an abandoned industrial plant of some sort. Seamus knew that this was one of many.
The downturn in the economy had hit this part of the country particularly hard. The unkempt, weed-ridden lawn was enough to tell him
that this place was no longer in use—at least not in any official capac-

ity. Not doing any business the IRS would be notified about. At the far corner he spotted a broken sign: Barlow Bros. Manufacturing. He gave no clue what the plant had made.

"You stay here," he told Arlo as he unbuckled himself.

"Okay," Arlo replied.

Seamus gave him a narrow-eyed look. "I mean it. You stay right here. I'll give you the car keys. If you see any trouble, leave. In fact, if you see anyone at all, leave. Here's a number you can call if you need help. Do not leave this car under any circumstances."

Arlo took the number. "Okay."

"I'm not sure I believe you're taking this seriously. I am serious. This could be very dangerous. I want you to stay out of it. Do not leave this car."

"I said okay."

"Yes, but your eyes are saying, 'I helped him once. Maybe I can help him again.' "

"I don't know where you're getting that."

"I'm getting it from twenty years of field experience."

"Look, I have no desire to get hurt. I'm not going anywhere. You're on your own."

Seamus's eyes narrowed still further. "And you mean that? You won't leave the car?"

"Absolutely. You want me to pinky-swear?"

"That won't be necessary. Just don't leave the car." Seamus pushed himself out. His ribs still ached where he had taken the boot several times. But he blocked that out of his mind. He had to focus on the task at hand: figuring out what, if anything, was going on in there, and then figuring out how to stop it.

The building was so expansive he assumed that the base wouldn't use all of it. Even if they had the most elaborate James Bond–esque headquarters imaginable, it wouldn't take up half of this facility, and Arlo had told him that the satellite control operation he envisioned wouldn't require that much space at all. What he had to do was figure out where they were and then go in somewhere else.

He hung close to the building—so he couldn't be seen from the inside—and called Zira.

"I'm there. Have you got the heat readings?"

"Yes. I'm sending it to your cell."

Barely three seconds later, he had it. Another trick in the CIA magic show—one not many people knew about—was that the United States had satellites capable of zeroing in on any building in the country and using infrared imagery to get heat impressions of what was going on inside. Was this constitutional? Well, who knew? With the current conservative Supreme Court, almost anything the government wanted to do was potentially constitutional. For the time being, what mattered was that it told him where the heat was—where the people were. And at the moment they were primarily concentrated at the north end.

So he moved to the south.

"I don't get that much definition on my cell screen," Seamus said. "Can you tell how many there are?"

"Not to any degree of certainty. Looks like about ten people."

Which meant they outnumbered him by nine. At least.

"Do you want me to send in reinforcements?" Zira asked.

"Let's make sure this is the place first. But have them standing by."

"It's not as if I have a ready army, Seamus," Zira said. "We're dealing with several national crises here. I'll have to pull people away from their current assignments."

"Understood. If I need reinforcements, I'll let you know."

He closed the phone and approached the south wall.

He had two means of entry: a door and a window. The door would be suicide. Even if they were trying to keep their numbers small, he had to assume someone would be watching all the doors. The window might be unguarded, but entering by that means inevitably would be noisy and, well, he never liked to risk his neck on a "might."

So he decided to try the roof.

He found a planter on the back end of the building that brought him four feet off the ground. Standing on that, with a concerted leap he was able to pull himself up onto the roof, though his ribs ached from the strain.

He didn't have many advantages in this situation. In fact, the element of surprise might be his only one. And he couldn't even be sure about that. By now, they must have noticed that the thug he left back at the mall hadn't shown up with Harold Bemis. So they might well be on their guard.

Seamus hoped not.

If this were a movie, he reasoned, by now he would've spotted a curved air exhaust that led to an extensive network of ventilation shafts that would allow him to crawl anyplace in the building, overhear key information, and then penetrate their ranks and blow the whole operation sky-high. But here in real life, he had never yet seen a building with a passable network of ventilation shafts, and even if there were one somewhere, he probably couldn't fit inside it. He was limber and in good shape, but there were limits.

He did find a door. Presumably the top of the stairs. He'd have to settle for that.

A chain secured with a combination lock was wrapped around the door handle—something about sixteen times stronger than the screws holding the door handle to the door, or the door itself. They must've comforted themselves knowing how hard it would be to open that lock. He wouldn't even try. If he knocked the door handle off the door, he wouldn't have to worry about it.

And he didn't. Four well-placed kicks to the handle and it splintered away from the worn and warped door. Lesson to terrorists: invest in a good carpenter.

He quietly stepped inside, gun at the ready. It was dark, but he could see a thin shaft of light coming from below.

A few steps closer and he could see the floor. It looked like a concrete slab, not something you'd want to spend the day standing upon. The lighting was poor. It looked as if someone had strung a line of electric torches along the wall. They weren't making the place homey—just operational.

No guards. Well, none that he saw. That would probably change.

How many punches had he thrown since this day began? Too many. He didn't need to add to the running total. Even the best-toned knuckles gave out eventually.

He descended the stairs, clinging to the west wall, and made his way slowly toward the opposite end of the building. He knew it would be several minutes before he reached the source of all that heat. The building appeared to be divided into several large sections. Back in the days when the plant was operational, each had probably housed a different part of the manufacturing process. Now they were just empty spaces that the current occupants—or squatters—didn't seem to need. Seemed wasteful, but perhaps there were advantages to using buildings that didn't conform to what might be expected.

Seamus had sidestepped along the length of the building for almost four minutes before he heard the distant sounds of activity: a low-pitched drone that could be anything, or perhaps nothing. But he didn't think so.

He crouched down and, even more carefully than before, inched forward.

He could see light, not just the bare-bones light that suffused the rest of the building but bold, bright overhead light—the kind you would need where people were working. There was a door between him and the northmost end of the complex, and the closed door was probably stifling a lot of the sound.

He crept close to the door and pressed himself against it. Was it possible he could open it and sneak in there without being noticed? He didn't see anyone patrolling the hallway or watching the door. What should he do?

He could call Zira, but he still didn't know what was going on or if these were the people he was looking for. He didn't want to come out of this looking like an idiot. Of course, he didn't want to be drilled by terrorists, either.

What the hell. Slowly, as gently as possible, he turned the knob.

It was always possible that a door in a long-abandoned building might squeak, so he didn't open it any more than necessary. He released the knob, then slid through the narrowest opening he could get himself through. Then he closed the door behind him, just in case someone came along later.

He was inside.

The first thing he saw was the back of a row of computer equipment. Beyond that, he spotted a satellite dish, a large tactical display, and the tops of the heads of several computer operatives.

He recognized the tactical display. It showed the location and range of all the ballistic missiles controlled by the computer system Zuko had seized.

He had found the terrorist base camp.

36

In the midst of the tumult that followed this revelation, Ben wasn't sure what to think. Everyone was reacting, but it was perhaps more subdued than he might have imagined. Perhaps that was because it involved race—no one in politics wanted to be accused of racism. At the same time, there were obviously sound nonracist reasons for recognizing that these newly revealed relationships—a son born of a Middle Eastern mother—could cause political problems for President Kyler.

That was something Kyler would have to work out later. Ben's job at the present was to save his job, and the only way he could do that was by demonstrating that his policies in Kuraq were not insane. Prejudiced by personal feelings, perhaps, but not insane.

The president remained strangely phlegmatic. Calm was good, and far better than some alternatives. Ben just hoped it was a stable calm—not the prelude to another irrational outburst.

"Why wasn't I informed of this?" Secretary Ruiz asked. "How can I attempt diplomatic relations with this nation when the president has secret relationships with the citizens?"

"Do we have any reason to believe Colonel Zuko knows about

this?" Secretary Rybicki asked. "If he doesn't know, I don't see what difference it makes. You were a senator, Kincaid. You remember what Lincoln said: don't assume your enemy knows everything you do."

"Whether Zuko knows or not," the vice president insisted, "it compromises the president's ability to perform the functions of the office!"

"Are we doing closing arguments now?" Ben said. "Because I wasn't even clear that we were done with this witness."

Cartwright pounded on the table. His palm must be plenty sore by this time, Ben imagined. "I want everyone to stop talking—now!"

The buzz in the bunker diminished but did not subside.

"I know there have been some startling surprises today, but we simply do not have time for this babbling. So please, show the court that you can behave as the professionals you are."

The chatter evaporated. Cartwright turned toward Swinburne. "Are you done with this witness?"

"Just a few follow-up questions, judge. A few questions I imagine are on everyone's mind. Mr. Zimmer, is this mystery mother still in Kuraq?"

"I have no idea."

"You never asked?"

"It's none of my business."

"Is she living?"

"I don't know."

"Has the president ever visited her?"

"Not to my knowledge."

"Does Colonel Zuko know about this?"

"Honestly, sir, how would I know?" Zimmer looked as if he was reaching the limit of his tolerance. "I'm his Secret Service agent, not his priest. The only reason I know about his son's background is that I of course had to perform a background check before the meeting, and his connection to Kuraq came up with a red flag. I still don't know any of the details. And I don't particularly want to."

"Fine. It's clear enough that these relationships compromise the president's objectivity."

"If you keep previewing your closing," Ben said, "the cabinet will be bored of it before you actually deliver it."

Swinburne didn't blink. "I thank the defense attorney for his valuable trial strategy. No more questions of this witness."

"Very well. Agent Zimmer is dismissed."

Zimmer stepped down. He walked directly to the communications station and yanked the headphones off Agent Gioia's head.

"Thanks for the help. Now scram."

Gioia did as he was told.

"Anything else?" Cartwright asked. "Or are we done?"

"Just one more witness, I think," Ben said. "But I have to talk to my client first. It's absolutely essential. I promise to keep it brief."

"Kincaid, we don't have time."

"Your honor, please." Ben lowered his voice. "I need to ask if he's willing to testify."

President Kyler's back stiffened.

"He has a constitutional right to remain silent, as I'm sure the court knows. If he's going to waive it, it has to be an informed decision. I'm sorry for the delay, but it is essential to a fair trial."

Cartwright frowned. "Very well."

"Thank you, your honor."

President Kyler immediately stood and entered the adjoining room. Ben started to follow.

"Just a minute, Mr. Kincaid. I'm not finished."

Ben stopped. "Yes, your honor?"

"You've got three minutes. If you take any longer, we're going straight to verdict."

"Understood."

Cartwright touched a button on his watch. "Your time starts now."

Ben raced into the adjoining room—and was astonished by what he saw there.

After all the surprises this day had brought, why would such a little thing make any difference? And yet it did.

The president was smoking.

"Forgive me, Kincaid," he mumbled as he took a long draw on his cigarette. "I need something to relieve the stress."

"I don't doubt it. Look, I know this probably sounds awful, and to be fair, it could backfire on us—but I think you should take the stand in your own defense."

"Why? I thought Zimmer's testimony went well."

"I agree, but it wasn't enough. At best, he justified your decision regarding Kuraq. At worst, he showed you were too personally invested to be capable of performing your job properly. But in any case, what's really haunting our jury is your weird behavior—talking to portraits and threatening to kill yourself. And let's not forget that two of the cabinet members and the vice president witnessed your last episode personally. That will be very hard to put out of their minds."

"So how am I going to do it?"

"I have no idea. And I don't have time to preview and vet your testimony. I'm just going to have to put my faith in the fact that a smart man will think of something."

"And how do you know I'm smart?" he asked, blowing smoke into the air.

"Well, a stupid man isn't going to be elected president of the United States. With one or two exceptions."

When Ben returned to the main room, there were only twenty-five minutes remaining on the countdown clock. That left maybe ten minutes for this examination, maybe five or so for closings, and then the vote. That would barely leave time for the president to take charge—or the vice president to call back the troops, depending upon the outcome.

Best not to think about that. He needed to concentrate on the job at hand. He couldn't think of another time in his entire career when he had gone into the critical defendant's examination so blind. How ironic that it would occur on the occasion when he happened to be representing the most powerful man in the free world and his performance could have global consequences—could quite literally determine whether thousands of people lived or died.

"Mr. President, I'm going to skip all the discussion about your professional background and qualifications. I assume everyone here knows who you are and pretty much knows where you've been."

"A fair bet."

"So without wasting any more time, let's get down to the heart of the matter. Is there any reason—medical or otherwise—you are incapable of executing your duties as president?"

To his credit, the president smiled a little bit at Ben's bluntness. "No, there is not."

"Are you sure about that? Because the vice president undoubtedly will suggest that a mentally ill man is not aware of his own condition."

"I'm about as self-aware as anyone on earth, I would imagine. In this business, you have to be. If I were crazy, I'd be the first to know. And I'd resign on my own and this proceeding would not be necessary.

But the truth is, I'm not, and this whole business is nothing but a trumped-up power grab by a party or parties with an opposing point of view on a complex matter of foreign policy."

Wow. Ben liked the sound of that. He made a mental note to steal that for his closing. "You're aware, sir, that the prosecutor has put on eyewitness testimony regarding unusual behavior attributed to you. And some of us have even witnessed it."

"Yes, I know."

"Can you explain?"

"I'm not sure what there is you think I need to explain. Here's the reality: I'm not as boring as everyone thinks I am. Or as some people want the president of the United States to be. I'm a free spirit, which is admittedly an oddity in the world of politics. I'm eccentric. Always have been. I don't think there's anything wrong with that. Sure, that's not the side I show when the cameras are rolling. But in the privacy of my home or my office, what's the harm? Not every president has to be the same stuffed shirt."

Ben pondered for a millisecond. He liked the approach the president was taking. It would appeal to all who considered themselves non-conformists, which was more or less everyone. But was it enough to cover some of the behavior the cabinet had heard described? Not on its own. Even though he hated to bring it all up again, they would have to delve into the details.

"I understand what you're saying," Ben replied, "but I'm not sure how it applies to some of the incidents we've heard about today. For instance, Sarie told us—"

"Sarie is a wonderful woman," the president said, interrupting. Technically, he should wait for the question before answering it, but no one was going to object to any attempt to move things along. "Efficient, organized, and on occasion ruthless. But she's also somewhat emotional. And conventional. She is disturbed by the slightest deviation from schedule. Nothing wrong with that. It's part of what makes her a great chief of staff. But it does influence her opinions. She is readily thrown when people are anything but perfectly conventional."

Out the corner of his eye, Ben saw Sarie's brow crease. It was probably hard for her to hear him speak these words. But of course, her testimony had not been a picnic for the president to hear, either.

"Sarie recounted three specific incidents," Ben recalled. "The first had you chatting with portraits hanging on the wall."

The president smiled. "Which was grossly exaggerated, and besides, talking to pictures is not a crime or a sign of mental illness. Let's have a show of hands. How many people in the room have ever talked to themselves? That would be everyone, whether you admit it or not. This was no different. Now, if I expected the portraits to answer, that would be bad. But I didn't. I was just speaking my thoughts out loud, basically."

"She said you were asking the portraits . . . philosophical questions."

"My recollection is that I did it once. Maybe twice. So what? I've long been a student of the U.S. presidents, and I'm interested in how they dealt with crises such as contracting polio, and in how a purportedly devout Roman Catholic reconciled his marital indiscretions with his faith. And I vocalized those thoughts while I was looking at the pictures. To me, that's no different from looking at yourself in the mirror and thinking out loud. I'd be willing to bet that even Sarie Morrell does that."

Ben marveled, not for the first time, at the vast power of a good orator. President Kyler, like other presidents before him, was a great communicator. His calm and measured accounts were almost eradicating the incriminating images formed by Sarie's earlier testimony. If he kept this up, they might just have a tiny chance of success.

"Ms. Morrell also recounted an incident involving you skinny-dipping in the White House pool."

President Kyler tucked in his chin. "Well now, that episode was embarrassing for the both of us. The only difference was that I tried to keep cool, while she just about lost it."

"Were you in fact swimming naked?"

"Yes, and what's wrong with that? Lots of people do it. It's my pool, for Pete's sake. I can swim in my birthday suit if I want. It's not as if anyone was there, or invited in there. I didn't ask Sarie to track me down. That was her idea. And she inexplicably hung around even after she saw that I was not dressed. If there was any odd behavior, in my opinion, it was hers."

"Have you done this on other occasions?"

"Yes. I like it. Haven't you ever swum nude?"

"I don't have a pool."

"Ever gotten into a hot tub naked?"

"No."

The president smiled. "What was I thinking? You're Ben Kincaid. You probably don't even get into the bathtub naked."

"Well . . ."

"Most people I know who own hot tubs don't bother with the swimsuit. You heard Sarie talk about guys swimming in the buff at the Y. That's how it was in my hometown, too. It's very cleansing. Supposed to be good for you. And at any rate, there's nothing wrong with it. Granted, if I had sought out Sarie while naked, that would not be acceptable. But that's not what happened."

"Is this something you've done on other occasions?"

"Of course. My whole life long. Why not? Here's what you need to understand about me. Even though I've been in politics for a good while, I have always been able to maintain some measure of a private life. Until now. These past four months have required an incredible adjustment from me. Even when I was governor, I didn't have this kind of transparent existence. I keep struggling to find opportunities to be myself, to express myself, to enjoy some personal freedom. But between the press, the Secret Service, and Sarie, that has become almost impossible. And that is very frustrating for me."

Nicely done, Ben had to admit. This examination, which he had expected to be supremely difficult, was almost effortless. He pitched softballs and the president knocked them out of the park. Could they really rehabilitate the president's reputation? Or was this just the calm before the storm?

He glanced up at the monitor to try to gauge the reaction of the all-important cabinet members. For the most part, they weren't showing whatever thoughts were buzzing around in their brains. But they were paying attention.

Something still troubled Ben, though.

None of the others could see it. They were too far away or sitting at the wrong angle. But Ben could tell. He could see the telltale movement in the upper leg. And when Ben "inadvertently" dropped a page of his hastily scribbled notes, he confirmed it.

The president's feet were tap-dancing again.

If he had started that, what would he do next?

37

"Sarie brought up one more incident, Mr. President. Perhaps the strangest of them all. It involved you up on the roof of the White House, a purported attempt to fly, and threats to kill yourself. What really happened?"

The president sighed heavily. "Well, you're right about one thing, Ben. That one was very different from the others. Very different indeed."

"Please explain."

"I suppose, at the end of the day, it does reveal an error in judgment on my part. Not insanity, to be sure. But a mistake. I thought I could trust Sarie Morrell."

Across the table, Ben saw Sarie's lips part. The sadness on her face was palpable. Ben keenly regretted this. He genuinely liked Sarie and thought she was the shining light in an otherwise middling staff. But her testimony had been damaging to the president. If he was going to win this trial, he was going to have to confront what she said head-on.

"Please explain."

"Let me say one thing up front. I don't blame her. She didn't want to testify. But when she did, she revealed things that were told to her in confidence, and honestly, if a president can't trust his own chief of staff, who can he trust? Apparently, no one."

Sarie looked as if she had been stabbed by a butcher knife, but the president continued.

"Yes, I went out on the roof. I was desperate for some privacy. Some time to myself, something I never seem to get. Don't you like to be alone occasionally? I think everyone wants some alone time every now and again. But I never get it, not unless I make it. So I ditched my keepers and climbed out on the roof. But I was there less than ten minutes when, what do you know, here comes Sarie, hunting me down. I was furious. I will admit I acted a little weird. But I did it purposely. I did it because I wanted her to leave."

"Did it work?"

"Hell, no. The weirder I got, the more determined she seemed to stick with me. It was a lose-lose scenario. Yes, I talked about flying. Who hasn't dreamed of flying, of just taking off and going wherever you want? Up, up, and away, right? I even pantomimed it a bit. But I didn't plan to do it. Why Sarie ever thought I might—well, who knows? I think she had already made up her mind that I was nuts. Or perhaps just too much trouble. At any rate, she told me she was done. Through. She was resigning."

The creases in Sarie's brow deepened. Ben wasn't sure if that meant she remembered doing this or didn't.

"How did you respond to that?"

"I tried to talk her out of it, of course. I told her we all get despondent at one time or another. That's when the topic of suicide arose. I confessed that on occasion I've had dark thoughts of doing dark things. I think that's universal. We all have that blackness at the heart of our soul. I was trying to comfort her, to bolster her spirits. Isn't it ironic, then, that she takes the words that were offered to help her and turns them into a weapon? Her desire to quit becomes my desire to die."

"Are you in fact suicidal?"

"Not in the least. Not even in my worst moments. Not even when I desperately want to be alone. Not even now. There were times when I was a kid when I may have entertained such thoughts—when a girl dumped me, or after rereading *Romeo and Juliet*. But it wasn't serious. And now I'm a mature grown-up and there's just no chance."

"Not even during a press conference?"

"I don't know where that bit came from. I don't recall saying anything like that. But to answer your question: no, not during a press conference. Or anywhere else. Absolutely not."

"You're sure?"

"Do I look suicidal? Honestly, if most people had to go through a day like today has been for me, I think they'd be doing a lot worse than singing sitcom songs. But I've been in politics a while now. I'm used to it. They can't get to me, not the real me. I have no reason to want to die."

"And since you mentioned the singing . . ."

"Thank you," President Kyler said eagerly. "I wanted to talk about that. I mean, forgive me for saying so, Mr. Vice President—but when did you become such a self-righteous, pompous ass?"

Cartwright leaned forward. "The witness will address his comments to the court and the jury. Not the prosecutor."

If the president heard this at all, there was no sign of it. "If I want to sing, I will damn well sing. It's a great way to relieve tension. Who hasn't sung in the shower? Sung along to their iPod when they're driving. There's nothing wrong with it."

"Your choice of song was somewhat . . . eccentric."

"So what? I like that song. In fact, I *love* that song. I'll sing it if I damn well please. Even the president needs a little something, some kind of release, every now and again. As long as I keep it out of the public eye, there's nothing wrong with it. And it's no one else's business." He paused, drew up his shoulders. "I'm the president of the United States, people. If I want to kick back and get silly, I will."

"And you have no trouble returning to business afterward."

"Absolutely not, and I haven't heard anyone testify that I did. Even Sarie acknowledged that after these so-called episodes were over, I got back to business as usual. So what's the harm? Forgive me for saying so, but I think they're making a mountain out of a molehill. And if the vice president weren't so eager to rest his butt in the Oval Office, he'd see how flimsy this case really is."

Ben paused for a moment, pleased at how well the testimony was going. This was better than he would've thought possible. Even though he hadn't covered every single point Swinburne raised, he'd covered enough of them. The president had argued in favor of his right to express himself freely in private, and who would deny a president that? Like a brilliant trial lawyer, he had framed the issue in a manner that made it impossible for anyone to rule against him.

And in Ben's book, that meant it was time to move on. He had intentionally started with the "crazy" arguments. He thought the jury would be most interested in hearing about that, and he didn't want to finish on that note, with the president having to defend himself. Better to get it out of the way and end with something more positive.

But before he could do that, there was one more matter that had to be addressed.

"Mr. President, we've just heard Mr. Zimmer testify that you have a son, heretofore unknown to the general public. Is that true?"

The president blinked rapidly, then looked around the room, making eye contact with many of the people there. "Yes, it's true."

Many significant looks passed through the room as President Kyler offered this confirmation, but nothing like the shock that had registered earlier. In only a few minutes this had become yesterday's news.

"Please tell us what happened."

"Of course. But I have a request first. I have no way of enforcing this. But I will ask that everyone in this room please maintain the confidentiality that goes with being in the cabinet or on the White House staff. This has become relevant to this trial, and while I regret that, I accept it. But there is no reason why this needs to be made public, especially if I remain in office once this trial is over. So I respectfully request, out of respect for my wife and children, that you keep this to yourself."

"I'm sure everyone will honor your request," Ben said, expressing a confidence he did not feel. "Please proceed."

"My son's name is Abe. That's short for Abram, of course, a very popular name in the Middle East. I met his mother when I was very young and naive, just finishing up at the School of Government and Law at Yale. Tovah—that's his mother' s name—was in some of my classes. She was a cousin of the royal family in Kuraq, which is the only reason she was there. Although the ayatollah in charge at the time was running the government, he had allowed the royal family to remain intact for symbolic purposes. Not unlike the royal family in England— they don't actually have any power, but the government still keeps them around. Most women in Kuraq wouldn't even be educated, much less at Harvard. But her family's prestige gave her special privileges."

"And I assume you came to know her there."

"It took awhile. I was a bit shy around women back then—not a ladies' man like you, Ben."

Ben blinked.

"But she was beautiful, absolutely beautiful. The smoothest, creamiest complexion and elegant light brown skin. Lovely. I'd never seen anyone before who struck me as so gorgeous. So I spent about half the semester stuttering around her. But eventually I managed to ask her out."

"And?"

"We hit it off almost immediately. We had a lot in common—our idealism, our desire to serve our people, our devotion to education and political theory. But what was most intriguing was how we were different. I loved words; she loved numbers. I loved poetry; she preferred nonfiction. I liked rock and roll; she preferred classical. We didn't duplicate each other. We complemented each other." He shrugged. "Is it any wonder I fell in love?"

"And were these feelings of yours reciprocated?"

"Absolutely. We loved each other with an intensity that few people before or since have ever experienced. And out of that love was born a child."

"Abe Malik."

"Yes. Malik isn't his surname, but it is a family name. It's Arabic for 'strong.' "

"Why didn't you marry?"

"I wanted to. She refused. Remember, she was from Kuraq. And although she was determined to bear the child, a marriage to a Westerner would be impossible, at least if she ever intended to go back. And she did. She had great plans. She wanted to make the royal family relevant again, to bring her country out of that stagnant theocracy. And she couldn't do any of that with me."

"Did you ever see the child?"

"No. She gave birth in Kuraq, in secret. I was not allowed to visit. I didn't see him for almost twenty years."

"What happened then?"

"She returned to America. Her plans for her country never materialized. It was not the royal family that wrested power away from the ayatollah. It was Colonel Zuko."

"I see."

"And as you might imagine, he was not as comfortable with the royal family's presence as his predecessor had been. He didn't want any potential threats to his supremacy around. Like the rest of her family, she fled. She returned to America—this time with her son."

"Did she contact you?"

"She did, although it wasn't easy. I was governor by then, and not the easiest person in the world to contact privately. But she was always a very smart woman. I met her in secret. She had never married, never had any other children. She was devoted to Abe and her cause, nothing else. She had, I think, hoped that we might be able to . . . to pick up where we had left off. But it was impossible. I was married to Sophie by then—very happily, I might add. And I was in the public eye. No journalist had managed to tumble to Abe's existence yet. We decided it was best to keep it that way. And so we parted." He slowly exhaled. "I didn't see Abe again for several years. Not until she sent word that our son was planning to join the Red Cross."

"And that concerned you?"

"It concerned both of us. You can see why he wanted a posting near Kuraq. That's his heritage. But I knew Colonel Zuko was on the warpath. He had already begun the invasion of the Benzai Strip. I knew trouble was coming. I knew U.S. intervention was likely. And I didn't want my son in the middle of it. It was dangerous for anyone—but imagine if Zuko discovered Abe was his archenemy's son. Abe's life would be in constant jeopardy."

"I gather you were not able to talk him out of it?"

"No. He's very stubborn." The president's lips turned up slightly at the corners. "He probably gets that from me."

"Did you hear anything else from him thereafter?"

"Precious little. I had a few people watching out for him, but I didn't want to make a big deal about it. The fewer people who knew the truth, the better. I didn't know how the American people would respond to the revelation that I have a secret son, but the connection to Kuraq could make that very tricky. Very dangerous politically. I hadn't heard much about him for some time—until I saw the passenger manifest on that downed helicopter. And found his name there. As the pilot."

"So of course you prepared to bring in troops. To mount a rescue operation and secure the country."

Kyler nodded. "I like to think that I would have done that in any case. But yes, once I knew my son was in that helicopter, there really was no choice. Not for me. No choice at all."

"Just a few more questions, Mr. President. Do you regret your decisions regarding Kuraq?"

"Absolutely not. That man—Colonel Zuko—is dangerous. A serious threat to the nation, as today's events have proved. If we let him go unchecked, it will establish a precedent that quite literally could rip this country apart at the seams."

"The secretary of state has suggested that your failure to withdraw the troops, now that Zuko has control of some of our missiles, is insane. Do you agree?"

"Ruiz is a good man, but I've never been able to get him to see the big picture. Zuko may be able to do some damage with those missiles, and I regret that. But if he does, he will earn the enmity of the world community and the UN. He will find himself cut off, unable to function, and he knows this. I think he's trying to scare us—after all, that's what terrorists do. But it's brinksmanship, and I don't think he's stupid enough to take it too far. In the meantime, if we withdraw, we lose a good deal more than a marble monument and the people in that helicopter. Hundreds of thousands of people will be slaughtered in Benzai. I won't have that on my conscience."

The vice president rose to his feet. President Kyler raised his palm and continued before he could speak.

"Now, I am keenly aware that Vice President Swinburne has a different opinion. He's entitled. But differing with the vice president does not mean you're insane. Personally, I think caving in to terrorists is insane, but you'll notice I'm not trying to have him committed." His tone dropped a notch. "But I'm not going to let him have my job, either."

"Thank you, Mr. President," Ben said. "Your honor, I have no more questions for this witness."

Ben wiped his forehead. He hadn't realized it before, but he was sweating profusely. It wasn't the heat; this bunker was perfectly temperature-controlled. He had been under enormous pressure, trying to figure out how to salvage this administration. But the testimony had gone well—better than he'd dreamed, actually. If the president could only survive cross-examination . . .

Unfortunately, that was a huge if.

38

Vice President Swinburne cleared his throat, then began his cross.
"Are you seriously suggesting that there's something normal
about dissociative episodes in which you revert to infantilism?"

"Objection," Ben said instantly. "Argumentative."

Cartwright didn't wait for any explanations. "It's cross-ex, son. It
isn't supposed to be friendly."

"But—"

"The truth is," he said, pointing at the clock, "we don't have time
for minor-league objections. So unless Mr. Swinburne does something
so bad it threatens to induce heart failure, don't interrupt."

Ben sat down, frowning. Cartwright had just given Swinburne vir-
tual carte blanche to do whatever he wanted on cross. That could be all
too dangerous.

"What I said, I think," the president replied calmly, was that if I
wanted to sing a song, that was my right, and so long as I get my job
done, as I always have, it's no sign of insanity and none of anyone else's
business."

"Just as you apparently feel the members of your family are none of anyone's business. That you can ask people for their vote but don't need to tell them about your Middle Eastern son."

"Well, you're sort of right. I think my private life is my own. Everything about me does not have to be up on display just because I'm running for office."

"You don't think the public has a right to know?"

"Of course, that's the excuse journalists always use for prying into people's personal lives. Or they say it's a character issue, when it's really just gossipmongering."

"It is a character issue."

"No, it's an excuse for reporting tittle-tattle instead of reporting news."

"Are you seriously suggesting that the existence of an illegitimate son is not reflection on a candidate's character?"

"I think we all made mistakes when we were young."

"This is more than a mere mistake. You brought a human being into existence."

"And he's a fine boy. What's your point?"

Swinburne put his fists on his hips. "My point is that you know as well as I do that this son, if revealed, would cost you votes. That's why you kept him secret."

"I kept him secret? I barely knew anything about him until a few years ago. He has no desire to be a part of my life. I can sympathize with his desire not to live in a goldfish bowl. So I respected his desire for privacy."

"Which coincidentally dovetails nicely with your own political needs."

The president's words were becoming terse, overenunciated. He was getting angry—the worst possible attitude for a witness on cross. "I don't believe that most people are so shallow and judgmental they would change their vote based upon a mistake I made almost thirty years ago."

"But you weren't willing to take the risk, were you? That's why you kept him hidden."

"I've already explained that decision."

"Your honor," Ben said, "I know you're not looking for interruptions, but this line of questioning is not relevant. Although the vice president seems to be enjoying it, it does not pertain to the question of whether the president is capable of performing his duties."

"I have to agree with that, Mr. Swinburne," Cartwright said. "Please move on."

"Let me address this in a way that is directly relevant," Swinburne replied. "Mr. President, is it fair to say that the fact that your son has gone down behind enemy lines figured prominently in your decision to send in the troops?"

"Of course."

"And you have indicated that you have no intention of altering that decision. No matter what Colonel Zuko threatens."

"That's exactly right."

"Would it be fair to say you would be incapable of making a decision that might endanger your son?"

Ben bit down on his lower lip. He knew Swinburne had not chosen the word *incapable* by accident.

"I would not say that I'm incapable of doing it. I'm saying I don't want to, at least not at this time. Of course, I always have to consider the greater good for the greater number of people. There might be a time when I have to change this position. But we haven't reached it."

"So at least for the present, you are incapable of rendering a decision to withdraw the troops."

"Not incapable. Unwilling."

"Even if Colonel Zuko sends missiles to kill thousands of American citizens."

"You know my position. We can't give in to terrorist threats."

"Yes, especially not when your son is out there."

"Is that so wrong?"

"No. That's the act of a considerate, caring father. And we've all heard your concerns that you've been an inadequate parent. Perhaps that's why you are so adamant about sending in the troops. But by your own admission, at this time, you are incapable of rendering a decision to withdraw, even if it is in the best interests of the American people. That makes you incapable of performing your duties."

"Objection," Ben said. "He's speechifying again."

"You'll have to forgive me, judge," Swinburne said. "I'm not a trial lawyer by training. But you don't have to go to law school to know the difference between right and wrong. And having a commander in chief who is compromised—rendered incapable—by personal entanglements is wrong."

"Since he's still doing his closing, your honor," Ben said, "can I assume he's done with this witness?"

Swinburne didn't wait for Cartwright's response. "No, sir, I am most definitely not done with the witness." He redirected his attention to Kyler. "Mr. President, do you honestly expect anyone to believe that your erratic behavior is caused by your . . . personal eccentricities? Because you're a rebel in a blue suit?"

"I certainly don't expect you to believe it," President Kyler replied. "You've clearly got your own agenda."

That irritated him. "Let's review some of the actions you have deemed harmless and goofy." Swinburne glanced down at his notes. "You intentionally ditched your security detail."

"I never left the premises."

"You held conversations with portraits."

"I was thinking aloud."

"You queried JFK's portrait about his sexual escapades."

"I queried him about his faith in God. I mean—" The president stuttered, stopped. His face reddened. "I pondered aloud whether he was a deeply religious person. I have always been interested in matters of faith. I am a man of faith."

Swinburne kept barreling ahead like a snowplow. "You were skinny-dipping in front of your female chief of staff."

"I didn't ask her to come in there!" His voice was becoming strained. He was getting defensive. "I didn't know she was coming!"

"Balderdash. You ditch your security people, it's a sure bet your chief of staff will come looking for you. That's her job. And if you didn't know it beforehand, you would certainly know it after the first ten or twenty times it happened."

"I did not know—"

"It was perfectly simple to anticipate that she would walk in on you. That's probably why you did it. So you could see the shocked expression on this poor young woman's face when she found the president stark naked!'

"That's a lie!" Kyler said, but the more he insisted it was not, the more it sounded as if it were. Swinburne was doing a good job of shaking him out of his comfort zone and putting him on the defensive. Ben knew that anytime a defendant appears to be stretching, making excuses, juries start to lose faith in him. He needed to find an excuse to intervene.

"Are you sure, Mr. President? Are you sure exposing yourself didn't appeal to your sense of goofiness?"

"Objection to the use of the term 'exposing himself,' " Ben said, finding his opening. "It's unnecessarily inflammatory."

"Oh, whatever," Cartwright said. "We all know what he's getting at. Let's move along."

"But he's talking about this minor incident as if he were talking to someone accused of a sex crime. That's totally inappropriate."

"Can I help it if the president has urges to flash the American public? I haven't even gotten to the nudity fetish yet."

"I object to the terms 'exposing himself' and 'fetish'!"

Cartwright looked as if he were about to explode. "Could you please use a different terminology, Mr. Swinburne? We need to move along!"

"Yes, judge. Of course." Swinburne continued working through his list. "You dangled off the edge of the White House roof and talked about flying."

"It's a universal dream," the president replied through thin lips. "I hope you noted that I did not, in fact, attempt to fly."

"This time." Swinburne kept blazing ahead. "You talked about committing suicide."

"In the abstract," President Kyler emphasized. He was becoming louder with each sentence. His voice was strident. It had a razor-sharp edge. "I never ever said that I wanted to kill myself, or planned to kill myself, or even could kill myself. It was a purely abstract, philosophical discussion designed to comfort Sarie. I'm sorry she didn't grasp that. She's very efficient, but sometimes she's a little slow. Maybe she didn't get her grits that morning."

Ben closed his eyes. That was not a smart play. Attacking his cute and spunky chief of staff was not a winning strategy. Ben wished there were a way to object to his own defendant's answers, but unfortunately, that objection did not exist.

"I think she could have had all the grits in Alabama and still not be prepared for the image of the president of the United States blowing out his brains during a live press conference!" Swinburne wasn't even asking questions anymore. He was just being argumentative, trying to agitate the president. And it was working. "I don't think anyone could be prepared for that!"

"I never said that! And I would never do that!" Kyler leaned forward. Beads of sweat appeared at his temples.

"I'm not going to give you the chance." Swinburne turned a page in his notes. "Earlier today, when faced with a national crisis, you retreated into a mentally withdrawn and delusional state."

"Is it a crime to laugh? To sing?"

"It's a bizarre and inappropriate response to a crisis situation. One that does not inspire trust."

"Look, Conrad, I'm the president. And if I find it useful to sing 'There's a Hole in the Bucket,' then I will sing 'There's a Hole in the Bucket'!"

Swinburne fell silent. He looked as if he had just seen a specter from the netherworld. Eventually, he said, "That's not what you were singing."

The president's left eye began to twitch. "It isn't?"

Swinburne's lips parted. "No." He laid his hands flat on the table. "My God, man—do you even remember what happened a few hours ago?"

President Kyler looked down at his hands. He was fidgeting. "Of course I do."

"Tell me what you were singing."

"What does it matter?" the president said, his voice cracking. Sweat dripped down the sides of his face. "I sing all the time. I don't happen to recall what I sang last. What difference does it make?"

"My God," Swinburne said, almost breathlessly. "You don't remember anything about it, do you? Did you totally black out? Has your brain erased it from your memory?"

"Look, I've been very busy. Just because I can't dredge up the details—"

"I remember all the details," Swinburne said. "They are indelibly imprinted on my brain." He paused. "But you seem to have undergone some kind of . . . mental erasure. As if the brain has erased memories that might cause stress or unhappiness. I believe the same thing happens after people experience seizures or bipolar episodes."

"Would you stop talking about mental!" the president shouted, before Ben had a chance to lodge an objection. "I'm tired of all this talk about mental! Maybe you're mental, huh? Maybe it's . . . it's . . . you . . ." All at once, Kyler reached forward, clasped his knees, and began to rock back and forth in his chair. "The itsy-bitsy spider went up the water spout . . . down came the rain and washed the spider out . . ."

Ben closed his eyes. No. Please, God, no.

"Out came the sun and dried up all the rain . . ." His eyes widened. He stared up at the ceiling, as if he were seeing something that wasn't there. "Then the itsy-bitsy spider went up the spout again."

This time, as Ben surveyed the faces in the bunker, what he saw was not so much shock as embarrassment. After all they had seen and heard this day, Kyler's actions no longer had the power to produce shock. What they produced, at best, was pity.

The president began the song over again. Swinburne shook his head sadly. "I think that's enough from this witness, judge. I've seen enough." He turned away. "Surely we've all seen enough."

"Thank you," Cartwright said. "If there's no redirect . . ."

Ben shook his head. What could he possibly do with this suddenly imbecilic witness?

"Then the witness is excused." Ben took the president by the arm and led him back to his chair. He barely seemed to understand what was going on around him.

"Now we'll proceed to brief closing arguments," Cartwright said. "And I emphasize *brief*. This trial has already consumed more time than we can spare.

"Understood," they both agreed.

As he spoke, Ben was already contemplating what he might say. What could he possibly do to salvage this mess now? He wondered if the noble thing would be just to throw in the towel. He couldn't possibly pretend that they hadn't seen what they had all just seen. And he couldn't explain it. He couldn't justify it. There was nothing he could do to prevent the inevitable judgment.

And he wasn't sure anymore if he should try.

It was all well and good to be loyal to an inspirational leader. A man who wanted peace. And of course he would always be indebted to anyone who did his wife a kindness. But how could he justify leaving this man with obvious issues in control of the country in the midst of an imminent missile crisis?

And yet . . .

Something was bothering him. Something was nagging him at the base of his spine, jabbing him in the cerebral cortex. Something was wrong here. Very wrong. And he wasn't at all sure that Vice President Swinburne was proceeding from altruistic motives. Everything he had seen suggested he was more interested in his own career than he was in the good of the nation.

What was it that bothered him? Why couldn't he put his finger on it?

He knew from experience these things never came when you wanted them. He needed to focus on the task at hand and hope the inspiration arrived serendipitously in the process.

"Mr. Swinburne," Cartwright said, "we are ready to hear your closing remarks. Members of the cabinet, please play close attention. As soon as these two advocates are done, I will poll you, and there will just barely be enough time afterward for whoever is in charge to take decisive action. In simpler terms: your vote may well decide the future course of this nation."

39

The noise was considerably louder in here, Seamus realized, although it sounded much like any office in any other place. A little talking, a few mechanical beeps, keyboards clicking. Nothing out of the ordinary.

He used the long row of silhouetted machinery for cover and inched forward, still careful to keep watch on all sides.

The first face he saw was that of a woman, dark-haired, dark-skinned. She was wearing an earpiece and typing into a computer terminal. Someone was hovering over her shoulder, a man in a white shirt. He looked more like a college professor than a terrorist. Another computer geek? Or some other kind of scientist? Neither of them looked managerial. They were employees.

Seamus could see the tops of at least five other heads. They all seemed glued to their screens. Who was running this show?

He tiptoed a few steps forward, trying to obtain a better view. It was basically three tiers of seriously complex-looking computers, including one master. If it wasn't a Blue Gene/L—the IBM supercomputer with a peak processing speed of 596 teraflops—it was something very near.

There were a few overhead monitors and one large dish—probably capable of transmitting signals to that deadly satellite in the sky. Probably would attract too much attention if they put it on the roof, but it seemed to function where it was. It all seemed familiar except for a large red button at the base. He didn't even want to think about what that might do.

Seamus supposed they had everything they needed to make this missile hijack work. Still, he would like to have some confirmation. . . .

Then Seamus saw him.

Seamus's spine stiffened. The hairs on the back of his neck stood on end.

The supervising figure who had just entered his line of sight was the man from the Washington Monument. The man with the scarred face.

The man who'd made off with the nuclear suitcase.

So he was involved with this missile hijack as well. Which meant Colonel Zuko was also involved in the Arlington suitcase heist. The dictator now had not only the East Coast missiles but a nuclear weapon.

This was bad. End-of-the-world bad.

"Tell me what is happening out there!" Scarface bellowed to the woman in the white shirt. She didn't look entirely comfortable working with him. Seamus guessed she was more likely hired technical help than a true believer.

She mumbled something in reply that Seamus couldn't hear. Whatever it was, it didn't appease her boss.

"That's not good enough!" he shouted back at her. "Will you be ready to launch when I give you the signal?"

"Of course I will," she said. "Everything is in place."

"When the colonel calls, he will want us to take action immediately."

"And we will!"

"Make sure that we do!" And with that, he raised his hand to strike her.

Seamus instinctively surged forward—then checked himself.

Scarface stopped his hand just inches short of her face. She flinched, then turned her head away. Tears trickled out the corner of her eye. "I'll be ready. I promise."

"See that you are. We must be strong. Though thousands may die, Kuraq will live!" He stomped off. The woman—and everyone sitting near her—seemed intensely relieved.

Seamus bit down on his lower lip. He would love nothing more than to knock that SOB down again—this time well enough that he didn't get up again. But that wasn't the smart play. He needed to contact Zira. Call in the troops. Then get Arlo out of here and let the boys with the big guns take over.

He lifted his phone and took a quick photo, then sent it to Zira. Moving like a ninja, he tiptoed back to the door and turned the knob.

Still no one seemed to notice. He was having a charmed day. This was the downside to bullying your employees. They tended not to be distracted by their surroundings—even when they should.

He eased his way through the opening, the same way he'd come in, and closed the door behind him. Now all he needed to do was make his way back to the stairs leading to the roof, or maybe just walk through the back door . . .

And that's when Seamus saw the guard. Who also saw him.

"Stop!" The man yelled.

Seamus bolted. The problem was, he had nowhere to go. The guard stood between him and his destination, and the computer ops base was behind him. So Seamus moved laterally, working toward the east side of the building.

Another guard heard the cry. A few seconds after that a third one zeroed in on Seamus. Where were they coming from? Had they all been on a coffee break a few minutes ago?

He reached for his gun, but they reacted by doing exactly the same. Mistake. He couldn't outdraw all three of them. He withdrew quickly and threw both hands up in the air.

"Sorry about that," he said amiably. "Didn't mean to scare anyone."

"What are you doing here?" the first guard barked. The three of them surrounded him.

"Sorry. No cause for alarm. Health Department." He pulled out a wallet and quickly flashed a badge—not his real one. "Just doing inspections on the abandoned property in the area. Had no idea anyone was in here."

"How did you get in?" Guard One had a serious and sullen expression. He was trying to look tough, but Seamus suspected it was more a case of a tough guy with a swagger being forced to actually do something for the first time. He would've probably been perfectly content to go on guarding for the rest of his life without ever encountering any trouble.

"Through the roof." In this case, honesty was the best policy. The doors might be wired to an alarm, and the windows were not broken. "We're allowed to do that. It's in the city charter."

"What do you want?"

"Just to make sure everything's clean and safe. Sometimes these abandoned buildings can become dangerous. Attractive nuisances. But I didn't realize anyone was working in here. Did you take out a lease?"

"I'll ask the questions!" the guard barked back. His two companions looked more relaxed. If Seamus worked it hard enough, he might be able to pull off this health inspector charade.

"Are you alone?" the guard asked.

"Yes. Look, if you have any questions about this, call my supervisor. She'll straighten the whole thing out."

He hesitated. "She will?"

Was he actually buying it? Praise God, from whom all blessings flow. "Of course. Her name is Zira. Just give her my name and she'll tell you that I'm legitimate. You can use my phone if you want. I don't mind."

"Well . . . I suppose it won't hurt to call."

Fabulous. Zira could think fast enough on her feet to carry this off. And if not, he'd knock them down while they were distracted by the phone. He punched the number on his cell and handed it to Guard One. "Here. Talk to her. She'll be able to give you a complete—"

"You! *You!*"

Seamus's eyelids closed briefly. He didn't have to turn to know whose voice that was.

A moment later, Scarface appeared before him.

"You were at the Washington Monument! You hurt me! You killed my comrades!"

The guards tensed. All at once, Seamus had three guns pointing down his throat.

"Where did you find him?" Scarface asked. The first guard answered all his questions succinctly. "Good work. He is a government spy." He reached inside Seamus's coat and took his gun. "Who sent you?"

"No one. I sent myself."

"Liar!" He cuffed Seamus's chin with the butt of his own gun. It hurt.

"I am not lying."

"Who else knows you're here?"

"No one."

"Liar!" He hit Seamus again.

"I'm telling you the truth."

"This is pointless," Scarface said. "And I do not have time to waste. Take him to the sleeping quarters. Strap him down. Make sure he cannot move."

Seamus didn't much like the sound of that.

The guards grabbed Seamus by the arms and shoulders. He made a show of struggling, but he knew it was useless.

"Once he is secure, come and find me. I will go find my tools."

Tools? This was not going to be pleasant.

Scarface grabbed his hair and jerked it back. "I saw what you did to my friends. Men of faith. I will do as much to you and more. You will tell us what we want to know. But I hope you will resist first. Because I want you to suffer as they did. I want you to suffer to your dying breath. Which will not be long in coming."

40

*B*efore Swinburne began orating, Ben took the president by the arm and led him gently to the other room. Kyler resisted a little, but not too much. He started to speak, more mindless babble, but Ben hushed him.

"I want you to stay in here," Ben said. "The jury does not need to see you acting like this during the closings."

The president pouted. "Don't wanna be all by myself."

"Tough. Stay in here and you can sing or rock or whatever. Just don't get too loud."

"Are you sending me to my room? I don't wanna be locked up. I wanna fly free. Free!"

Ben tried to stay calm. "I'm just trying to help. So stay put. At least until you're feeling better."

"You're mean." The president folded his arms across his chest, then began to sing. "The itsy-bitsy spider went up the water spout . . ."

It was just too sad. Ben closed the door and quietly slipped back into the main room.

Swinburne moved a few steps away from his usual spot at the

table, to a place directly before the webcam. Ben knew he was looking for a vantage point that would allow him to look directly both into the faces of those present and into the camera for the benefit of those cabinet members watching from the undisclosed secure location.

"Ladies and gentlemen, this is a sad occasion," Swinburne began. "We are gathered here to decide whether to retain the elected president of the United States or to remove him, as provided for by the Twenty-fifth Amendment. This is not pleasant for anyone, least of all me. I have worked with and admired Roland Kyler for years. This is perhaps the hardest and most unpleasant task that has ever fallen upon me to perform. But pursuant to the Constitution, this duty falls to the vice president, so I will not shirk from it, even though it gives me no pleasure."

Ben thought about objecting on grounds of profound insincerity, but decided against it.

"I don't know what more there is for me to say. This is a case where a picture is worth a thousand words, and I think the spectacle that you have just witnessed will likely linger longer in your memory than anything I have to say. So I will just briefly outline the main points for you to consider, and then I will sit down."

He continued. "First and foremost, the president's mental state is clearly unbalanced. I'm not a psychiatrist and I don't know the proper technical term, but I think we can all agree that what we have just seen is not something anyone should ever see from the president. And the testimony demonstrates that these irrational episodes, to varying lengths and degrees, have occurred many times in the past and with increasing frequency. This is not something we can turn a blind eye toward, not in such troubled times, and especially not in the midst of an enemy attack that puts this nation at dire risk. When it became clear that the emperor Caligula was hopelessly insane, the Praetorian Guard removed and replaced him. I'm sure it gave them no great pleasure, but they did it. We can do no less for our own people."

Although he had gotten better at reading faces over the years, Ben had no idea what was going on in the minds of those who would cast the deciding votes. They still seemed a little stunned by all they had seen and heard. He knew they were listening, but he had no idea what they were thinking.

"Second, the fact that the president has personal ties to the nation of Kuraq, and a son now behind enemy lines, obviously compromises his ability to render an objective judgment as to what course is best for

this nation—which again makes him incapable of performing his duties. You may feel that this is or is not his fault, but he has admitted that
so long as his son is in danger, he will only entertain one possible course
of action. A president who cannot or will not consider an action that
may be in the national interest should not be running the country.

"Third," he continued, "Secretary Ruiz testified about the president's extreme single-mindedness—you might say obsession—with regard to Colonel Zuko and Kuraq. Now that we know the truth about
the torrid affair in his past, and the love child it produced, that is perhaps more understandable. But it is still true nonetheless. The president
is obsessed with taking down the colonel, just as he is obsessed with
rescuing his son. Both of these two factors leave him incapable of performing his duties competently."

Ben got a sick feeling in the pit of his stomach. Some of the cabinet
members were nodding in agreement.

"Finally, ladies and gentlemen, we must consider the president's
physical ailments. Diabetes is a serious disease. It is unfortunate that
President Kyler was struck with this so soon after taking office—but he
was. My son-in-law has diabetes, which is why I know so much about
it. It's debilitating, and it may well be the cause of his current mental in-
firmities. The president should have resigned as soon as the diagnosis
was made."

Swinburne clasped his hands before him. "We are very fortunate,
my friends, that the Constitution has given us a means of ensuring a
ready succession from one leader to the next. Every four years, the people vote, and if there is a change in the executive office, the transition is
made smoothly and without the threat of upset or revolution. Similarly,
the Twenty-fifth Amendment provides for a smooth succession in the
event that the president becomes incapacitated—which is exactly the
situation we have here. Thank God we can make the necessary change
without the sort of upheaval that puts men such as Colonel Zuko into
power."

He leaned forward, balancing himself against the table. "My point
is simply this: I know no one wants to do this. But we must. And the
Constitution has made it possible for us to do it with as little angst as
possible. The Constitution has only been amended a handful of times.
The fact that it was amended not long ago to ensure an orderly means
of removing a disabled president shows just how serious this matter is.
We cannot take risks with the leadership of the nation when a foreign

dictator is threatening to kill hundreds of thousands of people. We can't ever afford to take that risk, because we know America's enemies are always looking for an opening. We will not give it to them. Not now. Not ever. So as distasteful as it may be, I ask you to do the necessary thing. Find the president incapable of performing his duties. Let me take the reins. You may or may not agree with what I do, but you'll know that someone dependable, someone unbiased, and someone sane is making the decisions. And that's what is most important here."

He pushed away from the table. "Thank you for your kind attention."

41

*B*en slowly pushed himself away from the table, still not really knowing what he was going to say. This was a occasion when, like it or not, he was going to have to follow his instincts. In past years he might've found that notion laughable, because he knew his instincts were so untrustworthy. Christina used to say that he liked everyone, especially those who deserved it least. Not anymore. His perceptions had become more finely attuned as time passed and he had more experience in the courtroom. And he had learned that the smartest thing a trial lawyer can do is to pay attention to the expressions on the jurors' faces.

What he saw on the faces of the cabinet members at this time did not fill him with confidence. But they had told him what aspect of the vice president's case he needed to address most, so he would do his best. He had agreed to take the president's defense. In fact, come to think of it, he had volunteered.

He would not let the man down now.

Ben made contact with each of the cabinet members in the room, then made contact with those on the other end of the blinking webcam. "Let me make one thing clear up front. I am not going to make excuses for what we have seen today. I'm not going to tell you it's no big deal. It's disturbing. Even bizarre. I won't attempt to sweep that under the rug. All I will tell you is that the Constitution is very strict in its wording. It did not intend to make the removal of a president easy, or something that can be done quickly for political reasons. It can only occur for one reason—because something has rendered the president incapable of performing his duties. And I will respectfully argue that, as disturbing as what we have seen and heard today may be, we have no evidence that the president is incapable of performing his duties."

Ben took a tiny step to the side. There was precious little room here to maneuver, but he knew that the tiniest change in gesture, expression, or anything else helped maintain the audience's interest. "I will address the points raised by the prosecutor in reverse order. First, the president's diabetes. I think we can safely assume that when the Twenty-fifth Amendment was passed in the mid-sixties, Birch Bayh and the other drafters were capable of inserting a clause providing for the removal of the president in the event that he contracts a serious illness. It had happened before. William Henry Harrison caught pneumonia and was incapacitated for a month before dying. Wilson had a stroke and never functioned at full capacity for the remainder of his term. But the framers did not address that. They only provided for removal in the event that something renders the president incapable of performing his duties.

"What evidence do we have that diabetes has left the president incapable? None. Absolutely none. Mr. Swinburne argues maybe this and maybe that, but he has no proof that this disease has impacted the president's ability to function in any way. So, with respect, not only do I not think you should make this a basis for your decision, but I believe that you cannot. The Constitution simply does not provide for the removal of a president because he has a disease.

"Next." Ben took a few steps in the other direction. Got to keep it moving . . .

"Mr. Swinburne alleges that the president should be removed because he is obsessed with Kuraq and Colonel Zuko." Ben paused and let his eyes run to all those in the audience. "Why is that bad? When we have a dire threat to this nation, I think it should be uppermost in the president's mind. I would think there was a problem if it were not. Let's be honest about what we all already know—Secretary Ruiz wants us out of the Middle East."

Ruiz swiveled around in his chair, a profound frown on his face.

"What Ruiz basically says is, 'The president has a different opinion from me, and anyone who has a different opinion from me must be crazy. Or dangerously obsessed. So let's get rid of him.' Well, that may be how it works in a dictatorship, but last I heard, Americans have the right to hold contrary opinions, and that includes the president of the United States. This is a purely political attack, and the Constitution makes no provision for removing a president because his positions are unpopular with one cabinet member or another—or even all of them. The president has autonomy to think for himself—thank goodness. Whether you agree with him or not, this argument is simply without merit."

Ben felt as if he was doing an adequate job of carving out a small space for success with what little was available to him. They might not like what they had seen the president do, but if he could bring them back to the high standard set by the Constitution, it was just possible he might be able to bring this trial back around.

At any rate, they weren't laughing out loud at him.

"Third, we must consider the matter of the president's son. I wish this had been revealed in a different way. I wish the president had informed the people of this blood relation on his own—especially after his helicopter crash made Mr. Malik a potential chess piece in a geopolitical conflict. But he didn't. And we are not here to judge whether the president's decision was right or wrong. Our only inquiry is whether the existence of the son renders the president incapable of performing his duties.

"Have we seen any evidence of incapability? No. All of Mr. Swinburne's examples are instances of the president not doing what Swinburne thinks he should do, or supposedly not having the ability to do in the future what Swinburne wants to do now. Is that evidence of disability? Only in the jaundiced eyes of the vice president, and probably the eyes of the secretary of state. But again, disagreeing with them is not tantamount to being insane. Let's hope that's never the measuring stick. Because frankly, I've disagreed with the vice president about forty-two times today, so if that's the standard, I'll be committed as soon as this trial is over."

That got a few small grins, which if nothing else showed Ben they were still listening. But now he was going into the tricky part. This was where he really had to do some work. This was where he really had to be good.

He heard a clicking sound on the other side of the room.

The president was reentering.

Jesus God—why now? Ben tried to hide his dismay from the others. It was the worst possible timing. Kyler seemed calm. Perhaps the episode was over. But his very presence, his return to the room, only reminded everyone of the disturbing sight they had seen only a few minutes before.

Ben took a breath and tried to block all those thoughts from his mind. Focus. Focus! "Finally, we have to consider the matter of the president's alleged insanity, based upon his unusual behavior both here in the bunker and on a few previous occasions. I think the president did about the best possible job he could of explaining those situations, and I won't repeat what he said. They were eccentric at best. Disturbing at worst. But ask yourself—was there ever any evidence that these episodes prevented the president from performing his duties?"

He paused, giving everyone a moment to think about it.

"Was there? I don't remember any such evidence. I don't think you do, either. Because there wasn't any. Even after the president had his chat with the presidential portraits, he returned to the garden and handled the Easter egg roll. Even Sarie, whose testimony did him no good, admitted that he always did his job. Agent Zimmer testified that he never saw the president's behavior interfere with the performance of his duties. And even today, as shocking as these spectacles may have been, the president always snapped out of it and returned to work a few minutes later. Even now he has returned to this room, even though I'm sure there are a million other places he would rather be. He has not been derelict in his duties. Not now. Not ever."

Ben spread his hands wide. "So where is the evidence that he is incapable of performing as president? Nowhere. It doesn't exist. All day today, he has been performing his duties and managing this crisis. Sure, he hasn't made the same decisions that Secretary Ruiz would. He hasn't pleased the vice president, which, let's face it, might well be impossible. But he has made decisions, and he has always been able to explain why he has taken them. Is he the first leader to refuse to back down in the face of terrorist attacks? Of course not. So why is it so controversial now? I understand that crises produce heated feelings, but this is a sober deliberative body, so we have to put those feelings aside and think clearly. The only question before us is this: has the prosecution presented any evidence that the president's disease, his personal life, his politics, or his odd behavior has prevented him from performing his duties as president? Has Mr. Swinburne been able to produce one example of a duty unfulfilled or fulfilled incompetently? He has not. And since there is no such evidence, the constitutional standard has not been met."

Ben took one final look into the eyes of those before him. "Being goofy is not the same as being incapable. And since there is no evidence of incapacity, the Twenty-fifth Amendment cannot be put into play. I urge you to respect the letter of the Constitution and to let the president remain in the office to which he was duly elected by the citizens of the United States."

Ben broke eye contact and took his seat. His throat felt dry, achy. It was probably the shortest closing argument of his life—and also the hardest. He had no idea whether they would listen to him, whether they could put aside what they had seen and think logically, as he had urged, to stick to the letter of the amendment.

And at the moment, he was too tired to think about it anymore.

Worry was pointless. In a few minutes, they would all know.

"Mr. Swinburne," Cartwright said, "you have about one minute for a rebuttal."

"I'll take less than that," Swinburne said, buttoning his coat. "I just have two sentences." He addressed the jury, gazing into the webcam. "At another time and place, we might have the luxury of doing as counsel asks, of giving the man some more rope and seeing if he hangs himself. But today, when ballistic missiles could be launched at any moment, we can't take the risk."

And with that, Swinburne sat down.

That rebuttal was all-time short—and probably a thousand times more effective for its brevity. Swinburne had put the jurors exactly where he wanted them: totally focused on the impending missile crisis and the potential danger of an unbalanced president calling the shots.

"All right, then," Cartwright said. "I thank counsel for their service. And now, members of the deliberative panel, it is time to vote."

42

Seamus was strapped down to a cot, his arms tied above his head, his legs tied down as well. After he was secure, they hoisted the cot sideways and mounted it against the wall. He didn't know how it was done. He couldn't see behind himself. Were there hooks on the wall? That would just figure. Scarface had done nothing for the décor, but he had made sure he had an efficient place to torture people.

Most of the security detail disappeared after he was hung on the wall. Apparently they thought he posed little threat at that point. His old sparring buddy, Guard One, stayed on, though, just in case.

"Hey," Seamus said, winking. "I'll make you a deal."

Guard One didn't even blink. From the looks of him, Seamus thought, he might as well have been guarding the Tomb of the Unknown Soldier.

"You're an American citizen, aren't you? You let me go and I'll make sure you aren't prosecuted for treason."

"Go to hell," Guard One spat.

"That may happen in time," Seamus said, "but I'd like to delay it as long as possible."

"You'll be there within the hour."

"All the more reason for us to make a deal first. Tell you what, I'll not only give you total immunity from prosecution, I'll give you an IRS waiver, too."

"A what?"

"An IRS waiver. Haven't you heard of it? You can file anything you want, and the IRS will never audit you. Guaranteed. It's like a tax-department get-out-of-jail-free card."

"Pass. I haven't filed a tax return for years."

Well, that must simplify his April 15. Seamus tried again. "You know, these guys are probably promising you virgins in heaven, but I can get you the best booty in the tristate area. Who wants a virgin, anyway? Wouldn't you rather have someone who knows what she's doing?"

Guard One's expression dripped with contempt. "I'm not Muslim."

"Then what are you in this for?"

"Money. Lots of it."

"Oh." No wonder he was hard to bribe. Uncle Sam probably didn't have a slush fund to match Colonel Zuko's. "Interested in real estate? I've got a great place for duck hunting on the coast of—"

"Would you just shut up?" the guard said.

"Well, if you're going to be unfriendly . . ."

The door opened.

Scarface stepped into the small room. He closed the door behind him.

He was carrying a tool belt. Like something Bob the Builder might carry, except with sharper edges.

"I am glad you are amusing yourself and having great fun," he said. He walked up to Seamus until they were practically nose to nose. "Now it is time for me to have some fun."

Arlo checked his watch again. Seamus had been gone a long time. It was possible he hadn't been able to get inside. But if so, why hadn't he returned to the car? It didn't make any sense. He knew Seamus wouldn't quit without making every effort. If he couldn't get in right away, he'd have come back for a tire iron or something.

So he must've gotten inside. Why hadn't he returned?

Could he still be looking around, taking notes? Stretching his legs?

Arlo could think of a far more likely explanation.

He couldn't forget what Seamus had told him. The man had drilled it into his head. He said it three times: do not leave the car.

Apparently he meant it.

Arlo had the keys. He could drive away from here.

And abandon Seamus? The man who had saved his life? No. Even if he weren't indebted to him, he wouldn't leave him hanging out like that.

But he had promised . . .

So many difficult decisions. He didn't know what to do. But he wasn't content just to sit here doing nothing. He needed a plan of action. If this were a World of Warcraft scenario, what would his avatar do?

One thing was certain: real life was a lot harder.

Seamus didn't know what he hated most: the fact that Scarface was invading his personal space or the fact that his breath was truly rancid.

"Why are you here?" his captor demanded.

"Well, jeez Louise," Seamus said, "isn't that obvious?"

Scarface slugged him hard, deep in the pit of his stomach. It hurt much more than it should have. That was because his ribs were still aching on the right side. But explaining it didn't make it feel any better.

"Why are you here?" Scarface shouted, even louder.

"Are you kidding? You've hijacked a nuclear bomb and the U.S. missile system. Did you think no one would come looking for you? Every federal agent on the East Coast is looking for you."

"How did you find us?"

Seamus didn't see any point in lying about that, either. "I got the address from that clown you sent to the mall to pick up Harold Bemis." That was true, more or less. "By the way, neither one of them will be showing."

Scarface was enraged. "We need him!"

"Oh, yeah? Got a glitch in the system?"

"Your fascist government is trying to interfere."

"You mean we're trying to boot you out of our computers. Imagine that."

Scarface pummeled him again, several times, all delivered to the same soft sore spot in his stomach. Seamus thought he felt something rupture. The pain was excruciating. Sweat trickled down the sides of his face.

"It does not matter. You will not succeed before the colonel's dead-line has expired. And if I sense we will soon lose control, I will fire all the missiles at once!"

That would be bad. And Scarface looked just crazy and pissed off enough to do it. Seamus knew Colonel Zuko was an extremist, but he didn't think he was totally starkers. He wondered if the dictator knew his first officer was so far gone.

"Who came with you?"

"No one. I came alone."

"Do not lie to me!"

"Look around you, pal. Do you see anyone? I'm alone." He hoped the creep bought it. Arlo might've had the sense to drive off by now, but then again, maybe not. He didn't want the kid dragged into this.

Of course, he didn't want to make Scarface mad, either. Truth to tell, his ribs weren't going to hold up to much more of this.

"Who else knows you're here?"

"No one."

"You must've called your superior."

"No time. Your top cops grabbed me just as soon as I spotted the control room, or whatever you call that."

Scarface paused a moment. Seamus could see he was considering, weighing the words, wondering if his captive could be trusted.

"How long would it take your colleagues to arrive?"

"They'd already be here," he lied.

"I don't believe you."

"Why would I lie about that?"

"How much do you know about what we are doing? How much does anyone know?"

"No one knows anything. I don't know anything. And I've seen the operation in action. But I'm still clueless."

"You lie!" He pounded Seamus in the stomach again and again. Seamus suspected he was bleeding internally. He was used to blocking out pain, but all the mental discipline in the world couldn't stop a hemorrhage.

Scarface brought his hand against the back of Seamus's face. "Talk to me!" Blood and spittle flew from Seamus's mouth. "Tell me what you know!"

"Do I look like a computer genius?"

"You are an American spy!" he shouted, battering Seamus's face again.

"I am just like you!" Seamus shouted back. "I take orders!" Not entirely true, but he thought it was the best way to appeal to this guy. The solidarity of soldiers and all that. "I do what I'm told!"

That seemed to give Scarface pause, at least for a moment. Not long enough. "Then your masters have ordered you to your death." He turned and reached for his tool belt. He returned with a pair of shiny steel pliers. "I do not have much time for this. I expect the colonel to call soon. So the question is whether you will die quickly and painlessly or whether I will have a chance to use my tools."

"You're not listening to me. I don't know anything."

Scarface slugged him again, this time with the pliers. That stung. Seamus could feel blood trickling out of his mouth. He felt around with his tongue. Damn—one of his molars felt loose. Not that he hadn't lost teeth before. But he didn't like it. There were only so many to go around.

Scarface pulled open Seamus's shirt, popping the buttons. The shirt hung in tatters, dangling from Seamus's shoulders. Scarface jabbed the pliers into his left pectoral. Then he twisted.

Seamus screamed. There was no shame in screaming, he told himself. When you feel pain, let it out. Holding it in only made it worse.

And this was bad enough already. Seamus could feel his flesh tearing, feel the muscle separating from the skin. Blood gushed down his chest.

"Still not convinced? Let us try the other side."

Scarface twisted the pliers around the right pec. Seamus screamed, a longer and louder cry. Blood and sweat poured down the sides of his body.

"And if that's not enough, we'll work on some of your other extremities. We will take you apart bit by bit. We will take away all that makes you a man." He paused, grinning with malice. "Before I am finished, there may be nothing left of you to kill."

43

"I think we can assume," Admiral Cartwright continued, "that the vice president wishes to initiate an action to remove the president."

"You can," Swinburne concurred.

"So I will poll each of the cabinet members, in order, and I will ask if you vote to retain or remove. Does everyone understand?"

There was general assent, indicated by nods.

"Good. Let's begin. Mr. Secretary of—"

"Excuse me!" It was Agent Zimmer, standing by the communications station, one earphone pressed against his right ear. "I have Colonel Zuko."

The president rose. "Put him on speaker."

Swinburne stood. "No, wait just a—"

"I'm still the president. At least for the next few minutes. And so long as I am president, I will do my job. So get out of my way."

Swinburne frowned but got out of the way.

"Colonel Zuko. Are you there?"

The deep, guttural voice Ben had come to dislike so strongly returned to the airwaves. "I am."

"What do you want?"

"I'm sure you've noticed, as I have, that there are only five minutes remaining on the clock."

"Is that right? I must've lost track."

"This is not a time for levity, Mr. President. Let me assure you that I mean what I say. The missiles have been targeted. They will deliver their payload to heavily populated residential areas."

"Where? Anacostia? Georgetown? Morgan? Cleveland Park?"

"Why do you ask? So you can begin an evacuation, as you did on the National Mall? I'm afraid I cannot answer your question."

"Because you want people to die."

"Because I can see from your failure to act earlier today that the taking of lives is necessary to make you understand that you have no choice in this matter. You must withdraw your troops."

Silence. The president chose not to answer.

"Have you changed your mind?" Zuko demanded.

"I have not," the president said, looking at Swinburne out the corner of his eye. "But . . . it's possible that things could change."

"I hope for your sake that they do. Because if I cannot see in the next few minutes that you are withdrawing the troops from my sovereign territory, thousands of your civilians will die. And you will be known forevermore not as the man who brought peace to his nation but as the warmonger who allowed thousands of his own people to be butchered."

"Colonel Zuko—"

Too late. The line was dead.

"And on that happy note," Cartwright said, "it's time for us to vote."

Ben pulled out his ballpoint pen, ready to tick off the votes. Please, God, he thought, please . . .

What did he really want? What did he think was truly best?

Please, God, do what's best for this nation and the people in it. He would leave it at that.

"Mr. Secretary of State?"

Ruiz answered, "Remove."

Ben cursed silently. Why did he have to be first? He hoped Ruiz hadn't started a trend that would be impossible to buck.

"Mr. Secretary of Defense."

Rybicki replied, "Retain."

Thank God. So the score was even, at least here in the bunker.

The president leaned toward Ben's ear and whispered, "However this turns out, Ben, I want to thank you. You've done a great service for me, and I appreciate it."

"I wish I had—"

The president squeezed his arm, stopping him. "You've done the best job anyone could possibly do with a virtually impossible case. And I will never forget it."

Cartwright continued. "Mr. Secretary of the Treasury."

"Retain."

Ben's eyes widened. They were ahead. Was it possible . . . ?

"Ms. Attorney General."

"Retain."

Ben closed his eyes. Yes! Keep them coming . . .

"Mr. Secretary of the Interior."

"Remove."

Well, there were bound to be a few.

"Mr. Secretary of Agriculture."

"Remove."

The score was tied again. And they still had more than half of the cabinet members to poll.

"Ms. Secretary of Labor."

She was shaking her head sadly as she answered, "Remove."

"Mr. Secretary of Commerce."

"Remove."

Ben looked at the president firmly. "Don't give up. It isn't over yet."

The president nodded, without much enthusiasm.

"Mr. Secretary of Housing and Urban Development."

"Retain."

See? Always hope . . .

"Mr. Secretary of Transportation."

"Retain."

Even odds again . . .

"Mr. Secretary of Energy."

"Retain."

Sweet God! Was it possible? They were ahead, with only a few votes outstanding. For the first time, Ben allowed himself to hope.

"Ms. Secretary of Education."

"Remove."

That's okay—still several votes out there . . .

"Mr. Secretary of Veterans' Affairs."

"Remove."

Well, it was predictable that he would side with the secretary of state.

"Mr. Secretary of Homeland Security."

"Retain."

Dear God, was it tied again? It could go either way at this point. On one hand, Ben was pleased to know that he had managed to persuade a few cabinet members—or perhaps they were simply loyal to the man who had appointed them. In any case, it wasn't the rout it could have been. But why did it all have to come down to one vote?

"Someone correct me if I'm wrong," Cartwright said, "but I believe that makes the vote of the Cabinet members exactly seven to seven. Looks like it all comes down to the last vote. Mr. Secretary of Health and Human Services, you're making the final call."

It was obvious he didn't want that responsibility. "I didn't ask for this."

"I know, sir. But you've got it, anyway. How do you vote?"

It seemed an eternity passed before he finally spoke. "Remove."

Ben felt as if his heart had just stopped. Damn! He knew the odds had been stacked against them, but to lose by one vote! He suddenly realized his whole body, especially his legs, were shaking. Had they been like that all along and he just didn't know it? Did it take the crash of the adrenaline infusion before he realized what was going on with his own body?

He looked beside him at the president. Kyler was shaking his head, fighting to keep his expression even. He had to be devastated. The temptation to shout, argue, or break into tears must be profound. But he was managing to keep it together.

"It's not your fault, Ben," he said generously. "You did everything that could possibly be done. I'm indebted to you."

"That's not—" Ben began, but he was cut off by the admiral.

"The vote of the cabinet is eight for removal, seven for retention. The majority favors removal. Therefore, in my capacity as judge of this constitutional tribunal, I hereby declare that the Twenty-fifth Amendment will be implemented. Although the amendment provides for a resolution to be provided to the Congress, under the circumstances I'm sure everyone will agree that we will not delay the transition of power, but will only ask that this technicality be fulfilled as swiftly as possible. The president has been found incapable of performing his duties and is therefore relieved of said duties. The office of the president will be assumed by Vice President Swinburne."

"The oath of office is in the football, with a Bible," the president said helpfully. His voice sounded as if it was on the verge of breaking, but didn't quite.

Did he mean the nuclear football? Ben wondered. The silver attaché case with all the codes for nuclear launch plus, apparently, a few other essential emergency items?

"Since I'm the judge, sort of," Cartwright said, "I guess I can be in charge of that. Mr. Swinburne, let's do it in the next room."

"We can do it later," Swinburne replied. "Have you noticed the clock?"

In fact, in the midst of all the excitement, Ben had actually forgotten about the ticking countdown. As he turned his head, the display changed to show only one minute remaining until Colonel Zuko's grace period ran out.

In less than sixty seconds, another missile could be headed toward a nearby residential neighborhood. For the first time, Ben found himself almost grateful he had lost the trial.

"Get out of my way," Swinburne growled, pushing away everyone who was between him and the communications station. "Let me talk to Zuko!"

Agent Zimmer glanced up at him calmly. "As you say, sir. We have a continuing connection. I'll see if he will pick up the line again." A few seconds later, he said, "I have the colonel for you, Mr. Vice President."

"That's Mr. President now," Swinburne said, snatching the headset away from him.

"Colonel? This is Conrad Swinburne. I don't have time to explain all the details, but I'm the commander in chief now, and I am immediately giving the order to—"

And then, without warning, all the lights in the bunker went out, including the lights on the communications station. Ben listened with horror to the slow, eerie dying whine of the electronic equipment powering down.

"What the hell just happened?" Swinburne bellowed in the darkness.

"I don't know," Zimmer said. Rustling noises told Ben he was trying a dozen things at once, trying to discern what was going on. "We seem to have lost power."

"I thought the bunker had its own generator!"

"It does," Zimmer said succinctly.

"Then what's going on?"

"If you could just give me a minute to investigate—"

"We don't have a minute! That madman will launch the missiles! Get him back!"

Ben heard Zimmer frantically pushing buttons, trying to raise a ghost in the machine. "I . . . can't."

"Then get me the Joint Chiefs. So I can give the order to have our troops withdraw!"

"At the moment I can't do that, either."

"Then let me the hell out of this bunker!"

"No." Ben didn't know how, but he got the distinct impression that Zimmer was restraining Swinburne.

"Get your hands off me, man. I'm the president now!"

"Which is exactly why you have to remain in the bunker. I'll send someone else to check out the power problem."

"Does anyone know the time?" Cartwright was asking the question.

Across the table, Ben detected a small green glow.

Secretary Rybicki had a glow-in-the-dark watch.

"The time . . . is up," he said in quick, clipped tones. "It's too late."

Ben felt his heart pounding in his chest. Sarie reached for his hand. He took it and squeezed tightly.

He could feel Swinburne crumbling to the table. "After all that. After all that. We're still too late."

The bunker fell eerily quiet. When Swinburne spoke again, he spoke for them all.

"Oh, my God," he said, and his words seemed to contain all the pain of tens of thousands of innocent civilian lives. "Oh, my dear God."

Part Four

The
Final
Betrayal

44

No one moved. No one spoke. They had known that missiles were on their way for two hours now, and yet, with the knowledge that they must have actually been fired, the horror of the situation struck home with an impact they had not yet experienced.

To Ben's surprise, the former president was the first to break the silence. "Is there any way to get confirmation about what has happened?" Kyler asked.

"Not until we get power, or a report from someone who's gone above," Zimmer said into the darkness. "I've sent agents topside to investigate. I assume they'll come down with information about any recent developments."

"How long will that take?"

"Hard to say, sir. My guess would be around ten minutes."

"Ten minutes of not knowing," Kyler said softly. "My God, how will we survive?"

"Is there any doubt about it?" Swinburne asked. "Zuko told us what he would do. He's a violent dictator, not a poker player."

"And how many people did he say would die?" Sarie asked, her heartbreak evident in her voice. "Thousands?"

"Tens of thousands," Rybicki reminded them all.

The room fell silent again.

"I guess there's nothing we can do but wait for information."

"For the moment," Zimmer said.

"And we can pray," Cartwright added. "We can still pray."

Ben felt certain that, at least for that one brief moment in time, everyone in the bunker, whatever their race, creed, or color, lowered their head and said a little prayer to anyone they believed might be listening.

45

Seamus gritted his teeth and raised his eyes to the ceiling. He was bleeding in so many places he couldn't keep track of them. It had all merged into one gigantic hurt. He had tried to hold in the pain, but he couldn't stop himself from bleeding, or screaming, or crying. He hated that. Not because it was a sign of weakness. Because it gave Scarface so much pleasure.

Raising his eyes upward was not simply an expression of his desperation. It was an old spy trick. You look away from whatever you don't want your assailant to see.

He had managed to pull one of his legs free from the cords that tied him to the cot. If he could loosen the other one, he just might be able to improve his situation.

Or die trying.

"You seem not so bothered anymore," Scarface said with unmitigated glee. "I miss the lovely sound of your screaming." Perhaps we need to try somewhere else." He removed Seamus's belt and jerked down his slacks. "I think the American testicles might be a good place to try next. Do you think you will feel my pliers on your American testicles?"

Seamus didn't withhold his contempt. It wasn't going to make any difference anyway. "I think you're going to do whatever pleases you. If you didn't have a strong sadistic streak, you wouldn't be doing this. You tell yourself you're doing it for some noble cause, but the truth is you're only doing it to gratify your own desire to inflict pain."

Scarface jabbed him in the stomach with the pliers. Seamus lurched forward. He felt his gorge rising. If he had eaten anything lately, he surely would have lost it. He thought it was possible he had broken another rib, but he had so much pain radiating from that region it was impossible to know with any certainty.

Scarface thrust the pliers between his legs. "Prepare to feel the pain of your own manhood slipping away from you. And then to lose life itself."

Seamus squinted his eyes shut, preparing for the inevitable.

Then he heard the crash.

He opened his eyes. Through the window, back in the main room with all the computer equipment—a car had just crashed through the north garage door opening. The car had been battered mightily by the crash, but it had made it through and it was still moving. It was traveling at a tremendous speed, which probably helped it get through. It—

Wait a minute.

It was Seamus's car.

Scarface whipped his head around. "What in the name—"

As soon as he looked in the other direction, Seamus made his move. Both legs free now, he pulled them upward. Using his ab muscles hurt like hell, but he ignored that and kicked back ferociously under Scarface's chin. The terrorist went reeling backward, stunned.

Guard One, obviously caught by surprise, raced forward. Seamus hoisted his legs up again and wrapped them on each side of the man's head. He hadn't been doing those thigh workouts for nothing. He held the guard's head in a lock and twisted it harshly around much further than necks were designed to move. Seamus heard a sickening crunching sound that told him this guard wouldn't be getting up again.

Scarface staggered to his feet, took one look at the situation, and ran.

Good. That would simplify matters. In the next room, Seamus could see his car was still speeding around the large open room, sending the personnel fleeing and crashing into the obscenely expensive machinery, from which sparks flew every which way. Good. This station wouldn't be controlling anything for some time.

He twisted around and, using his now free feet to push against the cot, pulled his arms free of the cords. They burned and tore his skin, but all that mattered was that he got himself unpinned from the cot. He fell to the floor in a heap, shrugged off his torn shirt, and ran.

The guards appeared to have fled—except for a handful who were lying on the ground after being smashed by a rampaging Dodge. The three computer operators, including the woman in the white shirt, were huddled beside the main computer, trying to stay out of the path of the car.

The Dodge squealed to a stop, and a moment later Arlo rolled down the driver's-side window.

"Seamus! Are you okay?"

Why would he ask that? Perhaps because he was limping and bleeding from a dozen places? "I'm fine, kid. Nothing the medics can't fix. What the hell do you think you're doing?"

"Um, trying to get you out before they kill you?"

"I told you to stay put!"

"No, you told me not to leave the car." He smiled. "I didn't."

Seamus bit down on his lower lip. Couldn't argue with the kid's logic. He flipped open his phone. "Zira? Send in the troops."

"Are you kidding? I did that a long time ago."

"I thought you needed confirmation."

"You sent me a photo of the base, remember? That was good enough for me. Especially after you stopped responding."

What do you know? Maybe Zira wasn't as totally useless as he thought. "When they get here, have them come in through the north side. I don't think they can miss it. There's a big hole in the wall."

He snapped the phone closed. He did a quick perimeter search but didn't find anyone. The toughs must've realized the jig was up and exercised the better part of valor. Smart on their part—treason was still punishable by execution, according to the U.S. Constitution.

"Nice work with the car, kid," he told Arlo. "That took some guts."

"Well," he said, "you can't spend your whole life playing computer games."

"True enough."

"Comes a time when a man has to stop simulating and try the real thing."

"And you picked exactly the right time to do it, too." Seamus grinned. "You can get out of the car now."

"Oh. Right. Thanks." Arlo opened the car door and slid out. "I think we should get you to a hospital."

"My people are on their way. They'll have a medic." He walked back into the debris that once had been a high-powered satellite control station and found the three computer operators still huddled together, hands over their heads, as if they were ducking and covering for a fifties nuclear bomb drill. "All right, you clowns. Stand up."

The woman was the first to speak. "We didn't want to do it. He made us!"

"Uh-huh. What'd he do? Threaten to withhold your tax-free treason stipend?"

"My mother is sick. We need money to—"

Seamus held up his hands. "Save it for the prosecutors. I just want to make sure this computer crap is totally disabled."

"It's history," the man who used to sit beside her said. "Smashed to smithereens."

"No more chance of interfering with defense computers?"

"None. I think they were maybe fifteen minutes away from booting us out anyway."

"So there's no way this stuff can launch a missile?"

"No, not—" He stopped, froze.

"What?" Seamus said. "What is it?"

The man swallowed. "This equipment is toast. But the satellite is still up there."

"And the satellite can still launch missiles?"

"Yes, but only if it gets a signal to—" His eyes widened. "They can launch everything at once. There's a fail-safe."

"What? Where?"

"It's on the dish. The satellite—" He thrust his arm out and pointed. "Stop him!"

Seamus whirled around.

Somehow Scarface had crept up behind him. He was making a bee-line for the satellite dish.

The red button on the base of the dish.

Seamus instinctively realized he could not let that sadistic madman get to the button, so he dove across the twelve feet that separated him from his torturer. Scarface kept moving.

Seamus fell a little short but managed to grab Scarface's right leg on the way down. He thudded down to the concrete slab floor with an impact that sent his whole body into spasms. His battered chest and ribs screamed out in protest. But he clung to the man's leg. Scarface had his arm stretched out as far as it would go. He was only inches short of the button.

Seamus's fingers slipped. Scarface edged forward a bit. Seamus dug in with his fingers and held him back with all his remaining strength.

"Arlo! Help!"

He heard the kid running up behind him, but in the meantime, Scarface kicked back. His boot caught Seamus hard on the nose.

The intense agony of compressed sinuses and bent cartilage radiated through his face. His eyes watered, but he gripped the leg as tightly as he could.

Scarface managed to gain another inch. He reached out—

He pushed down the red button.

"Oh, no," Seamus murmured. His head fell to the floor. "Oh, my God, they actually did it. They actually launched the goddamn missiles!"

46

"This should help a little," Zimmer said, and a moment later the bunker was filled with a bright illumination. "Glow sticks," he explained. "Which someone had the foresight to put down here with the first-aid kit."

Ben was amazed at how much a little light did to alleviate the pervasive gloom. Not that the circumstances hadn't left him massively depressed. If anyone could confront this tragedy with anything less, they must be missing the empathy gene. But being able to see a few feet around him, however indistinctly, left him feeling somewhat less vulnerable.

"Thank God," Ruiz said, standing cautiously. "I couldn't stand one more moment of that. I could've sworn something was crawling up my leg."

"The bunker is hermetically sealed," Zimmer explained. "It's actually not even possible for insects to get in here."

"Tell it to my leg," Ruiz groused.

"Any word yet?" Swinburne asked impatiently, if not desperately.

Zimmer shook his head. "I promise I'll let you know as soon as I hear something."

"You can see how we might be anxious!"

"Yes, but I'm sure you can see that my first priority is restoring power to the bunker."

"Damn it, man, do you understand that you are talking to the acting president of the United States? I want to know if the missiles have been launched."

"Whether they have or haven't," Zimmer said firmly, "there's not a thing you or I can do about it—unless I get power back to this communications station. So that takes top priority."

Swinburne folded his arms across his chest and frowned.

Ben was amazed at how still everyone else in the bunker was, as if somehow the thought of the great tragedy had frozen them all in place. It was enough to immobilize anyone. And yet . . .

Something caught his eye on the other side of the bunker. The door to the adjoining room was cracked open a little bit. Ben was certain it had not been that way before the blackout.

Had someone slipped over there after the lights went out?

Or for that matter, someone probably could have done it during the tumult of the verdict and Swinburne's frenzied attempt to call the colonel. Who would've noticed? Ben knew his attention had been focused elsewhere.

Ben remembered seeing a circuit breaker box in there during his previous huddle with the president. It was readily visible on the wall. It did not appear to be locked.

Could someone have slipped over there and sabotaged it?

And then Ben recalled another item of note he had observed in the other room. Slowly the pieces of the puzzle began to come together.

Ben scanned the room, making an inventory of all the parties.

He hated relying on his own memory, particularly when he had been so busy and so much was happening at once. But he was almost certain one person down here was not sitting where that person had been sitting before.

That would have to be the person who had taken a trip next door. But why?

It seemed incredible, unbelievable. But all the evidence, everything Ben had seen and heard, all pointed in one direction.

"Agent Zimmer," Ben said, "there's a breaker box in the next room."

"I know, but—" His head jerked up suddenly. "Hasn't everyone been in here?"

"Better check it out. It may have been . . . damaged."

"If that's what happened, it'll be a good deal easier to fix than anything else would be." Zimmer walked briskly into the other room. Ben didn't have to wait for news for more than ten seconds. "You're right, Ben."

"Breakers thrown?"

"Worse. Looks like someone loosened the panel and ripped up the wiring. But I think I can repair the damage. I've got a box of wire and tools in here."

He stopped talking, but Ben knew that was because he was hard at work.

"What are we talking about here?" Swinburne said. Even in the darkness, Ben could see that he was squinting. "Sabotage?"

"That's what it looks like," Ben said.

"But—that's incredible," Secretary Ruiz said. "Who could've done it? No one could've gotten down here without being spotted."

Ben nodded. "The only person who could have possibly done this is one of us."

Sarie gasped. "Impossible."

"Apparently not," Ben replied. "Remember, I told you earlier there had to be a mole down here. Someone who was in cahoots with Colonel Zuko."

"I don't believe it," Cartwright thundered.

"It doesn't matter who believes it," Ben said. "It's a fact."

"What are you trying to start here, Kincaid?" Swinburne said. "Some kind of witch hunt? You want us to start tearing at everyone's throats?"

"Not everyone's," Ben told him. "Maybe one."

Secretary Rybicki said, "Are you saying that someone intentionally shut off the power? Someone intentionally tried to prevent Swinburne from calling Zuko? Someone wanted the missile to be launched?"

"It is starting to look that way, isn't it?" Ben replied grimly.

"But that makes no sense!"

"That, I suppose, depends on what exactly is your ultimate goal."

"I refuse to believe it," Ruiz said. "It just isn't possible there could be a traitor at this level. Everyone in this bunker has been thoroughly vetted and investigated."

"And yet," Ben replied, "even the FBI can't investigate the many dimensions of the human heart."

"Balderdash!"

From the next room, they heard a cry. "Eureka!"

A brief moment later, the lights came back on.

"Thank goodness," Swinburne said, rising. "What about communications?"

"Powering up," Zimmer said, returning to his station. "Give it about two minutes and we'll be back in business."

"Two minutes!" Swinburne bellowed. "We don't have thirty seconds!"

"If I could snap my fingers and make all this computerized equipment come online any faster, believe me, I would. Unfortunately, violating the laws of physics is one of the few things still outside my power. And yours," Zimmer said angrily.

Ben looked away. Nothing worse than seeing a newly minted president totally humiliated.

The lights came up on Zimmer's laptop. One by one, all the lights on the communications station returned. Zimmer slipped the headset on and started pushing buttons.

"Are we ready yet?" Swinburne asked. "Get me Colonel Zuko. Immediately!"

"No can do," Zimmer said tersely.

"Why not?"

"Not sure. But I don't have an intercontinental connection yet."

"Damn it, man, time is critical here!"

"Yes, I know that, but I'm still going to need more time." Zimmer pushed a few buttons. He listened intently into the headset. "Yes, I'm here," he said to some unknown correspondent. "What have you got?"

Zimmer listened to his headpiece for the next twenty seconds. Everyone else in the bunker hung on pins and needles, waiting to hear what he was learning.

A few seconds later, Zimmer addressed the room. "I have some good news for you all. My people on the outside tell me there has been no detonation or launch of a missile. Repeat: no missile."

A loud cheer went up in the bunker.

"But," Ben asked, "why not?"

"We don't know. But for whatever reason, it hasn't happened."

"Thank God," Swinburne said. "Have you got Zuko yet?"

"Still waiting for a connection."

"Can you get me the Joint Chiefs?"

"That I can do." Zimmer began pushing buttons, putting through the call. "Message?"

"Tell them I want to withdraw the troops. Immediately."

"From Kuraq?" Zimmer asked.

"From the entire Middle East region. All of them. And begin dismantling the bases. Iran, Iraq, Kuraq. Even Saudi Arabia. Everywhere."

Kyler rose to his feet. "Are you out of your mind? You want to talk about insane—that's insane!"

"Just shut up, you insufferable has-been," Swinburne barked. "There's nothing you can do to stop me."

"I think maybe there is," Ben said.

"And I've had about enough of you, too, Kincaid. We put up with your little charade. We jumped through your hoops and took two hours to do what should have been done in five minutes. But the end result was the same. You lost. Kyler is out of power. And I'm withdrawing the troops."

"I can't let you do that," Ben said.

"Can't let me?" Swinburne said incredulously. "As if there were anything you could do about it. I don't need your permission! I'm the president of the goddamn United States!"

"But that's just it," Ben said. He stood up, steadying himself with a hand on the table. "You're not."

47

Seamus sprang to his feet, even though the sudden movement reminded him how much of a beating his body had endured over the course of this very long day.

He grabbed Scarface by the collar and jerked him to his feet.

"It is too late," the terrorist said, his face cracked with contempt. "Your people will pay the price for the arrogance of their president."

Seamus wanted to hit him, wanted to so badly it was like a primordial drive, but he held himself back. He wasn't going to descend to that level. Instead, he tossed the man into a nearby desk chair. He removed one of the cords still dangling from his wrist and used it to tie the man down.

"Is there any way to stop those missiles?" Seamus asked as he restrained the murderer.

"None. Once the signal is given, the rest of the process is instantaneous. Soon the East Coast will be in flames!"

Seamus tightened the cord around his wrist—probably tighter than was strictly necessary. "Is that right, Arlo?"

"Well, it's true that once the signal is given, it can't be countermanded," Arlo answered. "But the signal can't be given if the dish is unplugged."

"Wha—"

Seamus whirled around. About ten feet behind him, he saw Arlo standing with a self-satisfied expression on his face. He was holding an electric cord.

"You unplugged it?"

"Well, it seemed a lot simpler than flinging myself across the room like you did."

"Why didn't you tell me?"

"I tried. You seemed to be kinda wrapped up in your own thing."

Seamus ground his teeth together. "Kid, next time you've saved the world from the apocalypse, tell me!"

"Got it, chief."

A few moments later, the reinforcements arrived—just as soon, Seamus groused silently, as they weren't needed anymore. They fanned out on foot and in helicopters and managed to catch most of the scattered personnel. The computer handlers were taken away for interrogation.

And a few minutes after that, Zira arrived. In person.

She took care of herself, Seamus gave her credit for that. She had to be fifty if she were a day, but her skin was smooth and wrinkle-free. He didn't know what kind of skin care products she used, but Seamus would be willing to bet her nighttime ablutions took at least an hour. Her hair was probably dyed—hair just didn't come in bright yellow at that age—but who cared? If he were dating her, he'd probably think she was swell.

"Did I miss the party?" she asked.

"Pretty much. I've got everything under control."

Her forehead creased. "I would hardly say that."

"Why?"

"You may have prevented the missile launch, and we're grateful for that. But several of the men got away, the scarred man appears to have been physically abused, and the computer experts tell me that you interrogated them without Mirandizing them first. We'll be lucky if we can prosecute anyone."

"I thought the first order of the day was saving lives."

"That was part of your job. Not the only part."

"And if you want to talk about abuse," he said, "take a look at what that bastard did to my chest."

She did not appear interested. "I'm sure there will be time for full reports and debriefing later. I want you to head back to Langley immediately."

"Aren't you forgetting something?"

Zira looked as if talking to him were a chore that required infinite patience. "Please feel free to refresh my memory."

"The nuclear suitcase."

"A nuclear device was stolen today and you think I've forgotten all about it? I can assure you that I have not forgotten about it, Seamus. But what does it have to do with the matter at hand?"

"Colonel Zuko was behind that, too."

"You have proof of this?"

"I do. And there's more. We've got a mole somewhere inside the government."

"I suspected as much. But we had no evidence."

"Now we do. This computer invasion would have been impossible without inside information. And if you find out who had access to that information, you might be able to figure out who your Benedict Arnold is."

"I'll get people right on it."

"And your other possible source of information," he said, stopping her, "would be my close personal friend Scarface here."

"His name is Abdul Minoz. He was a lieutenant in Colonel Zuko's military when Zuko seized control of Kuraq."

"Thanks for the trivia. I feel better now."

"I'll have my people interrogate him thoroughly."

Seamus stopped her. "I'd like to do that myself."

She shook her head. "Sorry. You're too close to this. I can't trust you to behave appropriately."

"Zira. Look at me."

"No, thank you."

"Look at me!" He grabbed her arm, spun her around, and forced her to look at his tattered chest.

He was torn in half a dozen places. Dried blood caked his skin. There would be permanent scarring. There was no question about that.

"I think I've earned this," he said, looking deep into her eyes. "Give me a shot."

"I can't allow you to hurt him."

"Understood."

"I mean—not at all. Not even a tiny bit."

"Can I scare him a little?"

She tossed her head. "I don't think that violates any Company protocols."

"Thanks, Zira."

"You've got ten minutes. Find the suitcase."

He nodded. "I will."

48

"What in God's name are you talking about?" Swinburne demanded. "Of course I'm the president now. Were you asleep when that verdict came down? Let me send you a memo: you lost."

"I'm aware of that," Ben said, stepping right into his airspace. "But the trial was invalid because someone here was tainting the evidence. Someone was engaging in fraud, which invalidates any verdict. I'm demanding a new trial. And until that new trial takes place, President Kyler remains president, because the trial you won was invalid."

Kyler seemed just as baffled as everyone else in the room. "Ben, what are you doing?"

"And what are you accusing me of?" Swinburne said. "Where are my security people? I want this man arrested!"

A few of the Secret Service men inched forward, but Zimmer held them back.

"I didn't specifically accuse you of anything," Ben said. "I just said the trial was fraudulent. Because it was."

Cartwright stood. "I think you're going to need to explain yourself, Kincaid. Because as the judge, I think I'm the only one who can set aside the verdict. At least for now."

"True enough."

"So tell me what you know."

"I will. Because you see, we've all been proceeding from a false assumption. We assumed that the president's behavior is an indicator of his sanity. But it isn't necessarily so."

"What are you babbling about now?"

"I'm saying it isn't fair or accurate to condemn President Kyler for his unusual behavior when the fact of the matter is that he's been drugged. Against his will. For some time now."

"What?" All eyes focused on Ben. Not for the first time today, he seemed to have the complete attention of everyone in the room. Even Agent Zimmer turned, removing his headset.

Kyler looked at him with eyes wide.

"What are you babbling about, man?" Swinburne demanded. "Is this some pathetic lawyer trick to try to undermine the verdict? Because let me tell you something, now that I'm in charge, I won't stand—"

"But you're not in charge," Ben said firmly. "And you will listen, because you know as well as I do that if someone has been drugging the president—the real one—that invalidates everything."

Cartwright interrupted the debate. "What proof do you have of this, Kincaid?"

"Well, I'm short on proof, but I'm long on common sense and deductive reasoning, which are the best tools at our disposal so long as we're trapped in this bunker." He hesitated. "I'm hoping to collect the evidence as we proceed."

Swinburne was not placated. "I don't know what your game is, Kincaid, but I'm not going to have it. We indulged you once and gave you your little trial. We're not going to waste any more time on you. Don't you understand that we're in a crisis?"

"I know that, for whatever reason, the missile was not released. And I know that if I stand by and allow you to take over the government, it could result in a disastrous foreign policy scenario. I speak because I cannot remain silent."

"That's very poetic," Swinburne barked, "but I'll have you put behind bars before I'll—"

Cartwright held up a hand. "I think we can hear the man out. If he's brief." He glanced at his watch. "Kincaid, I'm giving you five minutes to explain. If you can't do it in that amount of time, I'll allow Swinburne to talk to the Joint Chiefs."

Swinburne was enraged. "You'll *allow* me? I'm the president."

"Maybe," Cartwright said. "We'll revisit that question in five minutes. Kincaid, go."

"I've suspected for some time that the president might be drugged," Ben began cautiously. "How else do you explain these sudden bursts of bizarre behavior that come and go without explanation? I come from a medical family, and I've been exposed to mental illness, but nothing I've witnessed looks anything like what we saw in here today. I've represented people with mental illnesses before, including those suffering from schizophrenia or bipolar disorder, conditions that might cause sudden irrational episodes. But I've never seen anything like this, certainly not from someone who otherwise seemed so sane. More than that—highly competent. And productive. It just didn't make any sense. But when I heard Sarie talking about the president up on the roof, longing to be free, talking about flying, it occurred to me that that sounded like nothing so much as someone under the influence of a hallucinogenic drug."

"Hallucinogenic?" Secretary Ruiz said aloud, but Ben noticed that he didn't say it in a way that suggested he was rejecting the idea out of hand.

"Yes. Mind-altering."

"What drug did you have in mind?" Cartwright asked.

"I'm not a doctor," Ben replied. "Or a pharmacist. But my suspicion would be that someone's been slipping the president something."

Ben was pleased to find there was no immediate reaction. No one screamed "Of course!" but then, no one reached for the hanging rope, either. But Roland Kyler looked intrigued. What Ben said evidently made a lot of sense to him.

Dr. Albertson was batting a finger against his lips. "I suppose you're suggesting a mild dose—to explain why these episodes come and go without ever lasting too long."

"Exactly. It's as if he gets a little jolt to his system, he runs amok for a few minutes, and then it wears off. Not a major acid trip. Just enough to affect his behavior for a brief time."

Albertson looked more concerned than anyone, which Ben supposed was understandable under the circumstances. "Just one minute,

Mr. Kincaid. I monitor everything that goes in and out of the president's bloodstream. There's no way he could be infused with something." He hesitated for a moment. "At least not without the president's participation."

"Or yours," Ben said pointedly.

"What the Sam Hill does that mean?"

"I'm just making a point," Ben said. "There's always a way to tamper, but it would require the participation of someone very close to the president. Like, basically, anyone in this room."

"Okay, Sherlock," Ruiz said, "explain to us how it was done."

"There are several ways it could have been done. Believe me, I've been taking notes. I just didn't think any of them were really workable—until I finally figured it out a few minutes ago."

"Don't keep us in suspense," Cartwright said. "You've only got five—" He made a check, then corrected himself. "Three and a half more minutes."

"I noticed right away that the president was using an inhaler, as I'm sure you all did. So he was ingesting whatever was in it. That could have been tampered with. Could've been infused with a hallucinogen."

"I keep that inhaler on me at all times!" Albertson cried.

"Exactly. So that wasn't a possibility—unless you're the traitor."

Albertson looked as if he were staring into the headlights of an oncoming car.

"The same is true," Ben continued, "of the insulin injections. How easy would it be to fill that syringe with a little something extra? Easy as pie. But once again, since Dr. Albertson keeps close watch over that operation, he's really the only one who could be the poisoner."

Dr. Albertson's lips clamped close together. "Kincaid, I have not betrayed my president. Or my country."

"And I haven't said you have. Yet. Please let me continue."

Albertson's face was red and he was breathing noisily, but he held his tongue.

"There was at least one other possibility," Ben continued. "Twice today I've watched Agent Zimmer bring the president his coffee."

Over at the door, Agent Zimmer slowly removed his headset.

"And I get the impression it's something he does fairly often. I don't know why. Maybe it's just convenient, since he's almost always around and not participating in the policy decisions. Maybe it's a standard protocol to make sure no one else has the opportunity to tamper with it. At any rate, I'm sure I don't have to explain to this august body how easy it would be to lace someone's drink. Particularly something as strong as coffee. The harsh, bitter taste of hot black coffee could mask any number of additives."

Zimmer cleared his throat. "I'll step down pending a further investigation. Agent Gioia, you're in charge."

"I appreciate your cooperation," Cartwright said, "but I'd just as soon you didn't do anything. At least till we've got this thing figured out." He turned back toward Ben. "You got anything more, or is that it?"

"Of course I've got more," Ben said. "If I didn't have more than that, I would've kept my mouth shut. I'm only speaking now because I figured it out—eventually. Took way too long, I know. But I didn't pick up the key clue until a few minutes ago. When I saw something I never expected to see."

"What's with all the dramatic pauses?" Ruiz said. "Just get on with it!"

"Right, right," Ben said, nodding. "Sorry. I'm used to being in the courtroom. Here's the thing. I've theorized about the president being exposed to foreign substances in all the ways I just described. But so far as I could tell, none of them led to one of these episodes. But a few minutes ago, I saw the president taking something. And not ten minutes later he plunged into the latest irrational scene—while he was testifying."

"What are you talking about?" Secretary Rybicki asked. "What did you see?"

Ben took a deep breath, then continued. "I saw the president smoking."

Lips parted. Brows knitted. Sarie was shaking her head.

"It's true. I was as shocked as anyone, because my wife reminded me earlier today that the president had given up smoking as a promise to his wife. No one wants to break a promise to his wife—or for her to know that he has. Which explains why he has been sneaking around so much lately. Seeking privacy—away from his wife."

Ben took the general wordlessness as a good sign. They were all processing this new information, running it through their brains, trying to make all the pieces of the tangram fit together.

"I never meant to hurt anyone," Kyler said softly. "I just . ... couldn't quit."

"You're not the first person to have trouble giving up smoking," Ben replied.

"If I had more time to focus on it, maybe," Kyler added. "But I don't."

"Exactly. And you're under enough stress already, without the added stress of trying to wean yourself off nicotine." He turned toward Dr. Albertson. "This is what you meant when you referred to the president being under the added stress of giving up bad habits, isn't it? You were talking about the difficulty he was having giving up this addictive substance. Nicotine."

Dr. Albertson frowned. Ben knew he still wasn't exactly on the doc's top ten list. "I was aware he was having trouble with it, yes."

"And this also explains why you kept ditching your security detail, doesn't it?" he asked Kyler. "You'd sneak off for a cig in the little boys' room or wherever. And that in turn would lead to another hallucinatory episode. So by the time Sarie found you, you would be in the midst of another crazy-seeming episode."

Kyler looked up at him, his mouth gaping. "I never put the two together. I just thought . . . well, I didn't know what to think. I didn't know what was happening to me. I was afraid . . . " He hung his head down low.

"I can imagine your worries," Ben said. "You were losing control of yourself—and you didn't know why."

"Speculation is all well and good, Kincaid," Cartwright said. "Do you have any proof of this?"

"Not yet. But Mr. President—and yes, I am talking about President Kyler—can you loan me a cigarette?"

With considerable reluctance—and embarrassment—Kyler reached inside his coat pocket and withdrew a cigarette.

Ben handed it to the doctor. "Dr. Albertson, could you examine this, please?"

"You trust me?"

"I do."

Albertson opened his doctor's bag and withdrew a small scalpel. He laid the cigarette on the black table and slowly cut it open.

The cigarette fell apart, spilling its contents. Ben saw lots of tobacco, a filter, and, when he looked closer, tiny white granules.

"Any idea what that is?" Ben asked.

Albertson touched a finger to a few of the granules, then touched it to his tongue. "Just an educated guess," he answered. "But I'm thinking it's LSD."

The reaction in the bunker was electric.

"That's lysergic acid diethylamide," Albertson expounded. "A psychedelic derived from ergot, a grain fungus that grows on rye. It traditionally produces effects such as the extreme reduction of inhibitions, a sense of time distorting, and irrational reasoning."

"In other words, exactly what President Kyler has been experiencing."

"Yes. It's normally ingested orally on an absorbent surface, such as a sugar cube or blotter paper. It can also be taken in liquid form. Inhaled as a crystal, like this, it would probably be less potent—but it would be enough to create the brief episodes the president has experienced."

Kyler slowly rose to his feet. His face was as stony as granite, but Ben sensed lava boiling beneath that surface.

"I want to know who did this," he said succinctly. "And I want to know now."

"I think we all do," Admiral Cartwright said. "Can you help us out here, Kincaid?"

"I can. Mr. President, where do you keep your cigarettes?"

"I have a silver cigarette tray—a gift from the British prime minister—that I keep tucked away in a desk drawer. I take a few out each morning and tuck them into my coat pocket."

"Is the desk locked?"

"Not during the day."

"So anyone with access to the Oval Office could have planted tainted cigarettes. Anyone in this room, to be blunt."

"But why?"

"That's a factor to consider, too," Ben continued. "Because I don't believe anyone would commit a crime of this magnitude for money. Or revenge, love, extortion, the desire to humiliate, or any of your traditional motives. It has to be politically motivated. Nothing else makes sense."

"Someone wants us out of Kuraq. Badly," Secretary Ruiz said.

"Or perhaps," Ben said, "out of the Middle East altogether."

Swinburne pressed a hand against his chest. "What are you saying? Are you accusing me of being the traitor? Is that what you're saying?"

"You don't have to speculate," Ben said. "If I decide to accuse you, you'll know it."

"How about it, then?" Secretary Rybicki asked. "Do you know who it is?"

"I do," Ben answered. "I'm surprised no one else has figured it out. I told you all a long time ago that we had a mole among us. I would've imagined everyone was trying to figure out who it was."

"Frankly," Cartwright said, "I thought you were just trying to stir up trouble. Playing typical lawyer games."

"Well, then, your infantile prejudice against lawyers prevented you from stopping a potential national catastrophe. That might be worth remembering in the future."

Cartwright looked appropriately chastised.

"Here's the thing," Ben explained. "Someone gave Colonel Zuko inside information. They told him the president was in the bunker, or was on his way there, and then later told him that the vice president was down here, too."

"I'm the president now!" Swinburne insisted.

"Oh, give it up already," Ben said. "You're not. Anyway, who was tipping Zuko off? No one could know the vice president was here until he was, and by that time we were all stuck down here. Cell phones don't work. Only Agents Zimmer and Gioia had access to the communications station. But would they have had access to the cigarettes? Doubtful."

"So how did the mole get the word out?" Sarie asked.

"Only one way possible. When Agent Zimmer gave three of us the chance to make a short phone call to the outside world. To comfort our loved ones."

He could see eyes rolling upward as everyone struggled to remember who had made a call.

"I was one of the three, but I knew it wasn't me, so that left two. And I'm certain it wasn't Sarie. For one thing, I think our spy gave Zuko the computer codes and passwords that helped him hack into our defense system. As chief of staff, Sarie would not have access to top-secret defense information. She was our eyewitness, the one who told us about the episodes she witnessed. If she had been the mastermind behind all this, she would have told far more dramatic stories. She would've said she wrestled the gun from the president's head, or had him threatening to blow up Australia or something. No, she was cast in the role of the observer, the one who would report all that she had seen—and her testimony would be all the more tragically believable, because everyone knows she loves and is devoted to this president. No, it couldn't be her. So that only left one other person who could have tipped off Zuko. Who could've made the cigarette substitution."

"Spit it out, Ben," Kyler said. "I want to know."

"Don't you remember?" Ben said. "The only other person who has had contact with the outside world was our dedicated secretary of defense, Albert Rybicki."

49

12:22 P.M.

Christina had reached her limit.

She had tried to be patient. She had tried to be calm. She didn't want to be one of those strident, pushy wives who were always keeping tabs on their husbands. But at the end of the day, she wasn't exactly the stay-home-and-knit type, either.

It had been hours since Ben had called her. Hours since she had heard any useful news. All she knew was what she heard on CNN, which wasn't much. She almost pitied those poor commentators. They had so much time to fill and so little to say. A dollop of information was buried in a mountain of pointless chatter. The news had turned into speculation and gossip, and now she wasn't sure what it was.

And now she was railing against the media when of course that wasn't really what was bothering her. She was worried about Ben.

She pushed herself out of her chair. She had waited here long enough. She was going to get out there and do something. Shake some bushes. She'd been in Washington for a while now and, as Ben's chief of staff when he was a senator, she had developed a pretty good rep as someone who could get things done.

So it was time she got something done.

Ben hadn't told her his exact location—probably wasn't allowed to tell her. But he said he hadn't left the White House. So that was where she would start. She had provisional White House clearance. She could get to the back door. After that, she would just have to take it one step at a time. Bully her way through. She'd done it before. Granted, not at what was perhaps the most heavily guarded private residence in the entire world . . . but she never shrank from a challenge.

She was going to find her husband, damn it, and make sure he was safe. And she had nothing but pity for anyone who got in her way.

50

The two men were back in the side room where Scarface had tortured Seamus. It was tempting to pin the man up on the wall and
get out the pliers. But Seamus resisted the urge. Zira would never approve, and even if she did, he didn't have enough time. He would have
to find his own way to instill terror.

He held Scarface—that is, Minoz—down by his throat and
watched his face turn blue. Zira had said he couldn't hurt the man—
which, translated into CIAese, meant: he couldn't leave any marks. So
he wouldn't. He wouldn't even punch the man in the neck, the usual
target when you wanted to do maximum damage without leaving a
mark. In his experience, strangulation had a strange way of getting
tongues wagging.

Minoz's arms flailed about uselessly. He was pinned down like a bug
and he wasn't getting up until Seamus decided to let him. It didn't take
him long to discover that. He only made a halfhearted effort at pushing
Seamus away. Lying flat on his back, he just didn't have the leverage.

Seamus pressed down hard on his trachea. "You already know
how I feel about you. So let's not waste time with the part where I con-

vince you I would kill you. You know I would kill you. You know I want to. And I will if you don't tell me everything you know."

Seamus let up on his throat for a second. Minoz gasped for air, but before he had gulped it all down, Seamus reapplied the pressure. The resulting sucking noise even sounded painful. "I want to know where the nuclear suitcase is. I will give you one second to answer. If you do not answer—immediately—I will choke you until you are dead. Understood?"

He took the eyes-wide expression for a nod and let go of the man's throat. "Talk."

"I do not know."

Seamus started to clamp down.

"I had it! I admit that. You know I had it!"

"Whom did you give it to?"

"I do not know his name."

Seamus squeezed his trachea tightly in his fist. Minoz squealed.

Ten seconds later, Seamus let up slightly. "Tell me!"

"I never knew his name. Colonel Zuko was the go-between. After we failed at the Washington Monument, I took the suitcase to a computer expert to have the triggering mechanism altered. Programmed with a fail-safe password. Then I left it at the designated drop-off point. I don't know who picked it up later."

"You left a nuclear device for a man you did not know?"

"I did what the colonel told me to do."

"What did Zuko call him?"

"He never used a name."

Seamus pressed in with his fingers.

"Wait! Wait, I do remember a time. It stuck in my memory because it was so odd."

"What?"

"Someone—not the colonel—referred to him as a secretary."

Secretary? Seamus's eyebrow knitted together. Colonel Zuko was working with someone's secretary? Perhaps a high-placed military advisor's, or—

Wait a minute. In these politically correct times, you couldn't call a secretary a secretary. He'd be an executive assistant. In this town, a secretary could only be—

Good God. Was it possible? Did Zuko have a cabinet-level informant?

Seamus felt cold fingers tickling at the base of his spine.

"What was the password your boss had programmed into the suit-case?"

"I don't know. That had nothing to do with me."

Frustrating, but probably true. They wouldn't tell anyone who didn't need to know.

"Listen to me, Minoz. This is very important. If you expect to go on breathing, you will provide me an answer. What is he going to do with the nuclear device?"

"He's taking it to the Middle East. Zuko said his clearance level is so high he can take anything anywhere."

Not anymore. As soon as he told Zira, every member of the cabi-net would be grounded. If they weren't already. "Did he have a backup plan? If he couldn't get the bomb overseas?"

To his surprise—and horror—Minoz smiled.

Seamus wrapped his hand around the man's throat. "Tell me."

"I will tell you." The sadistic pleasure in the man's eyes told Sea-mus that this was going to be something he did not want to hear. "I will tell you because there is nothing you can do about it."

And then he told.

Seamus shoved the man aside and ran as fast as he could back to the main room.

"Zira! Quick! We have an emergency situation. Divert all troops. Immediately! Divert all troops!"

51

"Me?" Secretary Rybicki said, pressing his hands against his chest. "You're accusing me? Seriously?"

"I am," Ben said. "Because you did it."

Rybicki stood on wobbly feet. "I don't believe it!" He looked at Kyler. "You're not buying this crap, are you?"

Kyler looked pensive. "I'm listening."

"This is an outrage. I'm glad you're so fond of lawyers, Kincaid. 'Cause I'm going to have a dozen of Washington's best shoved right up your—"

"I doubt it," Ben replied. "I think you're going to need all the legal talent for your defense."

"It's preposterous!" Rybicki insisted. "I'm the secretary of defense!"

"Which makes you one of the few people in the nation in a position to help Colonel Zuko hack into our defense computers. And, of course, your position gave you access to the Oval Office—and the president's cigarettes—anytime you wanted them."

"I'm not listening to this," Rybicki exclaimed. "It's insane."

"As if that weren't enough," Ben added, "you were the one who snuck next door and sabotaged the breaker box. Pity you forgot which chair you were sitting in."

"I noticed that he had moved, too," Secretary Ruiz said. "I just didn't put the pieces together."

"Passing me the note about Secretary Ruiz's connection to Apollo was a nice touch," Ben added. "It directed my suspicions to him—and diverted them from you. Briefly."

"This gets crazier by the minute," Rybicki said. He was pacing back and forth, practically wearing a hole into the carpet. "Why would I do such a thing?"

"I'm guessing you want the colonel to detonate another missile on American soil and inflict serious casualties. Because that tragedy will lay the foundation for whatever dramatic foreign policy shift you want."

"And what might that be? Since you have all the answers."

"I think you're in a better position to explain than I am," Ben suggested. "But it would appear to me that, like the vice president, you want America out of the Middle East. Altogether. To give the colonel what he wants." He paused. "But Swinburne wants us out because he thinks our foreign entanglements are compromising our national security. I don't know what your motive is—but it's more than that."

"So just tell us already," Kyler said. His teeth were tightly clenched. "I trusted you, Rybicki. And I for one would like to know what made you go rogue."

Rybicki sputtered. "But—but—"

"Damn it, man," Cartwright said sharply, "we all know you did it. It's written all over your face. So tell us why!"

"But I—I never—"

"Goddamn it!" Kyler bellowed, slapping his hand against the table. "We want to know why!"

"I—I—I—" Rybicki looked helplessly from one face to the next. "I just want what's best for the country! In this temple as in the hearts of the people!"

"I thought as much," Ben said. "What is it you were after?"

"I want the same thing you want, Kincaid."

"I very much doubt that."

"It's true. Don't you think the United States needs to commit to alternative energies? To end our addiction to oil?"

And all at once, Ben could see the whole picture all too quickly. "Oh, my God."

"Why do you think we're in the Middle East, anyway?" Rybicki asked.

Kyler answered. "To protect Israel. To give us a foothold closer to Asia. And, of course, to ensure the steady supply of oil."

"Yes, and let's face it, the last one is the one that really matters. That's the reason we keep invading over and over again. We need oil. We endanger our security and we enrich some of the most dangerous people in the world to feed our dependency on a rapidly diminishing fossil fuel. It's insane! And yet nothing stops us. Carter urged restraint, slower driving, energy conservation—and we practically impeached him for it. Americans think they are entitled to all the oil they want. Even when the price of oil went sky-high in 2008, consumption barely dropped. We simply can't quit. We're addicted!"

"So you were going to force our hand," Ben said.

"It's the only way! We can supply our own needs if we just practice conservation and make the relatively simple conversion to natural gas. So why don't we? Why aren't we seriously pursuing solar energy, wind, water? We've been talking about these alternatives since the seventies, but we're still not making any significant progress. Because the oil companies are too entrenched, too well connected. Because oil is cheaper."

"So you were going to fix all that?" Kyler asked.

"I wanted to make America safe again. In this temple and in the hearts of the people."

"I'm not following this," Ben said. "If that's your goal, why do you want our troops out of the Middle East?"

"So they won't be hurt."

A long line creased Ben's brow. "Hurt? How?"

For the first time, Rybicki smiled, and the smile sent chills up Ben's spine. "So I see there's at least one thing the brilliant lawyer didn't quite put together. That makes me happy."

"I still don't understand," Ben said. "What did I miss?"

"You're operating under the assumption that Zuko is the one who engineered the theft of the nuclear suitcase in Arlington. But you're wrong." A full-out grin spread across his face. "It was me."

52

12:29 P.M.

"You've got the nuclear suitcase?" Kyler said incredulously.

Rybicki smiled defiantly. "I used Zuko's people. But there was a quid pro quo: I helped them get into the defense computers, and they helped me get the suitcase. And they did."

"What were you planning to do with it?"

Rybicki opted not to answer the question. His hands were twitching. "I don't believe I care to answer that question. I want a lawyer." He paused. "And I don't mean Kincaid, either."

The president nodded. "Did you seriously think you could get away with this?"

No response.

"Does this betrayal mean nothing to you? Are you so self-righteous you believed you were justified in endangering thousands of lives?"

Rybicki looked away.

"Fine." The president's frustration rippled through his face. "Agent Zimmer, I think you can forget about stepping down pending an investigation. There's not going to be an investigation—of you. I'd like the secretary of defense placed in custody pending formal charges."

"Yes, sir. Gioia?"

The agent stepped forward. "Right here."

"Take the secretary of defense into the next room and restrain him until we get the all-clear signal to leave the bunker."

"Will do." Gioia took Rybicki by the arm and led him away. Ben was relieved to see that he did not resist.

"Mr. President." Zimmer had his hand pressed against his right earphone. "I've finally been able to contact Colonel Zuko."

"I'll take it," Kyler said.

"Wait just a minute!" Swinburne whined. "I won that trial. You have been relieved—"

"That trial was invalid," Cartwright said, "based on fraud tainting the verdict. I'm setting that verdict aside. If you want to institute more proceedings at a later time, you can—though I wouldn't recommend it. For now, Roland Kyler remains president."

Swinburne sputtered nonsensically.

"Oh, be quiet," Kyler said, shoving him aside. "And just in case you haven't guessed, I want your resignation on my desk tomorrow morning."

"But—but—"

"Just do it," President Kyler said. "You'll be saving yourself a lot of embarrassment. Now put the colonel on speaker."

Ben couldn't help smiling as Kyler stepped up to the communications station. He seemed strong, back in control, and—best of all—presidential.

"Mr. President," the colonel said in his usual taunting tone, "I have given you some leeway on your deadline, but no more! If you do not remove your troops immediately, I'll—"

"You won't do a thing," President Kyler interrupted, "and we both know it. You're not the forgiving type, colonel. If you had the ability to launch a missile, you would've already done it. I don't know exactly what happened, but I have to assume that one of my operatives succeeded in his mission and took down your petty little terrorist operation. And just in case you're wondering, yes, we know Secretary Rybicki was helping you. It won't happen again."

"You don't know what you're talking about!" the colonel fumed. "I can detonate your missiles at—"

"Yeah, sure you can. Now listen up, Colonel, and listen good. Our troops are going into your country, but they're going in for two purposes only: to rescue the people who went down in that helicopter, and to wrest control of Benzai. You are not going to occupy that territory, and you are not going to exterminate its people. If you stay out of our way, we'll accomplish our mission and go. If you try to interfere in any way—any way whatsoever—we will not stop until we have seized control of your entire nation, pulled you off the throne, and put you under arrest. I'm sure the entire world would rejoice to see you standing trial for crimes against humanity. And that's exactly what's going to happen if you don't stay out of our way. Do you understand me?"

Several seconds passed before he replied. "I understand. But—"

"Good." Kyler made a slashing gesture across his neck. Zimmer cut off the communications line.

"That was absolutely brilliant," Cartwright said. "You have my congratulations. I wonder what that sick buzzard will try next."

"Let's hope nothing. Is he trying to reconnect, Zimmer?"

The agent shook his head. "He seems to be done. I think you put him in his place but good, sir."

"Let's hope this means the crisis is over. I think we could all use a breather."

Ben couldn't have heard happier words. "Does that mean we can leave the bunker? Make a phone call?"

"Not just yet," Zimmer said. "I need an official all-clear from the CIA and the military task force investigating the missile crisis."

"How long will that take?"

"I don't know, Ben. But I'd rather keep you down here too long than not long enough."

A valid point. "I think I'll visit Secretary Rybicki. I still have a few questions I'd like to ask him."

"He won't talk."

"I've heard that before. You never know."

Ben crossed the room, opened the door, and entered the small adjoining room.

And gasped.

Agent Gioia was lying on the floor. A slow trickle of blood flowed from the side of his head.

Secretary Rybicki was gone.

53

Secretary Rybicki slowed as he approached the gateway to the north rear parking area. He didn't want anyone to know he had been running. But he knew that if he didn't get off the premises before the boys downstairs noticed he was gone, then he never would.

The 17th and Pennsylvania vehicle entrance was restricted to a limited few with clearance, and then only after passing through a series of gateposts and checkpoints. Of course, as a cabinet member, he had the magic blue sticker on the dash of his car that meant he didn't have to put up with any of that.

He smiled at the two marines stationed at the door without stopping. Just as he always did. Friendly, but not too friendly. Recognizing that they were there, but not too much. He was the secretary of defense, after all. Marines were under his supervision, not the other way around.

He had texted ahead so that they would bring round his car. As he walked down the steps, he saw an attractive redhead walking toward him.

Could it possibly be . . . ?

Someone up there must love him after all.

"Ms. McCall?"

Christina looked up.

"I'm Albert Rybicki. Secretary of defense? We met at the Press Club—"

"Of course." She smiled. "I'm sorry. My mind was elsewhere."

"That's understandable. This has been a very trying day. For everyone."

"I'll bet. Were you down in the bunker?"

"I was, yes."

"Can you get me in? I want to see Ben."

"Oh, Ben." His brain was racing. "Well, that's just the thing. He isn't there anymore."

"He's not?"

"No. He was released about a hour ago. To a . . . secret location."

"And he didn't call me?"

"I doubt they would let him."

She looked put out, but it was probably more worry than anything else. "Is there any way I can see him? Or at least get a message to him? There's something I really wanted to tell him. It's important."

"Maybe I could take a message."

"No. I want to tell him myself."

He snapped his fingers. "Well, I'm headed to the safe house right now. I don't think anyone would object if I brought you with me."

"Really?"

"You're married to a member of the White House staff. You already have provisional clearance, don't you?"

"How else could I be here?"

"Exactly. Hop in my car. We'll be there in ten minutes."

"I could just follow you in my car."

"Um, no. If someone saw you tailing me, they might send a fighter plane to take you out."

"That would be bad. Which one is your car?"

He watched as she clambered into his car, resisting the desire to smile. This was almost too easy. And too delicious. Another minute and he would be free. Then he would pick up his little parcel. And he and his newfound friend would travel together to their destination.

But only one of them would leave.

Good thing he had thought to take Agent Gioia's gun.

They might've stopped the missiles, but they couldn't stop him. He would fulfill his final mission.

And he would take his revenge against Kincaid, too.

54

"Zimmer!" Ben shouted. "He's missing!"

Barely a second later, Agent Zimmer was inside the small briefing room. "Where's Rybicki?"

"Exactly."

Zimmer crouched down beside his fallen comrade. "Gioia's not dead. Just unconscious. Rybicki must've had some kind of weapon. Or improvised a blunt instrument. Picked up a paperweight or something. Probably what he used on the breaker box, too."

Zimmer opened another door and entered the small foyer that led to the elevator. "He must have gone topside."

"You've got men up there, don't you?"

"Yes. But they don't have any reason to stop the secretary of defense. He has clearance to pass through the building as he wishes." Zimmer barked orders into his headset. Ben was impressed once more at how levelheaded Zimmer was. Even a snafu of this magnitude didn't faze him.

"He's left the premises," Zimmer updated him. "I'm sending people after him. There's not much he can do now that Zuko has lost control of the missiles."

"Unless he gets his hands on that nuclear suitcase."

"Wasn't he planning to use that in the Persian Gulf?"

"He was. But he can't do that now. God knows what he might try instead."

Zimmer frowned. "I'll double the detachment looking for him. Don't worry. We'll find him."

And Ben knew they would find him. Eventually. The question was whether they would find him in time.

President Kyler entered the room. "What's going on? Where's Rybicki?" He saw the bloodstained body on the floor. "What in the name of—?"

Ben filled him in as best he could as Zimmer continued to receive updates over his headset.

"We have to find that madman," President Kyler said.

Ben agreed. "But our first priority has to be the recovery of that suitcase."

Kyler nodded grimly.

"We have another problem," Zimmer said. He was frowning, which might be the most emotion Ben had seen him register all day.

"What's wrong?" Ben asked.

"I'm not quite sure how to tell you this. Probably best just to get out with it. Your wife was upstairs. At the rear receiving gate."

Ben's eyes bulged. "Christina? Where is she now?"

Zimmer swallowed. "She went with Rybicki."

Ben seized him by the arms. "What? Why?"

Zimmer shook his head, still listening to words streaming in from the other side. "I don't know the details. Sounds as if he offered to take her to you."

"Christina? With that . . . that lunatic? The one who thinks he can solve the world's problems with a bomb?" His voice fell. "The one who still has a bomb stashed somewhere nearby?"

"I'm afraid so."

Ben opened the door to the corridor and walked outside. A moment later he punched the elevator button. "I'm going up."

Zimmer stepped in front of him. "I can't allow that. We haven't gotten the all-clear signal yet."

"The president believes the crisis is over. The one from Colonel Zuko, anyway."

"If there's a potential nuclear threat, I can't—"

"The president needs to stay down here. I don't."

Zimmer held his ground. "Ben, I'm sorry, but I can't allow you to endanger yourself"

"I'm sorry, Zimmer," Ben said, looking him straight in the eye, "but you can't stop me, unless you're planning to draw your weapon. Is that what you're going to do?"

Zimmer's hand went to his holster.

"Really?" Ben asked. "After all I've done down here? You're going to pull a gun on me?"

Zimmer hesitated. "Mr. President?"

Kyler looked at Ben sternly. "I can't authorize the premature release of anyone from the bunker. I can't be held accountable if some tragedy should occur."

Zimmer pulled out the gun.

"Please," Ben said. "Just let me—"

"On the other hand," the president continued, walking back toward the main room, "I'm not in charge of Robert Griswold's legal staff. I can't keep track of everyone. How am I supposed to know what some renegade lawyer does?" He closed the door behind him.

Zimmer put the gun back in the holster.

The elevator doors opened. Ben stepped inside.

"Thanks," Ben said breathlessly.

"Godspeed," Zimmer said quietly as the doors closed between them.

Part Five

The Pages of History

55

*B*en stood outside the Lincoln Memorial, desperate to get inside. The authorities had cordoned off the building. Sirens were wailing. Any nonessential personnel were being hurriedly whisked away. Ben wasn't sure who was in charge—the CIA, the FBI, the local police—and he didn't really care. All he knew for certain was that he wanted in. And he also knew why he couldn't get in.

He'd had enough experience to know what this was. A hostage scenario.

Christina was in there. He was certain of it.

"Mr. Kincaid?"

Ben turned and saw a tall, strong-looking middle-aged man with sun-baked skin and a turnip of a nose. He was wearing a padded flak jacket. The strap of a holster on his shoulder told Ben he was armed.

"Mr. Kincaid, I'm Seamus McKay. I'm with the CIA."

"I know," Ben said, taking his hand. "We've met. When I was a senator."

"That's right," McKay said, arching one eyebrow. "I wasn't sure you would remember."

"The president mentioned you earlier today. Spurred my memory. I'm glad you're involved. Looks like your people have responded quickly."

"They're trained to do just that. Ever since September eleventh. No choice, really. As soon as I notified my people of the target, they set up this containment operation."

And that was enough of the pleasantries and small talk. "Is my wife in there?"

Seamus's shoulders heaved. "Yes. I'm afraid she is. How did you know?"

"An educated hunch. Rybicki mentioned Lincoln twice today. He even quoted from the inscription above the statue of Lincoln. 'In this temple as in the hearts of the people.' It's obvious the monument was weighing on his mind. He probably planned on using this as a backup target all along, in the event he couldn't get the suitcase out of the country. No doubt he sees some vast symbolic reason for the selection— freeing Americans from the slavery of crude oil, or some such insane rationale."

"But why take your wife?"

"That," Ben said grimly, "was probably done out of revenge."

"I'm sorry to hear that. We've got Rybicki in custody. Caught him leaving the building. The president called in an arrest order. Unfortunately, he had already triggered the countdown on the bomb. With your wife attached to it."

"Can you get her out?"

"No. There's a problem."

"The nuclear suitcase."

Seamus nodded grimly. "It's set to explode in less than nineteen minutes. She's handcuffed to it, and to the base of the statue."

Ben's lips parted. No. *No!*

"Can't you get her out of there?"

"They tried without success. Then they were ordered out, along with everyone else. We have a bomb squad on the way. They haven't arrived yet."

"But can't you cut her loose in the meantime?"

"No. Rybicki says the cuffs are made of titanium alloy."

Ben's brow creased. "What does that mean?"

"It means you're not going to cut through them with a blowtorch. And you're not going to pick the lock with a paper clip. And to make matters worse, Rybicki says that if we detach her from the laptop control device, the bomb goes off immediately."

"And you believe him?"

"I'm afraid so. I've seen this type of trigger mechanism before."

"There must be something we can do."

"We've been in contact with bomb squads across the country, but so far no one knows how to stop it from detonating. Apparently Rybicki rigged it so the countdown could be stopped by typing in a password—presumably as a safeguard in the event of premature detonation or his failure to escape. But no one knows the password."

"And Rybicki isn't talking."

"He's pretty damn stubborn. I tried some serious interrogation techniques."

Ben didn't ask what they were. He didn't want to know.

"But he didn't talk. And I didn't have enough time with him."

"Can't you just type some stuff in?"

"We had some people trying that. They did all the obvious ones. Happily, there's no penalty for a wrong guess. The countdown just continues. We've tried all his children's names, his wife, his dog, his favorite college professor. So far we haven't hit the right code word."

"There must be something you can do."

"Yes, but . . ." Seamus's voice trailed off. "Not in nineteen minutes." He glanced at his watch. "Seventeen now."

"You have to try!"

"We've already begun emergency evacuation procedures. Happily, the Mall was cleared this morning. But this bomb has a much wider range. Radiation fallout could affect people for miles around."

"You have to stop that bomb from exploding!"

"Believe me, Mr. Kincaid, I'm as frustrated as you. I've been chasing this suitcase all day. The good news is, in the process, I managed to stumble onto Colonel Zuko's satellite control station and booted him out of our computer system."

"You're the reason the missiles didn't launch!"

"Well, I had help. But the bad news is, I never found the suitcase. The operative I've been chasing since early morning left it at a predetermined location for Rybicki to pick up."

Ben looked at the monument. "I want to go in there."

"I can't allow that. Not even for a little while. It's too dangerous."

"I don't care. That's my wife in there. I have the right."

"I'm sorry, Ben. No. We have interrogation specialists working on Rybicki. Maybe they'll be successful."

Ben clenched his hands into fists. "Can you at least take me in there? So I can hear what's going on?"

"That much I can do. Follow me, please."

Seamus winced as he took the first step. He inhaled deeply, then started over again, clutching his right side. "Sorry. It's been a hell of a day. And I still haven't had much time with the medics."

Ben followed as Seamus led him through the cordon and into a makeshift headquarters at the base of the tall marble steps leading to the memorial. The interrogation area was just a concrete barricade and an impressive array of communications equipment. One agent was talking into a telephone. Two were huddled around what appeared to be a blueprint of the memorial and the surrounding areas. A video monitor showed the scene inside—Christina chained to the base of the statue of Lincoln.

"Christina," he said breathlessly.

"I'm sorry," Seamus said. "If I could do—"

"Can I talk to her?"

An African American woman dressed in a jacket like Seamus's answered. "I'm sorry. Not at this time. We don't have a communications device down there."

Seamus explained. "This is Special Agent Beldon of the FBI. She's the tactical commander for this operation."

Ben shook her hand. "Good to meet you."

"We have someone working on Rybicki. We're optimistic."

Ben pursed his lips. "I've heard the man rant. I'm not."

"Well, give it a chance."

Ben glanced at a nearby blackboard. "I see you're still employing the same four steps for hostile negotiation. Trust, contain, reconcile, resolve."

"We're treating this like a hostage negotiation—even though technically the hostage is not currently within his control. He knows the password that can save her and everyone else in the area, so it amounts to the same thing. You've been involved with prior scenarios?"

"Once or twice. What does Rybicki want? His plan is finished."

"He hasn't made any demands. I think he just wants the bomb to explode. It's possible he might change his mind, but . . ."

She didn't have to finish the sentence. It was evident that she very much doubted he would. And Ben very much doubted it, too.

56

Ben and Seamus followed as Agent Beldon led him to the area where they were interrogating Rybicki. His eyes narrowed when he spotted Ben.

"Kincaid. So nice to see you again."

Ben didn't answer. This wasn't his show. The interrogator, a tall, thin man with a badge that said Smithson, was talking from prepared notes. "Secretary Rybicki, I want to help you. I will consider any reasonable requests. And I won't lie to you."

Ben realized Smithson was trying to work his way through those key negotiation steps. But Rybicki wouldn't even let him get to first base: trust.

"There's only one person I want to hear from. Kincaid."

Smithson kept trying. "Sir, I know what you've been going through."

"No, you don't. How dare you say that when you don't. You couldn't possibly!" His voice sounded crazed, bizarre. "You don't know how desperate it is, how close we all are to the end. You can't know how frustrating it is to have the answer but no one will listen!"

"Mr. Rybicki," Smithson continued, "I want to help. I want to give you any reasonable thing you want or need to make sure no one else gets hurt by that bomb."

"Tell Kincaid his wife is going to die!"

"Sir, I know you're scared, confused. You don't know what's going to happen. You need someone you can trust. You can trust me. Make me your hostage. Let Ms. McCall go."

"No deal."

"Pointless," Ben muttered to Seamus under his breath. "This is not going to end up well."

Beldon's fists balled up with frustration. "Can someone please explain to me what this guy's problem is?"

"I can," Ben said.

"Then would you please tell me what I'm supposed to do?"

"That's the problem," Ben said, eyes widening. "There's nothing we can do. There's nothing we can give him he wants. And pardon me for saying so, but your approach is not going to work."

"Mr. Kincaid, I understand your frustration. But we have to play this by the book."

"I don't care about your book. I want Christina out of there."

"We can't—"

"And I want Mr. McKay here to take over the interrogation."

"Why? So he can torture the secretary of defense?"

"I won't use torture," Seamus said. "Not that it wouldn't be fun. But it wouldn't work with this zealot."

Ben didn't care if he did. He didn't care about anything except getting Christina out of there.

"Just tell us as much as you can," Smithson said to Rybicki. He had already blown step two: contain. Presumably he was trying for some hope of reconciliation, step three.

"I won't. Why should I?"

"Sir, innocent lives—"

"You have ten minutes left!" Rybicki screeched. "Then everyone will see that I was right!"

"Mr. Rybicki!"

Smithson continued to argue with the man, but Ben knew it would do no good. He wasn't going to change Rybicki's mind. The secretary of defense was way past reason.

"I can't stand to watch this. I'm going for some air," Ben told Seamus. He gave him his cell phone number. "Call me if anything changes."

"I will."

Ben walked a moment, made sure no one was looking. Then he quietly took one of the FBI flak jackets and slid it on.

He walked evenly, not too fast, not too slow, toward the monument. Seamus and the others were still watching the interrogation.

Ben reached the officers restricting access to the monument. "Change of assignment," Ben said, mustering as much authority as he could manage. "Beldon says she wants to see you immediately."

"Now? Who'll maintain the cordon?"

"I will. Follow your orders." The two men shrugged and started toward the interrogation area.

Ben skittered up the steps to the monument. The farther he got before he was spotted the better.

"Kincaid!" This was Seamus, about twenty feet below him, just before he made it to the top of the steps. "Freeze! Do not compromise this operation. We will use force if necessary to stop you."

"Then you'll have to shoot me in the back," Ben muttered. "I'm going in."

"Kincaid! I mean it!"

"I don't think you do," Ben said quietly. "At least I hope not."

"This is your last warning!"

Ben closed his eyes, said a quick, silent prayer, and walked into the memorial.

He was inside.

57

"Damn!" Seamus swore, holstering his gun. "Why didn't he listen to me?"

"Couldn't you have just wounded him?" Beldon asked.

"I'm not going to shoot a man for wanting to see his wife before—" He stopped short. "How long can he stay in there and still have time to escape the detonation?"

"We've got emergency transport lined up to get everyone out of range, but the last shuttle will leave when there's five minutes left on the clock. If he stays longer than that, he's doomed."

"He'll come out. He's not stupid."

"But his wife is in danger. He's not thinking rationally. I've heard he's a little off."

"Why?" Seamus snarled. "Because he cares about his wife? Because he doesn't want to trust her fate to your incompetent pussyfooting interrogators?"

"I don't think it's necessary for you to engage in—"

Seamus whirled on her. "I'm really not interested in what you think.

I don't believe you do it often and you're not very good at it. I want you to give me another crack at Rybicki. It's what Kincaid wanted."

Beldon pushed up on her tiptoes. "I'm running this operation. Not you. And not Kincaid."

"And you're accomplishing nothing. Let me back in there."

"My team has been specially trained—"

"No, he's right." It was Smithson this time, standing behind them. He looked exhausted. "I'm not getting anywhere. And we've got so little time left. If he can do something, let him."

Seamus grabbed Beldon by the shoulders. "At least let me try! What have you got to lose?"

Beldon pressed her lips together. Several seconds passed before she said, "All right. Go."

Ben passed between the tall Doric columns and entered the monument.

He checked his watch. Not much time left. Not that it mattered.

His cell phone rang.

"Ben? Can you hear me?"

He recognized Seamus's voice. "I can."

"You have to give them at least five minutes to get you out safely."

"Got it."

"Do you? Do you understand there's no point in staying longer? It won't help your wife."

"I understand."

"I'm going to work on Rybicki. If I get any password ideas, I'll contact you."

"Please do. I'll stay on the line."

At the other end of the cavernous monument, Ben saw her. Her face was red and streaked. It looked as if she had been hit in the face. There was a dark bruise under her right eye. Of course she never would have let Rybicki chain her here without a fight, even if he had Agent Gioia's gun.

Ben ran up and wrapped his arms around his wife.

"Thank God," he said, hugging her tightly. "I love you so—"

She pushed him away with her unchained hand. "What the hell are you doing in here, you chowderhead?"

"I—I came to be with you."

"Have you lost your mind? Did they not explain to you that this thing attached to me is a nuclear bomb?"

"Actually, I knew before they did."

"Do you understand why Rybicki is doing this to me?"

"Yes. It's, um, kinda my fault."

"It is not."

"Well, I screwed up his plan A. So now he's executing plan B. With you in the middle."

"Ben, don't blame yourself. That man is clearly unbalanced. He's become so obsessed with Middle Eastern politics he can't think straight. He's wants to detonate a bomb just to make his point."

"I know," Ben said quietly.

"And still you came in here? What did you think you could accomplish?"

"I . . . didn't really know. And it didn't really matter." He paused. "I wanted to be with you."

"Well, fine. You've seen me. Now march right back out of here."

Ben shook his head.

"When do you have to leave to get away safely?"

"They need at least five minutes."

"Fine." She glanced at the countdown readout on the laptop. "You can stay till then. You can sing me a song. Tell me some of your inane elephant jokes. But after that you're leaving. Do you understand?"

"I understand what you're saying."

"You are so exasperating!"

"And still you married me."

"You caught me at a weak moment."

He smiled. "I love you, Christina."

"So you came running in here to not save me?"

"No. I came running in to be with you."

"Ben, it's pointless!"

He took her hand. "Till death do us part."

58

Rybicki stared across at Seamus, his jaw jutting. Now that his plan had been exposed, his nervousness seemed to be replaced by self-righteous defiance. "Can't you see the beauty of it? No. Because people have always been blind to the realities out there. The evil that lurks outside, ready to cut off our head. You indulge yourself with talk about making peace, while ignoring the factors that are causing war over and over again."

"Pal, I've spent more time in the Middle East than you've spent reading about it."

"Then you know we have to do something! We're at their mercy."

"Because we need oil?"

"Yes, damn it, that's exactly why. That's the weakest link in our entire national defense. So what is the president doing about it? Nothing. He's going to stand around collecting accolades for his nice words while the country is destroyed."

"So you decided to take matters into your own hands."

"What choice did I have? What choice?" He was waving his hands in the air, looking wild-eyed.

Seamus spoke slowly, trying to fit everything together. "You wanted the colonel to send his missiles into an American neighborhood. So you gave him the computer codes and kept him informed of everything that was happening here—because a Kuraqi attack on American soil would set the stage for retaliation."

"Damn straight. After that, the American people would want Kuraqi blood. They would accept anything necessary, even a change in the way they consumed energy. Anything. And I wouldn't have to wait for this weak-kneed president to act. In exchange for what I gave Zuko, I got a nuclear suitcase."

"You're stark raving mad."

"I don't want to hurt people, not any more than necessary. I didn't want to explode the bomb here." He leaned forward. "Don't you understand? I wanted to set the bomb off in the Strait of Hormuz."

Seamus stared at him as the full magnitude of his twisted plan became clear.

"Not that many people would die, but the entire region would be irradiated for years to come, not just the strait but also the Persian Gulf and the Gulf of Oman. I'm sure you're aware that more than seventy percent of the world's oil supply passes through that narrow strait on the way to market. What would happen to those oil suppliers if the strait were no longer passable because it was drenched in deadly radiation? They would either have to ship their oil out over land—which would raise the price dramatically—or they would have to give it up. And you know what that means?"

"Really good news for Venezuela?"

"Don't be stupid. Venezuela can't service the entire world, and they'll jump at the excuse to increase prices once their primary competition is eliminated. Faced with less oil available, and even that at a dramatically increased price, Americans for the first time simply would have no choice but to start looking to alternative fuels."

Seamus shook his head. "You're wrong."

"About the Middle East?"

"No, about your sanity. You are—to use a CIA technical term— totally fucked up."

"You can belittle me all you want," Rybicki said, "but it would've worked. Sure, there would be a cost. You can't make an omelet without breaking a few eggs. But it would be worth it. We would not only end our dependence on foreign oil, we would be able to secure our borders and stop involving ourselves in the ongoing troubles of the Middle Eastern region. It's a win-win for us, man. Can you not see that?"

"It doesn't matter. Your plan is done. So why explode a bomb in Washington?"

"Everyone will assume it was Colonel Zuko. The president may even prefer to let that be the cover story, rather than admit that it was done by a man he appointed to office. The American people will demand retaliation. The president will have to grow some balls. He'll drop bombs. Maybe he'll even have the sense to execute my plan and take out the strait."

"Or maybe it will just lead to a lot of unnecessary bloodshed and death."

"There is no such thing as unnecessary bloodshed," Rybicki said. "The blood of the martyrs is the seed of the Church."

"The—" Seamus hesitated a moment. There was something about the way he said that. It was almost as if he were quoting something. Something very important to him.

He picked up his cell phone. "Ben? Are you there?"

"Still here."

"I've been talking to this whack job, hoping he would spill something important. Type in 'blood of the martyrs.' See if it stops the countdown."

"There's not enough space. It will only take ten characters."

"Then maybe 'blood'?" He heard the clattering of a keyboard.

"No."

"Martyrs."

"No."

"I think it's a famous quotation. . . ."

"Tertullian," Ben said.

"I'm impressed," Seamus said.

"I had a good rector. Well, till he went to prison." More keyboard clicks. "Damn. I thought there was just a chance. But that isn't it."

Seamus turned his attention back to Rybicki. "Listen to me, you son of a bitch. I know we're close. Tell me what the password is."

"Are you going to hurt me?"

"I might!"

"I hope you will. My lawyers will be able to use that."

Seamus felt his fists tightening. "Do you understand how many people are going to die if that bomb explodes?"

Rybicki only smiled. "Blood of the martyrs, my friend. Blood of the martyrs."

59

Ben and Christina were laughing uproariously. Ben was holding his ribs. Tears streamed down Christina's face.

"And—and then," she said, trying to catch her breath, "do you remember when the Capitol police made you strip down to your boxers? What I would have done to have a camera on that!"

"That's nothing!" Ben said, rolling on his side. "What about the time we were at the zoo and the birds attacked your hair?"

Her laughter slowed. "Well . . . maybe I did wear it a little big back then."

"Big? You looked like Cromwell."

"I did not."

He wiped his eyes. "No, you did not. You looked gorgeous. You always do."

"But the hair is better. Now that my hairdresser has it under control."

He smiled. "Maybe a little better."

She smiled back. "Why are we reminiscing like old people?"

He shrugged.

"It's because you don't think you'll ever see me again, isn't it?"

He glanced at the countdown.

"Hey," Ben said, changing the subject, "I've got big news."

"Really? So do I."

"You are not going to do that to me again."

"Perish the thought. What's your news?"

"Well," he said, his eyebrows dancing, "I've ferreted out the president's deep, dark secret."

"And?" she said.

"He's been sneaking cigarettes when his wife isn't looking."

"Smoking in the boys' room?"

"Exactly. In the White House."

"Shame on him."

"Well, it will probably be easier to quit once he's not being dosed with LSD."

"*Whaaaat?*"

"Long story. What's your news? Not that there's the slightest hope that you're going to top mine."

She grinned from ear to ear. "I decided to change my name. Already filed the paperwork."

He stared at her uncomprehendingly. "But I like the name Christina."

"Not my first name, you dunderhead. My last. I thought I'd take your name."

"What? But I thought you said—"

"I know what I said. Keeping my professional reputation,. blah, blah, blah. But you know what? We're a team. We're partners. We're husband and wife. We're a family." She laid her hand on his. "I think it's time we had the same last name."

"Are you just saying this because—"

"No. I've been thinking about it for a long time."

Ben looked back at her, his head bobbing. "I don't know what to say."

."Say, 'You're right, Christina. Your news is better.' "

He sighed. "Okay. You win. Again."

She squeezed his hand, then looked at the clock. Six minutes and counting. "Ben, I want you to go now."

"But—"

"I know what you're trying to do. I know what a—a noble soul you have. But you don't have to die just because . . . you know. You've done so much with the time you've been given. You've helped so many people. It would be a shame to throw all that away. I want you to go."

"But—"

"Don't argue with me. I'm your wife. And you know I'm smarter than you are, at least when it comes to practical matters. So go."

"But—"

"If you love me, you'll go."

Ben pressed his lips together, then slowly pushed himself to his feet. Eyes closed, he kissed her on the cheek, then turned and walked away.

"Hurry!"

He walked even faster, made his way across the monument floor, started toward the steps . . .

And stopped.

He came back to Christina, running all the way.

"I'm sorry. I won't leave you here alone. I won't. I can't."

She wrapped her free arm around him and sighed. "You are such an idiot." She squeezed with all her might. "And I love you so much."

"You know," Rybicki said, "I will not tell you the password. No matter what you do to me."

"I know," Seamus grunted, rolling up his sleeves. He could see Agent Beldon watching him closely from a short distance. "But it would still be fun."

"You would destroy your chances of convicting me."

"Do I look like a cop? I could care less about convicting you."

"The president might feel otherwise."

"Well, he's not here."

"Fine. Amuse yourself with your violent games. Reveal the beast that you truly are. It will soon be over."

"No, *you* will soon be over."

"What?"

"You're staying. After the last shuttle has left the station."

"You can't do that."

"Who's gonna stop me? It's your damn bomb. Only right that you should be one of the first victims." He leaned backward. "Have you read anything about what it's like to die of radiation poisoning? A slow, painful death. Your body just melts, starting with the internal organs. Your skin peels away from the bone. It's protracted agony."

Rybicki smiled defiantly. "You think that if you scare me I'll give you the password so you can stop the bomb. You are wrong."

Seamus squinted. "You're wrong, pal. You've been wrong all along. And your big master plan was stupid."

Rybicki scoffed. "As if you know anything about it."

"I've devoted years to knowing what people are like in the Middle Eastern region. And you know what I've learned? Whatever else they may be, they're tough. Resilient. They've been through a lot. They live in the harshest environment outside of the Antarctic, but they've survived. I don't think your little bomb would've changed that. If they couldn't use the strait, they'd find another way to get the oil out. Without raising their prices so high they killed the market."

"That would be impossible."

"Those guys do the impossible six times before breakfast."

"I understand that people like Colonel Zuko can be tough!" Rybicki shouted. "That's why we can't hold back! That's why we can't use half measures. Scorched earth! That's the only thing that works with these people. That's how the ancient Scythians took them out. We should do the same. Scorched earth!"

Seamus looked at the man's face.

Rybicki looked back at him.

The corners of Seamus's mouth turned up.

60

Fifty-five seconds left.

"Ben! Are you there?"

Ben picked up his phone. "I'm still here, Seamus. Shouldn't you have taken the last train out of town?"

"You should talk. Listen to me. Do you know anything about the scorched-earth policy?"

"My wife complains that I read too much history."

"Just answer!"

"It's a military strategy that involves destroying anything that might be of use to the enemy."

"Just the sort of thing a secretary of defense might know about? And bring to modern use?"

"I suppose."

Forty-five seconds.

Ben typed in first *scorched* and then *earth*. Neither was the password.

"He said something about the ancient Scythians."

Ben typed in *Scythians*. No good.

Thirty-five seconds.

"That's not it."

"He said something about the Scythians using it to take these guys out. Like it was a history lesson."

"That's right," Ben said, trying to retrieve the information from the far corners of his brain. "They were the first to use the scorched-earth technique and they did it in the ancient Middle East to battle a horrible dictator. They were nomads, and . . . and they had to retreat into the steppes, but before they left they burned all the food and poisoned the wells. The invading king moved in, but his troops started dying of starvation and dehydration."

Twenty seconds.

"What was the king's name, Ben? He's the Colonel Zuko of his time. He's the one Rybicki would obsess on. What was his name?"

Ben was thinking so hard it brought sweat to his temples. "I think it was . . . Darius. Darius the Great of Persia."

"Type it in!"

Ben typed. *D-A-R-I-A-S.*

Not the password.

Ten seconds left.

"That wasn't it."

"Damn," Seamus shouted. "I thought we had it."

"You spelled it wrong!" Christina shouted. "You just can't function at all without spell-check, can you? It's *D-A-R-I-U-S!*"

"Are you sure?"

"Just type it!"

Five seconds.

Ben typed it in, hit a wrong key, started over again. His fingers were wet with sweat.

D-A-R-I-U-S. He hit enter.

The countdown stopped. With two seconds remaining.

"That was it!" Ben screamed. "That did it!"

Christina threw her free arm around him and hugged him tightly. "Oh, thank God. Oh thank you, God!"

Her arms were trembling. Ben knew that she had been putting on a brave front. Only now was she allowing her true feelings—and fear—to show.

"It's okay," he whispered.

"Thank you for not leaving me, Ben."

He held her at arm's length and gazed into her eyes. "I will never leave you, baby. Never."

"Thank you," she gasped. "And as long as you're making promises, would you promise to stay away from crazed ideologues possessing nuclear weapons?"

"Deal."

Rybicki was furious. And that fury was the happiest sight Seamus had seen all day.

"Ben?" Seamus shouted into his earpiece. "We're going to call back the bomb people. They'll get Christina out of there and make sure that bomb never goes off."

"That's great news. We'll be right here waiting."

"You'll be happy to know that the secretary of defense is totally pissed off."

"Well, that is a happy thought."

"Congratulations, Ben. You showed a hell of a lot of—"

"Yeah, yeah, yeah. Seamus?"

"Still here."

"Are you with Rybicki?"

"Sure am."

"Would you do me a favor?"

"Anything you want, Ben. Just ask."

"I don't know how to put this. . . . I don't want to get you into any trouble. . . ."

"Just ask, Ben."

"I'd do it myself, but I'm staying with Christina. . . ."

"Spit it out, Ben. What can I do for you?"

"Seamus . . . that man not only threatened to kill my wife—he hit her. Hard. On the face. He left a mark."

"Say no more, Ben."

"Thank you."

"Of course."

Seamus turned back to the man in the opposite chair. Agent Beldon was still observing. "Got something special for you, my friend."

Rybicki looked at him, eyebrows pushed together. "What is it?"

Seamus smiled. "A special delivery. From my friend Ben Kincaid."

The blow hit so hard that Rybicki was literally lifted up into the air. It wasn't lethal, but Seamus was still certain the secretary of defense would remember it for the rest of his days.

61

Ben met Seamus as he was leaving the CIA office where everyone involved had been debriefed.

"I hope you didn't hurt Rybicki too badly."

Seamus shrugged. "Well, Beldon was watching. And I'm already in trouble for that sort of thing." He smiled slightly. "It would've been a lot worse for him if you hadn't stopped that bomb."

"Good point. I just don't want anything to undermine his prosecution."

"Ben, the man gave security codes to the enemy, stole a nuclear device, and tried to explode it in the heart of Washington. There is no legal technicality on earth that could save him. He's going to spend the rest of his life in prison. Or a mental institution."

"I'll sleep better knowing he's someplace safe."

"As will we all."

They fell silent for a moment.

"Are you sure you want to do this?" Ben asked.

"I'm sure. I don't know about you, but for me, April fourteenth was a hell of a long day."

"Wasn't exactly a vacation for me, either."

"Right. But you're a lot younger than I am. I've been doing this for way too long. I've served my country abroad, domestically, and what have I got to show for it? My wife left. My pension dried up when the stock market crashed. And all these supervisors who have a tenth as much experience as I do think I'm too mean to the bad guys. Enough already."

"The stock market will come back."

"Yeah, maybe. But I won't. I'm just too old to run around getting shot at all day long. I got the hell beaten out of me today. This is a younger man's game."

"But you're so good at it."

"I'm not going to give it up altogether. I'm taking a position with the NCTC. Counterterrorism work."

"You're taking a desk job?"

"Why not? It'll give me some time to, um, you know . . . pursue my hobbies. Something I've always wanted to do."

Ben held out his hand. "Well, you deserve it. Thank you for everything. And thank you for saving my wife."

Seamus shook his hand vigorously. "Aw, you did all the hard stuff."

"It was a team effort. Which is why I hate to see you go."

"Come visit me in Hawaii, Ben. Live a little."

Ben grinned. "I'm really not the luau type."

"The sun shines every day, it rains almost every afternoon—but not for long. There are endless beaches, and one woman in five dances the hula. What's not to like?"

"Pretty much everything you just mentioned."

"Worse things out there than watching the sunset and drinking rum out of a pineapple, Ben. Beats the heck out of chasing terrorists and getting beaten up by enemy agents."

Ben shook his head. "You won't be gone long. You'll be bored to tears out there. You'll be back in the field in no time."

"Not a chance."

"You will."

"What makes you so sure?"

Ben tilted his head. "I just feel certain we're going to hear from you again."

62

Ben and Christina were finally having their meal together, back at their own apartment, wearing their pajamas. There was much work to be done. The Kyler presidency had to be stitched back together again. Vice President Swinburne had already resigned, so the president had to select a new VP. The rubble in the Mall had to be cleared. But Ben knew it would all be done, and Washington would soon be back in business as if nothing had ever happened. Democracy was nothing if not resilient. And April 14 had turned out to be a very interesting day.

Ben fixed their very late dinner. Tuna fish sandwiches, chocolate chip cookies, Diet Cokes. No time for *Jeopardy* tonight, and Ben wanted to spend some time talking to his wife before he inevitably fell asleep. It had been a long and remarkable day.

"You think Rybicki will be convicted?" Christina asked later as they lay together in bed, gazing into the darkness.

"The president will want to avoid a trial if possible. But he'll be put away for good, one way or another."

"The president must be very grateful to you."

"Well, I'm very grateful to him, for—you know."

"Getting my sister out of trouble with the IRS?"

"All he did was make a few phone calls, but—"

"That stupid ex of hers was the one who didn't pay the taxes, not Chloe. But the president saved her a lot of legal hassles. And now she's free to move to Washington. Near us!"

"Really." Ben cleared his throat. "And that's a good thing? She is a little . . ."

"Benjamin J. Kincaid, you be careful."

" . . . wacky?"

"Well, all us McCall girls are loaded with personality. Ben—can I ask a favor?"

"Always."

"*Entre nous*, I'm not sure I want you working in the White House anymore."

"You have something against the president?"

"No, I have something against you throwing yourself at bombs and interfering with the plans of dangerous madmen."

"I doubt if that will happen every six months. But since you mentioned the job, I have news for you."

She nestled in closer, burying her face against his chest. "Me too."

"No! This is my turn!"

"Oh, grow up. My hero. What's your news?"

"The president is saying that because he's so grateful to me and all, he might appoint me to work at the International Court. In the Hague! In time I might even be appointed to a foreign embassy. He thinks I'm not only qualified but that Congress would approve me without blinking. Isn't that fantastic?"

She smiled. "I want to go to France."

"Well, duh."

"I'd settle for Belgium."

"I think we'll be lucky to get Liechtenstein."

She kissed his chest. "You know I'll go anywhere with you."

"I like the sound of that. Okay, so what's your news?"

"Oh, honestly, Ben. Have you really not already guessed?"

"How could I?"

"I've been giving you clues all day!"

"You have?"

She rolled her eyes. "And you're such a great detective. Except, it seems, in your own home."

"What are you talking about?"

"Ben, have you not been listening to me? I'm hiring an associate to help out in the office. Your mother is redecorating the spare room. I'm taking your name. Chloe is moving nearby."

"Ye-es?"

"Isn't it obvious?"

"Why do I feel so stupid?"

"Because you are!" She leaned up on one elbow. "Ben, when you stopped that bomb, you didn't just save one life . . . you saved two."

"Actually, I think I saved thousands."

She blew air upward, making her bangs flutter. "Ben—you're going to be a daddy."

His eyes expanded like balloons. "You're—you're joking!"

"Nope."

He grabbed her arms. "You're sure?"

"Got the ultrasound photo to prove it. So I'll need more help at the office, and your mother is turning the spare room into a nursery, and Chloe can be our nanny."

"I don't know if I'm ready for this."

"You're ready. I can't think of anyone better to raise my children."

"If I'm going to be the father of your children, does this mean you'll stop calling me a chowderhead?"

"No."

"Well, it was worth a shot."

He pulled her closer to him, feeling her warmth. "I love you, sweet-heart."

"I love you back."

"So . . . is it a boy or a girl?"

She grinned so broadly the freckles danced on her cheeks. "Yes."

Acknowledgments

As you may have gathered, Ben Kincaid feels strongly that we need to end our dependence on oil and move to natural gas and other alternatives as soon as possible. The best discussion of these issues I've read is in a book called *The Braking Point: America's Energy Dreams and Global Economic Realities,* by my friends Mark Stansberry and Jason P. Reimbold.

I hope you enjoyed meeting Seamus McKay. Seamus will return—now relocated to Hawaii—in my next novel, *The Idea Man.*

I also want to thank my early readers: James Vance, John Wooley, Barry Friedman, my editor Junessa Viloria, and Marcia Bernhardt. Their contributions greatly improved this book.

Most important, I want to thank my children, who have let me beg out of a Clue game so I could finish this book tonight, and my splendiferous wife, Marcia—my Christina—who showed me what it was like to have a real partner.

William Bernhardt

About the Author

WILLIAM BERNHARDT is the author of more than twenty novels, including *Primary Justice, Murder One, Criminal Intent, Death Row, Capitol Murder, Capitol Threat, Capitol Conspiracy, Capitol Offense,* and *Nemesis.* He is one of fewer than a dozen recipients of the H. Louise Cobb Distinguished Author Award given "in recognition of an outstanding body of work in which we understand ourselves and American society at large." He is also one of the country's most popular writing instructors, teaching at various conferences throughout the year. A former trial attorney, Bernhardt has received several awards for his public service. He lives in Tulsa with his wife, Marcia, and their children.

wb@williambernhardt.com
www.williambernhardt.com